Book 1 in the Seekers Series

CORREAE CHRONICLES

JEFF GAURA

ISBN: 978-1-961879-52-2 (Paperback)
ISBN: 978-1-961879-53-9 (Ebook)

Printed in the United States of America

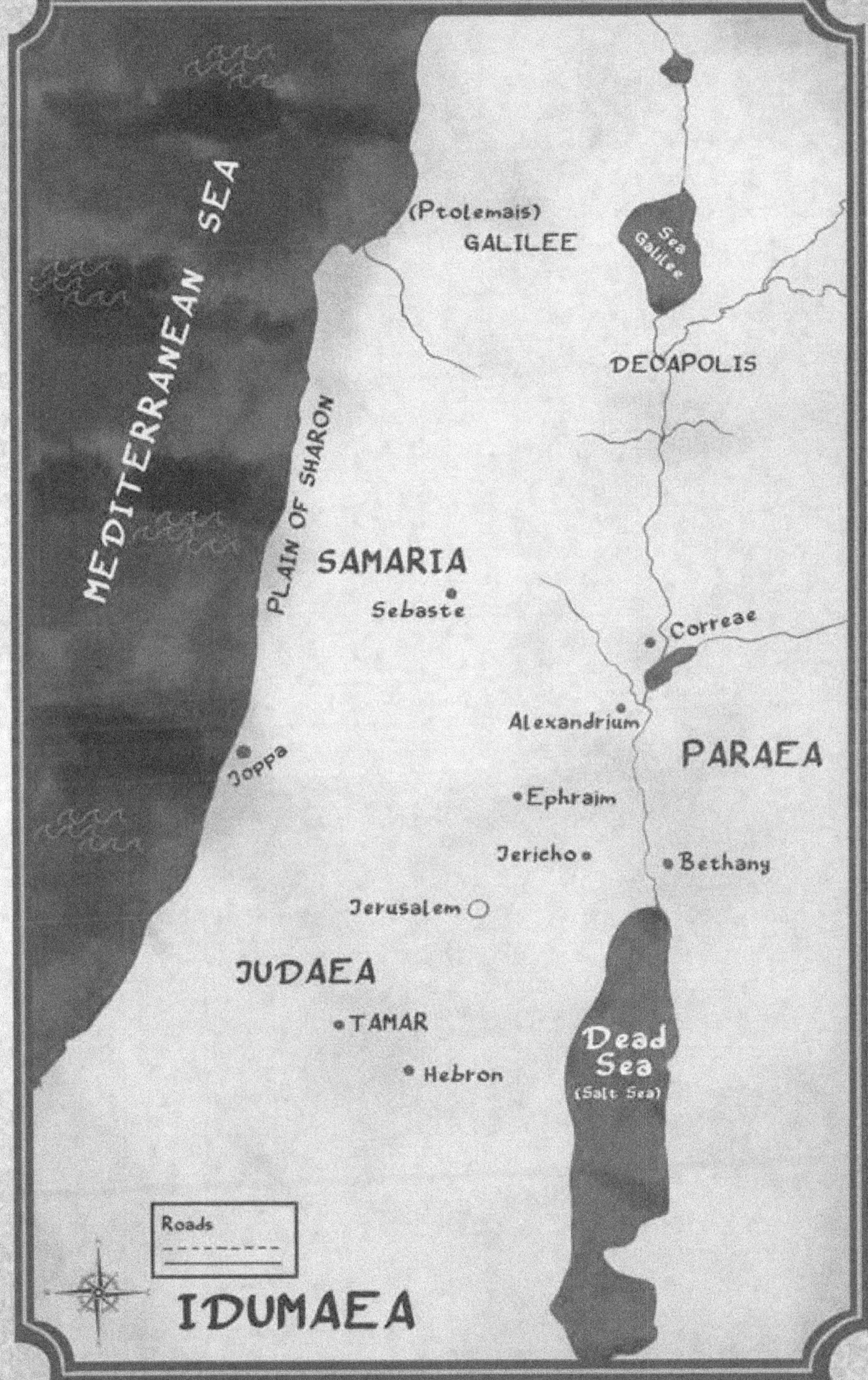

MEDITERRANEAN SEA
(Ptolemais)
GALILEE
Sea Galilee
DECAPOLIS
PLAIN OF SHARON
SAMARIA
Sebaste
Correae
Joppa
Alexandrium
PARAEA
Ephraim
Jericho
Bethany
Jerusalem
JUDAEA
TAMAR
Dead Sea (Salt Sea)
Hebron
Roads
IDUMAEA

Foreword to the
Second Edition

This book was previously published with the title Behind The Secrets In The Fall of Jerusalem (Trilogy Christian Publishing) in 2020. Between hand-written letters, social media remarks, and conversations with readers that I meet, the first three books in this series deserved a second edition. I completed the first editions in fast order, or so I thought. Books four through eight took half the time that it took to write the first three. As the story evolved, so did the need to change things in the background. I stayed true to history but the background needed more context, and the plot needed to evolve into something more.

This eight-book series is fictional but is based on events from the Bible and the recorded history of the Roman Empire. And I believe the eyewitness evidence presented from both perspectives. Please allow those two thoughts to permeate all that you read, think, and feel over these following few thousand pages.

Foreword to the First Edition

Just like excerpts of Roman history, every scene in the Bible has people, places, and things that are not described. There are colors, smells, sounds, and sights that we must imagine. The author didn't give us the details, but that does not mean that they aren't there. When I read, I see landscapes and imagine the activities of the times and, within moments, my mind creates an entire canvas from incomplete information. I do it every day.

I have ideas about what color clothing Jesus wore. I had an idea about the tone the teenage boys used when they grumbled as Jesus told them to cast their nets one more time. I see the size and shape of the leaves in the tree that Zacchaeus occupied, and not as full of green leaves and lush with life as others might. I see a brown tree without leaves, perhaps in an off-season, making it easy for Zaccheus to climb and look down from. I have an image that I can construct my understanding with. To pretend those don't determine how I interpret the Bible is dishonest. The items we add matter. But we don't know if we added them. This series is my addition both to Roman history and the biblical account in an admittedly fictional manner.

Adding to context is part of being human. Indeed, you will add context as you read this series. You will meet Caleb, with his beard and his powerful physique, and try to figure out how to place that next to his developing character as a nurturer and a healer. You will fall in love with Eliza as she alternates between a woman of courage and a scared little duck. Domitian Flavian seems to have earned everyone's hearts, even though history contains no records that he accepted Christ. I certainly don't, either. And little Oren, from the last books, is my all-time favorite. She starts life at the bottom and ascends to the top, surrounded by men and women sold out on Jesus

Christ or hell-bent on selfish motives and the fleeting desires of this world. She walks the razor's edge of sanity with the cloak of humility as her primary armor. That isn't listed as the whole armor of God, but it works for her.

Sometimes, readers add to the timeline of events that may or may not have happened, and we will hypothesize the outcome. When I read the Bible, I ask questions like, "What did the 5,000 do the day after they were all fed?", "Which one of the disciples suggested that the disciples go back to fishing?", and "Who ended up with Goliath's sword after the battle was over?" The disappearance of the Ark of the Covenant spawned a series of Hollywood movies that ask the same questions that I did as I constructed a world that includes these items of apparent insignificance.

In my books, I add depictions of the events at the royal palace, inside and under the Temple of King Solomon, in the Hippodrome, on the battlegrounds of the Roman Empire, riding on horseback through the countryside of Serbia, and living on the edge of a lake in Switzerland. Keep in mind that everything you read has been picked over and slept on too many times to count. I have wept and rejoiced as these characters came to life.

My spiritual barometer comes from the end of the book of John. We receive a nugget that creates credibility for the existence of other stories. That line of scripture turns my imagination on fire like no other verse in the Bible.

> *There are also many other things that Jesus did, about which, if they were written for everyone, I suppose that even the world itself could not contain the books that should be written.*

> (John 21:25)

Yet, my brain proteins continue to create new neural pathways as I imagine what those might be. I have wondered what the vineyards and olive orchards outside of Jerusalem looked like when Jesus was approaching riding on a donkey. I imagine the kind of landscape that lined the roads that the Good Samaritan traveled. I speculate the lighting in the manger when Jesus was born.

This series is a result of a guarded imagination to tell stories of first-century AD people who are living in trying times, doing the best that they can to take care of each other and their families while also trying to minimize what the government takes from them. Yes, this is a familiar tale.

These are fictional accounts of people who struggled to live and be at peace with who they thought God was. They discovered that their idea of God was incomplete. A Messiah had come, and He left behind unfathomable power. For whatever reason, they all missed it.

The act of leaving my old profession to embark on something new meant that my imagination would go to paper and e-books. In the event that these fictional yet compelling accounts of what the first church experienced offend your view of the contents of the Bible, I apologize in advance. Please refer to the first two claims of this introduction for additional clarification.

This book would not have happened without the positive affirmation from my followers on my blogs and videos.

I want to thank Scott, Chris, Marty, Greg, and Le for their companionship during our unscripted Thursday morning gatherings. You created a place for me to safely ask questions like, "I wonder why God picked that kind of person to make His point?"

I want to thank Zack, my editor for the first two books, for holding my hand. As a trained physicist, I needed someone with a Ph.D. in English Studies to referee my writing with no genuine concern about my opinion of his work. Good job.

I want to thank God for making this book possible through my life events. I am in Your vine, forever.

Lastly, I want to thank my pre-readers who agreed to consume this work and give me feedback before I send it for publication. There are too many of you to list. You know who you are.

Chapter 1:
Secrets

The small Ebreet hamlet of Correae had a secret that was over 50 years old, and it looked like their hidden gold mine was ripe enough to celebrate its 51st birthday. However, that morning, the secret meant nothing to Yael, and Yael hated secrets.

Yael stepped out of the front door of her house and turned around to look over her roof. The views of the snow-covered mountains behind her house were the stuff of King David' and King Solomon's poetry. The dry and cold air that struck her cheeks as she stepped outside of her family's stone and wooden home each morning made her feel happy to be alive. Correae's secret was hidden from the Roman Empire, and the Ebreet who called this place home lived with an economic freedom that few in ancient Judah enjoyed. Every citizen of Correae was wealthy beyond measure, yet they lived simple and Yahweh-fearing lives without apology. Yael's simple clothing could disguise her as a poor girl selling fruit on the side of the road outside of Jerusalem. Yet, her education and advanced maturity were what separated her from other teenage girls anywhere in the Roman Empire. Every young man and woman had grown up with private tutors helping them learn to read, write, and speak many of the languages of the lands; as well as do advanced mathematics like the kinds taught to Egyptian engineers who had designed the pyramids. They all knew history and economics at levels that could earn them jobs as administrators within the Roman Empire, and most could play musical instruments. These residents of Naphtali were not traditionally impoverished Ebreet. They were set apart.

Looking at Yahweh's Creation in this moment gave her awe and she was grateful that she didn't take it for granted. The color palette of the mountains took Yael's breath away: white on top, brown below the white and rich green from the middle to the land below. Yet, her best efforts to get her cousins Despy and Nava to stop and look at God's creation seldom worked.

"Wow, girls, look at the mountains this morning! Do you see that reflection off the snow near the top?" Yael shook her head from side to side as she expressed wonder.

Giggles were all she heard. Yael got nothing more. They didn't listen and didn't care. Yael put her hands on her hips and shifted her focus toward her two cousins.

"Why don't you two ever stop and look around? You are both idiots."

Despy replied in her familiar, condescending tone, "Look at the nice stones on the path under the sheep manure. Wow, Yael, that is so beautiful!" Despy looked at Nava as the two of them began to laugh. Yael dismissed them and looked back at the mountains.

"You are both idiots," she repeated, returning her gaze to the northern hills. They didn't hear her. They were too interested in talking about what they were going to wear for Shabbat later that evening.

She told herself that she was done trying to convince them. They were too interested in their conversations about people and things. She couldn't figure out how to share her love of God's creation with them. She had tried convincing them that no one would ever remember what they wore on Friday night. It didn't work to counter their indifference. They would soon be of age to marry, and they wanted to look their best.

She tried telling them the mountains behind them would stand for tens of thousands of Friday nights. They didn't seem to care. She knew they were the idiots; she wasn't. Shame on her for trying to convince them. Her rabbi told her never to place pearls before swine. She failed in that regard. She wished she had different cousins.

As she went back inside with a bucket of water from the well, she told her mother that Despy and Nava were stupid. Her mother and older sister Kayta smiled at her and touched her head lightly to let her know that they loved her. She told her mother what happened and her mother halfway listened as she washed off the beans she would soak and then cook for the family. Her mother told her that changing a person's heart was a job for Yahweh and not her burden.

"Little One, Jehovah is the Creator, and we reflect that Creation. We are made in His image, but we are not Him. He will present His glory to them when their hearts are ready, not when Princess Yael thinks that her cousins are ready."

Yael didn't buy what her mother was selling. The girls were acting stupid. She wanted answers to questions that she knew her mother couldn't provide; that is what teenage girls do.

"Mother, why do you spend so much gold investing in having the greatest and best Rabbis visit our village and teach both the boys and the girls everything? We know more than a Roman centurion and his counselors. What is the point of it all?"

Being stupid didn't make sense to her. It almost seemed wasteful. She knew that she needed to wait till her father got home to talk to him about this. Maybe she could get his attention before he got drunk.

Yael and her older sister were top students. All the rabbis knew Yael could recite Roman history better than Roman senators, and Katie knew Ebreet customs better than some Rabbis. Yael's mind for language was exceptional. Despite her young age of 16, she already spoke Ebreet, Aramaic, Egyptian, and Greek fluently. Both girls could calculate compound interest in their heads and convert between gold, silver, bronze, and copper without hesitation, regardless of the amount. What was the point of all this knowledge if you couldn't use it to change another person's heart?

Yael sighed. She didn't need to talk to dumb cousins. She preferred to talk to merchants from faraway places than her own family of idiots. They had a desire to accumulate good stories, and they seemed to appreciate beauty. Her cousins only wanted to accumulate fancy clothing and jewelry. It didn't make sense to her. Their parents would select their husbands for them. The clothing wouldn't matter. Every girl in Correae could have any boy in any of the twelve tribes that they wanted, as their dowry was massive and the girls were considered to be of the highest quality. Their expensive and high-quality diets gave all of them strong and disease-resistant frames. Yael knew she wanted to marry a warrior or a rabbi. Despy and Nava wanted to marry and be pampered. Their aspirations stopped there.

Kayta went by the name Katie when she was around people she knew. Katie listened to her little sister when she would talk about her dreams. Katie didn't feel compelled to let her mind run into the clouds as her little sister did, but she would listen when Yael described her future. Yael wanted to see the world. Yael wanted to explore those mountains and the lands beyond them. Once she conquered the mountains around her home, she wanted to see Jerusalem and Alexandria. Perhaps one day, Yael would go to Rome and see the famous statues that littered the city like sheep litter the highlands in the summer. She wanted to see a chariot race in front of thousands of screaming citizens. Once she had seen that epic event, Yael could sail home and bring back epic stories and exotic relics that no one had seen. Then, she would do it again, perhaps traveling to Uz to meet the descendants of Job. He was her favorite character from scripture. She also wanted to visit Caledonia. Something inside of her told her that in the future, knowledge of that place would be necessary. She knew that one day, it would be necessary and it called to her to come and visit.

Katie was always polite when her little sister talked through her dreams. Katie didn't share Yael's passion for seeing the world. However, she knew her little sister thought these first few steps into the village each morning created sights like what a walk in Heaven would be. Seeing snow on mountain peaks while listening to the sounds of rushing water gave her the courage to dream, all the while trying to hide the village's secrets for another day. Those secrets, after all, would be what pay for her to explore the world once she has the courage to do so.

"Your day will come when you will see the world," Katie would tell her. "Just be smart when it does." Katie cared for her sister and she didn't want to see her get hurt.

All residents knew that if the Roman soldiers discovered their gold mine, they would enslave the residents and begin extracting tariffs. In the worst-case scenario, they would kill everyone to make a point that secrets should not be kept from the Emperor. This threat loomed over all community activity. Yael hated secrets, but the wealth that came with hiding the truth had its benefits. Her education was one of them. Her physique was another. Both she and Katie were physically strong and well-developed, as they grew up always having excess food in their home. Their slaves were strong and their children were strong. Life in Correae was good for everyone.

Her village gold mine must keep the secret. It was best for everyone. Yael had a secret of her own. One day, she would do more than talk about her dreams to her sister. One day, she would leave this village on a long journey and see the world.

Chapter 2:
On Correae

It was now fall. The seasonal majesty of the valley where Correae was built was perhaps the most spectacular. From the village square, snowstorms were visible on the summits of the Golan Heights, a mountain range both north and east of the city. Soon, bitterly cold air would begin its winter descent into their valley, and the mornings would be cold. Frost would come from everyone's mouth until midday suns warmed the valley, and the air would get so dry that people's lips would crack. For these next three weeks, Correae was Eden on Earth.

The "Northerns", as the locals called these mountains, were rocky and steep, with no commercially viable trails leading over them. The southern-facing slopes, less steep and more walkable, could not sustain enough grass to feed the flocks of goats and sheep that Correae's residents relied upon. Not even the toughest of shepherds took their livestock to the higher flanks of those mountains for more than a day. That terrain was the wilderness of Naphtali that the Torah spoke about.

Last fall, however, a shepherd had decided to venture north to graze his family's flocks. He thought the distance would be shorter than that of a regular trip to the valley floor and the shepherd was looking for a way to do less work. His laziness proved to be a costly decision. The family lost all six of their goats to lions, and the old man returned to the village badly injured. His description of the lion attack convinced all Correae's residents that it wasn't worth venturing into the Northerns. They could buy slaves to handle the care of the flocks if it came down to it.

But despite the danger, Yael desired to explore those beautiful mountains. It was the sole direction that offered adventure within sight of her family home, and she was convinced that no other exploit would make her feel alive.

The eastern border of Correae was a tributary of the Jabbok River. It was the village's water source but had intermittent water flow, and the river's unreliability represented a great blessing as it protected the village's secret wealth. During some years, water coming from the Northerns would create currents in the river so fast and deep that a boat placed in it could make it all the way to Jericho in a long day. Last year, the river had been merely a trickle and no boats could travel either up or down it. This year, there was enough flow to water a few herds of livestock and Correae's residents; but not more. Since no one could depend on the water on this part of the Jabbok, there was no trade route associated with it. Nearly every other river in the provinces of Naphtali and Manasseh was a trade route, as moving goods over the water was always easier than by camel or donkey. The Jabbok's unreliability kept Roman officials uninterested. This year, there was hope for heavy snow, which would boost the water supply and make going downstream to Jericho easy. The village elders said they were due for a wet year.

The other side of the valley leading down to the river was steep and covered in loose rock. It was impassable for all but the lightest and fittest of travelers. Villagers had twice tried to create a road, but it washed away at the first rain or rockslide that hit that side of the mountain. After the second effort, they abandoned its construction and ongoing maintenance. It quickly returned to a home for wild mountain goats and marmots, but never anything bigger like lions or bears. Between mountains, snow, unreliable water flow, and impassable routes in and out, Correae stayed hidden from Roman attention.

Elders from the villages within Naphtali called their oppressors "filth", much like they described the Babylonians a thousand years earlier. These Romans currently occupied not just Naphtali but all the twelve tribes of God's chosen people. Even though Judah was merely one province, most Roman administrators and military called the entire land by the name of Judah. Israel was a profane word and the Ebreet themselves seldom used it, fearing death if they were heard repeating it. However, residents of Correae were proud to claim membership from Naphtali. They were never a part of Judah and they didn't care what the Romans called their native land. It would always be Naphtali to them and their children.

Their history and their faith carried them through the horror stories that were a part of foreign occupation. The traveling Rabbis who came to Yael's village to teach and educate would always tell them that Yahweh would send a Messiah one day to rid them of Roman oppression, in the same way as He had freed them from bondage and slavery many times in the past. However, no matter what the Rabbis said about a savior and final freedom, the residents kept their gold mine a secret. Everyone knew the story that their ancestors spent 400 years in Babylon before they were released. They might need to spend 400 years living on the wealth from this gold mine before this aforementioned Messiah arose from the land to save them. Until there was a savior, there would be a gold mine to provide for their needs.

Yael sensed that the village elders treasured secrets more than their faith and this hypocrisy made Yael pessimistic about a Messiah. If anything, Ebreet people didn't deserve a Messiah, at least not yet. They first needed to repent. Repentance was a part of their faith and she knew it was missing somehow. Otherwise, these Romans would not have come and stolen their freedom.

Correae's geography kept its residents distant from the impact of this controversy. The singular commercially viable way into the village was a low mountain pass to the south. Those hills were less ominous and were rarely covered in snow. They were also the hills the families in the village used most often to feed livestock in the spring and fall and to plant crops in the summer. They provided the cover story for anyone who did arrive in town and sought to investigate the economy of the village. In those rare moments, when a traveler did pass through and stop in, they would usually ask how they survived in such an isolated place. The alibi that grains and legumes provided enough food to eat when combined with meat from livestock was short and credible. People would stop asking questions after that.

To maintain this ruse, each morning, one of the stronger patriarchs would take the village livestock into the lower hills, bringing with him a pair of falcons. Anyone viewing the village from a random mountain pass would see signs of agricultural and livestock activity. If someone were spotted coming up on the main road from Alexandrium or as far south as Jericho, the man tending the livestock would be able to see them long before they could see Correae. If someone was seen coming, a falcon was dispatched to carry the warning back to the village that strangers were en route. That falcon's arrival would signal that it was time to hide mining and smelting operations before there was any chance of discovery. The small contingent of slaves owned by residents of the village was moved indoors upon the arrival of a falcon, as nothing gives away the presence of wealth like the presence of a crew of slaves. Pale-skinned people from Gaul and Brittania don't belong in Naphtali, and that would lead to more questions.

Their village secret was immense in magnitude yet small in size. A short walk south of Correae, on the steep section of cliffs, there was a vein of gold unmatched in all Judah. All who lived in Correae knew that if outsiders learned of the gold, someone would turn this information over to the Romans in exchange for something of much lesser value. The Romans viewed this part of the world as a resource waiting to be used to suit the needs of the Emperor, his family, and the rest of the Empire. All Correaen residents pledged closed lips so that no one outside of the village would know the source of their great wealth.

Years of debate have always led to the same conclusion. The wealth that came from mining the gold was contingent on their ability to sell it without attracting any attention. As such, the village always took the least conspicuous approach to liquidating gold in exchange for goods and services. To begin, none of the gold would be sold or traded in Correae. Any gold that was extracted and made into valuable items would always be carried away from the village at least one night's distance before it was offered for sale on any market. When asked, this metal was "gold from a distant land", not something from a nearby town.

Second, the gold would always be carried by at least one older and one younger person from the village. Any one person carrying great wealth draws attention. Any large group of men would also gather attention. A father and son or uncle and nephew team would be of lesser interest. A father and daughter provided no interest to passers-by looking to pillage. So far, no Roman soldier had searched any Correaen travelers who had been sent out in this tactical arrangement. Romans were predictable. The Ebreet were clever. That was their advantage.

Third, these teams would exchange the gold for Roman currency and use that currency to buy what they needed, regardless of whether the net transaction cost more - the less of a connection back to Correae, the better. Trading smelted and refined blocks of gold for goods in an open market always caught someone's eye.

Lastly, every traveling family would have to leave the market as soon as trading was complete. There would be no loitering and listening to stories. No family would stay back and indulge in the enticement of brothels, wine, or dice. Items must be purchased first thing in the morning. Everyone agreed that once the trading was complete, nothing could be wiser than to put as much distance as possible between the teams and the town.

The village didn't measure the amount of gold a family took when it left the village, but everyone agreed that the amount of gold carried and sold should be based on the village's present needs. During the wedding season, when more goods were needed, more gold was sold for Roman coins. During periods when everyone had their needs met, yearly pilgrimages that the men of the village would make to Jerusalem to seek forgiveness of sins must always include a tithe for the contingent working at the Temple of King Solomon. Since the beginning of recorded history, Ebreet had given their first fruits and Correae's leadership was committed to keeping that tradition alive. They didn't want to be spiritual hypocrites like their neighbors to the south from the tribe of Manasseh.

Ebreet women lived in safety that few women, Roman or otherwise, could fathom. At any given moment, Correae had enough grains, spices, legumes, dried meats, and fish to last an entire year, in addition to iron for tools and silver and glass for ceremonial use. They also held vast reserves of soaps and spices, and all their children were exceptionally healthy. There was literally no better place to have children and raise a family than Correae.

Their good fortune did not stop with their inventories. Women from Correae were more educated than even Roman aristocrats. Anywhere else in Judah, girls secured half the education that boys collected, if that. In Correae, girls and boys stayed in school until the end of Bad Midrash, the final level, before becoming rabbis. Girls and boys were equally educated and the village knew this made their daughters more valuable in marriage negotiations. It made them better mothers and community caregivers since they knew more and had the confidence to learn what they didn't already know.

The village owned several hundred scrolls that they kept in an underground storehouse near the buildings that held the meats and grains. Their library was as extensive as the one in the Temple, and every Shabbat, the elders would read one of these ancient scrolls out loud. They also had writings in Egyptian, Aramaic, Greek, and others in the new language of Latin, which seemed to be growing in popularity. All children would learn how to read, write, speak from the sacred scrolls, and do arithmetic and geometry. Ebreet had learned long ago that invaders could take their lands, their wealth, and their lives, but they could not take their faith or their education. Correa's leadership also saw the dividends associated with the mother in a family having book knowledge equal to that of the husband. Ebreet girls from Correae had perhaps more education than any other sect of Ebreet, including the Sadducees and the Pharisees. Yael and Katie were at the top of this pecking order of knowledge and their parents were proud of them.

One day, though, Katie knew Yael intended to leave and test all of her knowledge in the real world and explore like the boys. Book knowledge had made her hungry for real knowledge and she looked forward to the day when she could put it to the test.

Chapter 3:
Speaking Out

There was no such thing as overcommunication in Correae. Leaders reminded residents all the time that their way of existence was compromised for generations if one family said too much or got their instructions wrong. Village elders visited homes before sunrise most days and reminded the adults and children of their duties for the day. Often, this was a reiteration of what they had been told the night before. It didn't matter how simple or complex the task; getting it wrong was not acceptable. Some mornings, a family was reminded that they were on shepherd duty. On other mornings, they would be working on ore transportation or excavation on the side of the mountain. There were always several people on smelting duty, carrying in coal for melting gold or cleaning up the residue left behind when they mined. There could be no trace in the event a nosy squad of Roman soldiers arrived, looking to find a way to get something for nothing.

This morning, Yael and her sister Katya were in the house when a village elder entered before the first meal. The elder was wrapped in a colorful wool blanket and his sandals were crisp leather. He looked at the girls, for he knew that they would be the ones doing the work.

"Today, the mid-day meal is your responsibility." Both of the girls gave him a thumbs-up signal. They liked this job more than any of the others.

"Have extra water and salt, as this afternoon will be hot." Yael's father had already been told this the night before, but he had been too drunk to relay the message to the girls. Katya told him thank you but stopped short of telling him that this was the first she had heard about it. That would get their father in trouble again for his excess drinking. Both girls were good at covering for him.

As a community, the village decided that a grand mid-day meal was a luxury that everyone who lived in Correae would receive. Most people in the remote provinces from Egypt to Gaul to Brittania and Judah ate twice a day: once after morning chores were done and again at the end of the day. The village council decided to spend part of their wealth to add additional nutrition to each day. This additional allotment of food was shared with their slaves as well. All residents knew that a slave's longevity and usefulness depended on their health. Healthy slaves weren't the result of blessings from the Roman gods, as they were told when they purchased them in nearby markets. Health came from ongoing proper care. The children also seemed to be less susceptible to disease if they had more food in their bellies, less dirt on their skin, and more herbs in their diet. And when girls from Correae would be matched with boys from other villages, the girls were often as tall as the boys.

Yael and her sister loved it when her family's turn to cook the mid-day meal came up. Making others feel at home was their gift, and they enjoyed the work that went into preparing food for 50 families.

"Thank you. My sister and I can lose ourselves making food for everyone," Katya said to the elder as he blessed them and left. Many of the families loved it when they heard that it was "the girls" turn to prepare the meal, as they knew it would exceed expectations and that everyone would be greeted with a cool towel and perhaps a foot washing if time allowed for it. The community often said that whatever man was lucky enough to get either of these girls as his wife would be blessed beyond words. Both Katya and Yael would graciously receive their praise and remind them that a good meal brings joy to the heart.

Everyone in their home worked all morning to get the meal ready. Yael's mother would call it a "near wedding feast" because of the volume and quality of food. Today, an older goat had nearly died birthing a kid two nights before, and it was decided that it would be slaughtered and eaten. One of the slaves did the slaughtering with

Yael's father, and Yael's mother and Katie cleaned the animal. Yael's father placed the hide out to dry in a tree behind their home. The hide would serve many roles and last for up to ten years. The baby goats had already found a new home and both of the girls fed them during one of their mid-morning breaks. Preserving livestock was part of being a good steward; it was an extra blessing that both girls loved animal husbandry and caring for the animals.

Yael gathered spices from the village gardens that had been planted on the path, leaving the village going north. She also took a basket and filled it with firewood, as she needed a lot of it to keep the fire hot. Katya cooked rice purchased from Egyptian merchants in one pot. Another contained the goat, seasoned perfectly and sautéed in oils and savory flavors. A third contained roasted chickpeas and unseasoned meat, as several women were pregnant and had to abstain from eating spicy food until their child was born. All of the food was thoroughly cooked before the first villagers arrived. And once they arrived, Katya and Yael absorbed all the praises with grateful hearts.

Once the meal was over and everyone returned to the mines or their homes, the act of clean-up began. Without fail, other families would contribute their slaves to assist with the clean-up, as the care of the cooking utensils had spiritual meaning. The Ebreet laws required that the pots and utensils must be cleaned and dried before any other task commenced. Yael couldn't find where it said that in the Torah, but she trusted her grandmother and knew it must be in Moses's writings somewhere.

After the mid-day meal, the parents dismissed their children to attend "Bayt Safir", or school, with one of the teaching rabbis they paid to have brought into the village. Bayt Safir would happen at a building near the village square next to a building that housed the traveling rabbis. The youngest children, both boys and girls, visited Rabbi Andrew's house, where they heard stories from the sacred scrolls and focused on learning to read them out loud and memorize them. They sang songs, learned to count, and learned the history of their people. They were taught Ebreet law, and they learned that knowing and complying with God's law is what defined them. It was their identity. All Ebreet history is the story of the good that happens when one submits and follows God and the bad that happens when one rebels against Him.

The teenagers attended Bayt Midrash, where the focus was on in-depth reading and oral skills, as well as writing and recording the events that they saw and heard. They also applied mathematics and constructed small-scale items to demonstrate they could use what they learned. Each year, the students who were new to Bad Midrash would get to read the writings of those who had come before them, each time challenged to outperform the previous generation. The best of their writings would be taken and sold in Jerusalem, along with gold. Sometimes, the efforts were given as part of the village tithe at both nearby synagogues and Solomon's Temple.

Rabbi Thomas led Bayt Midrash and he was well-compensated for taking the assignment. During his storytelling, he emphasized the Socratic method of instruction. He acted as if he were portraying a stupid man and his "dumb" questions made them challenge what they thought they knew. Learning how to reason using intelligence and not emotion was a part of survival in this occupied world for every successful Ebreet settlement, and Correae was no exception.

Today, Rabbi Thomas asked, "What might have happened if Joshua had not answered his calling to write the events of Moses' life? Boys and girls, imagine a world in which the events that occurred during the forty years of travel in the wilderness were not recorded, and we didn't know what happened between Egypt and the Promised Land."

Yael was in Bayt Midrash and she loved these kinds of "what if" questions. They posited an alternative outcome to the one that she had already learned. They helped her imagine what life might be like outside of Correae. After all, she knew she was going to leave one day.

"Rabbi, we would have missed stories about why we should obey the law and how our life's work is to learn to follow Yahweh. We would know nothing of manna or the parting of the Red Sea, and we would not have been taught that the Lord is mighty to save. We might have found ourselves believing in pagan gods like the Romans, unsure of our identity." These words came to her with ease and she didn't look towards any of her peers for acceptance or approval.

She knew in her heart that the recording of that story defined how Correae operated. The elders of her village always talked about the law at public meetings when it was time to make a decision.

"Well done, Young Yael. You understand what it means to be a part of God's chosen people." Rabbi Thomas liked her and he always valued her insights, so he asked her a direct question.

"Little One, what would you have done if you were in Joshua's position, knowing that you were writing someone else's story? Would you have written it as instructed, or would you have changed the words?" He looked at her, as did the rest of the class. There was a heightened sense of tension in the room as the Rabbi attempted to make Yael spend a moment in the shoes of an ancient Ebreet leader.

She paused for a moment before speaking. "Yes, I would be tired each day after walking with Moses all day, but I would write that story of our day's events, no matter how tired I felt. Until that moment, everything that our people had experienced in Egypt and the desert was a secret to the rest of the world, and that needs to be recorded. I may have used different words and said more, though." Her emotions overcame her, and she blurted out, "I hate secrets! I hate secrets and those who think our lives revolve around keeping them!"

Katya always sat next to her little sister and she visibly showed that the outburst took her aback. The other students began to whisper and Rabbi Thomas could tell that the lesson he was trying to teach was lost on Yael's usage of the word "hate". After all, there are no more powerful words in any language than "hate" and "love". In the Ebreet culture, the word hate was reserved for the worst people and the worst behavior. It was not used to describe feelings for Roman occupiers who exploited Ebreet at every chance. Rabbi Thomas saw that he would not be able to teach anything more that day. "Everyone is dismissed to go home. Yael, I need you to stay."

After everyone left, Rabbi Thomas approached Yael, who had her head down in shame. She knew that she had disrupted class and it cost the village a lot of money to keep Rabbi Thomas in residence. He sat on the bench next to her, placed his hand on her face, and turned it towards him. He thoughtfully smiled. He knew that pleasing her teacher was important to her.

"Young lady, that outburst will not be forgotten. You struggle with a deep issue. Your community depends on you guarding your words, for if one small lapse of self-control regarding your village's livelihood escapes the village boundaries, all that your parents and your grandparents worked for is gone. You understand that I have to tell your parents about this?" She bowed her head in shame, acknowledging that she understood. He kissed her on the head, as he knew that she was not being punished. She was being disciplined.

"You are dismissed, Little One," he said, with what affection the circumstance allowed.

Yael walked out of the room with her head down, knowing that she had to repeat this conversation with her family at the end of the day. Soon after that, everyone would know about what had happened. She was mad at herself.

Hours later, Rabbi Thomas stood at the threshold of Yael's house before dinner was served. Seeing him, Yael felt a different kind of shame than she had experienced earlier. She was embarrassed for her teacher to see what life was like inside of her home. Her mother tried to keep it a secret that her father was a drunk, but almost everyone knew. Yakob worked hard during the day, but the end of each day wasn't a family celebration in Yael's house like it was in the other homes in the village. Although Yakob had not started his evening drinking yet, she knew he would start soon. Yakob was the first one to make eye contact with the teacher as he stood at the doorway to Yael's home.

"Greetings from your servant," Rabbi Thomas said. "May I enter?" Before getting an answer, he took off his sandals, bowed his head, and stepped into the house. He immediately sat himself next to Yael's father. The Rabbi told him the story of Yael's behavior. Yael was mesmerized as he spoke and she couldn't believe how much he had focused on all the good things she had done before he described her outburst.

"Sir, I don't think she will do it again, as I think she knows the consequence to the whole village if she has another verbal explosion.

If you don't mind, I will handle this outburst personally. I will let you know if it happens again. I don't think it will." Yakob nodded and accepted the Rabbi's strategy for disciplining the young girl. However, Thomas could tell that Yakob was not acknowledging his daughter and her gifts. It was as if he was dismissing this event like the story of a lost goat who was found at the end of the day.

"Father, your daughter has a desire to make a difference in the world and has been given the skills to do so. She is a female version of young David before he slew Goliath. She is the best with language in this village, and she understands economics and geometry without any need for practice or advanced instruction. She has a memory for history, and many of the boys consider her to be out of their league. They don't compete with her in my contests. She and Katie are the two brightest, and Yael is this village's best student."

For the first time since entering, Rabbi Thomas made eye contact with Yael's mother and did not focus on her father. He looked at both Katie and Yael, making sure that they heard him repeat what he said. They needed to know he was speaking the truth. Yael's father shook his head and finally decided to say something.

"I don't know if my youngest will amount to much. If she keeps her mouth shut and behaves like the Pharisees tell her to, she will be ready to marry off soon. I can't imagine her keeping her mouth shut. Erusin for her would make all of us happy, but I am not holding my breath. I don't want to listen to this. You all can start eating. I will be back later," he said, standing up and leaving the room.

The girls looked at each other, knowing now that the Rabbi had observed their father's unwillingness to be there and his low standards for his daughter. As the leader of a house from the tribe of Naphtali, he should have led the family in evening prayers before dinner and spoken a blessing upon his wife and each of his children. Instead of following customs, he was gone, probably to go down the road to get a flask of alcohol. Rabbi Thomas saw the shame on the three women's faces. He stayed seated and said a short blessing that Yakob should have said, stood up, touched the two girls on their heads, and left. Moments later, their father returned with a small pot of wine under his left arm. He sat next to Yael's mother and started his regular evening monologue about his day at work while he drank the entire pot.

He didn't speak to either of his children for the rest of the evening. Yael went to her room and she and her sister lay down and cried. Katie held Yael, forcing themselves to smile at each other for something they knew they didn't deserve.

Yael wanted a normal family. She wanted the love of their father and the acceptance in her own household that everyone else got. She heard Despi's father tell her that he loved her, but neither she nor Katie had memories of that occurrence. She and her sister had a hole in their hearts; they wanted their father to be proud of them. Unfortunately, Yakob seldom listened to input from Yael's mother. Yael saw how the other men listened to their wives as they led their families, and Yael was sad and sometimes bitter that her dad didn't participate in the lives of his own family. Yael and her sister would often commiserate about their father's drinking. Sometimes, she and her sister hated him, choosing to be so alone and disconnected from his family. This evening, Yael had wanted him to be present and active in front of Rabbi Thomas. It made the hole in her heart bigger.

More than anything, she wanted to see life outside of Correae. Did other villages look and act like theirs? What were big cities like? What did a synagogue look like? What did a Roman soldier look like? Her father had promised both she and her sister that he would take them both one day to see the Temple in Jerusalem, but with his drinking, she doubted that this day would come to pass.

Soon, she and her sister were asleep.

Chapter 4:
In Need of a Companion

Yael dreamed of exploring the Northerns and she hated that she could not get either her sister or her cousins to go with her. At the heart of her desire was how much she hated her fear of the unknown. What she needed was someone who shared her passion for exploring Creation. In fact, that was her daily prayer.

Yael disliked a lot of other things about her village life, but being a girl in a male-dominated society was perhaps the biggest one. Boys got to travel with their male relatives. Girls seldom did. And with her father being a drunk, she would not have that opportunity, as he didn't travel. As a response, she took it to the Lord in prayer with all the boldness she could muster. "Yahweh, please send me with a way to travel."

Unfortunately, there was no one in Correae interested in going with her. She always got the same reply when she would talk to someone about joining her on one of their days off. "Yael, you are crazy. Don't you remember what happened to Grandfather Haim? Why would you want to take that risk when all that we need is here?" What they said was logical, but it didn't appease the calling on her soul. Something bigger than living a happy life in Correae was in her heart, and she couldn't ignore it. She was called to more than being a good student and one of God's chosen in a wealthy village. She was not a wife in the making. She was an explorer.

Her sister gave a constructive response. "Why don't you take up other challenges that don't risk your life and mine? There are other ways to explore outside of walking where lions roam." Her sister was a rule follower, which to Yael meant she was boring. She appreciated her sister's gestures to be safe and smart, but they didn't give her any peace. She suggested traveling with her aunt to visit the coast, but she didn't want to spend a week in the house of someone else's family where she didn't know anyone. She wanted adventure.

Yael lost count of the number of times she committed to going into the Northerns by herself. The evening of every Sabbath, she would tell herself that tomorrow morning, she would do her share of pre-Sabbath chores, make up a story to tell her mother, and quickly leave to walk into the Northerns when no one in the village could tell her not to.

The morning of the big day would come, and she would finish her chores and ready herself. She would start her walk north of the village, leave the last man-made outcropping, and every time, her courage would fail. Words from her sister would creep into her mind, and if that didn't stop her, the fear of being alone would take its place. She couldn't do it. She would turn around and come home, dejected. She would sit by the river and throw stones, watching the trout go up and down the river with no boundaries other than the water itself. And she was jealous of the trout.

What she needed was a companion who didn't say no or come up with reasons not to go. She knew that courage doesn't magically appear. It is nurtured. "Please, great Yahweh, send me the courage to travel," she prayed.

Chapter 5:
Colch

Education was foundational to the residents of Correae. Reading, writing, and storytelling are how the Torah was passed from one generation to the next, and it was also how the children learned the ways of Roman commerce, mining, smelting, seamanship, orienteering, geometry, algebra, and problem-solving. All education was directed by the local community of elders and school teachers, and it was customary for elite Rabbis to take a sabbatical from the Temple in Jerusalem to teach in remote villages. These rabbis would often invite people outside the village to join them when they came in to teach, but they always sought permission from the village leadership, who paid their hefty salaries.

During this fall season, Rabbi Thomas made such a request. When he explained to the village elders that his nephew Colch was training to become a Rabbi, they quickly approved. Since Colch would soon have his Bar Mitzvah, an in-depth study of the Exodus from the land of Egypt and the tyranny of Pharaoh would help prepare him for his transition from child to adult. Exodus and the formation of ancient Israel were Rabbi Thomas's upcoming subjects, so he brought Colch to join them. Colch would reside with them for a moon cycle and his status as a nephew of a rabbi meant that he was sworn to protect the village's secret.

The students looked forward to having a new member in their classroom. Colch arrived nearly unnoticed, as he arrived separate from his uncle, wearing a traditional Ebreet outer cloak and came with a small bag of his belongings. He stopped and greeted an elder on his way into the village and asked which home belonged to his uncle. Yael and Katya watched him enter the village without speaking a word to each other. When the old man turned and pointed towards Rabbi Thomas's temporary residence, Yael made eye contact with Colch. The boy smiled and waved at her, dropped his gaze, walked towards his uncle's house, and entered.

Katie looked bemusedly at her sister's face.

"He thinks you are cute!" she said, with a smirk on her face. She knew her sister well enough to know that she was already wondering what this new boy was like.

"Shut up, Katie," said Yael, and her sincerity made Katie laugh. Yael had no response, as her sister had caught her staring at the boy. The blush on her face was her words, and it made Katie laugh harder. Yael stuck her tongue out at her sister.

"I hate you, Katie," was all she could say before Katya put her arm around her sister and pulled her in for a hug. That made Yael laugh.

"Was it that obvious?" Yael said. Katie smiled and nodded yes.

Once the laughter subsided, Katie took a moment to be serious. "Don't do anything stupid, Yael. Remember that you are one of God's chosen, the same as that boy is, and are meant to live to a high standard. We aren't Romans."

"I know," said Yael. She stared at her older sister's feet. Yael felt embarrassed that her schoolgirl crush was easy to see.

"Come on," said Katie, breaking the silence. "Let's go get fuel for this evening's cooking fire before Mother starts yelling again."

Yael was glad to have Katie as her older sister, but it didn't change the fact that, over the next few days, she kept reliving the glance she had shared with Colch.

Correae's boys and girls got to know Colch over the next few days as he was actively engaged in his uncle's teachings. They soon learned that Colch had the gift of gab. His words came out so fast that he would sometimes refer to Rabbi Thomas as "Uncle" instead of "Rabbi", and he would have to correct himself quickly. When this happened, everyone in the class laughed, including Rabbi Thomas. Yael continued to stare at him, and once or twice a day, he would make eye contact with her and smile. He liked her, too.

Colch joined the boys and girls to listen to stories from the teens who had traveled to the market. One boy, Malachi, had recently returned from Joppa to bring back items from the seafarers. Malachi spoke about how long the docks that led out to the boats were. He claimed that it took longer to walk down a dock than it did to walk across the village, and he was amazed that every step he took was on wood. Some of the boys asked Malachi questions and he answered with great authority and confidence.

When he was done, Colch softly spoke into Yael's ear as everyone paid attention to Malachi.

"It isn't that big. That dock supports three boats on each side at a time, and I could walk down and back holding my breath." Yael looked him in the eye and was enamored with his worldly experiences. She was a bit jealous that he had already done things that she had dreamed about. When she learned that the two of them shared the same birthday, she felt more companionless in her pursuit of grand experiences.

"Where else have you been, Colch? Have you been to the Temple?" she asked eagerly.

"I have, but we stayed for a single day," he said. "My father --" His voice cracked, and he went silent.

"What is it? What happened?"

"He was killed at the Temple. It was an accident. It happened during some of the construction projects that the Romans had been funding. My father was carrying stones to one of the new projects on the Temple Mount and a column fell on him. It killed him, as well as two members of the Sanhedrin." Yael's heart broke. Her father was a drunk; Colch had no father at all. Perhaps they didn't have a tapestry of shared experiences, but they each had a father who wasn't there.

"Colch, I am so sorry," she said. It began to make sense to her why Colch's uncle had made it a priority to bring him to the village. She sensed his grief and it seemed sincere. She reached over and held his hand for a moment. He smiled weakly. "I have always wanted to leave this village," she said, hoping to distract him from his pain, "but I don't think I will be allowed to go. I guess that's a small complaint compared to your burden." Of course, he didn't know about her father's habits and what that had done to her.

Soon, everyone left the village center and began making their way to their homes to prepare for the evening meal. Yael was almost there when she felt someone tap her on the shoulder. She turned around and Colch was standing there, albeit a bit winded. He had obviously run to catch her before she entered her home. Once the sun went down, he could not be allowed in to see her again until the morning. He needed to get to her before that happened.

"I was thinking about what we talked about. Yael, you can go to these places, Pretty One."

"What?" she asked.

"You could travel to these places, too. I am sure of it. Thousands of people visit them every day. You could do it, too. You could go by yourself if necessary."

"Really?" was all she could say before she heard her mother yell.

"Girls come inside! It is time for dinner!" Reluctantly, she turned to go inside. She stared at the ground the whole time, a smile on her face that she didn't want anyone to see. "Thank you," she said to Colch.

His word choice had been deliberate. He chose to use the word "pretty one" when he spoke to her. "Pretty one" was meant for those who were engaged to be married or who were already married, not a word to be used between friends or family members.

What he thought of her was now her secret. She didn't know if she could tell Katie without hearing another lecture about Torah and the law. Add that restriction to the list of secrets.

Chapter 6:
The Northerns

Katie continued to tease Yael about Colch for the rest of the week. But, of course, her sister didn't know the words he had said to her. Katie saw that Yael was enamored with Colch and she talked about him all the time. He had real experience and had traveled. Colch was also a bit mysterious. But his words that day had been intimate, especially since he didn't know her. She wondered if he could be her husband one day and they could see the world together.

No one had called her "pretty one" before that moment. Her dad could have used those words since they reflected both romantic and familial love, but he didn't. Receiving affirmation from him became nearly an infatuation that she thought about often. When she would look at herself as she combed out her hair each evening, she would look at her image and say to herself, "pretty one," diligent in getting her hair as straight and as perfect as possible so he would think that when he saw her again in the morning at school. Sometimes, she put it up using pure silver needles customarily reserved for formal ceremonies, but her sister thought she looked beautiful when she did it.

Colch continued to spend time with Yael and Katya. He liked sitting with them at lunchtime and he told stories of how far he would sometimes walk to find drinking water in his home village outside of Jerusalem. He told the girls stories of life outside of Correae whenever he could, but he was wise enough to withhold the use of "pretty one" if other people were listening. Yael had not reciprocated the intimate words, as she was taught to withhold their use until she became engaged. She wondered if Colch had been taught the same message, but she didn't dare to ask him what he meant by his choice of words. In a way, thinking about what he meant was scarier than leaving the village.

At the end of his third week in the village, Colch was talking to several of the boys and girls in their class when he began to speak of the Northerns in a poetic manner that described their natural wonder in a way that mesmerized Yael. He told everyone that they didn't know how great a picture of Creation they lived with. He said it was more beautiful than Jerusalem and more mesmerizing than the sea at sunset.

Despy and Nava looked at the admiration on Yael's face. Once Colch finished, they giggled, saying, "Did you hear him, Yael? He thinks like you do!" they said, giggling again.

Yael replied with an air of indignance, "Of course he does! The Northerns are a gift from Yahweh from the time of Creation. They are the definition of beautiful! They are not meant to be a background for gossip!" She refused to look at her cousins, as she knew she was right, and Colch thought the same way. As soon as school was over, she stepped outside and looked up at the Northerns. She waited for her cousins to join her outside, and she spoke to them, still angry from this morning.

"All of creation is meant to be explored. What if Adam and Eve had not explored Eden and named all the animals?" she said out loud. Her cousins had long since forgotten that conversation and were ready to go home for an afternoon snack.

"Come on, Yael, school is over. Let's go home and get something to eat," Nava replied. Colch joined them on the walk back, as he did most days. He spoke in a soft voice meant to soothe Yael, but he knew everyone else would hear his words.

"I agree with you. Creation is meant to be explored." Despy and Nava looked at each other and giggled again. However, Yael's heart raced. Had her prayer for a companion been answered?

At that moment, they were all interrupted by the village crier. They were told to go to the village center for an announcement. These were common and were intended for adults and not children, but everyone was required to attend. Colch asked Yael to stand in the back, and when Yael was confident no one could hear her, she found the courage she had been praying to receive. She had made a decision. She whispered, "I have to tell you about the Northerns one day, Pretty One."

Colch stared at her for a moment before speaking. He grinned and said, "I would like that very much. In fact, that is what I wanted to talk to you about. There is nothing to do on Shabbat once the ceremonial activities are done. Do you want to walk up high into the Northerns? "

"Yes!" Yael answered with enthusiasm. "I have always wanted to go up there, but everyone thinks I'm crazy."

Colch didn't hesitate. "I will get my aunt to make us some food for the trip, and we will leave after breakfast."

Yael couldn't keep her excitement to herself. When the announcements were over, she told Katie and received a mixture of amusement and approval.

"You two have fun. Come back if you think you have reached an unsafe place. Remember, it is the Shabbat, so don't do any work. And please wear sandals that you can run in in case the lions show up again!" She paused for dramatic effect. She knew that they were looking for something from her other than advice about footwear.

"And yes, I will keep this a secret. Just don't do anything stupid."

"Thank you, Katie," Yael said, hugging her sister.

The next day, immediately after breakfast, Yael gave her sister the biggest hug she could. "I will be back before dinner," she said to her sister, anticipating her response. She added, "I promise."

"Mazel Tov," Katya replied in her usual teasing manner. "Perhaps Elisha will help you when you reach the top. Or are you going with Moses, too, so you can warm your hands with a burning bush?"

Yael rolled her eyes, but the girls shared a look of deep affection before she walked away. Yael walked as briskly as she could to get to the old house before anyone spotted her and asked her questions.

She didn't have to wait long before Colch arrived. "So, what path shall we take?" he asked.

"You mean, what path shall we *make*? The rabbis taught us that true exploration meant going where no one has gone before."

"Well said," said Colch, looking into Yael's eyes.

"Has anyone told you how pretty you are?" he said as he pointed at a ridgeline in the distance.

"You have no idea how good that makes me feel," was what she wanted to say. Indeed, that feeling occupied her heart.

"Lead the way," was what she said instead.

They walked together along the western edge of the valley, which received the morning sun first. Once they reached the top of the first ridge, they were sweaty. They stopped and drank from one of the flasks of water Colch had brought. It felt cool and refreshing. When they turned around, Correae was not much more than a speck in the distance.

"Wow. That is beautiful," said Yael. She turned to look at Colch and he was already looking at her. She wondered how long he had been doing that, as she had been gazing down into the valley for more than a moment or two before she looked at him.

"We need to keep moving if we want to reach that far ridge over there to get views of the River Jordan," Colch said.

"You know, my eyes have never seen the River Jordan," Yael said as they huffed their way to the top of the ridge.

"Really? How is that possible? You live so close to it. Well, actually, I guess I do know why. There is no way to get there without going south and around the mountains. It would take a couple of days to walk it."

That was one reason. But the truth lingered, unspoken. She was scared to go alone.

They chatted during the next quarter of a day's walk, and as they crested the ridge, they saw the River Jordan. It took Yael's breath away. She could audibly hear the water striking the rocks on each side, and she was speechless as she listened to the distant roar. She watched the water travel down the canyon walls, kicking up white foam as it struck rocks as large as Yael's home. Before she could find the right words to use to describe its beauty, Colch had made a snowball from the patches of snow on the ground and thrown it at her. He missed, and when she returned his attack, she missed as well. Try as they might, they could not hit each other. Soon, they were laughing so hard that had there been any lions there, they would have been scared away by the noise.

After a few more playful tosses, Colch walked up to Yael and embraced her. He wrapped his hands around her waist and pulled her to him. She instinctively lifted her hands and placed them on top of his shoulders, as she had seen her aunt and uncle do on Shabbat. Her heart was racing, and she felt his desire. She felt like his "pretty one". It was a new and exciting feeling.

Yael did not understand what was happening. In her paralysis, Colch leaned in and kissed her.

She didn't know how to respond. She knew of kissing, but the experience was foreign. Her father did not show interest in doing this with her or her sister. What was she supposed to do in return? Was she doing it right? Is this where her lips were supposed to be?

He stopped after a few seconds and asked, "You have never done this before, have you?"

"You mean hike up this high?" she replied. "Never. I love how it feels, though." He laughed, and they kissed again. This time, she got more than his touch.

"Yael, you feel wonderful. Your lips, they are so soft," he said. It made her close her eyes and allow him to kiss her with more passion. He changed his head from side to side as he pulled her in closer and closer. She had not experienced an emotional high like the one she was feeling right now. His lips were making her body react in ways that she didn't know about. She felt like she was in a trance, following a carrot like a donkey might when they would hold it on a string in front of him.

Colch took off his outer cloak and carefully laid her on the ground so she wouldn't get either wet or dirty. Gently, he guided her to the ground and took off her sandals. He placed her on her back and lay on top of her. He ran his hand along her chest, and he stopped at her breasts.

"Can I?" he asked. Yael responded as she continued to wear her smile.

"Of course," she said. She had heard one of the women talking about her wedding night at the river a few years ago, and she remembered hearing her say this is what happened when her husband was ready to become one with her. It seemed appropriate, as this was a secret moment that was uniquely hers and not one to be shared with the village. She closed her eyes and let him explore her body in a manner that no man had. She and Katya were well-developed women and both of them had moments when they would catch the boys staring at them. This moment, though, was different. It was powerful, and she had no boundaries.

She had grown up in a world full of barriers keeping her safe from exploring creation. She couldn't travel. Her world was too restricted. She had no stories of faraway places. At this moment, she was going to explore creation, and that now included this young man. She was going to experience something that other girls don't get to experience until later in life. This time, she was not going to let her lack of courage hold her back. Right now, she pushed the teachings of the Torah out of her mind.

"You can keep going," she said with her eyes closed. And with that permission, Colch kept going. She knew from the sacred scrolls that men and women were meant to become one flesh once they had left home and cleaved together. In her mind, they had done that. That is what happened when they climbed up high in the Northerns. And she had already imagined him as her husband one day. She was not ready to let a beautiful moment be destroyed by fear again. She had already done that too many times and regretted it every time she let fear hold her back. She was done with letting fear govern her decisions. And before any joyous climax could happen for her, Colch was done.

Once they got dressed and began their trip back down to the village, they held hands in silence. Yael felt close to Colch and she casually looked at him as they navigated boulders. She envisioned herself as his helpmate once he became a Rabbi. Colch was to be hers. She wanted to have his children. Yet, she knew she had broken the Torah, and something about what happened didn't feel right. Yael gathered her newfound courage and asked Colch a question that she feared the answer to.

"What are we going to do when we return? Will you tell anyone about what we've done?" She didn't know if she could tell her sister and she was so nervous about what Katie might say.

"I am absolutely not telling anyone! If my family finds out, I won't be able to continue my family's tradition of being a Rabbi. This must be our secret." He spoke with an authority she had not heard from him. His voice had a commanding tone to it. It wasn't a negotiation. It was a notification.

Yael knew Ebreet law was stricter concerning issues for women than men. A man could make love with other women before Erusin, the Ebreet betrothal tradition, but not after. Women from the twelve tribes, however, were required to be virgins until marriage. Colch would suffer consequences for today's act, which is uniquely related to his wish to become a Rabbi. For Yael, the situation would be more dire. Indeed, in some Orthodox societies, she could be stoned for what they had done. At the least, she was now ineligible to marry a man from any of the twelve tribes.

His comments aside, she was not done dipping into her well of courage. Everything about today was new and this emotional rush was another part of today's experience. She wanted to keep going.

"Colch, I think we should commit to Erusin and marry, and you should take me with you to your next destination. You should talk to my father and begin building a house."

Colch looked perplexed as he listened to her. He obviously did not see what had happened the same way that she did. He was obviously not prepared for a clingy response and was expecting a more relaxed approach to sex.

"I like you, Yael. You have more courage than most people. But I don't think you see what happened the same way I do. We simply had a lot of fun!"

Yael's breath went shallow. She had felt deeply connected to him, bound to him, and brought alive when he touched her. How could that have been "simply a lot of fun"? It was more than that. Why did he suddenly stop calling her "pretty one"? None of these responses were good. Colch broke the silence with a statement that he should have told her long before they left to take this morning's hike.

"Last night, my uncle said that I need to return home and begin preparations for my Bar Mitzvah. Before we left to come here, he said that I must leave tomorrow. And that is what I intend to do. I'm sorry."

Yael took off, running ahead of him, crying uncontrollably. Her wound was great enough so that the village she was trying to run away from was now the only place that she wanted to be. No rejection from her father had felt this strong. The shame from Rabbi Andrew was nothing compared to what Colch had just done to her.

Her brain raced as she returned to the Torah and imagined the consequences if anyone found out what they had done. Had she destroyed her future? Would she now be forced to marry outside of the twelve tribes and become the wife of a Philistine? How could she possibly repent and be made new? These thoughts crushed her. She just kept running, trying to let the fatigue of the run pull the thoughts from her mind.

Once she reached her family home, she sat against the back wall outside and lamented what she had done until she could put on a brave face and go back inside. Certainly, her father would be drunk, and her mother would have no interest in what she had been doing. Katie, though, would be on the lookout. She needed a story. She made one up and put on a face to cover her shame. She needed a secret to navigate her sister's inquiring spirit. Perhaps her father had done something like this, and that was why he was a drunk as he coped with his pain. Once her heart had returned to normal and the sweating had stopped, she stood up and entered her home, acting like nothing happened.

As he promised, Colch left the next day to return home. He came to her home to say goodbye, but she was too ashamed to come outside. She told her mother to tell him she wasn't feeling well and to wish him the best.

Chapter 7: Katya's Erusin

It seemed almost cruel to Yael when, less than a week after Colch had left, her sister's Erusin began. Erusin was a critical part of any "real" Ebreet marriage. The couple and their families make it known through a ring and gift exchange ceremony that they are committing to a life together. From the proposal to the marriage ceremony, Erusin lasts up to one year, and for both bride and groom, it is the most exciting and talked about time in their lives.

Custom dictated that the groom enter the childhood home of the bride on the day of the engagement to declare his intentions to build her a home, where the two of them would begin their lives as a couple. Until that house was completed and the groom had set up a place for them to eat, cook, and sleep, there could be no marriage ceremony and no consummation. "For this reason, a man shall leave his mother and father, cleave to his wife, and the two shall become one flesh," was what Rabbis taught every child from every one of the twelve tribes in every village in the Promised Land. It was in the first scroll of Moses and essential to following the Torah. No Ebreet man could marry until these requirements were met. The families were very involved with the build-up to the start of Erusin and there was seldom a surprise on the day of commencement. Katya and Matthew's parents liked each other and their children had grown up together. It made sense that they became one flesh, married, and had children.

Matthew arrived wearing new, beautiful clothing and covered in perfume. He took off his sandals and walked into his future in-laws' small home. First, he gave Katya's mother some cakes his mother had made. Katya's mother received a beautiful prayer shawl that his family had bought at the markets in Jerusalem. Matthew approached Kayta's father, Yakob, as is tradition.

"Father, with your blessing, I intend to marry Katie. I ask your permission for Katie to be my bride, and we promise not to shame you with either our words or our actions." Matthew stared directly into Yakob's eyes as he spoke.

"Do you promise to love her as you both age?" Yakob asked. Yael watched her father get very serious and involved in the ceremony. She was not expecting him to care.

"I promise, as my father and mother have done before me." Yakob nodded his head in approval and motioned for Katya to stand beside Matthew.

"Katie, do you want him as your husband?" Yakob asked.

Katie reached out and took Matthew's hand in front of their father, and Yakob smiled as the two of them interlocked their fingers. Katie turned to face her father and nodded yes. That affirmation was all he needed to approve.

"Congratulations, Matthew. You have earned my first daughter," he said, drawing the young man in for a hug. Everyone began to clap, and Katie's mother went outside and yelled out.

"My daughter is engaged! My daughter said yes!"

Once their mother came back, Matthew spoke to his new fiancé. He was a soft-spoken man at school, and he seldom used unfiltered words the way he was about to. He turned to face Katie, and he held both of her hands. A few others came into the room, including Despy and Nava, and everyone could see the sincere joy on Matthew's face.

"Katie, I desire to marry you. Before your family, I bring you a ring from my forefathers. If you accept this ring and accept our family's offer of marriage, I promise you that I will do to you as we have been taught in the Torah. I will look at no other women besides you. I will guard my mind and my body to keep myself pure and conscious before we marry so that when it is our time, you will be the only one whose flesh I ever will know. I will fight for you and defend you with all my strength. And, I make it known to all that, if necessary, I will die for you. You will be the mother of my children, and I will father them with all my heart."

He maintained his gaze into Katya's eyes. He had known her since she was a little girl and he was a little boy. Now, Katie and Yael were two of the most beautiful young women in the village, and Matthew knows that he has "a good one". Katie was an ordinary Ebreet girl and she was feeling the bliss of unconditional acceptance from a boy who had just publicly told everyone that he wanted her as his wife.

"Katie, your family shall be my family. Your hopes for a family shall be my hope. I ask of you the same that my father asked of my mother when she was a young woman. I ask that you preserve yourself for me and that you make ready your heart to become one with me. I promised your father that we would follow the wisdom of the Torah. We both shall leave our parents' homes, and I will build our home and take ownership of our affairs. We shall become one." He paused long enough to wipe the tears from his eyes before he continued with the part of his speech that his grandparents had asked him to include.

"If you cannot or have not been preparing yourself this way, I cannot marry you. If you have been with another man, I cannot marry you."

Matthew extended his right hand, holding open his palm, exposing his grandfather's Erusin ring that he gave to Matthew's grandmother about 50 years ago. It was made of pure gold inlaid with diamonds. He got down on one knee, bowing his head towards her feet so that when she looked at him, all she saw was his Yamika on the top of his head. After a momentary pause, he looked up at her and met her gaze. Katie blushed and she could look Matthew in the eyes for a moment before bashfulness overtook her. Her heart had melted while Matthew had spoken and she was happy beyond words. The truth was that she didn't care where they lived. She wanted a man who was willing to commit all of himself to her before they married. And she didn't want the life that her mother had. Matthew was not a drunk, nor were his parents. All Katie wanted was to distance herself from that sort of evil.

Katie knew Matthew was coming over to propose, so she wore a beautiful white gown that accented her feminine curves. Her hair was perfectly lifted and held in place by two long, silver ceremonial nails. She, too, smelled of perfume and had fasted all day, praying to have a hunger not merely for food but for the leadership that a good man provides. Katie picked up the ring and put it on her ring finger.

She had scripted her response, as every little girl knows that this day would be a part of her future and a life-changing moment. She had looked in the mirror and practiced how she would respond to her Erusin request, as all the girls in the village had for generations. She knew what to say and how she was going to say it. This was her singular moment to apply what she had practiced.

Instead, she lost herself in the moment. She saw that a single tear was falling from Matthew's right eye. Matthew exceeded every expectation that she had for her future husband and her passion was bursting from her to the point that she couldn't control it.

"Matthew, I see your heart. I--" Overcome with emotion, she had forgotten the words she had prepared so long ago and practiced so many times. Matthew put his hands on her face to wipe away the tears. She apologized, collected herself, and continued.

"Yes, Matthew, I have been pure. I also have followed the wisdom of our people. I shall take you as my husband and bring you honor. We shall make a house together and live in accordance with Yahweh. We will serve together every day. I will take care of you and our household, and it is my prayer that we will have many children whom we can teach the ways of our ancestors. Matthew, yes." At that, she broke down again.

Matthew took the cleanest part of his all-white tunic and wiped the tears from her face again. It made both of them laugh. Finally, Katie gave up, threw her arms around him, and cried with joy and satisfaction. Abruptly and in front of the family, Matthew kissed Katie on the lips for the first time. Despy and Nava both cried as they watched the intimate exchange. Although uncommon, a first kiss was considered a part of Erusin. Matthew told Katie that she was the most beautiful woman in the world and kissed her again.

Katie couldn't speak but continued to let Matthew embrace her as she closed her eyes and laughed.

"Katie, I will build our home as fast as I can. Your father and my father will help me. It will be beautiful, and we will live there!" The tears were all gone now and Matthew swelled with happiness.

All the while, Yael watched and felt like she wanted to die. Her heart was getting shredded by the truth that she was ineligible to have what her sister did. She admitted that Katie was receiving what she wanted from Colch. Now, Colch was gone, and she was alone with her memories of that selfish boy who took her virginity. She said a half-hearted prayer to God for a second chance at life and marriage, but her tears of self-pity and self-loathing interrupted the prayer. All of her family thought she was crying tears of joy for her sister. They had no idea that what they were seeing was regret at what she had given away when she had given herself to Colch. She wanted to redo her life and take away that moment and the choices that led her there. She was now coming to terms with the fact that her election to have sex with Colch in secret came at the cost of what her sister was getting to experience. She felt dejected and did her best to congratulate Katie and Matthew.

Later that evening, as Yakob announced to all in the village square that Matthew and Katya had consented to Erusin, dancing and celebration began. Yael's father was not getting drunk that evening, and that also made Yael feel hurt and angry. How could he stay sober for Katie but not her when Rabbi Thomas had come to their house? Why was her father deciding to take ownership of his responsibilities for Katie and not her? What was wrong with her that he didn't love her as much as he did his first daughter?

She tried to get lost in the joy of the Erusin party. Matthew's family had killed a goat and all families ate the meat as they celebrated. Despite 50 homes in the village, the excitement in town made it feel like there were 1,000. Yael walked among the crowds, filling people's cups and serving food. Staying busy was her antidote to sadness.

The village gathered by a fire in the center of the village square and celebrated with ceremonial wine and tales of their own Erusin moments. They spoke not of the joy of forming a family but also of the hard work and suffering. And nothing got more story-telling attention than the extra workload a young man took up when he committed to building his first house. Per tradition, young men during Erusin do not get time off to build their homes. They must continue to serve in whatever role they already occupied, like farmer, miner, or shepherd. In the early morning and late evening, they must work on the home. Men often built or helped build ten or more houses in their lifetime, but it was the first one and the first alone that Ebreet society used to judge their skills. As such, the groom would run his ideas past the best construction minds in the village for commentary and assistance, and it was considered a great honor to be asked to help. In this moment, the groom's skills as an organizer, leader, and foreman must stand and be recognized despite his lack of experience. All men are considered carpenters and stone masons once they have completed their first home, and they knew that their first works would be the singular judge of their skills.

One part of the conversation captured Yael's attention. Both men and women told stories about the difficulties of staying celibate. Many grooms used this project to distract themselves from the awakening sexual desire now raging inside them. For the betrothed couple during Erusin, waiting was the hardest part.

Yael stared at her sister as she walked around the village, holding Matthew's hand. She knew that her sister would wait patiently and loyally for their wedding night. She wanted to be happy for Katie, but all she felt was bitterness and soon, that bitterness turned to hatred. She hated her sister for staying pure. She hated her father for choosing this day to finally start acting like a father. But, more than anything, she hated herself.

Chapter 8:
The Wedding

For Yael, every day in the build-up to Katie's wedding felt more painful. Katie was honorable and she followed the rules. She kept no secrets and she was destined to be a good wife and mother. Despite Yael's initial desire to tell her sister that she had sex with Colch as soon as she returned from the Northerns, she couldn't. She didn't have the courage for that task, either. She knew it would crush her sister, and she wanted her to rejoice in her upcoming wedding without thinking of her little sister's failure. Yael's fornication got added to the list of secrets as part of life in Correae.

Katie played the part of a soon-to-be bride with natural ease. She spent her final day with her childhood friends, laughing and giggling that this would be her last night in her old world before she would move to her new one. Everyone was happy for her and a few of the older women came into the room when she was putting on her marriage gown, trying to tell her what men like and what she was supposed to do. Yael listened but didn't laugh. The women were exactly right with what men liked. It gave her a sense of melancholy that she could visualize everything the old women were telling her. It reminded her of how badly she messed up by giving herself to a man who disappeared from her life the day after.

Katie politely listened to their advice but she told the older women that she couldn't wait to give herself to Matthew. She couldn't wait another day to consummate herself with Matthew, and Matthew had worked his hands nearly raw to have their house ready as soon as he could. Yael almost lost her stoic sense of control when Katie told her what Matthew whispered into her ear. His intention to bring her to a climax with complete abandon mandated that Yael bury her betrayal in a new way. Colch never concerned himself with her pleasure; he exclusively sought out his own. Yael stared as Katie glowed with bliss. Katie felt no shame telling her sister of Matthew's intentions to touch her body, and perhaps that was the lone moment Yael was happy for her sister. Speaking with her friends in the hours leading up to the big event, one of them heard her use the word "home," and she got softly corrected. "You mean childhood home, don't you? Matthew has built you a new home, and beginning tonight, that is your home."

"Of course," Katie replied, beaming. "I will always cherish my Erusin with Matthew, and I know it was worth it. But I can't wait to be intimate with that man. He has sacrificed everything for me." She made a final adjustment to her clothing. She entered the tradition of Badeken, or veiling, by donning a thin cloth brought home from Jerusalem by her grandfather many years ago, the same as Jacob had for Rachel. All in the room became quiet. Katie was beautiful in a way that no words could describe.

"Yael, the bedroom in your father's house is now only yours. Okay, girls, let's go. It is time," said Rabbi Thomas' wife, coming through the door and into their four-room home to let them know everyone in the village was ready for her grand entry. Katie took a deep breath and began the walk to the ceremonial location on the edge of the river.

Katya's friends walked in front on the path leading down to where her marriage ceremony would take place. They each took a corner of the Chuppah and carried it down the path to the river's edge. Music played and younger girls danced on the path in front of them as they moved towards Rabbi Thomas and the ceremonial ground. Once they finished their walk to the river, they set the portal awning down close to the riverside, and both Matthew and Katie stepped underneath it. Rabbi Thomas had been waiting for them with the Torah opened to a specific section on the history of their people. Throughout the procession, he read aloud from these ancient Ebreet texts what the responsibilities of the bride and groom would be once they are married. He ended with, "Be fruitful and multiply," and he closed the scrolls and handed them to a young boy to secure for the rest of the ceremony. The crowd quieted and the procession stopped. Then Rabbi Thomas held his arms out to the side. Two village elders stepped under his outstretched arms and held them up as he prayed for the village and their ongoing success in their struggle against Roman occupation.

Rabbi Thomas asked, "Will the bearer of the ceremonial Ketubah please step forward?" This pre-nuptial document outlined the terms of the Ebreet faith that each bride and groom were expected to comply with. Each was asked to sign it and read aloud what they were agreeing to do for their new family and each other. Most Ebreet women were illiterate. However, since every girl in Correae attended both Bad Safir and Bad Midrash, they could read and write and it made this part of the marriage ceremony all the more meaningful.

Yael saw the joy on the faces of both her sister and soon-to-be brother-in-law, but she didn't share it. Her emotional tank was empty. While everyone else was full and ready to celebrate with the new couple, she wanted to yell out, "Colch, you are a jerk!"

"Because of you, I cannot experience this!" she whispered under her breath, fighting back the tears that came from seeing her own sister's joy and the truth that no pathway existed to experience what Katie was now feeling.

When everyone in the village yelled "Mazel Tov" as the wedding glass was broken, signifying the end of the ceremony, Yael almost jumped back. She hadn't been ready for it, even though the sound and the celebration were expected. At that moment, Yael realized that in her self-centered discontent, she had missed the ceremony. It was an ironic outcome, considering that no one other than the Rabbi was standing closer to the couple than she was.

Matthew took Katie by the hand and led her to their new home for yichud, a short period of seclusion where the bride and groom would break their two-day fast together before emerging to the cheers of the crowd. During this brief interlude, some couples opted to consummate the marriage, but Katie and Matthew had discussed this and agreed to wait until later when there would be no pressure on them. While they were in the tent, the girls could hear Matthew say,

"Please, Katie! Come on. I don't want to wait," and everyone whispered that they thought Matthew might be changing his mind. The old woman laughed when Matthew said that and she reminded the other girls that Matthew was not the first man to change his mind.

The yichud moment aroused stress for Yael. All the other women in the village kept asking her the same question. "Yael, your Erusin is next. Are you getting excited yet?" Yael and Katie were two years apart in age. Before Yael could answer anyone, they would embrace and congratulate her on the upcoming event. These comments made her feel more awkward. "I think I will be ready when that time comes," was the best answer that she could muster. What she wanted to say was, "I have a sin that I don't know how to reconcile and until I do so, the thought of Erusin terrifies me more than seeing a hungry lion in the Northerns."

As is to be expected, the wedding celebration went into the late hours of the night. Yael had to carry her father upright as she took him home, as he once again had too much to drink. There was a part of her that was satisfied to see that he was no longer acting in the role of the perfect father. She wondered how her father had helped Matthew build their home, considering how drunk he got in the evenings. Yet he had helped him every day and their future home was beautiful. It sat next to her house and that made her sad. She would see Katie's perfect world every morning as she got up, reminding her that her sister had something that she couldn't.

Either way, both she and her father missed out on the spirit of the ceremony and they must both live with the consequences of their choices. After putting her father under the feather quilt on the floor of their home, Yael sat in darkness, listening to him snore. Despite her distaste for his behavior and her own pitiful state, she had a moment of clarity. So, she did as she was taught and prayed to Jehovah.

"Yahweh, please hear your daughter's prayer. May my sister's marriage bring you great glory, even though I don't want to watch it do so. I ask that you give her a fertile womb so she can have children for both of us. Please let her maintain her incredible strength. She is my hero. Yes, I want what she has, but I know that I am a failure. I need Your hand to come down and touch me, great Yahweh."

As her sobbing escalated, she started praying aloud rather than in her head. With her father drunk and asleep, she felt no concern that he would hear her.

"Please give me a chance to experience what she did tonight; allow me a chance to bear children of my own despite my sins. I promise to serve you all my days and beyond. Save me from the Pharoah of my sins."

After a few moments, she collected her emotions and stood up. She knew what to do next. She had two things on her list. One of them was urgent, and that one would have to wait until morning.

Chapter 9: Running

Even on the night of her sister's wedding, Yael preserved her secret, telling no one of her intimate afternoon with Colch. In the weeks leading up to the wedding, she perilously reflected on relieving herself of the secret by telling her sister. The weight of the secret was a burden beyond words, but sharing it would break her sister's heart and ruin her wedding. Her mother would warn and her father would be required to wear sackcloth, adding to the family's embarrassment. The penalty for sin was death and she decided to own that punishment alone.

Sleepless nights gave her only two choices. She was going to die alone, without an Ebreet husband and children, or she had to travel to the Temple of King Solomon to offer a sacrifice and receive a bead of atonement. The thought of going to Jerusalem by herself was overwhelming and the task of seeking atonement was beyond her station in life. Her father had been encouraged to go by the rabbi and he, too, was scared to travel a week to confess his sins. How could she possibly do that? She needed Colch to have the courage to hike into the Northerns.

She remembered one of her Rabbi's teachings: When all else is impossible, the probable alone will remain. The sleepless nights gave her determination and daring. His words, combined with her guilt, gave her spunk. Her sister's wedding night was the best time for action and put behind her life of paralysis and capitulation to fear of the unknown. And, no one would know she was gone until she was one of many traveling the Jerusalem highway.

"Father, wake up." She shook her father's shoulder until he awoke. He remained a bit drunk and attempted to sit up, but he couldn't sit up without her help. Once he was upright, she started with her first of several courageous acts: confession. She spoke to her father as if she were in a trance. She needed to tell him of her sin if she was going to begin to heal from her shame and guilt.

"Father, about a year ago, Rabbi Thomas' nephew Colch stayed in our village for a few weeks. Do you remember that?" She had seen her mother try a communication tactic when she needed his input: asking him simple questions that required short answers.

He replied that he did although his speech was slurred.

"Father, I broke our tradition and gave him my body. I can't get married until I atone for my sin. That means I must travel to Jerusalem and offer a sacrifice in the Temple. I need your coins to pay for my travel and to purchase an animal worthy of sacrifice equal to that of my sin. I must go alone, as I don't want to shame you or anyone else in our village. This is my mistake and I must be the one to fix it."

Her father didn't respond. She had counted on that. It was a complicated speech and she had expected him not to be able to follow it. But she needed some acknowledgment before she could act.

"Father, listen to me! I need your coins and your promise that you won't let anyone come after me. You can tell them anything you like. People will not be aware that I am gone for at least a day or two."

"Yes, yes," he grumbled as he reached into his tunic. He took off his bag of coins and handed Yael the whole bag. It was much heavier than she expected. She was unaware of how much currency her father carried until that moment. There was enough gold to buy half of a village. She was not expecting what he said next.

"I meant to give that bag to Matthew, but it sounds like you need it more. I think you are a good kid. I am sorry I was such a horrible father to you girls. You both deserved better than an ass like me. I love you, Little One," he said. He collapsed back into the bedding, turned his head, and fell back asleep.

She stared at him, nearly breathless. Perhaps he did care for her. She looked at the bag of coins and spoke out loud, knowing no one could hear her.

"My father gave me Katie's dowry," with a near tone of disbelief. Speaking out loud made her choke up. Her father never carried this much money, nor was he a big spender or hoarder. This purse of coins was not uncommon. It was special.

She needed to meditate on that truth. Drunk or not, she took a moment to embrace that he willingly gave her the gift meant for his son-in-law and the father of his grandchildren. He said that she needed it more than Matthew did. His words had not been slurred when he said it either. After a few more glances at the bag and her sleeping father, she took a deep breath. Today was not going to be like all the other days when she fell short of courage as she started a hike by herself into the Northerns. She felt more than courage. She felt a missing love in her life take form. Today was a day to act and not play the role of victim any longer.

"Thank you, Father, for saying that. You don't know how much your words meant to me. I don't know how I could do this without you. I think I have my courage. I can do this. I love you, too." She leaned over, kissed him, and stood up. She put the coin purse on her inner garment and secured it. She grabbed the bag she had packed and turned towards the door to her childhood home and took her first steps on a very long journey.

Slowly and deliberately, she walked out of her house and started onto the path that led out of the village. "Yahweh, I am going to Your Temple right now to make things right. But, I do not know the way." She could feel tears coming down her face, and she paused to take a deep breath and survey the world. She put her head down and walked as briskly as she could. Then, she tightened her backpack and began to run. This time, she wasn't running from Colch. She was running toward the God of her fathers, who promised a way of escape from her sins. She was going to the temple of Jehovah Jirah, a place of extreme holiness. She carried her sister's all-white wedding robe in her pack so she could put it on once she had atoned, as God promised to make her new once she had atoned for her sins.

"Thank you for a full moon tonight," she said as she left the village perimeter and headed towards the southern mountains, the lone route out of the valley. It would take her nearly two hours to get through the passage and beyond the Southern, followed by another four hours to get to the main road leading to Jerusalem. Once she reached the main road, she would be one of thousands of people going about their business, and she would be anonymous.

Yael felt alive. She was finally the traveler she had always wanted to be and no one would know she was gone until she was halfway there. She was going to Jerusalem for the first time and she had her father's blessing and some of her village's wealth to make sure she could finish what she was starting.

Her meditation was for sustained courage to finish what she started. She was done with being a coward and making bad choices. She was educated and strong and she needed to get herself right before God if she wanted to have a family like her sister. Acting like a powerful woman who could make decisions was the best idea she had in a long time.

So she thought.

Chapter 10: Growing Up Roman

As a Roman citizen growing up isolated in distant Caesarea, Rufus could sense at an early age that he was getting the "special" treatment afforded the most elite of citizens. His father was Cornelius, a renowned Centurion in the Roman military. He had risen through the ranks of the military and knew the last four emperors on a first-name basis. But Rufus knew Cornelius as his father and the military titles didn't matter. Cornelius loved his only son unconditionally and he shared everything he could with his son.

Cornelius liked to carry a maple staff to signify his role as Centurion over a squad of the best and most well-equipped soldiers the residents of Manasseh had ever seen. He no longer needed a sword to do his job, as his tongue and his parchment and quill had become much more powerful tools to get his job done. Cornelius was synonymous with success and was revered by the Ebreet, whom he governed, as well as the Roman senate, whom he reported to every year with his requests for budget resources. His report on the growth and successes in Caesarea was circulated to all areas of the empire. Cornelius was famous; the emperor himself told him that when he was a little boy.

Cornelius' professional success was a shadow over Rufus's view of his father. In fact, there was no doubt that Rufus would join the military one day and follow in his father's footsteps. He had introduced him to the emperor when he was much younger, and he swam with the children from the House of Caesar. During that time, while playing with other children in Rome, he learned that his hometown was named after the name of the Emperor.

Cornelius, Valentina, and their two children lived in a gated home at the top of a hill in Caesarea, and no one entered or exited without a member of their household knowing of it. The walls surrounding their compound were patrolled at all times by a squad of soldiers and there was no discussion as to how to handle anyone seen attempting to scale the wall. Judgment was fast and fair if you were Ebreet. Those who were of age to understand what they were doing were killed. Those who were of school age were beaten and sent off. If the school-age children returned and attempted to scale the walls again, they, too, were killed. Cornelius always thought this was the greatest tragedy associated with protecting assets like his family. If you didn't learn the lesson, you were not given a second chance. But he also knew that using the Torah against them shut down the vilest of encounters. All people from the twelve tribes learned that the penalty for sin is death, and a holy god does not tolerate the presence of sin. Ebreet already had rules for dealing with sin. He did not need to explain himself if he merely reported the rules of their faith as they broke them.

Cornelius' family kept a small allotment of indentured servants. Still, the workers were well paid, and the children of these indentured servants attended school with his children at no cost to the family. Cornelius mandated that his family do hard work along with the servants, and all of them came together to celebrate holidays and honor Shabbat on Friday nights. Despite being Roman, their outpost in Caesarea was far from Rome, and Rufus and his sister attended Bad Safir with other Ebreet children, who wore the same uniforms that the Ebreet children would wear. The family shopped for food in the local markets like everyone else, and they did not negotiate an unfair price for goods and services. They would always yield the right of way to those who were unable, like the lame and the blind, and they gave joyfully and graciously to beggars and lepers in their area. Cornelius would often strike up friendly conversations with beggars to get to know them as people. People felt comfortable approaching him and telling him about issues that they were facing in the city. The people he governed universally considered him righteous and just. To some, he was the "Roman equivalent of a rabbi."

Rufus' father, more so than his mother, defined how they would interact with the people whose land they occupied. Rufus had strong memories of one moment when his entire family was walking at the edge of the forest on a road leading inland towards Jerusalem. A group of Ebreet were gathered in a clearing, taking a short walk into the forest and preparing to celebrate a holiday. One of the younger men began yelling obscenities at Cornelius as he made no effort to control his rage at seeing a Roman defiling a solemn ceremony. In his words, he blamed Cornelius for everything done by the Roman empire, and Cornelius allowed him to finish his tirade before he did or said anything. Once the man was done, Cornelius took his wife by the hand and slowly walked into their satyr meal and asked them if those ugly words were part of the ceremony.

The group was fearful and speechless, for once he got close, they identified him as the Roman man in charge of their region of Judea. Yet he received no answer to his poignant question. With that, he leaned onto his staff with both hands and spoke to them like an old man. He knew these people honored the elderly more than the Romans he grew up with.

"Very well. I do know something that is a part of the ceremony," he said.

With that, he closed his eyes and blessed them from the Book of Numbers, bowed, and left. After taking a few steps from their gathering spot, he stopped and turned around. Every eye remained fixed on him, as he was much larger than any of them, and they could tell that he was a powerful man.

"I would like to come back here with my family and see this countryside next week on the Shabbat. I think we should all meet here again, and perhaps this time, we should practice the Golden Rule and treat each other as we wish to be treated."

His family turned and left, and Cornelius held Valentina's hand. He and Val slowly left the forest and returned to the trail. Rufus looked back as they were nearly out of sight. He saw that they all remained paralyzed as he departed. "Father, they are scared," he said.

"Son, they aren't scared. They are feeling sorrow, for in their hearts, they know that they committed a crime for treating us poorly.

They are lamenting. Make a man lament using the words of his own mother and he will always act honorably in the future. They don't want to admit that they need to humble themselves before me to make things right. Let them have a week, and let's return."

True to his word, the following week on the Shabbat, Cornelius and his family returned to the clearing. This time, Cornelius was wearing a Yamika and a prayer shawl over his flowing white and purple robes of the sort that a Rabbi might wear. His wife was dressed appropriately for an Ebreet woman, with her head covered and a robe that flowed down below her knees but well above her feet. Rufus' sister was also wearing flowing robes, as she was now becoming a woman. Many of the Ebreet boys looked at her in awe as she was beautiful and old enough to catch any man's attention.

One of the older Ebreet women in the family gestured towards Valentina and their daughter to come and join them at the cooking fires. The eldest amongst them embraced and kissed her, apologizing for how her family acted last time.

Speaking to her softly, the old woman said, "Your husband is a man of God; that means you must be a woman of God. We are so embarrassed by our family's behavior. Please accept our apology. We felt much shame after you left last week."

Valentina laughed and told her not to fret. She reached under her robe and pulled out fresh coriander and sage. Everyone's eyes perked up as it was considered an honor to bring fresh herbs at the start of a meal. "I harvested some of this before coming here. I was hoping we could season the meat with it."

Once Valentina and the old woman cleared the air and apologies were accepted, the other women began talking incessantly to Valentina, each thanking her in their own way. Many of them had no experience speaking to a Roman woman who was friendly and sincere. They all wanted to know more about her garden, asking what else she grew. Soon, all the women were smiling and laughing, and they struck up a conversation as if they had known each other for years.

The camaraderie wasn't isolated to the women; their younger daughters were laughing and giggling with Rufus' sister. Soon, the girls were carrying pots down to the river for water while the women washed the grains and cut the vegetables for the meal. Cornelius looked over at his wife and knew she would be occupied for hours. Nothing made Valentina happier than getting to meet new people and serve them, and he knew his wife was in her element.

While the women started food preparation, the Ebreet men remained transfixed on Cornelius and Rufus. One of the men finally approached Cornelius, embraced him, and began to weep. He looked at the larger-than-life man and apologized for judging him. This was the man who yelled obscenities, and he regretted everything he said. He was embarrassed, unable to cease his apologies. He called forth his son and told his son what he did wrong, challenging the young man not to be like his father, and Cornelius was impressed.

"See?" Cornelius said, quickly looking at Rufus, showing him that time and sin can create repentance without the need for a sword or a whip. Rufus looked up at his father and laughed. Cornelius' softness was sharper than his blade and Rufus stood in awe at the reverence he showed to his father. Cornelius could tell that Rufus would remember this lesson for the rest of his life.

Other men from the family approached the great Roman leader, apologizing repeatedly. They explained their actions, hoping beyond hope for understanding and forgiveness. They claimed that there was no way for those in captivity to know that their captor was a man who knew their Lord and could recite His word from the Torah. These Ebreet sensed that they were observing something unique, as Roman administrators during the first century did not express their faith in public.

Rufus knew from school and from reading letters in the family basement that allegiance to the Emperor was both expected and demanded of all Roman citizens. Worshipping or calling another a god not ordained by the Emperor was criminal. Each one knew that Cornelius was the adjudicator appointed over their region, with the power to pronounce death, and they were fearful of him. However, none of them had a relationship with a Roman citizen, making his presence a novelty.

"We can't understand why Rome is torturing us. Can you explain it to us?" they asked.

They wanted to know the purpose of the occupation. They wanted to know why there had been many changes in Emperors in their lifetimes. They wanted to know why Cornelius was different than other Romans and how he knew part of their language. Cornelius quickly discovered that each answer he gave created a new question, but he was patient and answered all of them. The boys interrupted them throughout their talks, as boys often do. He told stories throughout, knowing that men remember a tale more than a philosophy. He knew the boys would be gone soon enough.

During one of his stories, two of the older boys returned carrying a small deer. Rufus offered to help clean it and before any of them could approve, he had taken his steel knife from his belt and began cutting into the animal's hide. None of them had seen Damascus steel before, and they were amazed at its silvery hue and its razor-sharp edge compared to their iron sickle. Long before they had finished cleaning the first deer, all of the boys thought it would be too small to feed everyone, and they decided to leave to go hunting again. One of the Hebrew boys offered Rufus a spear, but he said that he would run home and get his bow if the other boys would wait for him.

This was Rufus's finest moment as he tried to integrate and be accepted by the boys from the tribe. Fitness was Rufus' greatest strength. He could run and maneuver faster than nearly anyone he had met. He ran home, grabbed his bow and a few arrows, and was back before the other boys finished cleaning the first deer with the knife he let them barrow. Some of the younger boys had taken the stomach from the deer, tied off the ends, and filled it with air. They were now kicking it on the ground, trying to hit a tree that each team defended. No one was allowed to touch the stomach with their hands. If they did, they had to perform twenty pushups.

"That looks like fun," said Rufus as he handed his bow to his father and ran to play with the boys. He immediately figured out that one team was much stronger than the other, and he joined the weaker team. He was able to help them tie the score before the eldest boy said, "Let us go harvest more meat." So, all the commotion of teenage boys playing rough was nothing but a memory. Rufus took his bow from his father's hand without speaking a word before turning and leaving.

"Wait for me," he yelled at them. In an instant, all the boys were gone.

Cornelius finally had an audience in front of the men without any distractions.

"Ask me anything you would like to know about Rome," he said, smiling at the group and extending his hands in a neutral, hands-up gesture. Slowly, at first, the men began asking him questions about Roman citizenship, property rights, voting, commerce, and anything else that came to their minds. Soon, they were asking him questions rapidly to the point of interrupting his answers. Cornelius was consistent in making his points.

"Everything remains yours, but it is under our authority. We demand taxes, and in exchange, we provide roads, water, commerce, and protection from foreign invaders." Eventually, the men in the community understood the subtleties of this new occupation.

Through this sharing, they could see that Cornelius was different than other Roman administrators. In addition to acting as the mouth of Rome, he also spoke to them from the Torah, using it to answer questions about Roman citizenship. The Ebreet were amazed at the freedom afforded to them by the power of Rome. They could travel without permission from anyone, and they were exempt from paying a tariff when they reached their destination. Their currency was accepted throughout the Empire and the only words that were not permissible were words against the Emperor or his edicts. Although Rufus was not there when any of these teachings occurred, he saw the impact that his father made. From that day forward, when any members of that family saw or came within sight of the Centurion, they gracefully greeted him with "Shalom." He responded to them not as a Roman soldier might but as a Rabbi by striking his chest with his left hand, bowing his head, and reciprocating with "Shalom."

From that encounter with the local citizenry going forward, Cornelius taught often at that clearing in the woods. Soon, more than a hundred people would gather monthly to listen to him teach and answer any question without fear of rebuke. Cornelius integrated with the Ebreet community, as did his wife, Valentina. Not long after that, he began attending synagogue on Wednesday nights. When he did, he wore Ebreet clothing, discarding his uniform and blade, which made him the most powerful member of the Roman military in the district.

Above all, Cornelius demanded that no one in the family strike anyone either without cause or with emotion. Any such attempt to use their position of power without a warrant was worthy of a serious reprimand. No matter what their eyes can see, a man should always be allowed to explain his actions before suffering the consequences. If someone did something that was not allowed, and their excuse was either selfish or driven by an emotion that they chose not to control, the Centurion was swift to send them to their death, as he was with Ebreet uprisings.

Rufus did not generally watch his father when he would issue judgment on a man's actions. However, when he did watch him, he was always absorbed by the look on the faces of the people whom he was judging. His father remained stoic throughout the process, yet the Ebreet on trial would almost always be fearing for their lives, and the look of desperation on their faces always led back to the same question in his mind.

"Why did they let their lives come down to a single decision made by my dad?"

He was positive that there were ample times before this moment when they could have done something to avoid this deciding moment, but they didn't. In his way, Rufus felt sorry for the Ebreet. Despite their outward focus on education and tradition, those values were useless when there was a chance that they were about to be beheaded or crucified. Their pleadings were always the same.

"Please, Honorable Centurion. I promise never to do it again. I am sorry!"

The tears would flow, and the screaming and pleading would come next.

For his part, the Centurion was consistent in his answer. "Yes, I believe you. Right now, you sincerely mean what you are saying when you proclaim to everyone in attendance that you will never do this deed again. However, you have done it, and you must pay the consequence for your deed. At least you and I both agree that this deed is something that you should not have done."

And with that, he would most often pronounce their death. For his part, his father was consistent in his response to their pleas. As instructed by the Emperor himself, Cornelius would nearly always state this position by quoting from both the Torah and Roman law. And with so many crimes deemed to be deserving of the death penalty, this task was not difficult.

Chapter 11: Obedience

Rufus was away in Rome with his mother and sister when the most important event in his father's life occurred. One night back in Caesarea, while he slept, Cornelius received a vision from an angel of the Lord that his prayers had been heard. A messenger of the Lord spoke to Cornelius, telling him that he had a higher calling than that of a Roman soldier and judge of the Ebreet. This angel told Cornelius to send the men who worked in his household to Joppa on the coast of Judah to find a man named Simon Peter and to bring him back to Caesarea.

When Cornelius woke up, he obediently complied. Before the first meal, he sent four soldiers to Joppa. They found Simon Peter living with a tanner named Simon. At the other end of this spiritual communication, Simon Peter knew they were coming and he spoke a story to Cornelius' men, but they did not understand it. After a period of polite listening, the men escorted Simon Peter back to Caesarea, per Cornelius' request.

When his men brought Simon Peter inside the walls of their compound, Cornelius fell to his knees. He prostrated himself before the short and overweight man known as the leader of the disciples of Yeshua of Nazareth. His men had no experience seeing their Centurion behave in such a manner, and they became scared. The soldiers had spent the last few days with Simon Peter and saw nothing about the man that justified the sort of reverence that Cornelius was showing.

To further add to their shock, Simon Peter was the lone person who stepped towards Cornelius and helped him stand back up.

His men and servants watched as Simon Peter showed no fear of Cornelius in his afflicted state. Simon Peter began to speak with power and authority that no one expected from the chubby man.

The remainder of that day and the next, Cornelius and his soldiers learned about a humble Ebreet man named Yeshua. Yeshua was the prophesied Messiah. He came to proclaim the forgiveness of sin and freedom from the oppression of the evil that all men do. Yeshua gave His disciples a great messenger called the Holy Spirit, and He taught that this messenger's power dwells with us today, available to those who believe based on their faith.

During this teaching, Simon Peter became animated with both word and song, and all present began speaking in languages unknown to anyone in attendance. Some of the soldiers on duty concluded that the men were getting drunk. This conclusion made no sense to them, as no one was consuming either food or wine; alas, there was no other explanation. All the men who had escorted Simon Peter back to Cornelius and all those in attendance began to praise and worship the Lord using the name of Yeshua. It was as if they had become insane.

Rufus listened to the recanting of this story from several of the servants when he came home and he found his father to be different. Cornelius woke up earlier now and he spent much more time in the basement studying and writing letters while everyone else was asleep. While away at work, he became less likely to administer the death penalty. Instead, he would offer forgiveness of sin, telling lawbreakers to turn from their ways and to sin no more. He continued to call for the beheading of men who had themselves killed other men. However, laws involving crimes of theft or deception were forgiven now more often than they used to be as long as the offender promised not to break the law again.

His home life and the stories he told also changed. Whenever a dignitary from a distant land came to their house, his father would tell of the time that Simon Peter spent in their house. He retold stories of that day and how Yeshua was the Messiah who had been foretold to come and save the world. However, Cornelius lacked the passion and power of storytelling that Simon Peter did, and not all believed him. Silently, many agreed with the soldiers who thought he was drunk.

However, some parts of Cornelius' routine did not change after Simon Peter left him. Cornelius continued to train every day with a bow and blade, and Rufus always wanted to compete against his father. Cornelius promised him that if he joined the military, he would spend hours every day getting paid to become proficient in these tools, and the optics of that lifestyle created a fantasy in Rufus' mind that consumed his dreams of the future.

Rufus remained interested in joining the military, but watching his father's new view on life impacted his view of his father. Rufus now thought his father had become soft in his judgment and leadership, and he was concerned that his father's new approach to crime would be taken advantage of. Some of the men he released back into the public were bad men and he feared for his father's well-being. He had learned in school that Emperors are often killed by those nearest to them when they are found to be lacking in toughness and slow to make decisions. He was concerned that this same fate awaited his father.

Cornelius also insisted that both Rufus and his sister stand in front of him and their mother before leaving their compound each day to receive prayers and blessings. His father's prayers now ended with the strangest of phrases, ones that no one else in school received. Rufus knew this because he asked his peers if their parents did the same. None of them did.

Every prayer also ended with "In the name of our Messiah, Yeshua, Amen!" Rufus heard him say it so often that it seemed normal within a season.

All the men who worked for Cornelius in their household received the same prayer. Cornelius trusted all of them, whether they were Roman or Ebreet. This bothered Rufus, for he knew that any one of them could quickly kill his father, as Julius Caesar had been killed. He and his sister thought that their father and mother were now religious zealots and they were concerned for their well-being.

Cornelius had other visions that he acted upon, but they didn't result in further contact with Simon Peter. Rufus recalled one morning when his father woke everyone up early and told them that they needed to go to the mountains to the south and look for a mountain goat that was trapped in a thicket near the snow line. They were told that the goat was injured and needed to be found and set free. Cornelius sent two of the best soldiers toward one mountain and two more toward another. Their order was to find the goat, set it free, and give praise to God in prayer.

Rufus asked his father about this event while it was happening. "These men are going to find and release a goat of no meaning to us. Why are you doing this?"

Cornelius was a towering man of great size and strength. He put his hand on his son and drew him near. "This word regarding the wild goat came directly to me from God. He gave me this word not to help the goat but to teach me to be obedient to Him. Perhaps my men will not find a goat. However, if they do find a goat, it will grow their faith." Cornelius looked down on his son and smiled. Rufus was occupied with the notion that God could tell him to do something and not deliver on his part of the transaction. Rufus thought that those words didn't sound like words from God but rather the thoughts of an uncontrolled mind.

"But father, what if there is no goat? Are you not concerned about what they think of you? Will they not think you believe in another false god or another incomplete Messiah, as others have claimed?"

Cornelius paused to formulate his response. Everyone who knew him knew how thoughtful he was with the words he chose. "No, son. I am a man who fears the Lord, and if he tells me to go free a goat, I will be obedient! My obedience is not contingent on the goat actually being there. My obedience is also not contingent on my orders being understood. I do the next right task without questioning the motives."

Rufus thought that this bordered on wasteful behavior. Why would a God ask us to do something, knowing that the very task He asked us to do couldn't be done? He gave a brief chuckle when his father was done. He knew better than to make eye contact with him at that moment. He got up and quickly ran off to play.

In the hours after his father's men returned, he learned that no goat had been found.

Chapter 12: Becoming a Solider

Rufus joined the military and immediately connected with the history and culture within the city of Rome. Finally, he was training with men of a like mind, and he loved it. Learning from master archers, navigators, sailors, and blade men exceeded Rufus's expectations. Since he was a third-generation Roman soldier, his father's success allowed him to enter the most elite training camps and academies in Rome, led by the best soldiers and military leaders alive. However, the special consideration afforded him during the admissions and placement process ended the day training started. From that moment forward, it was up to him to demonstrate that he belonged. That meant hard work every day, with lots of competition and testing of his resolve.

The family pressed for Rufus to attend the school in the mountains outside of Rome but within site of the city. It was staffed by people Cornelius had trained with, and he trusted them to prepare his son for combat. Once the family dropped off Rufus at the gated entrance, his mother, sister, and father kissed him goodbye. Rufus knew he wouldn't see them for nearly a year. He courageously picked up his bag and the coins his father gave him to cover his first month's expenses and went inside to meet his fellow grunts and the leadership who would make him into a man. Within a minute of everyone checking in, they closed the doors of the camp and the grunts had basic fitness evaluations. The staff measured how far each man could run in one minute, how high they could jump, how long they could hold their breath, and how far they could throw a stone. By the end of the first day, the young men competed at everything, including how fast they could each eat a chicken. The Romans had learned that competitive men get better quickly, but this worked only if they were challenging each other every day.

The days in training camp started early and ended late, and he loved everything about the competition and the drills that made him better. He loved the early morning runs. He loved the strategic and tactical planning sessions led by elderly Legionnaires who had more experience than his father. He loved the survival training that helped the soldiers identify and live on the plants and wildlife in the foreign lands that Rome occupied. He loved the strategy sessions about how to select the correct weapon in a battle. He loved the cross-cultural training associated with occupying and dominating a foreign land. He loved learning how to cook foreign meals and preserve the food using techniques that he would otherwise not have learned.

Yet, above all those things, he loved the camaraderie. Men were always paired up and they were forced to complete tasks together despite not sharing the same language. The military leadership had learned that the best armies contain men from multiple ethnicities who communicate clearly, regardless of language barriers. It made them more cunning than their opponent, and they were not paralyzed by the need to analyze a situation before acting on their instinct. And they were proficient at following orders.

Attendance at this camp was limited to landowners and their children. Care was taken to ensure that elite Legions were filled with mostly landowners and landowners' children to inspire cohesiveness during difficult combat moments. Leadership knew that those who enlisted without land would be the first to abandon difficult combat. After all, if they had departed before battle, there would have been no family to shame and no disgraceful family legacy left behind. Those who owned land were comparatively wealthy, and their communities and families would be at a loss if they did not return. Those who owned land fought until the very end nearly every time, and their loyalty was unmatched.

Roman leadership also focused on completing campaigns. Their best leaders were always available if their skills were not needed back home in the fields where their family and village crops were grown. "Let's do this tomorrow and take this day to rest" were words seldom spoken by the better soldiers. Soldiers knew that they got to return home once the campaign was complete. If they could finish quickly and receive the same pay, they would be rewarded with more time off. In addition, any completed campaign meant that they would receive a bonus. If the Empire felt like it had acquired more than expected, the bonus would be greater than the total of all their monthly salaries. Certainly, there were lifetime soldiers, but most of the work was completed by mercenaries. Payday mattered at least as much as honor and glory.

In the soldier selection process, preference was given to certain professions, specifically blacksmiths and butchers. Weavers and tavern keepers were not suitable for military service and were often told to go home and learn something meaningful for military service. In addition, all men were required to be taller than the average population and nearly no exception was made for this rule, even amongst the sons of the Senators. Lastly, there was a mandatory medical exam. Good vision and good hearing were the minimum requirements.

If they met all these requirements, they were given three pieces of gold as a signing bonus and a training location and date. There was a Roman adage that those first three gold coins were the first steps on a pathway to 300 gold coins. Soldiers would often claim booty after their battles and would carry home any wealth they could after a campaign. More than one Roman village was transformed overnight when a young man would bring home a chest of gold from Gaul or silver from Sicilia. There were no professions in the Empire that offered such a great chance of overnight wealth as that of a soldier fighting in a foreign war in places that the Roman Empire had not yet reached.

In addition to the possibility of booty, Roman soldiers had something no other military in the world had, and that was regular pay. Each man, whether they fought in the front lines or cleaned dishes, received at least the equivalent of the salary of a tavern employee. The soldiers were paid with coins that had the Emperor's face on each side, and men were reminded of who he was every time they looked at their wealth. Despite a predictable monthly salary, there was little opportunity to spend wealth while at war. As such, the Emperor mandated that all men must save a portion of their earnings. These savings were kept in special rooms at the forts that security guards protected with their lives. Savings were compulsory and an allotment was received each quarter to pay for tombs and end-of-life processing tasks like the shipment of corpses back to their villages. Although soldiers who were newly enlisted complained of this unfair practice, the older soldiers would speak of how many families were left in the dark when their son was killed. Still, nothing would be returned to acknowledge their grief.

Early in training, each soldier received a dummy shield, a sword, and a javelin that weighed twice as much as the real ones. These heavier tools created muscle and endurance that their opponents would not have. On days that the soldiers worked with these weapons and tools, they received extra meal rations to ensure that bodybuilding occurred as fast as possible. Still, the wine was withheld until several consecutive days of training had passed, and the men appeared both stronger and faster in their weapon use.

Once the new soldiers had proven themselves with these tools, the Empire provided them with standardized chain mail that would absorb any sideways blows and most jabs from swords and spears, but this armor did little to protect them from stabbing attacks of knives or arrows. As such, the more elite warriors received plate-based armor that was held together by leather straps. Plate mail stopped all forms of attack.

Marching was a large part of participation in military service. Soldiers were expected to cover fifteen leagues in half a day, wearing their armor and carrying weapons. This rate of travel required that they not stop for food or water, and they needed to demonstrate that they could march both up and downhill at the same speed. Protection of the head was also thoughtful. The Roman helmet was designed to give its wearer maximum protection without blocking any of the senses. The Roman shield was made of layers of wood glued together and bound with metal and leather to keep it in one piece as it absorbed blows from all forms of weapons. The shield's curvature protected all around the body, and it was easy to rotate, allowing one Roman soldier to engage several enemy warriors at the same time.

First and foremost, all warriors were trained in javelin. This was the first item used in combat. All soldiers would engage the enemy with the javelin before they would get in range to use a sword and shield. Recruits who could not pass the javelin tests were not promoted nor taught how to use a sword. They were often sent home with a few coins and a "thanks for trying" decree signed by their commanding officer. On the occasion that an upcoming campaign required much travel, these non-throwers would become cooks and tailors, staying well behind the battle lines.

The last item each soldier was issued was a gladius or short sword. The weapon was meant to stab in close combat situations, for few enemies could afford armor to protect them from the thrusts of the iron or steel blades. Although these weapons were seldom swung at high speed or with great force, those who wielded them won the world for Rome. Any weapon that stabbed into the core area of the enemy had the highest mortal wounding rate.

Men were organized into Legions, and Legions were the smallest unit sent to do the Emperor's bidding. No unit smaller than a Legion would travel to new territory, nor would any unit smaller than a Legion report to the Emperor. Each Legion consisted of nearly 5,000 men under a single commander, and this commander received an audience with the Emperor or the Senate any time he was in need. Each Legion was broken down into ten cohorts of nearly 500 men each. Each cohort was broken down into five Centuria, led by a Centurion. Cornelius was one such Centurion. Lastly, each group of eight men would share a tent. The organization and structure of each subunit had a unique support staff and professional advancement path.

Rufus, for his part, wanted to be a Centurion like his father. He had no interest in becoming the leader of a Cohort or a Legion. As such, all his thinking and planning were meant to make his path into that role as fast as possible. He trained frequently and wore plate mail to strengthen his body. On days when he did not successfully defeat his training partners, he would eat uncooked food, using it to motivate himself to try harder.

There was a better reason to be a Centurion than to follow in his father's footsteps. It wasn't until a soldier became a Centurion and became full-time that he was paid all year, regardless of any active campaign. Centurions were the first type of lifelong soldiers and many soldiers would work part-time for fifteen years before they got a promotion to be a centurion.

Rufus knew from his time in Caesarea that the Ebreet people had no sustainable alternative but to accommodate the Roman military presence there. However, the Ebreet were used to occupiers, and they made money from their presence. Towns were formed everywhere where soldiers set up bases, as the soldiers' regular pay meant regular spending. These towns would provide the soldiers with food, gaming, alcohol, and women. Women were especially important since none of the recent Emperors allowed Roman soldiers to marry while serving. Many Roman soldiers would have children, but the soldier would not marry until his military service was complete. For many soldiers, the towns outside of their assigned military outposts became their retirement homes. Soldiers who retired would move their possessions a short distance from the Roman outpost and make the nearby town their final home. These men were usually well-received. They continued to receive regular pay, meaning regular money would come into the village where they purchased their supplies. In addition, their military and political experience made them ideal candidates for service as sheriffs and mayors, and they helped keep the towns safe. They could also muster resources quickly to defend the town if a threat presented itself. Some retired soldiers continued to work in the community as security guards at the local synagogue or administrators in larger Ebreet operations. Although they remained forever forbidden to speak negatively against the military or its leaders, they enjoyed not having to participate in the war engine of Rome.

Despite the benefits, life wasn't all good for the new soldier. All new soldiers knew that part of their early years of service would include road and aqueduct construction. Both the Emperor and the

Senate agreed that connecting the Empire helped everyone; the military always received the gold they asked for if there were construction plans in the request that serviced the homes and countries of the voting Senators. No one objected to clean drinking water or shorter and faster paths between locations, so there was little political resistance. On these well-groomed Roman roads, goods flowed faster, and commerce safely increased. Commerce meant more taxes and the Roman leadership knew that whatever investment they made in roads and aqueducts would come back many times over.

Also, an army full of soldiers who were busy completing tasks meant an army with little time to plan political overthrows. Rufus and his father had seen how several Emperors would come to power and quickly lose it, in part due to the military having little to do during periods of peace. The current Emperors learned that keeping the troops occupied in non-campaign times required making soldiers into construction workers.

Unlike Empires and the nations that had risen and fallen before them, Romans made it a point to end their battles before everyone was killed. They consistently offered the losers the ability to join the Empire and bend their knee to the service of the emperor. In some cases, the leaders and remaining soldiers could immediately become Roman citizens with all the rights that came with it, including the ability to take slaves and relocate their families anywhere in the Empire safely. More than one army surrendered before they lost to join the Roman Empire. As Rome grew, it made its enemies into allies at an unmatched rate in the history of the world.

For all his efforts to be a great soldier like his father, Rufus was continuously troubled by his father's choice to become a follower of this new faith based on a risen Messiah. During his travels to Rome to join the military, Rufus often wondered why his father and mother picked a God full of ambiguous callings and standards. At times, he felt ashamed of his parents' circumstantial religion. In some ways, he wished to emulate his father. But in other ways, he thought that he could become a better man and not trust a god who tells them to chase after goats that aren't there.

And that is the real reason he joined the military.

Chapter 13: Too Late to Go Back

It was late into the night but before sunrise. Yael's mind had stopped worrying about what the people back in Correae might say when they woke up in the morning and did not see her walking around the village. Instead, she thought about the road ahead and the excitement of meeting new people and seeing new things. Sunrise meant the start of a new day, and the first light was beginning to show to the east.

"I make all things new," Yael repeated to herself a dozen times as she looked up and saw the light coming up from the distant horizon. She had been walking nearly all night, talking to herself to maintain her steadiness. She revisited her father's last words to her before she left. He could not have picked a better time to be the father she always wanted.

"God, if you really do make all things new, please let me start a new life as I walk to your sacred Temple. I promise I will do things right this time," Yael said. Dawn was approaching and the early morning cold would have bitten her to the bone had she not packed a thick cloak and wool socks and mittens. Yael anticipated success, but her preparations were thorough to address shortcomings with food supplies along the way. Her bag was full of provisions. She had enough bread, hummus, dried lamb, oil, and salt to last a week. All the boys told her it was five or six days to Jerusalem. She planned for seven. She had a comfortable bedroll, a wool hat, and thick socks to wear, as she had heard many of the men speak of horrible nights of sleep because they forgot to bring comfortable bedrolls and clothing that would keep them warm at night.

"I have got to get out of the valley before sunrise. Once I get on the road to Jerusalem, I can find a quiet place and rest," she told herself as she allowed herself to be guided by the moon and stars. The road was well-traveled and there was no way for her to get lost. Her steps were methodic, and she allowed herself to sip water while she walked. It tasted so good to her, but she dared not sit down. She had to keep going as the first checkpoint of her trip was somewhere ahead of her.

"I am coming, my Lord," she would say when she would accidentally kick a rock as she walked during the night. She had been looking at the maps in the basement of the school for weeks and she had memorized the names of each town she would pass through. One of the elders in the community had recently told a story of his trip to Jerusalem with his twin grandsons and she paid attention to everything he said. She felt like she knew the way.

Her inventory was as complete as it could be, as she had all kinds of items she had brought with her from the wedding feast. She had two large skins filled with water. The unknown of walking made her remember that water is the one thing that she cannot go without. She knew she was crossing a part of the desert of the land of Naphtali; next, she would cross the land of Issachar. After Issachar, she would be in Manasseh for a few days before she would enter the land of the tribe of Benjamin. The City of Jerusalem was in the land of Benjamin, on the top of a hill made famous in all the poetry and writings of the great prophets. That meant her first trip out of Naphtali would include the lands of four of the ancient tribes. That was enough to think of herself as a traveler and adventurer.

She reached into her cloak, feeling for her father's coin purse. Her anxiety disappeared when she heard the sound of gold and silver moving inside the bag. Once she felt it, she reached up higher and touched the smaller pouch containing two small coins near her breast pocket. Perhaps the best thing that Colch had taught her was to keep a small amount easily available for bandits to discover should they come searching. As another part of her cover, she carried two scroll cases filled with some copies of the prophet Isaiah so she would have a story if Roman soldiers stopped her as to what she was doing.

They couldn't read Ebreet and would believe her story before she finished telling it. At least, that is what Colch told her. Her sister could fashion and deliver a believable lie, but Yael was not adept at it. She thought about what lie she might fabricate as she walked through the night. Between praying for courage and practicing the lie, she stayed awake.

Finally, she passed beyond the last of the rock outcroppings that formed the pass through the Southerns and stopped to catch her breath. She knew the intersection of the Jerusalem highway was only a few steps ahead.

"I did it!" she thought as she looked at the forested region beyond the southern pass. This was the furthest she had traveled from home and a break was long overdue.

"Now that I am here, I shall rest. Today will be stressful, and I need to sleep," she told herself. She looked around for a place to lay her bedroll and sleep. She cited a good location, left the road, and walked into the forest to lie down and rest without attracting any attention. She found a small clearing that she guessed had been used for this purpose by others, and she laid out her bedroll and quickly fell asleep. She had many dreams and her sleep was restful. She woke up startled by sounds all around her as morning activity on this road had started. She could hear horses and oxen pulling carts as well as the sounds of some villagers talking in some dialect of Greek that sounded new. That meant the intersection of the highway was near.

She quietly packed up her bedroll and put it on her pack as securely as she could before she stepped out of the clearing and began walking back towards the road. She didn't know how long she had slept, but the skies were already bright and clear.

"Thank you, Father," she said to herself as she began walking. She reflected for a moment as she saw the landscape in the light of day. Her plan to leave the wedding and atone for her sins would not have worked if her father hadn't gotten drunk and given her Katie's dowry. She also knew his words had given her the courage she had been lacking. She looked around to see if anyone from her village had followed her, but none of the distant figures looked familiar.

"I am so glad I told Father about Colch. My soul feels lighter," she said to herself. Even though he was drunk when she confessed, it felt good to remove the burden of secrecy. She felt another joy as she reached the Jerusalem highway and took a path next to the main road that was obviously well-used. She quickly returned to her marching rhythm as she began her adventure going south. Yael felt alive, and she had a purpose. She had already taken out a dried fish and some of her grandmother's bread and she ate them as a reward for reaching her first landmark.

The road was just as everyone had told her. It was dusty and she occasionally covered her face with her outer robe when a team of oxen passed by. She was already drinking the last of the water in her second skin and didn't realize how dehydrated all the walking in the cold had made her.

"Yael, let's go. You have already gone further than you ever have. Let's go to Jerusalem," she told herself. She had dreamed of this moment of seeing new places and new people, and she was excited about her big chance to explore. However, roadside trash was every-where, and there were signs of cooking fires every few minutes of walking. All the pollution underwhelmed her. Correae was cleaner and nicer than any of these roads. These people were not following God's plan to be good stewards of the land. This must all be the work of Gentiles and Romans, she thought.

As midday approached, she came upon a crossroads that she remembered from the maps. She had heard stories of this place many times. This was the first great crossroads between the road she was on and two other more traveled paths. On her far right was the road to Meddigo. This road eventually led to Joppa and the coast. It was constructed of stone and sand and it seemed impervious to weath-ering. The other road led to Jerusalem by way of Shechem, Shiloh, and Bethel. It was an Ebreet road and it was not maintained by any central government but by each village that it passed through. It had many ruts in it from wagons trying to pass during heavy rains, and there was no drainage on the sides like on the Roman roads. No one had told Yael that the Romans did roads better than the twelve tribes. She began to wonder what else these Romans excelled at.

Looking at the sun, she knew that she would not reach Shechem today. She had heard the stories of how people would sleep under the stars and sometimes see and hear Yahweh speak to them on this road. The Torah was rich with stories of the Lord speaking to people in the wilderness, and this road was one such place. Yet, she didn't want to sleep alone and have no one with her if she heard from God. She always slept with Katie, and now that Katie is sleeping with Matthew, she will have to learn to sleep without her. Her anxiety convinced her to keep walking.

"I can do this," she said as she kept walking down the road all morning. She had slept under the stars many times during herding season; but this time, she would be doing it alone. Fear crept into her heart and her positive self-talk helped.

"Yahweh, please give me companions this evening to help me keep safe. But don't let them be like Colch." She laughed as she spoke her prayers out loud. She was using Colch's behavior as a measuring stick of right and wrong when she knew she was in the wrong as much as he was.

For the first time in her life, she saw a traveling caravan. It was nearly noon and the long line of camels and carts was coming towards her from the direction of Jerusalem. She paused to watch the beasts walk towards her and they were all carrying some form of cloth. Although she dared not ask them any questions as the first of them passed her, her natural curiosity was hard to reign in. She stepped a bit further off the path to give the beasts the right of way and made eye contact with the first camel rider. "How far on foot is it to Jerusalem from here if the weather holds?" She thought it too risky to ask where the caravan was coming from or where it was going.

"Five more days if you are slow. Three days, if you are fast!" he replied. All the camel riders began to laugh. She could tell that the men were not Ebreet, and they could tell that she was from Naphtali by her accent. From that moment on, she decided that speaking Greek would be wiser. It was the common tongue thanks to the Romans and their fixation on global commerce. Thankfully, the Rabbis who had taught her had insisted that everyone learn it, even if they had no intention to travel outside of Correae.

Within the hour, Yael saw a second group coming towards her. This group included larger wagons. As they neared her, no story or tale could have prepared her emotionally for what she was seeing. As the caravan came closer, Yael saw that slaves were pulling the large carts. Six men led the first wagon and the cart was full of salt. The slaves were almost naked and they had obviously been worked to near death. They wore no shoes and they had lacerations on their back from being whipped. She had heard of people being used as pack animals, but she had not imagined what it looked like. From a distance, it seemed odd to her that men would ride horses while humans pulled carts, as that was inefficient at best and cruel at worst. She guessed that they would all be dead within the month.

The men sitting on the cart were yelling at the slaves to maintain their effort and speed. Yael had stepped many paces off the road, but not so far that she couldn't see their faces as they neared. The lead men on horseback were of a much darker skin color than she had seen and their hair was knotted and short. Behind the lead wagon were smaller wagons pulled by a single person at a time. Each wagon contained items bound for trade markets. There were bolts of brightly colored fabric and numerous tools foreign to her. The wagons also carried large barrels, but Yael could not tell what their contents were. The men on horseback rode next to each group of single-person wagons. The men on horseback were in good health and appeared fit and strong. Yael was shocked by the injustice of the arrangement, but for once, she kept her mouth shut. Her mission was not to save them. She needed to reach Jerusalem as quickly as she could so she could save herself.

She was not prepared for the sights that the second half of the caravan would bring. Behind the last of the carts were perhaps fifty women, all of them wearing well-worn sandals and they were chained together. There were older women in the group, but some were younger girls, perhaps Yael's age. What shocked Yael was that all of them were naked. Yael was in disbelief that a naked woman would appear outdoors. When she and Katie bathed, they were partially covered by colorful cotton wraps, and one of their slaves stood on watch to prevent men from walking upon them when they took everything off to change. She felt shame for these women.

One of the older women stumbled and fell. A horseman grumbled something to one of his companions. The first man dismounted and walked towards the elderly woman. The other women in the chain gang began to scream hysterically. When he reached the woman, he removed her shackles. He grabbed her by the arm and walked her in the direction that Yael was standing. He moved behind the woman, and in the blink of an eye, he unsheathed his sword and decapitated her with a single stroke of his blade.

Yael vomited and fell to her knees. She could not believe what she had seen. The murderer made eye contact with her for a brief second and his face showed no emotion. It was as if he were killing a goat or chicken. Yael wanted to scream, but she knew that if she did, she might find herself in shackles with the other women.

The caravan kept moving, and soon it had passed her. Still in shock, she rose to her feet. She had to keep going.

"What was that?" she said to herself, in disbelief that something like that could happen. No one had told her about that. It was her first experience with the worst part of humanity, and she was distraught.

After the caravan passed, she continued on her way. As she walked and stared at the ground, she wondered what these women had done so wrong as to justify enslavement. They looked like her, and they spoke Hebrew. Where were these sisters from, and where were they going? She could not help but wonder if this was what the elders had seen when they created the rules about keeping their wealth hidden from the Romans. They all said that if the Romans found out what they were doing, they would all become enslaved. If this was what enslavement looked like, perhaps that secret is worth keeping. Her secret had to be her top priority, and that thought kept her going.

She tried to push the memory of the decapitation from her mind, but it was too extreme an event to banish. A fear arose within her unlike any she had known. Could she end up like those women?

Maybe she had made a mistake leaving her village. But it was too late to go back now. Second-guessing would slow her down. She had to get to the Temple. Atonement awaited her.

Chapter 14:
Two Soldiers

Before the evening of her first full day away from Correae, she had passed no fewer than ten other traveling groups. There was a group of Roman soldiers prepared for battle, and Yael stepped far off the road to observe them. She was in awe. None of the descriptions given to her by the men and boys who had seen a trained member of the Roman army could do them justice. All of them wore matching clothing, and they rode their horses in a synchronized manner, going two abreast. Each of them wore a large helmet that was adorned with furs and feathers. Their skin was well-oiled and their hair was well-kept. Many had shaved heads and thick beards. They spoke amongst themselves in a tongue that she could not understand, but she speculated that it was a Greek dialect that she didn't know. One of the men turned towards her, gesturing for his wingman to follow him. His wingman complied and they advanced on her position. Yael's heart raced and she stood motionless in her fear. She had heard stories about how the Roman soldiers would rape and enslave any Hebrew woman they saw.

In her fear, she prayed. She remembered the story of when David combatted Goliath with a sling and stone and was victorious. Hebrew tradition spoke of God giving David both the confidence and skills needed to win that day, and David eventually became Judah's king. She needed the same kind of confidence.

"Yahweh, grant me David's courage. Let me see these soldiers as the men that they are." Before she could finish her prayer, the two horsemen had covered the ground from the road to where she stood. As the pair approached them, she spoke to them in Greek, the kind she had learned from Rabbi Thomas. "You are a long way from home!" she said with as much authority as she could.

They both laughed before responding.

"Yes, we are," one of them returned, speaking Greek back to her. Yael knew that many men in the Roman army were captured from other countries, and she guessed from his use of Greek that this man was not from Rome. They dismounted their horses. The size of the swords that they wore around her belt were large enough to slice through their horses' necks in a single swing.

"We are nearly out of water, and we must let our horses drink if we are to keep moving. Where should we go?"

"Today is your lucky day! I can help you at no cost!" She spoke in what she hoped was an amusingly eager tone. Perhaps she could keep them chuckling. A laughing soldier was a happy soldier.

"My name is Roan," one of them said. "This is Meeran. We are with the Emperor's second Centuria in the 10th Legion, and we are patrolling this area. Your humor is a breath of fresh air. We seldom find people who wish to make us laugh. Where is the water?"

Yael's heart rate began to slow. She had made a connection with the enemy of the Ebreet people. She had her first traveling story. For the first time since the wedding, she let herself dream about a return to Correae once she had atoned for her sins and how she might frame this moment when she told others about this encounter with Meeran and Roan.

"There is a clearing about 10 minutes back up the road. There is a spring there. You can't miss it, as everyone uses it." She held up her leather flask of water and shook it so they could hear that she had recently filled it up.

"Thank you. You shouldn't be traveling by yourself. Bad things can happen to young women like yourself on this road," Mereen said.

"If anyone stops you, tell them that Roan and Mereen are looking out for you. We each lead a decurion of men and are charged with protecting the innocent. That includes you," they said. Yael couldn't believe these men were willing to offer their names to protect her as she traveled.

Roan regarded her with interest. "So, where are you going, young girl?"

"I am going to Jerusalem to atone for a sin. My name is Yael." She had no idea why she answered him truthfully. But they did seem trustworthy. Two other men on horseback had now approached, but they stayed on their horses as the three of them talked.

The men looked at each other, and this time, Meeran spoke to her.

"Our Emperor has sent 40,000 men and all of his war machines to take Jerusalem, and the war efforts are near ready to commence. It is possible that by the time you arrive, Jerusalem will no longer be an Ebreet fortress but a pile of rubble. If you can avoid Jerusalem, you avoid war."

Yael was speechless. Why hadn't anyone told her that the Romans were destroying the holy city and all within it? Certainly, someone in the village had to know this. "I have no memory of this story. How long has this been going on?" she asked. They could tell she was upset.

"I am so sorry that we had to be the ones to tell you. We have been building our battering rams and bringing over our beasts of war for several moon cycles now. This is not a new story. Your village must be very isolated. Where are you from?"

She was becoming overwhelmed with fear. "Please excuse me. I need to go." She picked up her staff and left them as quickly as she could. They spoke to each other, but they did not call out to her to stop. They had gotten her name, but it was a common one. They had not gotten the name of her village. Correae remained safe for another day.

"Take care, Yael. It was nice to meet you. We spoke truthfully. Use our names," said Roan as he got back on his horse and caught back up with the rest of the soldiers.

It now made complete sense how Rome had been able to take over the world. Those men were polite, considerate, and honest, and she was expecting the opposite.

Chapter 15:
A Man Who Speaks
with Authority

As the day started to come to an end, Yael decided that she was feeling strong and would walk into the night a second time. The new scenery in all directions enthralled her, and this part of Manasseh looked majestic under the canopy of stars and moonlight. She passed through smaller hamlets that she had heard her uncles and the other men in the village talk about since she was a little girl, and she waved at the people there as if they were long-lost friends. She spoke to a few of them, but she protected her name and hometown from these strangers. She kept her water skins full, and one woman gave her a small sample of olive oil on fresh bread. It tasted like home, and the familiarity warmed Yael's spirits.

Late in the afternoon, she stopped at one village, where she knew that the old woman made the best bread in all of Issachar. She found her cart, asked for a loaf of her famous bread, and paid her with a gold coin. The woman looked down at the coin and inspected it.

"You can keep the change," Yael said. The woman's countenance changed, and she reached out to take Yael's hand.

"Oh, you must be from Correae," the old woman said, looking into the teenager's eyes.

Yael smiled. She nodded her head in affirmation. This woman obviously knew about the gold mine.

"I have heard all about your bread from my uncles since I was a little girl," Yael said. The woman smiled. Yael's exceptional memory now guided her words.

"And I know you have the gift of prophecy like Isaiah and Jeremiah," Yael said. The woman understood that the gold coin was a tithe, not payment for bread. She put away the coin, closed her eyes for a moment, and said a prayer.

"The Spirit tells me you are on your way to the Temple to seek forgiveness of a hidden sin; otherwise, a young Ebreet girl would not walk this road alone," the woman said. Yael expected her to know that. That is what prophets could do.

"I am, and I seek your words. I don't know what I am doing."

"Sit and speak to me," said the old woman, and she made room for Yael on her stool. With that, Yael told her the story of Colch, her sister's wedding, her drunk father, and the beheading she had seen in the morning. Yael took a deep breath and let go of the woman's hands.

"And you are the first person I have told all of that story." The woman looked at her and smiled.

"Well, I have heard worse." That made Yael laugh until her belly hurt and tears began to flow. She was feeling the joy of iterations of secrets and the telling began to heal her.

"I am glad you have the courage to try to atone for your misconduct. As you spoke, I prayed to the Lord. I saw that your future will be one filled with difficult choices, but I can see that you will have children of power, and the hand of the Lord will be upon them. I saw that your family and your grandchildren have been called to redeem the lost and minister both to the Gentiles and to the twelve tribes. The Romans who rule this land will also sit at the feet of your offspring and listen to the tales of a risen Messiah. Indeed, Yahweh showed me that your children and their children will usher in the Kingdom of Heaven." Yael looked at the woman and tilted her head to the side. The proclamation of prophecy was both extreme and confusing to her, and the old baker's words were remarkable.

"My children and grandchildren will usher in the Kingdom of Heaven?" Yael said rhetorically.

"In my vision for you, I saw both a small man and a larger one standing beside you as you fulfill Yahweh's calling on your life. You had a son, but his future is blurred to me." It was now the old woman's turn to take a deep breath. Others were approaching her cart to buy bread and she needed to serve them. Before she changed to focus on the next customers, she shared one final thought with Yael.

"Here. Take this bread for the others you shall meet today who will repeat part of the message that I told you," she said. She handed Yael two additional loaves of bread and blessed her as Yael moved to the side to make room for the next customers.

For the rest of the afternoon, Yael thought about the woman's words. Certainly, she did not believe that she would live to see her children's children usher in the Kingdom of Heaven. Perhaps this was a prophecy for thousands of years from now. It certainly wasn't like the other prophecies that her uncles told her about. Normally, the prophetess focuses on weather, finance, and fertility. This prophecy seemed like nonsense, especially the part about a risen Messiah. There has been no Messiah, let alone a risen one.

As twilight approached, Yael paused long enough to get some hummus from her bag to go with the fresh bread. She continued walking while eating her meal. She was nearly out of water and she would need to refill by the morning.

As darkness settled on the road, there were fewer and fewer travelers. There were many caravans camping off the sides of the roads in nearby forests. Most had cooking fires and people were sitting around these fires. She could hear them telling stories and laughing. As she came close to one group, she heard a man telling a story with great enthusiasm. Something compelled her to stop and listen, and she stopped at the edge of the place where they camped. She put her hands on her hips as she watched and listened.

"Yeshua knew the Pharisees had heard that He was baptizing and making more disciples. So, He left Judea and returned to Galilee. He had to go through Samaria on the way. Eventually, He came to the Samaritan village of Sychar near the field that Jacob had given to his son Joseph. Jacob's well was there, and Yeshua, tired from the long walk, sat wearily beside the well about noontime. Soon, a Samaritan woman came to draw water, and Yeshua said to her, 'Please give me a drink.' He was alone at the time because His disciples had gone into the village to buy food. The woman was surprised, for Ebreet typically refused to have anything to do with Samaritans." Yael was mesmerized by the story, as she had never heard it. She listened with intent and stood motionless as the man continued.

"She said to Yeshua, 'You are a Jew and I am a Samaritan woman. Why are you asking me for a drink?' Yeshua replied, 'If you knew the gift God has for you and who you are speaking to, you would ask me, and I would give you living water.'

'But sir, you don't have a rope or a bucket,' she said, 'and this well is very deep. Where would you get this living water? And besides, do you think you're greater than our ancestor Jacob, who gave us this well? How can you offer better water than he and his sons and his animals enjoyed?'

Yeshua replied, 'Anyone who drinks this water will soon become thirsty again. But those who drink the water I give will never be thirsty again. It becomes a fresh, bubbling spring within them, giving them eternal life.'

'Please, sir,' the woman said, 'give me this water! Then I'll never be thirsty again, and I won't have to come here to get water.'

'Go and get your husband,' Yeshua told her.

'I don't have a husband," the woman replied.

Yeshua said, 'You're right! You don't have a husband. You have had sex with five different men, and you aren't married to the man you're living with now. You certainly speak the truth!'"

With this, Yael's breathing stopped. She didn't know this story or the people in it, but she could see that her life was on track to be like the woman at the well.

"'Sir,' the woman said, 'you must be a prophet. So, tell me, why is it that you, an Ebreet, insist that Jerusalem is the proper place of worship while we Samaritans claim it is here at Mount Gerizim, where our ancestors worshiped?'

Yeshua replied, 'Believe me, dear woman, the time is coming when it will no longer matter whether you worship the Father on this mountain or in Jerusalem. You Samaritans know very little about the one you worship, while we Ebreet know all about Him, for salvation comes through the Ebreet. But the time is coming—indeed, it's here now—when true worshipers will worship the Father in spirit and truth. The Father is looking for those who will worship him that way. For God is Spirit, so those who worship him must worship in spirit and in truth.'

The woman said, 'I know the Messiah is coming, the one who is called Christ. When He comes, he will explain everything to us.'

Yeshua told her, 'I am the Messiah!'"

Whatever had paralyzed Yael's tongue lifted and she spoke without thinking.

"Excuse me, Rabbi. Who are you talking about?"

The man telling the story stopped and called to her.

"Come and sit with my family," he said, standing and gesturing for her to enter their circle. Yael briskly walked into their gathering and sat next to an old woman who must have been the old man's wife.

"You seem like a smart girl. Do you know the Messiah? What have you been taught?"

Yael began to recite the teachings that she received from her Rabbis. She talked quickly and interrupted herself repeatedly as she told the stories and prophecies about his coming. Within a few minutes, she exhausted all that she remembered of the Messiah who was to come and save the world.

"Did you know He has already come and has traveled here?" said the man.

She shook her head. "Here? This road? No, that can't be true. If He had come, we would no longer be under Roman rule and cruelty. Just today, I saw a Hebrew woman beheaded for no crime other than stumbling." The man looked down and smiled.

"I think it is Yeshua who has placed you here with us this evening. For now, I think you need to rest and let Yeshua work on letting His story settle into the depths of your soul. You are well-schooled in the Torah, and you recalled the writings of our prophets. You have made your Rabbis proud. And I believe Yeshua wants you to use your skills to spread His kingdom."

Yael felt a pull upon her heart, and this new idea began to get her attention. She took out two loaves of bread from the woman and handed them to the man.

"These are for you," Yael said with a rescinded tone.

"Ah! I prayed that someone would send us fresh bread. Yeshua always answers prayers if we call upon his name," he said.

"How did you know that I would come with fresh bread?" she asked. Yael was obviously perplexed. The old man didn't answer her but did offer a smile. He knew she wouldn't believe him.

"Before you go to bed, I want you to know that I met Yeshua when I was a young boy. The day I met Him was important, but the months and years afterward were the times that He changed me the most. Like you, I learned of him while walking on a road by myself late one evening, traveling at night, hoping no one could see the secret I was carrying."

"How do you know that I have secrets?" Yael stammered.

"Your countenance gives you away, Little One. For now, lay out your bedroll and go to sleep. You and your secrets are safe with us, and you need not be anxious."

With that, the old man stood and prayed over his family and the others in his group, using words like, "Thy will be done on Earth as it is in Heaven." He spoke casually about Yahweh, and Yael had no idea how to respond as he casually used Aramaic to describe the God of the Heavens. She had been taught never to do that, as it was a breach of the commandment not to use the Lord's name in vain.

She was more perplexed by the ending to his prayer. How could it be that they were asking God for His will to come to pass here on earth? How is it that His will is done in Heaven? Was this heaven the same one that her grandchildren would be ushering in? Did Yahweh intend for the prophets to return and use their power to make men change? If that was true, why was God waiting? Did that prophetess hear his prayer for bread from half a day away? She had no answers. She took a deep breath and took her bedroll off of her pack.

"That is enough for me for today. I can't understand anything," she said.

She unrolled her bedroll near the fire, where everyone else intended to sleep. As she lay down and covered herself with the thick wool blanket that her mother had made, she looked up at the twinkling stars. This old man and his stories were far beyond what she expected to encounter when she left Correae.

Between the baker and this old man, there was a rift in her thinking. The questions she found herself asking and the thoughtful answers that came to her mind were new, as well. Who is this Messiah that both of them were talking about?

Of course, she did not believe that the Messiah had already come. Visions of the woman's decapitation today were enough evidence that any Messiah had not yet rescued the Ebreet. These travelers must be delusional; she had seen no salvation on earth.

As she lay there trying to fall asleep, she couldn't deny a simple truth. These people were at peace, and she wasn't. Everyone in her village, as well as all the travelers whom she had spoken with along the way today, were anxious about the events of the future. Roan and Mereen were powerful soldiers, but they had shown concern about the future. Preparation for what was next was always on people's minds. How was it that these people could live in such tranquility when danger and tragedy were occurring around them?

Her thoughts slowly faded into sleep, and Yael slept soundly that night. All she could conclude was that, whatever the source of their peace, it was permeating her and demanded a response.

Chapter 16:
Barnabas

In the morning, Yael woke up when the group began to stir. With the sun rising over the horizon, she could finally count that there were about a dozen people present. All of them appeared to be Ebreet from other tribes. They were of all ages, from Yael's age up to the old man.

After packing up her bedroll and placing it strategically in the bottom of her pack, she quietly approached the old man who had spoken to her last night. As she approached, he looked up at her and reached out to her with his hand and she extended her hand until it met his. He spoke softly. "What is it? You look very troubled. Did you not sleep well?"

She set her pack down and sat next to him.

"I don't know. As I slept, my mind processed your words and those of the woman who gave me the bread to give to you. There is no way that the Messiah has already come. What I saw yesterday alone makes your argument invalid."

His wife brought her both of her water skins as she had filled them. After Yael thanked her, the old man asked her a question. "Tell me, what was it you were taught in Bad Midrash that the Messiah would do when He came to earth?"

She was impressed that he could tell that she had attended Bad Midrash. It was an honor for anyone, let alone a girl, to be considered worthy of such a high level of education.

"He was to save us from our oppressors," the old man chuckled. He knew she had read the scriptures he wanted to discuss.

"Who is it that oppresses you?" He asked. Yael hesitated, so he asked the question again, differently.

"Is it your sin, or is it these Romans who enslave us and cut off our heads like the woman yesterday? Which one oppresses this young girl?"

She held her cup of hot tea in both hands and stared into the fire. Its warmth felt wonderful this time of day and she didn't want to move. Yet, she didn't have an answer for him that she could offer with conviction.

"The Romans have done nothing to me or my family as of yet. Indeed, we are rich compared to most of the people I met yesterday. I guess my sin oppresses me."

"Well done! You are wise beyond your years. All peoples, including those who are not yet born to us, shall be oppressed by sin. We know that one day, these Roman occupiers will be gone and the Kingdom of David will again be home to God's people." He waited for Yael to nod her head before he poetically delivered his point.

"Have Philistines and others occupied not this land before? Have our ancestors not been oppressed by the Babylonians? The element that remains constant in all generations is the oppression caused by our sin. And I think your heart is confirming this as I speak." Yael noticed that everyone in the group was now staring at her. Some were smiling, and some were praying, but no one appeared to wish to speak to her. They all seemed to trust what the old man was doing.

Yael wanted more information. She asked him questions about his understanding of the section of the sacred scrolls describing the attributes of the Messiah. And he told her stories of his time walking with the saints and prophets, trying to teach others what she was now hearing for the first time.

"I am impressed that a young woman like yourself knows the text of our forefathers as well as you do. Indeed, you know it better than many who teach the contents to those of us who follow The Way."

She didn't know what he meant by The Way. She bashfully accepted his compliment and he put his arm around her shoulder.

He had a presence about him. She had heard many of the boys from Correae return from travels and tell stories that were lies. She could sense that this man was not lying.

"Join us for breakfast," said the old woman. She handed Yael a large plate with vegetables, spices, and freshly made flatbread cooked in olive oil. It smelled like home. She offered to pay for it, but they would not accept coins or payments. Yael ate in silence. She felt no peace telling them her name or where she came from. Fortunately, no one had asked.

During the meal, the old man told another story. Yael looked around at the group and realized she was not alone as she listened with zeal to this man's adventures. Two other young men in the company also asked him questions. They sounded like she did. She heard that she was not alone in her disbelief that the Messiah had already walked on Earth.

The old man shared a lengthy story of a man called Paul, who used to be called Saul. He described the many ways that Paul persecuted the early followers of The Way.

"I traveled with Paul after Yeshua had called him, listening to what he called 'the greatest persecutor of the faith to have lived' proclaiming the Good News of the Messiah."

One of the men asked, "I can't believe that all of this is true. How can someone go from a large-scale murderer to someone who teaches the opposite message at the risk of his own life?"

The old man smiled. "Perhaps seven years ago, when I was in Salamis in Cyprus, I had to flee for my life. The Romans placed a high price on my head to ensure that I would be killed if I were found. I now travel to places where Romans do not go so that I can continue to spread the Good News. My life is forfeit, but the Good News must continue to be spread."

Yael could not understand what this man was sharing, but she felt ready to trust him. She had another question.

"I see no evidence that the Messiah has come to save the Ebreet from oppression. Yesterday, I watched a woman get her head cut off by a sword. The soldier wielding that sword treated her as if she were a farm animal. He killed her without emotion or anger in his heart. It was as if he was culling part of a flock. How could the Messiah have come and there remain innocent people killed like animals?"

"The grace of God is here with us and you are struggling with what has been revealed to you. Your questions are beautiful, Little One. The desire for peace is universal. The idea of peace means much more than the end of political hostilities. The Hebrew word 'shalom' has the idea of 'completeness' or 'wholeness.' Because of sin, we are all 'incomplete.' This is the very desire of God. Our great King and psalmist David said, 'The Lord will bless His people with peace,' and the great Prophet Isaiah said that the Messiah will be called 'Prince of Peace.' In fact, when Messiah reigns, peace will be His Kingdom's theme, according to Zachariah." The old man took a deep drink of spring water and continued. "This universal peace of the Messiah is based on each of us first having a personal relationship with Yeshua. It is said that 'You will keep him in perfect peace whose mind is steadfast because He trusts in You.'"

Yael was trying to process the connections he was making. Of course, she had heard of the prophets that he had mentioned. However, she hadn't seen where their messages overlapped. But what he was saying made sense.

"Rabbi, keep teaching," she said, taking another sip of tea as she listened with intent.

"The scriptures prophesy that the peace promised by the Messiah would be rejected when it was offered," continued the old man. "Isaiah the prophet wrote that the Messiah would come to make peace between God and His people and that His message would be rejected. When the Messiah would be rejected, the peace He brings would be rejected with Him."

Yael spoke up. "The scripture predicts that He would be killed instead of listened to. He was brought as a lamb to the slaughter, as a sheep before the shearers are silent, so He did not open His mouth."

The old man nodded to affirm the young girl's knowledge of the scrolls.

"He is upon you!" said the old man.

She thought of Rabbi Andrew's teaching on this topic.

"'Many will come teaching of false Messiahs. Do not be deterred from the faith by their blasphemy,' we are taught."

"Are you saying the ancient scrolls are no longer true? Should we leave their teachings?" Yael did not hide her tone or her use of the Socratic method as a learning tool.

"No. Yeshua completes the scrolls. He does not replace them." The man laughed for a moment. He was enjoying his conversation with her.

"So, who is our Lord in this matter?" she asked.

"Yahweh is our Lord. Yeshua is His son. The two of them are one."

She was lost again. That made no sense. Yet, she could sense that it wasn't an accident that she was here, talking to an old man who spoke in riddles and circles. Yet, she knew she was a sinner. If she weren't, she would not have needed to manipulate her father or abandon her sister and mother. She would not have lost her freedom to speak honestly of her life. Her face was blank. She didn't know what to say to his claims. Father and Son are the same? Two in one? This was borderline ridiculous.

"Young Lady, your choices before this day that brought you to this meeting with the person of Yeshua. Do not regret those decisions in your life that brought you here. Yeshua, the Messiah, suffered and was killed under Roman leadership. He died and was buried, as scripture predicted. He arose from the dead on the third day and He visited many people, including me."

"What? You saw the Messiah after he arose from the dead?" asked one of the young men who were, like Yael, not yet believers. "How is that possible?"

The old man smiled. "Yeshua was not a false Messiah as the Romans claim. I am here to tell you that I saw Him after He arose from the dead and that He is not a false Messiah."

Yael's thoughts drifted. She began to relive the afternoon in the Northerns with Colch when her reaction to his touch and perceived feelings had caused her to sin. She wished she had paused during the experience. Had she followed the Torah and the command not to fornicate before marriage, this journey would have been unnecessary.

This circular conversation with a delusional yet intelligent old man would never happen, and she could be home with her idiot cousins bathing in the river and putting on perfume to prepare for Shabbat.

The old man stood up. "Our Lord uses all things to bring glory to his kingdom. Your sins are part of His plan for you to meet His son and find peace. The Christ was crucified for your sins so you can find peace."

"No! How could you possibly say that I shouldn't regret the damage I did to her family?" She was both mad and indignant at what he said. And she had more to add.

"How is it that God can use all things, even sin, for His purposes? I am walking all the way to Jerusalem to atone for a grave sin that I have committed against my family. I will not be made new until I have offered a sacrifice at the altar in the Temple. I need a bead of atonement before I can marry a man from the twelve tribes. I made a big mistake. That is why I am even talking to you." She felt confident with her rebuttal.

"As you wish. Yeshua will be here for you when you discover that your way will not bring you peace." She wanted to tell him to leave the prophecy to the bread lady, but she bit her lip instead. Yet, she could not deny that he cared for her and sincerely believed he was helping her.

The old man approached Yael, opening his arms, and she found herself compelled to melt into them. She had no idea why his lunacy pulled on her. It made no sense, but she felt safe holding onto him and crying. Could it be that all of the events of her life were meant to lead her to conclude that the Messiah had already come to set her free, not from the Romans but from sin? Or was this about decapitation and its impact on her soul?

She looked up at the man's face when she had no more tears to shed.

"Rabbi, I have no freedom from my sins. I agree with your teaching. But how can I trust you? Are you of the twelve tribes? I can't determine if you follow the Torah?"

"Yes, I am Ebreet and I believe all things written by the prophets of old. None of that is nullified by accepting Yeshua as God's

Messiah. Allow me to trust you first. My name is Barnabas. Give that name to any Roman soldier you meet and my life is forfeit before sunset. You will be rich with the reward the Romans promise to any man who brings me to justice and I will be killed. Perhaps now you can trust me."

Yael's eyes opened wide. She had heard that name! She knew of a man called Barnabas. A long time ago, a boy came back from the coastal towns talking of a man who traveled and did great things and was now being hunted by the Romans. That man's name was Barnabas. This had to be the same man. He maintained his gaze into her eyes and she knew he was telling the truth about everything he had said.

"Rabbi, I will not share your name with anyone I meet. Your secret is safe with me. And I know how to keep secrets, even though I hate them."

Another secret. How did this happen that the very thing she hated she embraced as her own?

"Little One, you need not travel to the holy city and sacrifice at the Temple. Believe in Yeshua as the Son of our Lord and your sins are forgiven."

Yael turned around and began to leave. "I don't believe that. I can't believe that. The temple is our faith. It is where the spirit of the Lord lives. I am going to Jerusalem to atone for my sins. This is the way of all Ebreet and I am no exception. I cannot rest until I do so." She thanked everyone and said goodbye with the words her family taught her, and she accepted theirs in return.

She left them and restarted her journey to Jerusalem, wondering what she had experienced. She had met a female prophet and a Rabbi named Barnabas, who told her she didn't need to atone for her sins at the Temple. There was no way she would take that path as long as the Temple stood as the symbol of their ancient faith. Yahweh of Abraham, Isaac, and Jacob would not let such a thing happen.

She kept walking.

Chapter 17: Important Questions

Over the next two days, Yael crossed the land of the tribe of Issachar and entered the land of the tribe of Manasseh. That meant she was more than halfway to Jerusalem. It lifted her spirits and she felt like her march on the highway was nearly routine. She occasionally spoke with others taking the same route that she was and they would fill up their water skins at the same stop. They were very respectful of Yael, as many were Ebreet families en route to celebrate Rosh Hashanah either at the temple or with family outside of Jerusalem.

The road was well-used and well-maintained, and she passed without seeing conflict. The river Jordan stayed on her left, and she could sometimes see and hear it as the road crested hills part of the landscape. She noticed that the ancient continued to widen, as her uncles told her it would. There were huge fields of grains nearly ready for harvest, and she began to see others on the road who had the darker features and thicker hair that had made the Benjaminite tribe famous. Yael had light conversations with people when she would stop for bread and water, but two questions remained unanswered in her mind.

What if the Roman soldiers were telling the truth? What if Barnabas was telling the truth?

If the Romans were telling the truth, and Jerusalem was about to fall, she *must* get there before this transpired if she is to sacrifice and receive forgiveness for her sexual sin. Her faith demanded this. She had heard about atoning at the Temple of Solomon since she could remember hearing that the penalty for sin was death. She wanted to marry and have children, so receiving the bead of atonement and forgiveness for sin was not an option.

But what if the Temple was destroyed before she got there? How could she find atonement from sin if the sole place of atonement was destroyed? She has seen that the Romans were a formidable force. She had seen with her own eyes their ability to kill. Her people and her faith would crumble if they couldn't go to the temple to find forgiveness of sin.

Yet what if Barnabas' tales of a risen Messiah were true? If it were true that the Messiah had already come to Earth, it meant that it was possible to receive forgiveness of sins from Yeshua without having to go to the Temple. Barnabas also said that Yeshua didn't come to replace scripture but to complete it. How could a man who had already died complete the Torah?

These questions kept her mind occupied as she walked to Jerusalem over the next few days. The things she saw along the way meant almost nothing compared to the zeal she invested in answering those two questions.

She recited her plan for arrival in Jerusalem. Once she entered the city and reached the outer courts of the Temple, she would use some of her father's coins to buy a pure white lamb. She would find a Temple Rabbi and pay him to help her complete a blood sacrifice that would remove her from the guilt of sin. Her sin would be forgiven, and she would receive an atonement bead. That atonement would allow her to marry without shame, assuming she did not turn out to be with a child. This was the exception. According to the Pharisees, any woman with a child outside of wedlock could not marry. She had already bled since her encounter with Colch, so she knew she was not with child.

But she wondered if her sacrifice would be pleasing enough to God to forgive the horrible choices she had made. Would it be pleasing enough for her future husband's family? Was she expected to tell her future husband of this event? She didn't know. She hoped that the Rabbi at the Temple would help her answer that question. She would sometimes laugh when she thought that it would be easy if he told her to keep it a secret.

Yael repeated her conversation with Barnabas a hundred times over the next two days. She decided that his words demeaned what she was doing, which was offensive to her. He had taught that no one needed to go to Jerusalem to pay the blood price because Yeshua paid this for everyone when he was crucified. If this was true, why weren't there more people teaching this message? Why had neither Rabbi Thomas nor Robbi Andrew mentioned Yeshua? And how could a man pay for a sin before the sin happened? Yeshua, she learned, had died about thirty years ago. That didn't make sense to her, either. If that were true, her uncles would have heard about it and brought that story home with all the others they brought home.

At the same time, she admitted to herself that she wanted Barnabas' story to be true. At the end of the second day, she finally gave up all of her thoughtful ruminations and went to Yahweh in sincere prayer.

"Yahweh, I do not know what is true or what to believe. I do not want to fall away from your teachings any more than I have. My choices have hurt me. I want to follow the way of my elders, teachers, and family and atone for my sins by sacrificing at the Temple. I am on my way there now, and I intend to follow our ways, as I am one of your chosen people. Yet, there also appears to be a new way. Show me which one is true. Please show me if Barnabas was telling the truth that the Messiah has returned, as you promised in the scrolls of Isaiah. Please provide me with a teacher in Jerusalem who can explain this more clearly to me. I am your humble daughter, crying out to you for relief from the pain that I am feeling."

She didn't know what she would do with the answers she received, but she committed to reaching Jerusalem by the next evening.

Chapter 18:
Another Old Woman

Before the sun was halfway down, she reached the outer walls of a small city at the bottom of a valley. She allowed herself a moment to sit, drink some water, and celebrate. The holy city was now visible ahead of her, high up on a hill. She had reached another milestone on her trip, as the City of David, now called Jerusalem, was visible. The days of long walks through the unknown were a thing of the past. Soon, she hoped to be free of her sin and on the road back home.

Looking up towards Jerusalem was like staring into heaven. Jerusalem, the center of the Ebreet faith, was nothing short of majestic. Its ramparts were thick and tall, and they wrapped around the summit of the mountain. The city looked unconquerable. The outer walls had been painted in brilliant colors on the top and she could see people walking on the tops of the walls, purveying the situation below. The city was as glorious and eye-catching as her uncles had said it was. She could see the top of the Temple above the city walls, and it gave her great hope to see that her final destination was in sight. Yet, the majesty of the view was soon washed away as she saw evidence that the two Roman soldiers were telling the truth. Directly below the city walls in the valley lay an army of tens of thousands of men working on the creation and positioning of war machines, preparing to breach the city walls.

Yael lost her spirit to celebrate. She stood up and quickened her pace to get to the other side of this adjacent city as fast as possible.

An hour later, she had passed through and stood within earshot of the first of the Roman troops. She could hear their conversations and the sounds of their hammers and saws. The Roman Empire was constructing towers that men could use to climb over the walls. They were putting the towers on wheels. Near the back of the army camps were forges and the sounds of metal on metal. She could see there was a mass effort to make swords, arrow points, and knives to be used to war against the people both on the wall and in the city.

Fear overtook Yael. She stood motionless as if she were seeing the two soldiers again. She could not go into the Roman encampment and tell them to stop. Certainly, she wanted to, but wisdom overcame her impulse. Instead, she turned and walked back through the city gates and into the city at the bottom of the hill near Jerusalem. As she passed through those gates, despair entered her heart. "Mereen and Roan, now what do I do?" she said. If those two men were here, she would have done whatever they said, as she had no idea what was next. Instead, her mind was racing as it sought out alternatives to quitting.

How could she get into the city to offer a sacrifice with a Roman army in between her current position and the city gates? How could she find a teacher who could show her more about the Messiah? Her mission was on the edge of failure.

She leaned against the city walls as a feeling of powerlessness overtook her. Her mind relived the events of the last week - first, the beheading. There was the meeting with the prophetess who said her children and their children would preach the Messiah and usher in the kingdom of Heaven. Barnabas came next, and he shook her soul with a tale of faith that she could not stop thinking about. Now, the center artifact of her faith was about to be attacked and likely destroyed. She would be lost and so would a part of her faith. She could already see herself rescinding to marry a Philistine who never bathed and be relegated to a life ridden by shame.

Her desire to quit was strong and it was about to overtake her spirit. She wiped the tears from her eyes and approached a street vendor selling food from a small cart. The operator was an Ebreet woman about her mother's age.

"Older sister, how long has this army been massing? What are they going to do?" Yael asked.

The cart owner replied, "I would not be here if I were you. I can't tell you the number of times I have seen Roman patrols round-up younger girls like you and take them to their camp, vanishing from the earth. I can't imagine what they are doing to those young girls, but it can't be good. You need to be inside these city walls when the next patrol comes!"

"Where should I go, then? I have to get inside that city and get to the Temple." The panic in her voice was obvious. The old woman could tell that Yael was panicked. The old woman also was aware that Yael was trying to be courageous and must have come a long way. Certainly, Yael needed a bath after sleeping on the side of the Jerusalem highway for several nights.

"Older Sister, do you think you could find a way inside that Jerusalem that the Romans do not know about?" Yael asked. She looked like a puppy dog as she spoke to the old woman.

"Look at how many more of them there are than you! Trust me, you aren't getting through those walls until they do!" said the old woman.

This naysayer sounded nearly the same as her cousins. But Yael was no longer a girl from Correae. She was a traveler with her own stories. She used the woman's words to fuel her deep desire not to quit.

"You don't understand. I have got to get in there! My family's future depends on it."

"Good luck with that! What are you going to try to do? Sneak up at night? Jump over the wall? Dress up like a Roman and go into battle with them? I don't know how much longer they will be in this valley before they attack, but it can't be very much longer."

"You are wrong," Yael replied dismissively. Why was she trying to convince this woman of anything?

Soon, the city gates closed, and she approached a different woman at the market and asked her if she had a room for her. Ebreet tradition allowed traveling women to stay at the home of a widow in any city in which they found themselves. It was not appropriate to stay at an inn or home that men also occupied. Everyone knew that. Yael was not about to break another rule.

"Katie would be proud of me for following the rules this time," she said to herself.

This old woman was much quieter than the first one, and she nodded, saying she had a room for her. She finished packing up her cart and escorted Yael back to her house. Yael needed a safe place to sit and think about her next move, and she also needed a bath.

That evening, Yael took a bath outside. The woman had an outdoor shower with water that poured on her head each time she pulled a rope. It was filled by a natural spring and Yael washed all of her body twice. The area was secure from onlookers and the old woman gave her a thick cotton towel to dry off. Yael took out her other set of clothes from her pack. She felt a bit refreshed and the clean clothing smelled of lavender.

"Your shower and towel were wonderful gifts. Thank you," Yael said. She kissed the old woman, offering to help her prepare the evening meal. The woman looked at her with tenderness and concern in her eyes. "What troubles you, Little One?"

"That which I want to do, I can't do. That which I want to know, I can't know. I forgot who said that to me, but I can't help but think about what it means." Yael smiled but not at the old woman. Her external refresh had done nothing to heal her brokenness on the inside.

"You carry secrets both in your heart and on your tongue, don't you?"

"I do."

"Don't throw your life away over something you did in the past. And don't give up hope because you don't have an answer today. The Romans have come to destroy, but they can't take away our hope. You must not give that to them. We are God's chosen people, and we have survived worse occupiers than these Romans. Perhaps it would help you to tell me what troubles you." The old woman poured Yael a small glass of red wine and told her to sit next to her. Yael confided in the woman every detail from before she met Colch until she met with Barnabas. When she was finished with her tale, so was the wine. Yael finally felt relaxed.

Yael thanked the old woman, finished her dinner, and went to her room. The old woman's comments had helped her come up with a plan, and that, along with a good meal, had steadied her. Perhaps she had all the hope she needed.

Chapter 19:
The Tunnel

The next day, Yael started the day helping the old woman serve customers at her cart. Most of the old woman's customers were servicing the Roman army. Livestock farmers were chief among them, as the Romans paid a fair wage for all the cattle and sheep that they purchased. After all, they knew that after defeat, there would be a need for commerce with the remnants of the surviving members of the tribe of Benjamin. She was grateful that she paid attention when the rabbis taught her Aramaic, as that was the primary language of the Benjamite farmers who serviced Jerusalem.

There were wagons of fruits and vegetables that passed through the city's gates and the sellers walked up to the old woman's cart with vast sums of coin, ready to spend it on hot food. They didn't seem to care that the cultural center of their world was about to tumble. The Roman occupation had worn them down and they were looking to their economy to stay alive. One younger man discussed how he would service the community once the walls of Jerusalem were preached and the Sadducees evicted. They both paused their services to take an afternoon nap, but they returned two hours before dinner to service the last of the city customers.

As the city gates were preparing to close for the evening, Yael went against the flow of traffic. While everyone else was entering this final outpost town for the night, she walked in the direction of the Roman encampment. After the metal gates came down and the large wooden doors were closed, she leaned her back against the walls and waited for darkness to come.

Activity in the Roman camps slowed as the sunset. She could see a few flickering lights, probably coming from Roman torches and cooking fires. The Roman military didn't concern themselves with anyone trying to get inside the great-walled city during the night. Yael counted ten lights on the perimeter. If one man had one torch, that meant that there was fewer than one torch bearer per 4,000 men. She suspected that many of the men were already drinking and sitting by the campfires telling stories. She even wondered if they acted like her father, getting drunk and falling asleep with everyone watching them.

Her next moves required that she smartly apply her intelligence. The fear of decapitation was at the forefront of her mind. Visions of the beheaded woman kept her footing secure and her steps light. She began to walk toward the walls of the great city on the southern edge, where she had heard stories of hidden tunnels under the city. The Torah and the Mishnah both spoke of secret passageways under the great city that the old kings would use as escape routes in cases of insurrection or marauders breaching the walls and attempting to kill the king or the high priest.

It was easy to navigate in the dark that evening, as the sky was void of clouds, and the moon was full. She intended to travel parallel to the encampment on what she thought was likely to be a goat trail on the south side of the city wall. Her path around the Roman camp was not as circuitous as it first appeared it would be. She went south before the trail started ascending the Mount of Olives. In fact, the trail went so far south that she couldn't see the lights from the Roman encampment anymore. That feeling of concealment provided her courage to continue looking for a way under the city walls.

She stepped into a small clearing of rocks below a dried-out spring. She guessed that it used to be an area where shepherds would take their flocks for water, but the spring had long since been depleted of its natural water source. She touched several of the rocks, and she turned them over. Despite the darkness, she could see that they were wet, an undeniable sign of an underground spring. The trail continued both east and south, and Yael decided to leave it and head straight up the Mount of Olives towards the city walls and the source of the spring. She knew that wherever water had flown, there were paths, valleys, and tunnels left behind. Straight uphill seemed like the best way to find that source and one of the famous tunnels of King David.

She decided to stop at an outcropping of rocks about a quarter of the way up the side of the mountain for some food and a drink from her water skin. She sat on a smaller boulder and brushed off the stones that sat on top of it, wondering how much work it must have taken to carry all the stones to make ramparts on the top of this mountain. As she kicked around some of the small stones, lost in thought, one went tumbling down into a hole that she couldn't see.

Yael stopped chewing the bite of bread that was in her mouth and rose to investigate. She moved aside one of the larger rocks near where she was sitting and felt cold air coming out from underneath it. The source of that colder air must be coming from underground, she knew.

Her imagination raced as she recalled poetry from a thousand years ago about how kings and queens had used tunnels to escape enemies. Perhaps she had found one of them.

For the next hour, Yael carefully and quietly moved boulder after boulder until she found herself standing at an entrance to what must be an old cave or tunnel. Since it was too dark to explore it now, she decided to set up camp at the entrance and get some sleep. When she woke up to the sound of distant roosters, she was pleasantly surprised at how comfortable she was. The temperature at the entrance to the cave was much cooler than the outside temperature and her choice to sleep in her cloak had been a good one. However, there was no moisture or dew present on her clothing when she woke up. This puzzled her, as the caves she had explored south of Correae were very moist. Something about these caves was different than the ones back home, but she didn't know what.

She ate a couple of bites of yesterday's bread and dried meat. She said her morning prayer and moved away a few more boulders to allow additional light into the cave. She could see now that this was not a cave but an ancient pathway, hopefully leading into the city. Her heart raced with excitement. This is exactly what she was hoping for.

"Thank you, Yahweh," she said. The weight of her sin loomed over her, but she was also excited. The most sacred place on earth was ahead and above her. She could almost feel God's presence. She was excited now and her fear was gone. She had evaded the Romans and was attempting to do something that no woman from her village had done: traveling into Jerusalem on her own.

Before she left Correae, she had packed candles. She pulled one of them out of her pack and lit it with a flint, using the light to follow the ancient path at the back of the cave. She traveled with her flint in hand in case the candle went out.

As she walked, she talked to God aloud. "Great Yahweh, I want to make things right with you. Please let me come into your presence to fix this madness that I have unleashed!" She felt that she was near the Temple now, and she prostrated herself. "Thank you, God. Please let me inside your sacred temple so I can be rid of the burden of my sins!"

As she walked, hopefully, closer and closer to an entrance to the city, she thought about what the cave might have been used for. She had been walking straight enough for a long enough time to tell that she was underneath the city walls now. She imagined herself in King David's army, walking secretly in and out of the city, seeking wild animals to feed her king. She imagined traveling to the city after a long journey, looking forward to coming home to the sounds of trumpets from the city ramparts.

The path turned left, and she was suddenly in front of a flight of steps carved into the floor. Every eighteen steps ended with a landing that was large enough for ten men. She climbed. At the end of the seventh flight of stairs, the path was blocked by a pile of rubble. She noticed that the rocks that made up the rubble were not very large. She concluded that they must have been put here on purpose. The ceiling did not look collapsed, and she quickly formulated a new plan.

She was convinced she needed to move the rubble to get to the other side, but she had enough experience to know that she needed to light a second candle and place it somewhere in case the one in her hand went out. To lose her light source now would be dangerous, as she didn't know this tunnel well enough to walk out without light. She mounted the second candle on one of the ornate torch holders she saw on the wall and began to move the rocks.

Yael had been prepared to find a way to enter the city. Although she couldn't have foreseen her discovery of this tunnel or the entrance at the end of it, it had not truly surprised her. She felt like God was directing her path. But what she met on the other side of the rubble was something that she was not prepared for. A better question to ask might have been "who" she met. The young man was as least as shocked as she was. He looked like a Philistine, with dark skin and a frail body shape.

"Who are you?" he asked. And all Yael could do was wonder the same thing.

Chapter 20:
Titus

Rufus was a long way away in Caesarea, but Rufus found himself thinking about his father's words when it came time to pick who he would spend his time with during non-training and non-combat periods. He didn't get to choose who fought next to him, but he did select who his friends would be.

"Son, seek out boys with whom you want to become men together," his father taught him. Now that his father was on the other side of the empire, his guidance made sense.

"Make friends out of boys who train hard and are successful, not with those who dream big and drink bigger. Remember: a dreamer may or may not succeed. A hard worker will be successful."

Certainly, there were plenty of men in his training regimen who learned to drink and whore very early in training. But Rufus could see that they weren't getting better as soldiers as fast as he was.

"Support the boy who works hard and keep him on his course, and you won't regret it." Rufus was quick to complement a man when his effort was complete, regardless of the outcome of the training. Rufus desired men who always worked hard as friends. He intentionally sought out and initiated deep relationships with the boys who had skills and talents like his or were better than him.

There was a reason Cornelius was highly regarded. Guidance like this was one of the many ways that Rufus would describe his father when he was asked about the origin of his work ethic. When his commanding officer gave him his review, Rufus was quick to quote his father. At the end of each 6-week training block, Rufus received "best in class" accolades more than any other soldier. It was as if his father was with him each time he was corrected, and he got continually better at his job.

He told his Legionnaire that before leaving for Rome, Cornelius took Rufus on a walk out of their compound near the place where they met the Ebreet family. He spoke in solemn tones to his son.

"You have great physical strength, and you are both courageous and fast. You will certainly progress further than I have, so long as you remain in close relationship with those who are as good as you. Do not give in and accept an easy assignment. You have the ability to change the fate of the Empire and our family by doing as I say." Those words had taken root, and a tree was now growing from them.

Over the months of teaching and training, Rufus stood out in every training group as the instructors changed the collections of trainees. Rufus was always able to carry the greatest amount of weight over the greatest distance. When asked, he shared his story.

"My father made me carry a newborn cow around our compound each day for six months, knowing that the calf would weigh more each day. This game of baby cow carrying is what made me stronger every day," he would say. His instructors would yell at the other trainees to work as hard as Rufus, and those words gave Rufus the affirmation he needed to continue being excellent.

Rufus was not the only trainee with an inspired background and a famous father. He was not as strong as Rufus, but he was faster. Indeed, he won any of the competitions that included running up or down a hill with time to spare. Rufus was unable to catch him, even when Rufus cheated and started a moment before he should have. Instead of basking in the glory of his accomplishments, this soldier would deflect the praise and would often tell the instructors how to help the other recruits achieve his speed. Rufus was impressed with this man, and he did not withhold his desire to compete with him and get better.

"We need to have our competitions," Rufus told the man.

"Done!" said the other man, without any fear or bashfulness about competing in front of everyone else. Their instructors complied with their requests with joy. Soon, the two men were not only the best soldiers but also entertained the training class.

They both wanted harder training and more realistic combat practice, including the use of live swords and real arrows. They fell short of receiving their wishes, but they kept the instructors' attention, and they were often called upon to demonstrate the correct way to do things. This positive affirmation made both boys grow in confidence and develop their leadership skills. And they both got better, faster, as a result of their "let me compete against him" mentality.

Before long, each was given a squad of men to command and, with the help of the instructors, they would formulate activities each day that would challenge the men and make them better without creating monotony in their training. One-eye-closed sword fights and javelin throws were lots of fun, and putting armor on while blindfolded helped the men understand the correct fit better than any instructor. Rome provided a year of training to the most elite of soldiers before dispatching them into campaigns, and each day was a meaningful investment. Both boys pressed that point to each member of their squads. They wanted the men in their squads to improve every day, with no holidays during training.

Rufus was now mentally engaged in his development as much as he was physically. He knew that leading men by a strong example was the formula for long-term success in the military. He became the voice of the Emperor and the Emperor's instructors almost naturally, and he learned how to encourage as much as direct. Soon, the instructors left the task of training the 100 men in their group to the two young men who were addicted to competing with each other. Others followed their lead more than they followed the instructors, and others of like ability began seeking each other and pairing off for one-on-one competitions.

Rufus's rival was named Titus, and his father, Vespasian, was a member of the Senate. The family was close to Emperor Nero, but Rufus didn't care about politics or alliances. He had met the emperor when he was a young boy, and he knew that the position of emperor was nearly always temporary and wrought with corruption. When training ended, Titus invited Rufus to their home in Rome to meet his family. Both men knew that they would be traveling the world and conquering it together; getting to know each other's families seemed natural.

When he entered Titus' family home, Rufus was introduced to everyone. Titus' mother asked questions about his family, and Rufus told everyone, "My father is Cornelius, the Centurion." Vespasian took notice that his son's friend had a wonderful father and he expressed his appreciation that his son was to be welcomed as a son.

"Your father is a good man. Your father fought alongside mine back in the early Gaelic wars. I have heard tales of Cornelius, and they were good tales," said Vespasian.

"Let me get some wine so we can celebrate," said Vespasian as he left the room. The two young men were alone, and in the comfort of his own home, Titus opened up to his training partner.

"I wager that the two best from our batch of men shall also be two of the best in the future of our great empire."

"I was about to say the same thing," said Rufus. They put their hands on each other's shoulders, and their eyes burned into each other's as the strength of their grip increased. No force of earth or heaven could interrupt the bond that had formed.

As they awaited their first assignment, the two men lived in Titus' home, training together daily. When it was finally time for their graduation ceremony, Cornelius came to Rome with his wife and daughter to see the Emperor acknowledge their successes as the top recruits in the class. Each of them received helmets made of Damascus steel from the Emperor's hand. Normally, this was reserved for the top recruit in a century. In this case, however, both men performed exemplary work and they both received their helmets from the Emperor at the same ceremony.

"The fastest young man and the strongest young man are now bonded to be the best pair of recruits in all of Rome," said the Emperor to the crowd of family and military leadership that was gathered in the meeting room outside the Senate. At a young age, people around Rome could not say the name "Rufus" without also saying "Titus." They were a powerful pair who had shown great potential.

After graduation was over, the two men were approached by Optius, the leader of the Legion to whom they were both assigned.

This man was twice their age and served as a Senator. He knew Titus' father as a friend and adamant supporter of the Empire. He also knew Cornelius, and he held him in the highest regard. Optius spoke stoically, holding his ceremonial javelin in hand.

"You are like Castor and Pollux, the Gemini twins. The emperor and I have decided that you are needed in a distant part of the Empire to rectify a situation. Prepare to go to Gaul. We have some unfinished business for you to complete. You may be gone for a long time. We promote you to the rank of Standard, and each of you will report to Centurion Cartha."

Optius made eye contact with each man and paused before speaking again. He took so long that Rufus thought Optius must have been his father's teacher. "You shall each receive an additional promotion if you are successful. You need to decide what you want. We all know that anything is possible for you two."

The two men looked at each other and smiled.

"We accept," they said concurrently. Their fathers stood behind them, smiling with pride at the men their boys had become.

Chapter 21:
Gaining Power

The time in Gaul for these two upcoming military leaders was fruitful. As everyone in leadership expected, both men earned the rank of Centurion, affording them the dream life of receiving full-time wages. After a successful campaign against some coastal tribes, they both were promoted to Imperators, each now leading twice as many Roman troops against these barbaric uprisings. Their notoriety grew and the Legionnaire referred to them as "the first aid of conflict" at the ports around the Western Mediterranean.

Both men had grown in their administrative skills as well, as they now relied on the strength that came from the vast numbers of Roman troops at their disposal. However, they both learned that fighting tribal entities was an unending battle. Cornelius was a linguist, but his son never developed many language skills. As such, neither man knew any of the languages of Gaul, and investigating marauding groups through translators occupied nearly all of their time when the Gauls were not engaged in farming. They could never find the right people to talk to, nor could they get a consistent answer when they asked where they were. Cornelius had repeatedly advised Rufus to learn the language wherever he went, but Rufus placed that as a lower priority than his father did. This deficiency left him confused when he sought reliable information.

Titus, for his part, invested greatly in learning the tactics and supply chains of the enemy, ensuring that their supply chain always included Roman assets. He knew that attacks against the Romans would end if they were deemed to be providing a critical resource that the Gauls could not do without. He petitioned the Senate and the Emperors to permit him to provide the Gauls with great roads but not to tax them when they used them for commerce. This way, he could keep track of their comings and goings. He told the engineers to have the roads terminate at Roman outposts and the ones that Gaul needed at the other end. He introduced the Gauls to commerce across the Mediterranean and let them see how much they stood to benefit by shipping their great mineral and timber resources to other parts of the Roman Empire. He built shipyards in all the major cities, and he paid an above-average wage to get the best men to come and learn how to make vessels that could traverse the empire.

Meanwhile, Rufus engaged the people at the grassroots level, learning what they desired the most. He provided what they wanted in exchange for acceptance of Roman military presence and Roman commerce. Some tribes sought greater harvest reserves, as many would find themselves impoverished at the start of each summer when their winter supplies had depleted before the fall harvest could start. He worked with Optius and his logistics manager to ensure deliveries of grain each summer in exchange for unrestricted access to surplus livestock and timber. The trade agreement greatly satisfied both peoples. His engineers showed the Gauls how to build one-way boats that could be used to ship cattle and timber downriver and then disassembled. The timber that was used to construct the watercraft could be sent to distant outposts that lacked quality lumber for additional revenue. After several years of fine-tuning, Roman incursions into Gaul and surrounding provinces stabilized, and both Rufus and Titus were called back to Rome. Nero gave each of them a miniature copy of the golden and emerald scepter he used when he opened the Senate each year as a token of his gratitude.

Titus was promoted to Legate, the head of an entire Legion, in addition to battlefield commander, and Rufus was named first in charge of all non-battle operations. Both men were pleased with these promotions. Each came with impunity from any law while they were away, Roman or otherwise, and each man was given access to Roman coffers for military and provincial spending purposes. They no longer needed permission from the Senate to implement their budgets as long as they continued their successes. More land, more trade, and less conflict were their only measuring sticks for triumph and achievement.

With their campaign complete and the formalities of promotion and celebrations over, the Emperor himself called them to the royal palace to receive the details of their next assignment. The emperor invited all the local senators to join him and offer their support while Titus and Rufus sat next to him.

"Men, we are having problems in another remote part of our Empire. I am sending these promising young men to correct the situation, address the source of the problem, and make recommendations for change to prevent it from happening again. Come forward, Historian, and educate us all."

With that, the Emperor's Historian jumped out of his chair on the side of the chamber and briskly walked to the Emperor. Once he arrived, he began speaking in an almost practiced manner. He told of Rome's attempt to conquer and control the remote land of Britannia, home of the Britons. The Historian was verbose and included lots of details, such as names of houses destroyed by counterattacks, names of ships lost, and the amounts of monthly gold shipments that were not accounted for in the Roman treasuries. He used his knowledge of the minutiae to develop his hypothesis. Rome was losing the battle, and the losses were measurable.

On Britannia, there were several tribes scattered across the island, but they were not unified. The Romans had selected a few tribes to befriend, calling their leaders "client kings." They taught them smithing and forgery skills and advanced combat training. The Romans anticipated that those with additional skills and knowledge would be used to beat their competitors for resources such as land and food. Rome selected a few tribes to educate and teach them to use their technology. By doing so, the Romans created a pecking order amongst the tribes that would nearly always prevent them from uniting against the Empire.

This strategy was economically sound. Despite hundreds of thousands of men and women living on the wet and rainy island, the Romans could maintain peace and extract tariffs from all of them with a fighting force of less than 2% of their population. With such meager resources poured into such a valuable territory, Rome antici-pated great revenue for its investment.

One of the client kings, King Prasutagus, had received special favors from Rome, and his tribe knew how to craft projectile weap-ons of great accuracy. When he died, he left his land and estate half to Rome and the other half to his daughters. Although the Roman leadership in Britannia considered this more than fair, Nero decided to set an example for those who did not give all to the Empire. He ordered the Legion to whip the surviving queen and rape both of the king's daughters publicly, take them to the largest of tribal commu-nities on the island, and repeat these horrid acts.

This atrocity gave the Britons a reason to unify and fight back. That single twenty-minute public raping in their home fortress led to thousands of deaths in the Roman Legions during the ensuing attacks. The Roman leadership watched the Britons respond with fury and organization of the kind none in military leadership had seen in Roman territory. The queen waited for the Romans to leave her castle once the public raping was complete. Once out, she coor-dinated the surrounding tribes to push the Romans off the island. It was during that push that most of the 70,000 Romans were killed. Taxes were no longer coming into the Empire from Britannia and traditional attack-and-conquer politics would not work. Once the historian was done, the emperor dismissed him and took a deep breath before speaking.

"And that is why I am sending these two to clean up Britannia," spoke the Emperor. The emperor told them to take whatever they needed and depart Rome as soon as possible. Their vacation-style work in Gaul was over. It was time to lay down the law of Rome. They had heard complaints that the island was rainy most of the time; otherwise, they were ready to do as instructed by Nero.

Both men had changed their appearance during their time in Gaul. Titus now sported a short beard and he had one of his soldiers who would groom it for him often. Rufus now wore a mustache. Both men kept long hair and had a single braid coming out the back of their helmets. Each of them had a feather woven into the end of their black, straight hair. Many of the soldiers knew how to find them in battle by the presence of the feather.

Their differences on the inside were also significant, as would be expected of men who were deemed to be above the law. Titus had learned to love to collect sexual experiences with the women of the provinces that he visited. More than one tribal conquest was deemed a waste of time by him if it didn't include intimate time with a woman with a unique body feature. Body part size and shape were all intriguing for Titus. One time, he decided to have a woman with white hair and long legs, and he deemed the siege in progress incomplete until such a woman was found. While fighting in Northern Gaul near the eastern border with Germania, Titus fixated on finding women who were taller than he was. He sought them out during combat. Once found, he would have the soldiers bring these women to him. Titus loved the power that he felt when he was having sex with these women, and the fear on their faces aroused him. He was addicted to the experience of new sex, and everyone in his Legion knew of this fetish.

Rufus, for his part, loved finding and taking home artifacts from the tribal religious places. Although he cared nothing for the name of the religion or people group, he was interested in what the items were called and the names of the places from which they came. He had carvings from the druidic temples and stones from the monuments in Gaul. He tried to learn the words in the native language and would often have the scribe who traveled with the Legion record the details of the acquisition. He had been in the Senate many times and had seen that knowing the history of a people, place, or thing created immense power and that the one who possessed that knowledge controlled the conversation. The best part of the process was the acquisition. Once he had the artifact, it would go into storage, and perhaps he would forget he owned it. Gathering and storing was the burden of wealth, and Rufus suffered from it.

What Rufus and Titus liked the most about combat operations was that they were above Roman law. They were given all the labor and financial resources that they needed to shield themselves from bureaucracy and the processes of the chain of command. The

Emperor also knew of their fine tastes and would protect the perceived fulfillment of their "acquisitions." Many treaties were signed with foreign lands, including agreements not to rape or pillage, but Rufus and Titus were considered exempt from those clauses within the treaties. Rome allowed these two men to break the rules at will since they possessed skills of immeasurable value. They knew how to finish what others could not, and Rome accommodated their behavior. Emperors came to power and repeatedly were killed while Rufus and Titus stabilized remote parts of the Empire, but all the Emperors knew these two men as the "clean-up crew." These two men were, in the eyes of the Empire, some of the most powerful weapons an Emperor could ask for.

Chapter 22:
A Call to Service

Titus and Rufus spent no time calling their men to action, and they departed two days after the emperor gave them directions. The flotilla of ships took two full weeks to reach Britannia, as their navigator had predicted. The travel to the island was uneventful for Rufus and Titus, other than the amount of time they spent each day with the court Historians learning the rudimentary language skills of the Angels in the south so they could interact with the primary tribes. Both men learned much of the tribal politics of these uniquely pale-skinned and yellow-haired people, in addition to military tactics associated with extended combat in rainy weather that minimized the role of fire. Provision management during a campaign this far from Rome meant that communication to nearby outposts was critical. It took too long to get messages to and from Rome, so for all practical purposes, Titus was the acting emperor. Since one of the ships was filled with gold, he had all the financial resources he needed to get what was required to complete the job.

The men knew the importance of timing. When they arrived, they waited for the Britons to be occupied in the harvest before engaging them, knowing that they would be reluctant to resist and fearful of the consequences of leaving the fields to participate in combat. If the harvests were interrupted because of a need to swing a sword, their families would lose much of the crop and starve by the next year.

The Britons stood no chance and quickly surrendered once they knew that crop loss would be the price of victory. Reinforcements arrived later and the men executed nearly perfect attacks, completing their campaigns to restore order and taxation in two days and one month. Some 80,000 Britons were killed before the surrender was complete. The two leaders sent letters back to Rome with their fastest ship.

In their letters, they detailed how the loss of people on both sides could have been prevented, and they included the original decree from the Emperor. They concluded by stating that 150,000 people could have been spared if they had accepted the king's original offer to give half of his land to Rome. The men speculated that his half of the land would feed perhaps a village of 500, and the population of the Empire was now 149,500 fewer as a result of that choice. In essence, they chose not to fear Nero and instead spoke to him using truth.

Their letter was received and spread throughout the Senate, creating much unrest. Nero killed himself over this and many other reasons. Over the next year, Rome saw many rulers take up the scepter and the throne. While working on a wall across the northern part of the island, a group of messengers sent word to Rufus and Titus to come back to Rome immediately. The Senate had voted and made Vespasian the new Emperor, and Vespasian had a job for the two of them. Instead of visiting Rome as two fighting men, they were coming as the son of the emperor and his best friend.

Upon their return to Rome, the men were given a grand entrance. Vespasian sent out a delegation to greet them when they entered the outskirts of the city. They received an escort to the center of Rome, led by chariots and trumpets. In the front was a crier who yelled in intervals to the crowd, "Remain standing where you are and honor the Legion that brought order back to the province of Britannia!"

Once they got off of the carts inside a protected region of the capital, the Emperor himself came out to greet the warriors and his son.

"Well done, boys. I have read the reports. Your work was beautiful and made Rome appear in a positive light. You bring glory and honor to all soldiers in the Empire, and you have restored order and hopefully peace in a part of the world where this is no easy task."

The Emperor embraced Titus and Rufus, as well as another ten men before he asked them what their hearts' desires were.

Rufus quickly spoke for all of the men. He knew he could have anything he wanted, but what they wanted were the most mundane of items. "My men and I have seen much and lived by a schedule fraught with danger for years. For a time, we would like to sit by a fire without any weapons or armor, eat meat, and drink wine. We would like to have no one come in and wake us up, and --"

Two of his men interrupted him. "Rufus, you would be the one waking us up for fitness. If you don't do it, no one is going to do it!"

The men, including the Emperor and the Emperor's guards, all laughed, as Rufus' fame as a disciplined fitness instructor was the stuff of legend.

The Emperor spoke again, this time as a command. "Be normal men for a while." The Emperor offered them a garden on the northern side of his palace. They all accepted his offer, and they retrieved their gear from the wagon.

They were already carrying their gear towards the stairs leading up from the bottom floor when the Emperor yelled to them, "You may drop your bags! Someone else will take care of them. You have done enough carrying on behalf of the Empire. Now, go upstairs, eat, and rest. Some of the Senate will come to you for a report on the status of Britannia, but not until tomorrow. You have my promise."

The men went upstairs and found several slaves following close behind them. They were not carrying their gear and goods—instead, they carried pots of fresh water and new, lighter clothing. The slaves gave the men a bath in one of two pools in the garden. They each groomed and dried off before donning new clothing.

Two of the soldiers began fondling the servant girls, but Rufus quickly put an end to that, giving each slave one gold coin for enduring the men's lack of self-control. "And that coin I gave those Ebreet women shall come from your pay, by my life, I swear it!" yelled Rufus.

Titus turned and spoke to his friend Rufus. "Leave the men alone. They have not tasted the flesh of a woman in many months. Let them follow their heart's desire."

"You and I are different. My father taught me to take for myself exactly one woman. Do as you wish, but the men who report to me will follow my rules. Leave the honor of this woman intact, be they slaves or citizens," said Rufus.

For most men, this was the first time they had seen Rufus and Titus disagree, but none of them spoke against either of them. For his part, Titus saw no reason to fight Rufus in front of others, and he left the topic of sex with slaves alone. He lay down and quickly fell asleep before the smells of freshly cooked food awakened him.

Throughout the late fall afternoon and into the evening, the men told stories of the events of their conquests in Brittania. The weather would certainly not be missed. The extended rains that seemed to soak all the way to the core of the body were miserable, and the long darkness of the days of winter often left men depressed. The men repeatedly toasted to not returning there again.

The men were grateful to be back in the South of the Empire, as they all agreed that women with yellow hair weren't as attractive as the dark-haired women of Rome. Indeed, much of Britannia followed religious practices that recognized the presence of witches. Titus' men agreed that any credibility to the claim that some of these women were witches was related to this yellow hair.

With the gift of uninterrupted relaxation, the men got drunk and fell asleep on the roof of the palace. Several of the slaves and guards also drank and did the same, though not until Titus first requested confirmation from one of the Emperor's attendants that he had permitted them to do so. No guard or slave could deviate from their assignment and expect to live without direct permission from the Emperor. That night, the emperor gave all the slaves the equivalent of a holiday. The men were used to taking care of their affairs while away on the Emperor's missions, and they extended the gift of uninterrupted relaxation to the slaves who had cared for them. Rufus learned all of their names and he offered the oldest one a place on his bed with him so he could rest in comfort.

Six Senators arrived the next morning and took a quiet place in the garden next to the palace. As they woke up, groggy from the night's drinking, Rufus and Titus changed nothing of their morning affairs. The Senators watched as the two men ran into downtown Rome and did calisthenics in a field adjacent to the garden before returning to bathe and eat. They stripped down and bathed naked and cared not that there were Senators present.

Rufus could see the Senators wanted stories of victory, and he gave several tales that distracted them from the state of the Emperor. The average Roman soldier was stronger and faster than the best warriors from Brittania, and it wasn't uncommon for Rufus to suffer no casualties while bringing a village of one thousand men to their knees in submission. The Senators loved hearing that all their investment in military training camps was creating the best soldiers in the world.

Once they were done with their questions, Rufus suggested the creation of a Roman project on the island that no single tribe could tear down. Rufus saw that much of what the tribes had established on that piece of rock was either small or temporary. Rufus suggested importing marble from captured lands and sending lots of engineers to build public works that would traverse the island between feudal factions. He knew that the people who lived there would greatly revere and respect what was built and those who knew how to build. He suggested using Britannia as a training ground for the next generation of architects and engineers to learn their craft in a way that could not hurt anyone in Rome. He also suggested sending younger, skilled, and multi-lingual Romans, as it would be easier for them to learn the languages of Britannia than an older yet more experienced engineer.

The Senators nodded their head in agreement to all of Rufus' proposals. They asked many other questions before Vespasian joined them in the garden. The soldiers bowed down once the Emperor arrived, as did the Senators. Vespasian spoke when he had everyone's attention.

"At the recommendation of both the Senate and the men under you, I am promoting you to the rank of Imperial Legate. You will have four Legions under your command. You will have Tiberius Julius Alexander, the governor of Egypt, as your second in command, but only because tradition dictates the inclusion of a Caesar." No one was expecting the Emperor to openly reveal his disgust towards the political requirement of including a Caesar in the line of military command. "Instead, Rufus shall be your second in command for all aspects of what is ahead of you."

Both Titus and Rufus bowed their heads but quietly smiled with delight. They looked up at each other like they were boys again in the first week of military training. The Emperor handed each of them a sword worth more than everything in a single village. Each piece of crafted steel had an ivory hilt made from an elephant's tusk. The scabbard was covered in precious gems, gilded in gold and silver. The blades were sharp as razors and usable in combat, and they made a sound when unsheathed that made both men laugh with joy.

"Your Grace!" They both took a knee and looked at the ground as insignia was placed on their uniforms to display their rank. It was a grand ceremony that Vespasian knew would fill their souls. For the rest of the next two days, the men walked around Rome, wearing their blades, going from house to house, and accepting the adoration of the families of nearly all the Senators.

On the third day, the men directly under Titus and Rufus gathered for breakfast. After their morning calisthenics, Vespasian entered, commanding all of them to get up and follow him. The group walked to the edge of the garden that looked down on Rome. From the Palatine Hill, where the Emperor resided, the view was magnificent. It was from here that the Emperor would impart his will on the world. The last four Emperors had lasted less than a year combined, and Vespasian wanted his to be a lifetime appointment. He turned to the men whom he had written into history and spoke to them, with the Senators, slaves, and warrior friends all listening.

"Titus, for the last several years, Ebreet leadership has pushed the Empire out from Jerusalem, arguably the most powerful city in the world aside from Rome, and we can't regain control. The resistance has formed their government in direct defiance of ours, and they have appointed their best as leaders. Ananas ben Ananas, the former High Priest of their faith, is one of the government heads. Over 500,000 people visit Jerusalem each year during their feast of Passover and Rosh Hashanah. They have made their currency and laws so as not to need any of the resources Rome normally offers to its captured territories." He paused to make eye contact with all the other senators before finishing his edict.

"We are taking a different approach, and I am placing you two in charge." He gave his words a few moments to distill their impact before he continued.

"Those who have come before me have extracted minerals and wealth from Jerusalem as people travel to seek out blessings and forgiveness from a false god. The Ebreet have defied us at each step, and for the last several years, we have not made it clear that Rome is in charge, not Jerusalem. Despite all the investments that Rome has made in developing the Temple Mount and making Jerusalem into a worldwide attraction, I want you to destroy it. Specifically, I want you to tear the Temple down. I want no stone standing on any other stone. We must send the Ebreet a message that history will burn into their souls. Otherwise, I am not the Emperor of Rome."

The two men unsheathed their blades and accepted the challenge. Vespasian waited for them to look at him before finishing his directions.

"You have the full Roman military at your disposal," the Emperor continued. "I will give you as many Legions of men as you need. Make your supply chain the largest one in the world; make it bigger than the one that serves the city of Rome itself."

No one spoke, but the Senators feared that this would mean taking from the resources available to Roman citizens and their constituents. Vespasian knew that he would think like that, so he gave his men some time to implement change.

"We have not been in control of that disgusting city for four years. We can wait another few months. Take your men and take time to heal and rest before leaving. You are going to Jerusalem to destroy it. Take our Historians with you and prepare to go, my sons. If you are successful, you will change history."

Chapter 23:
A Growing Sorrow

"I hate this heat."

That sentence summarized what nearly every soldier felt about the late summer afternoons in the heartland of what all of them called Judah. The maps stated that they were walking on land that was part of the tribes of Dan, Ephraim, and Benjamin, but they didn't care. It was all ancient history that would soon be lost once they finished their siege. They liked calling it all "Judah," so they did.

Roman thinking did not apply to working with supply chains on the way to Jerusalem. Navigating the land of Benjamin differed from anything else in the empire - North, South, East, and West defined direction. In Benjamin, everything was either up or down - there was no flat. Combined with the summer heat, Benjamin, at midday, was hell on earth.

Rufus was done with riding on horseback. He walked the final day's distance to the outer walls of the city of Jerusalem with his men, carrying his gear like any other soldier. He was certain that these next months would be some of the most difficult ones that he had been exposed to as a soldier, as the Emperor had told them to starve out the Ebreet. No campaigns. No cultural strategy. They were to stand their ground, preventing food and supplies from entering the massive hilltop city. That meant enduring numerous attempts to negotiate as well as lots of escape attempts for those trying to save themselves. They would need to dig several wells for all the animals and soldiers, and no one had anticipated that. And, there would be lots of time sitting around when it was too hot outside to think. He could tell that he would need to make structures to provide shade to all his men. Fortunately, Lebanese cedar trees were some of the largest in the world, and they were easy to purchase and get delivered to the city; building the shade would be easy.

Titus and Rufus had everything they needed to win. The Emperor had empowered them with enough men and gold to compensate for a gross tactical mistake that cost them as many as 5,000 men. The force of four Legions of soldiers had not been seen in this part of the world ever, and the organization that the Romans brought with them would be overpowering. Their contingents had engineering and architectural resources without match, and there would be remnants of their contingent here for years to come. It would not be the act of tearing down that would consume the most time. Once the temple was torn apart, they were to begin rebuilding Jerusalem as a city to meet the needs of the Roman administration. That would mean new buildings, roads, walls, and waterways. Rufus stood at the front of the world's largest caravan, and for hours, he affirmed each man who walked past him.

"Come on, boys. Let's surround that city like ants surround sugar cane on a hot day." He hit each man on the shoulder as they went by him, and he tried to motivate them to keep their focus. This was going to be an endurance event, not a show of great force. When they thought they were done, a second job of equal importance and longer commitment would begin. Rufus didn't like this climate, either. He didn't want to be a part of Brittania, and he was wondering if he wanted to be a part of the rebuilding of this city once his job was done.

The final details of the plan were written out and a copy was given to each legion communications officer to make sure every soldier knew and understood their mission. The primary job of these four legions during the first three months was to deny access to the food and supplies needed to survive. After a brief interval, they would destroy the outer walls and move in to destroy the Temple. Lastly, there would be a multi-year effort for clean-up and rebuilding. Titus and Rufus were engaged in a project that no field leaders had undertaken in the history of the Roman Empire. Their work would require three phases with three different skill sets. Ironically, no one in any of the Legions was skilled at all three. Jerusalem's destruction and subsequent rebuilding was the most unique affair that the Roman empire had ever undertaken.

The historians organized the boat ride from the port of Ostia outside of Rome to the port of Joppa in the province of Dan. These men used meal time to teach and educate Rufus and Titus on Ebreet history. Rufus repeatedly took over the teaching of the historian's recitations when he heard a story that his father had taught him during his education in Caesarea. Rufus' memory impressed the historians, and he spent half of a day teaching the Exodus to Titus and all the other field leaders.

Rufus taught that their name, Ebreet, meant people of the crossing. They began their occupation of this land after a 40-year journey through the desert from Egypt to Israel, and it ended when they crossed over the River Jordan. They earned their namesake once they got to the other side of the river and they were instructed to kill all the occupants and build for themselves this great city upon a hill in the middle of their land. Since their God was not a real god and did not give them the power to kill all of the people who occupied their land, they struggled. Their history was a parody of success followed by failure, as their God would come and go from their presence. Throughout all of that, Jerusalem remained their sacred city, and it sat at the top of a hill that went by many other names. Sometimes, they occupied it; other times, it was rubble.

Titus was impressed with his best friend's vast history of this place. He had visited Cornelius at his home when he was younger, but he didn't realize how adjusted Rufus was to the people and their history. He could sense that Rufus would feel at home in the presence of Ebreet.

As the weeks went by and Rufus got to interact with the local Ebreet for supplies, his childhood memories resurfaced. He remembered the children he played with when he was younger, and he found himself talking to and telling jokes with the merchants who were supplying them with food and provisions. He did not reveal to anyone the passion he was developing for this place and its people, but his assistants could tell he liked being in Judah.

He was impressed at how well the historians had found and recorded stories from their ancient past. He knew that they must have found a copy of the Torah and had it translated into Latin. And he routinely smiled when the historians would state their disbelief and wonder why the Ebreet remained a global presence.

For example, there was the tale of a young boy who was sold into slavery by his family and later became a king. In another, a boy used a sling and a stone to kill a giant, and he, too, became a king. His father told him those stories and it felt good to hear them from Roman historians. Despite what Titus was thinking, they seemed more real to Rufus, especially now that they were in Judah.

Rufus convinced Titus to be impressed by the great courage these early leaders displayed. He liked them. Unlike the Gauls or the Britons, the Ebreet hoped that a Messiah would come and rescue them. The incredible tales from their history led them to believe that God had rescued them before and would do so again. Rufus was sad for them that none had yet to come. Certainly, he remembered all the prayers his father spoke when he was a boy back north in Caesarea.

The Emperor knew this story and had expressed concerns about this belief before they left.

"Do what you must. There must be no place for this Messiah to return to. Destroy their obnoxious Temple and clean up the mess afterward. Do not let them have hope that the Temple will be built again. Haul away the debris as soon as you can and restore a normal appearance to that place. We want to wipe the memory of that Temple from their memories. We want the next generation to know only Rome. Instill the spirit of commerce and public works there as we have done elsewhere. Build for them what they want and repair anything that is not the Temple."

With their directive clearly explained, the men began settling into life below the decorated walls of Jerusalem. As far back as they could see were the lines of the soldiers and supplies required for four Legions of Roman war engines to travel.

After a few weeks, most of the men in the four Legions had arrived. Titus climbed to a high spot and spoke. "Behold, the city of the mythical King David. Before we leave, it shall be ours, and its temple will be destroyed. We shall make history with our efforts. Starting now, no one shall enter or leave this city. We shall starve our enemy unless they allow us to come inside and destroy the Temple. Make it a point of displaying harsh judgment on those who do try and leave. Our Emperor sent us here because the Ebreet defied him. We shall not let them defy us."

A well-thought-out plan to blockade the city was in place and the men began implementing it before the end of the week. Since they would be there a quarter of a year before the first stone was thrown, extra attention was given to sanitation, water management, and fuel in the places where they camped, as they would need to keep all Roman troops healthy for ninety days before they would begin fighting.

As the starvation began, Rufus was disturbed by his growing feelings of empathy. He felt deep sorrow. His normal, talkative self was gone. All he could see in the faces of his youth as they passed through the small cities and towns was fear. Yes, the job that the emperor gave him and his best friend would be accomplished. He had sworn an oath to the Emperor. Yet something was changing inside of him that he did not understand. He felt sorry for the Ebreet. He lacked empathy for the Gauls or the Britons. The Ebreet world was much more mature and older than anything he had seen, and it was about to change permanently. Their most revered monument was about to topple.

His father's voice returned to his consciousness, as it did during the early days of training.

"Treat all people as you want to be treated. If a man has done you no harm, it is not right to harm him. If you do, there will be a consequence for your actions. You must not sin, especially when your heart desires to extract tribute."

Rufus tried to ignore his internal conflict between what he felt and the task he was required to perform by throwing himself into his work. He took the task of designing the weapons of war seriously. They were needed to breach the city walls and be portable enough to take inside the city for use at the Temple Mount. Pouring himself in his work was his numbing medicine for the conflict he was feeling.

Titus spent a lot of time with Rufus, waiting for the blockade to do its job. He saw that something had stirred inside Rufus. "These are the people of your youth, aren't they? We visited your family a couple of leagues north of here, didn't we? Do you remember the language of these people? What has made you soft, my brother?" Titus was sincere and patient as he awaited his brother's response to these and other questions.

Rufus had always been able to tell Titus anything. This moment was no different.

"These people did nothing wrong. Those in the city who defy the Emperor deserve to pay the price for their behavior, not the poor and simple farmers who care nothing of the affairs of priests and Emperors. The pilgrims inside who came to worship the God of Exodus have also done nothing wrong. They have been doing this for thousands of years. It is not their fault, either."

"Don't tell my father, but I agree with you. You must separate yourself from this situation and do your job. Remember that."

Rufus knew that Titus was speaking to him both as his leader and his brother. All that Titus had said was true, but he didn't know how to separate himself from their current situation.

"Perhaps you should drink more wine each evening, my friend," said Titus. He laughed, but he wasn't joking. He had nothing else to offer his brother.

Rufus had a hole in his life, and it had spread to his heart. He didn't know what to do with it. Something about this story that he was a part of writing seemed wrong.

Really wrong.

Chapter 24:
Wise at a Young Age

Despite a near-perfect memory of their lives since arriving in Jerusalem, the memory of the time before that was blurred. Mishi moved when he was eight. He had heard both his parents and grandparents tell the story, and all the different versions of the claims confused him. Yes, they had migrated from rural Edom, a land that was part of Philistia, to metropolitan Jerusalem. However, the variety and renditions of that story were uncountable. The story they told was of an incredible journey that got a bit bigger each time they told it. Mishi always felt compelled to tell a more truthful version, but that would have been disrespectful to correct his elders. When he called them out on it, all they could say was that that was how they remembered it. This disconnect between what happened and how it was told was a central theme in his life.

Sometimes, the story would be one of "a few days of travel." Sometimes, it would be a few weeks. Sometimes, during one version of the story, the family watched a lion attack their livestock. Sometimes, they saw a swarm of locusts descend on the wheat fields one week before harvest as they passed through a small village a few days south of Jerusalem. His grandfather watched the residents scream in terror as the village's primary food supply for the following year was consumed in minutes. His grandmother saw hordes of starving children. In other renditions, two families asked Mishi's father to take them as slaves so they wouldn't starve to death the following Spring. Mishi's father would tell them no, but they would kneel in front of the pack animals, pleading their cause. Mishi remembered every rendition like he remembered every face that he had seen. His mind could recall any memory vividly and realistically; unfortunately, no one else in his family came close.

One day, Mishi promised his father that he would make the journey back to Tamar with him and find out how long the journey would take. But that wasn't today. His life in Jerusalem was too busy for a trip. Even the short trips that he had taken to nearby cities and villages always left him wanting to return to the Temple Mount and continue his work. Mishi was a career academic and he was in the best place in the world for those who loved studying and learning. His detail-ridden memory was best used in a place where there were the greatest number of scrolls to read and people to talk to. Jerusalem was the center of his faith and his life and he was at the top of the system of people who were allowed to study their 1000-year history. It always intrigued him how his mind could remember every word in the scroll of Isaiah but not what color house he lived in for his first eight years.

Mishi seldom spoke of anything from the trip. When he did speak and add to what his parents were saying, he would tell of Roman soldiers stopping them at intervals along the way, asking for their destination and a coin to pass. This was, after all, Roman territory in all ways that the territories were measured. The Romans protected the surrounding feudal tribes and maintained roads and water sources. In exchange, they took portions of crops, freshly butchered meat, harvested lumber, and fish from the sea. All along the way, Mishi would hear his father speak to the Romans. He listened to his messages about Hebrew history. It wasn't until Mishi had been in school and could read and write that he concluded that his father had told the Romans the truth.

"Son, people have always taken what is not theirs from us, Ebreet," he would say to Mishi. "We Ebreet have lost our land to the Babylonians. We were enslaved in Egypt by Pharaoh. These Romans and their ever-changing Emperors are the latest manifestation of our history of captivity. But you must remember this point, as it is our identity. We are Yahweh's chosen people and He keeps his promises. Our God knows of our captivity and hears our prayers. He has always provided a deliverer for us, and he will do so again. Yes, He punishes us for our sins, but if we repent, He will provide a deliverer for us. He will come, this Messiah. We will be freed again."

Mishi's father's tone was filled with confidence, but its impact on his only son was not limited to his spoken words. His memories of his father included feelings of love and reflections of affirming touch. He would often put his hands on his son's shoulders and tell him that he loved him. Mishi's father was a good man and a great teacher.

His father was known for other things, as he spent most of his days with a hammer and chisel. He was a skilled artisan who made designs drawn on parchment into monuments. During the solemn moments when he worked, he would think about the Torah and meditate on it. Mishi enjoyed listening to these meditations.

"In our past, God sent Moses to deliver us from Pharaoh. God sent Cyrus to deliver us from the Babylonians. Soon, he will send a Messiah to deliver us from these Romans. I am sure of it, and you should be, too. Your mother and I hope you will be one of the helpers of our ancient faith, speaking and praying to Yahweh on behalf of all of the twelve tribes." His father was very proud of his young son as he knew that he was intelligent and educated. Mishi's vision to become a powerful rabbi and great teacher came from his father's investment of kind and loving words.

Mishi also remembered the miracles. As Jerusalem appeared on the horizon for the first time, Mishi's father told the whole family to begin praying so that God would provide housing for them. Prayers of prosperity were among the most common ones that villagers remembered when the scrolls were read out loud. Mishi's father had his family memorize one of these prayers, one he called the prayer of Jabez. "Bless me, indeed; let me expand your horizons for Your name!" When they entered the city, they found an apartment within quick walking distance of the Temple Mount. The rent was high, but they had prepared for this and did not hesitate to accept the terms that their new landlord gave them.

Once they had given the owner a deposit, Mishi's father reached into the family cart and took out a small vial of lamb's blood that had been packed in dried meat to keep it cool. He also took a previously unused water skin that contained water taken from his family's well in Tamar. Holding the vial of lamb's blood in one hand and the village water in the other, he walked to the front door of their apartment. As he walked toward the entrance, Mishi's grandfather began chanting and dancing. Once his father reached the door, he opened the vial and rubbed the contents on the door frame and lintel of their home. As he did so, he said, "May the God who delivered our people from Egypt protect us when evil spirits pass over our home as He did during the days and weeks leading up to the Exodus."

Mishi remembers that it took three twists to open the water skin and pour a small amount on the ground in front of the door. "May this water from our past show that we carry the essence of our faith with us, no matter where we travel, no matter where we rest our flesh."

He passed the flask to each family member, who drank. "May this last drink from the village of our past stay with us as we take the first drink of our present and our future." Mishi's mother swallowed it and passed it around for everyone to drink. Once everyone was done, Mishi's mother and grandmother took two large clay pots and set out to find their new water source. Until they came back, everyone sat down in the coolness of their new apartment, awaiting their return.

When the women returned, and everyone had taken a drink of the Jerusalem water, Mishi noted how no one had anything positive to say about the taste. They all compared it to the past and found it lacking, speculating that it tasted like Marah. He spoke up in a way that he thought might dispel their negativity without offending them.

"Millions of mouths are given this water every week, including people smarter than we are, and its quality doesn't seem to be inhibiting their success. Did you see how big Solomon's Temple stairs were? The people who carried that marble drank this water, I bet!"

Everyone nodded. Mishi's grandfather spoke up. "You are wise at a young age. May your insight into this water be a foreshadowing of your insight at this school. The first taste is not an indicator of something's worth." His grandfather rubbed his head back before he removed his hand.

Things were about to change in Mishi's life in ways that his father predicted.

Chapter 25: A Home in Jerusalem

After a few weeks of settling into life in the largest Ebreet settlement in the world, Mishi found that his family's migration story was much like that of others who lived near them. Their neighbors were also skilled artisans who had relocated to Jerusalem to take advantage of construction jobs at the Temple Mount. The Romans were expanding it, as Jerusalem was a tourist destination and a cash cow for taxation. The temple was a place that Assyrians and Gauls would visit, even though they did not share faith in one true God. As such, there were unlimited jobs for those in construction as this part of the Roman empire was expanding.

Since a new governor was installed, both skilled Ebreet and Roman workers labored to build the Temple Mount into an ever-growing global attraction for all pilgrims. Jerusalem's place both in the Roman Empire and Judean world overlapped in this shared passion to make the Temple Mount better. Ebreet were required to atone for their sins by sacrificing at the temple. Tourists wanted to come for commerce, to visit the hotels with grand views, to eat the cuisine, and to see the largest synagogue in the world. It was rumored that the Lord himself resided within its hallowed walls.

For most Ebreet families, the patriarch and sons would make the journey once a year. Occasionally, the wives and daughters would also make the journey, but not without securing an escort, as the inbound roads could be treacherous. They all came to sacrifice and become clean, but they also came to see the great walled city and Solomon's Temple. With all roads leading to and from Jerusalem under the careful watch of the Roman military to prevent brigands from deterring these tourists, more and more people visited Jerusalem each year. That required more resources.

Both Roman architects and Ebreet Pharisees saw great value in making that experience better every year. At first, accommodations were constructed exclusively for the "wealthy sinner," with nicer hotels, restaurants, and furnishings placed on the pathway leading to the Temple Mount to inspire a future return. Roman accountants recognized each year after the Temple census that many of those who would like to visit could not afford the cost of being there, so additional, lower-cost facilities were built outside of the city. This appealed to the Ebreet farmers, who could not justify the one-week wait that often came with the reality of several million Ebreet men trying to visit one Temple to atone for their sins at the same time.

The Romans and Ebreet alike worked together to build a second Temple to service those with limited resources who wished to cleanse themselves of sin. This allowed twice the traffic and, therefore, twice the taxation. The Romans had an agreement with the Pharisees, who oversaw the forgiveness ritual, to share a portion of the taxes in exchange for protection as they traveled in the area and special consideration for the interpretation of certain laws. Pharisees, Sadducees, and Romans prospered under this agreement.

Yet none of those outcomes could have happened without skilled and well-fed laborers working to make the Temple Mount bigger and better. Mishi's family arrived at Jerusalem in one of the waves of artisans, looking for the work and the wealth that Jerusalem offered.

There were parts of the migration story his family told that were always the same. Back in Tamar, Mishi's family grew crops and raised livestock, and their village of perhaps fifty homes was not far from the Wadi River. Despite its proximity to the Dead Sea, the land around Tamar was rich in nutrients, and the rainfall was consistent, making agricultural living both peaceful and manageable. While others traveled to all parts of Egypt and Judah as gatherers and seasonal hunters, the founders of Tamar decided to set their roots in a single place and build a community based on farming and tending livestock. They seldom suffered from drought, and the soil was loose enough that it could be tilled without metal plows and strong animals. As the older men in his family were quick to note in their storytelling, the health of all residents in Tamar increased with each generation. Boys were taller and girls were stronger, with wider hips and thicker torsos. Wheat could be grown two seasons a year instead of one, and the sale of the excess crop provided money for the village. There was always a reserve of Roman coins available for ceremonial investments and occasionally for a traveling Rabbi to spend a few weeks with the younger boys, teaching them to read and do mathematics. If there was a middle class in the Promised Land, the residents of Tamar were it.

Unlike the elders in Correae, Tamar's leadership used their excess wealth to hire seasonal workers from nearby Ephraim and Reuben to help in the fields, and the amount of farmed land increased year after year. Roman roads made it easy to travel to find these migrant workers and to bring them to their village safely. Otherwise, conflicts with surrounding tribes would make this act too risky.

Tamar was in Judah proper, but it was removed from the main thoroughfares that connected Jerusalem to the coast and other cities. Few in the Roman administration ever visited Tamar. Romans were concerned with establishing a presence in places that had vast wealth or populations prone to uprisings. They quickly judged a village to have wealth if they had a synagogue or a large population. Tamar had neither. A yearly visit from a foreign tax collector was the single noticeable Roman presence. Since few Romans learned to speak Ebreet, the tax collectors remained unaware of the vast sums of grains and livestock that the village possessed, as their stay was too short for them to learn of Tamar's hidden treasure. Even though some of the younger village boys had learned Greek from traveling Rabbis, they were instructed not to speak it when the tax collectors arrived, fearing it would create additional questions and inadvertently reveal their secret wealth.

During more than one village council, the elders would discuss building a synagogue. Each time, the idea was shot down. If they chose to build a version of the great Temple in Jerusalem, as many other towns had done, a Roman contingent would be stationed near it to collect taxes. More Roman presence meant more taxes and less freedom. It was agreed upon that once the Roman invaders left Judah, they would build such a house of worship. Until that came to pass, they would exist without their synagogue.

When Mishi was seven, it was decided at one of these meetings that it was his family's turn to offer their next born to the Temple in Jerusalem as a Rabbi. After considerable discussion amongst the men in the village, it was determined that Mishi's parents' firstborn son would be a teacher of the Torah. Unfortunately, his mother had many complications during Mishi's delivery, and she didn't expect to have any more children. The elders in the village concluded that her infertility was rooted in a great, unconfessed sin in her family's past. Although no one could pinpoint any specific moral crime, someone in her family lineage must have done something very wicked for her womb to close. She would spend her life with one child. No one challenged this point.

In Ebreet custom, all male children grouped their talents and resources and took responsibility for caring for their parents in their old age. With Mishi likely to be his parents' lone son, his success dictated his parent's quality of life in their old age. The village decided that the best course of action was to invest both their time and money into Mishi's education. The family sold a piece of recently converted forest that was now farmland and all their livestock to Mishi's uncle, except for a few animals that would journey with them. They decided to use the proceeds of the sale to travel, pay for temporary housing, and find the best schooling for Mishi in Jerusalem.

Even before they left Tamar, they discovered that Mishi remembered everything that he saw. It was obvious to all his relatives that Mishi would be admitted to the competitive Temple school once the headmaster could see his perfect memory. The elders agreed that this offering was the best chance for Mishi to succeed as a provider for his parents, the head of household, and successor to his family name. An Ebreet education of the highest sort was the way to refine his talents and keep him safe from all but the worst of Roman threats. It was decided for Mishi's sake that both of his grandparents would also leave and go to Jerusalem to study. Once Mishi was of age, he would

Bar Mitzvah, take up the phylactery of the Rabbinical life, marry, and return to their village to teach.

That was the story that was told to all who would listen.

But there were portions of the story that were omitted. Tradition mandated that the Kohanim were to be dedicated to learning the ways of the priestly cast. The family's choice to sell a piece of land would help them argue with any of the temple priests that the requirements for priesthood specified in the Scrolls of Joshua had been met. However, they didn't sell all of their land nor all of their livestock as they kept receiving proceeds from the sale of crops and livestock while they were in Jerusalem. That indicated that they were not fully committed to letting the Lord provide for them on their holy journey. "Yahweh is the inheritance of the Kohanim" was the answer Mishi was told to give when asked about his family's provisions outside of Jerusalem.

Mishi entered the city for the first time a day before his ninth birthday. The pathway to the city was lined with vendors buying and selling goods of all sorts for people who were making the pilgrimage to the holy city for the holy season. Men were yelling in languages that were foreign to Mishi, looking both to buy and to sell. Bolts of multi-colored cloth sat in large piles on a horse-drawn cart at the base of the city hill. Next to it was a portable iron cauldron with a small fire inside, cooking bread to sell to hungry travelers. Mishi's mother bought two loaves as the family stepped off the pathway leading up to the city to eat their first meal on the holy hill. Camels carrying grapes on each side of their humps passed by while the family ate their warm bread, set on carrying their harvest of fruit into the city center. The camel driver paid no interest to any of the street merchants trying to buy his goods. A young girl carried a large stick over one of her shoulders, and each half of the stick was weighted down with a dozen squawking chickens, all tied together at the feet to prevent them from falling off as she carried them. A large cart carrying a single clay pot, the size of which no one in Mishi's family had seen, was being pulled by a pair of oxen out of the city. Whatever was in it didn't smell very good. His mother wouldn't tell him what it was when he asked other than not to ask again.

Once the family passed through the city gates, they spent the next hour mesmerized by these sights and sounds. There were snake charmers grouped together in the middle of the street, playing flutes to get the snakes to stand on their tails and stare at the other travelers. Nearby, there was a cart full of meat from a freshly slaughtered sheep, and next to the butchers was an older man selling oil that he claimed would cure leprosy and make blind people see. Another baker was selling fresh bread, and a farmer had a basket full of mangos of an astonishing size that was not found in southern Judah. Mishi remembered his mother joking frequently, suggesting that they may live near the "Shopping Paradise of Jerusalem."

This first entrance into Jerusalem would remain one of Mishi's strongest memories of the first part of his life.

Chapter 26: Temple Education

As foreigners in their kingdom's capital city, Mishi's family chose to live as inexpensively as possible until everyone had secured work and Mishi was enrolled at the Temple school. They lived in a small two-room apartment for the first season. Mishi was too young to realize that they were poor. He was young and absorbed everything, and his mind thrived. Other Ebreet immigrants occupied this part of the city, and he found lots of friends whom he could speak to using his mother language of Aramaic. It was almost as if a part of Tamar had relocated to Jerusalem. Mishi made it a point to talk to all of them. He wanted to know their stories, too.

His father found work as a carpenter and stone mason on the Temple Mount, and his mother found work as a job site meal preparer. King Herod and those who came after him had been investing as many resources as they could to develop the Temple into a place for Roman tourists, not merely a holy place for Ebreet pilgrims. With the additional buildings and structures, both pilgrim and tourist tax revenue increased. Secondarily, the prosperity associated with all the new jobs brought peace. The Ebreet benefitted as much as the Romans did. Despite their adversarial relationship in other matters, both sides agreed that any task that resulted in more revenue and more employment was a task worth undertaking.

In addition to completing walls around the Holy Temple, the Herodian leadership constructed ornate towers and paid to have great statues and works of art created and strategically placed in the city. During the occupation, the Roman Emperors had the city gated and covered in precious metals and ornate wood carvings. In addition, the sides of the building, originally carved from the stone of Solomon's original imports, were now covered in elaborate carvings and lavish tapestries. The horse stables looked like Royal palaces from a distance, with intricate carvings of camels and beasts of burden that carried holy men into the city to worship at the temple on the sides. And, for a small fee, you could park your beast at the "holy manger" while you visited the Temple Mount to have your sins forgiven.

Despite the stress placed on city water and sanitation resources, the Romans and the Ebreet Sanhedrin leadership saw no reason to curtail either the development of the city or its policy of flooding the area with pilgrims during the holy season. Sanitation was problematic during these times, but with ample supplies of money and slaves, the influx of human waste was removed from the city walls once the pilgrimages were complete and the travelers were gone. Mishi figured out that must have been what was in the large clay pot on the first day, but he didn't talk about it as his mother told him not to.

Mishi's father's skills place him in the right place at the right time. The construction projects and associated maintenance tasks required skilled labor, specifically carpenters and stone masons. Mishi's dad was both. Mishi's mom thought that she would not have any marketable skills. Still, her assistance in preparing all her villages' Bar Mitzvah and Bah Mitzvah meal requirements made her equally valuable as a job site caterer for joint Ebreet and Roman crews. She could please the taste buds of both groups, and she was often sought to serve a grand meal when dignitaries from Rome visited to tour the temple grounds. As such, the family saw no end to the opportunities to create wealth while staying in the holy city. Although no one else from their village lived in Jerusalem, nearly everyone who came to visit pondered the possibility of joining them once they saw how much money the family was accumulating.

With both of Mishi's parents out of the house with gainful employment during the day, life in Jerusalem was much busier than anyone in his family anticipated. Mishi got to explore the city like few children do. He walked with his grandfather around the city, sitting through discussions with other men his grandfather's age. While his peers played with unused construction materials like iron, wood, and polished stone, Mishi listened to the old men talk of older times as well as current events. Many compared the Romans to invaders from Judah's past and these stories always came to the conclusion that Jerusalem was now half-Roman, based on the agreement to build and tax. However, a few of the men thought that all the work and improvement were great for reducing crime and keeping people employed, both of which had been problems for the last several decades. Everyone who wanted a job now had one and crime was at a low. No one could deny it.

Mishi quickly learned to be a negotiator. He had Lebanese friends with whom he would trade a loaf of his mother's bread for a story of the great animals that once inhabited the land or tales of cedar trees higher than the Temple Mount itself. He visited the Roman soldiers' break areas for no other reason than to eavesdrop and practice speaking the Greek that he was learning in school. He would sit with the slaves from faraway places at the start of the day, listening to their tales of their toil. Many slaves were thin from years of labor, but some were strong, especially those tasked with carrying marble and other precious stones that could not be dropped. These slaves' masters took precautions to keep them as dependable as possible. These masters had long ago learned that two or three extra servings of food were cheaper than replacing a piece of broken marble that dropped from the hands of a weak slave.

In this way, Mishi learned some of the languages of Egypt, as well as those of Gaul and Britannia. All in all, he was able to engage in conversation in no fewer than five languages by the time he was twelve. More importantly, he learned to listen to arguments from many perspectives. He would wait until everyone else had spoken before he would ask questions. His thoughtful interrogation helped to sort out any peculiarities of their position. His rhetoric was thoughtful, and people would change their minds when he spoke to them. Soon, he became addicted to changing people's minds.

The old men often debated the fate of the city and its residents. There was much Ebreet uprising, and the Romans dealt with it strongly, yet the outbursts and attacks on soldiers continued. Some were convinced that the Ebreet would soon be either killed or enslaved, as in the stories of ancient Babylon. This possibility hung over all of Jerusalem. Others thought the city would withstand the test of time for no other reason than that it always had.

Mishi sided with the men who did not fear execution or widespread Roman enslavement. Why would the Romans invest so much money into construction projects if they intended to destroy them? If they were going to destroy it, they would have already done so. They might kill the occasional member of the local tribes in public in order to keep peace, but that was all. If construction and maintenance were important, they wouldn't kill the people who constructed it.

Ebreet culture did not allow Mishi to openly debate with older men in a group setting since he was too young. Yet, with all the social upheaval and Roman military presence in the community, he did it anyway. No one reprimanded him in Jerusalem, but he speculated that he would not be able to do this when he returned to Tamar one day.

"I think the Romans were smart to build up this city and extract more money. Once they have no more money to gather, they will leave. I don't see them wasting their time killing or enslaving us if there is no money in it for them." His logic was good. Men would nod in agreement and occasionally stare at him with fierce eyes, and he watched them change their minds.

"I speak with Roman soldiers all the time. Romans want to keep the peace; but more than peace and fear of an uprising, they want wealth to grow their Empire. Jerusalem is their fatted cow and they are going to get every coin they can from her."

Arguing and listening to rebuttals became a game to him. One day, he convinced a group not to drink the water from the Temple Mount. He then convinced the next group to drink some of it and take some home with them when they left. He took pride in his skill with words.

Gaining admittance to school was much easier than the family thought, despite Mishi being twelve. The shortage of qualified Rabbinical students was equal to that of qualified carpenters and masons. The Pharisees in charge of admission quickly discovered Mishi's ability to memorize what he read, and he was brought into the school and introduced to the Rabbis the day he applied for admission. Since Mishi also lived close to the Temple Mount and his parents worked there, the Rabbinical staff considered him trustworthy by association and he was asked to do extra tasks for them. As such, he was granted permission to learn to write with the older students, and he got to use Roman paper and Roman ink pens to practice writing the Ebreet, Greek, and Latin alphabets. The Rabbis all knew that he grew up speaking Aramaic, and they would sometimes ask him for alternative meanings of sentences. His language skills were second to no one on campus and he received permission to learn the other languages of the area, including ancient Babylonian. He knew it was a matter of time before he would learn Egyptian, travel to the ancient lands, and read the hieroglyphs on the sides of the pyramids of his forefathers.

Greek, Roman, Latin, and Ebreet came easily to him. So did mathematics and music. He was gifted with a quick understanding of patterns and pattern recognition. Once he showed his father and mother what he could do, they teared up, for no one in their family had learned these skills before. Many could read Ebreet, but none could write. They were impressed when he wrote down their names on paper, which they were seeing written for the first time.

"Son, I am proud that you can do these things and no longer have to live a life like your mother and me," his father said. "God has gifted us all. You will not be a laborer but a man of God like the Pharisees and a teacher of the scrolls. We are proud of you. God will use your goodness and intelligence to help us."

In the weeks that followed, Mishi began taking care of the family finances and all correspondence with Tamar regarding their residual farming activities. He knew that he could not discuss these letters and certainly could not be caught carrying them on the Temple Mount, but he did it for the good of his family. It was his secret.

Chapter 27:
How to Change People's Minds

Early in his life, Mishi had to come to terms with public executions. No visit to Jerusalem was complete without witnessing one of these horrible events. At least twice a week, someone would defy the Emperor's dictates or those of his appointed leaders, and the Romans dealt with non-compliance with consistency and immediacy.

For the pettiest of crimes, the Roman soldier who observed the event would strike the perpetrator dead with his sword. For the vile crimes in which others were hurt or robbed, the Ebreet would be taken outside the city and crucified on one of the hills that overlooked the city. There was no fewer than one crucifixion a week and many who were caught stealing lost a hand or foot without a single question being asked of them.

The first crucifixion was the most awful event that Mishi witnessed during his first year in Jerusalem. An old man accused of not making way for a cart carrying Roman supplies took nearly an hour to die once he had been nailed to the cross and stripped of his clothing. Mishi watched, speechless, as he listened to the man plead for mercy repeatedly, but it was as if the Roman soldiers were deaf. Once he died, two soldiers took down the cross and removed his body. They carried it a short distance and tossed it into a fire. The flames were hot, and the blood quickly boiled out as the body began to catch flame. Dogs circled the fire, waiting for the soldiers to feed them freshly cooked meat. Mishi was disgusted, but he couldn't stop watching. That expression of Roman authority always captured

Mishi's attention, as it was seldom done with any sentiment or emotion. It was as if the soldiers had stopped and gone to the bathroom. Nothing more.

Yet Mishi held to the promises of his forefathers that one day, a Messiah would come and free them all from the bondage caused by these oppressors. However, until that day came, it was his job to learn as much as he could so he could teach the next generation all that he knew. His Temple education was not limited to scrolls, books, and the words of old Rabbis. As he engaged in conversation with temple workers from around the world, Mishi had no choice but to hear alternative perspectives on what a good life was and what good living was. He was taught that the Roman Empire's presence represented God's judgment against the atrocities committed by the Sadducees that went unpunished. Although he knew not what the atrocities were that they referenced, he could tell that there was a time in the distant past when life was not as it was today.

Mishi loved the fact that the Temple Mount was a busy place. It prevented any chance of boredom. He always came home with stories to tell about what he had done or learned that day that his parents and grandparents would listen to with great interest. They were very proud of their "future Rabbi," and they would always introduce him as such. He liked thinking of himself as a Rabbi.

Mishi's conclusion used words that possessed both power and content. Mishi wanted the power of words that all the Pharisees had. He wondered if his future might be to stay and work in Jerusalem and not return home to the simple villagers who weren't interested in new and exciting. They wanted to be Ebreet, farm, raise their families, and enjoy the simple pleasures in life. He wanted to engage people who thought differently and perhaps change their minds.

Mishi was also one of the few Ebreet who found there to be something to gain by listening to the Roman soldiers. Spending time with folks who people told him were the enemy became a part of his everyday life, and his curiosity kept him engaged with this new culture. They were soldiers when he first met them; they became people later.

He did not find the Romans inherently evil, as many around him had concluded. He would invite himself to join them while they were playing games with dice without fear of consequence. He engaged with them to learn both their spoken and body language. They would laugh at him as he mispronounced Greek words or used the wrong word when talking about a simple matter. Instead of feeling shame over using a wrong word, he would laugh with them and wait for them to correct him. That sequence of experiences made it easy for him to learn from it.

His mother wasn't shocked to learn that the soldiers grew fond of him. Everyone liked Mishi. The Roman soldiers in residence knew that they were shunned by most Ebreet who lived and worked in the city for no other reason than they were obediently doing their jobs. The tasks that they performed were often horrible, but they were generally not acting out of emotion. Mishi saw no reason not to treat each one of them as part of his life in Jerusalem. He knew that acquiring their language would give him an advantage over other boys in his class when it came time for them to be selected to follow a Rabbi. The boys were taught that one of the most life-shaping events in a man's life was who selected you to follow them when your education at the Temple was complete. Mishi wanted to be called by a Rabbi who had an interest in working with everyone, not one focused on serving the wealthy Ebreet, who would receive large sums for cleansing of sins.

More important than learning about their culture, Mishi got the soldiers to tell stories of their life back home. He learned that most of these soldiers were not from the city of Rome, and several were from places that were distant and not found on any maps within the Temple archives. They all spoke some Greek dialect, but few of them could read or write. When they discovered that he could, they would often seek him out and ask him to read out loud whatever decrees that they had been given and told to enforce. He discovered that they knew nearly nothing of the plans of the Emperor.

Best of all, Mishi had a service he offered to Roman soldiers that no one else did. He would write letters for them and have them sent home. He charged a fair wage for each letter and it gave him spending money. He limited his services to writing on a single piece of parchment, and he charged them for the parchment separately. Although he did not earn anything close to what his father made, he was beginning to support himself, and that gave him greater confidence that he would be fine the day his parents left to return to Tamar.

Mishi didn't know a life that didn't include Roman occupation and he was one of the few who understood that the soldiers dreadfully feared death if they disobeyed an order from a superior officer. Indeed, he found them to be more like Pharisees than his fellow Ebreet thought. The same emotions drove them. Romans celebrated holy days of their own, feasted, got sick, cried over sad stories, and laughed when people did stupid things. The Roman empire was different, but the Romans he got to know were more similar than different. Mishi found himself defending the Roman occupiers. He would use subtle words instead of abrasive claims, as he didn't want to admonish those whose approval he needed. Instead, he used stories of individuals. The Ebreet, who most hated the "devilish occupiers," were the ones he would invite to join him when he went into the Roman parts of the city. He would also tell them mundane stories when he returned to make his point that the Ebreet had more in common with the Romans than they realized.

Mishi had no memory of observing Roman soldiers do anything bad that they weren't first told to do by their superiors. The soldiers would warn all who listened to them in advance of what they were going to do. They would tell everyone how to prevent them from getting hurt. In some cases, Centurion leaders would speak first to Mishi and ask him to explain to the crowd what the will of the Emperor was and why they should not resist. He was sometimes taunted for acting as "the mouth of Rome," and he would get asked how much he got paid to say, "Clear the square and go home; otherwise, you will be beheaded."

Mishi didn't care in the least about this name-calling. He concluded that if he could help one person avoid injury or death at the hands of the Emperor's troops, he had done a good deed. That would make his mother proud. She knew he would be a good husband one day.

On one occasion, he suggested to the Centurion in charge that they approach the man in the household first, instead of the first person whom they met, in order to extract the taxes due. The Romans had been instructed to "demand from whomever you meet," and Mishi's suggestion was directly against protocol. However, a few tax collectors hated the resistance that they encountered and they tried Mishi's method. They reported back the next day that the strategy was effective, took less time, reduced the likelihood that anyone would get injured, and shortened the workday. By week's end, nearly all the tax patrols had adopted Mishi's idea. From that day forward, the centurion in charge always greeted him by name and nodded his head at him. Mishi was barely into puberty but was already a respected member of both Roman and Ebreet society.

Give one person one good idea and let them dwell upon it. That is how Mishi changed people's minds. But he withheld that one good idea until he had spent lots of time listening to and sitting with them. He learned that words without relationships are useless.

And that is how Yahweh would use him to change history.

Chapter 28:
Inside the Temple

Despite all the changes in Roman leadership between Herod and the present governor, there was always money in the budget to pay for Temple Mount expansion and improvement. The return on investment was good, and the sales pitch to the Roman senate always included an invitation to "Some see it yourself." Alas, Judah was too far away, and no senators ever made the journey to see the famed temple.

The current Emperor, Vespasian, was old and had not stepped foot in any of the Eastern provinces, but he was very supportive of construction and anything that brought more people to the Temple. According to the last census, nearly seven million Ebreet were living within the boundaries of the Roman Empire and Vespasian knew that these Ebreet meant revenue for all his projects, not uniquely the ones on the Temple Mount. He didn't like their disrespect, but he loved their taxes. He spoke to them calmly and without dissent when one of them would find themselves in an audience with him.

There were great lessons to be learned from recent history. The previous three Emperors were in power for less than a year each. Some of the Rabbis questioned whether or not they held actual power. Prior to these leaders, Emperor Nero ruled and much of his behavior defined what Ebreet citizens deemed to be the worst part of Roman character: cruelty. Nero was adopted and his mother nominated him for Emperor. Later, when he no longer liked what his mother had to say, Nero had her murdered. Later, he arranged to have part of Rome burned down to make room for one of his projects. Fortunately, Nero died with no surviving offspring, which was great news for the

Ebreet. The Sanhedrin and Pharisees in power at the time believed that Yahweh must be preparing to send a prophet to save them. Some Pharisees anticipated the appearance of the Messiah and the corresponding exodus from this latest form of slavery. Unfortunately, the head of the Pharisees investigated these claims and hopes, but they found no evidence that such a savior appeared.

Over the next years, as Emperors came to power and suddenly died during the night, Ebreet leaders would bring attention to someone whom they claimed to be the Messiah. Each was declared to be the one who would save them from the oppression that they lived under. But once each Messiah was announced, the governor in charge of Jerusalem and Judah would send for his death. These Messiahs would fade from memory and the people would anxiously await for "the real Messiah" to come.

Mishi was keenly aware of how, after years of chatter about prophets and saviors, the typical member of one of the twelve tribes was pessimistic that Yahweh was going to send a Savior anytime soon. The more accepted response to this current enslavement was to evict the Roman occupiers themselves. The Pharisees taught that God helped those who helped themselves. Certainly, that applied to the residents of Jerusalem.

While this underground movement was taking shape, Mishi's father was challenged with a new project as soon as each old one was completed. He avoided all the clandestine meetings about throwing out the Romans, as they were paying his family's bills. To him, it was more important to use his work to teach Mishi some life lessons.

Once, his father came home from work and enthusiastically invited Mishi to his worksite early tomorrow morning. After an early breakfast, the two of them walked into the Temple Mount and directly into the section he was upgrading. The area was full of the smell of fresh cedar and there were shavings of wood and broken stone on the floor. The sun was shining through the openings above their heads and Mishi could see the intricate carvings in the wood that made up the wall of that part of the inner Temple. There was a cool breeze blowing in the Temple, as the upper windows received air without obstruction.

Soon, the slaves responsible for cleaning the Temple would arrive and the residue of the construction would be removed. The area would be closed off for all but the highest of privileged Temple leadership. Mishi's father knew this might be the best day he would get to give his son an intimate view of this part of the Temple. They were one curtain away from the Holy of Holies, and Mishi always wanted to know what this area was like. He had met the High Priest while he was in school, but he never thought it to be his place in life to see what was behind these curtains.

As the two of them entered, Mishi was immediately awed by the art and workmanship around him. He had read in the sacred scrolls about all the gold and wood inside the original Temple, but he had no idea that what his father was doing was an improvement on it. Shiny metals of many sorts covered many surfaces. There were statues made of obsidian and black onyx that were taller than any man that had lived. Depictions of angels made of pure gold covered in white cloth sat on each side of the doorways. The ceiling and walls were covered with interwoven thin sheets of Lebanese cedar, painted in many colors and inlaid with precious gems, depicting all the ways that Moses had tried to convince Pharaoh to let his people go. Mishi's father pointed to one of ten large panels on the eastern wall. Each panel was five cubits by ten cubits in size. He put his arm around his son and walked him to it.

"Son, I spent a year carving that one piece. It is made from the best wood from five different cedar trees. I had the help of many slave laborers and all the tools a man could desire. Once the piece was mounted, I had less than a minute before the Roman architect called me out of the room to take me to my new job site. In fact, this moment with you is the longest that I have had to look at my finished work without being asked to do something else. The High Priest will not waste one second to look at it, and none of the slaves who clean up here each night look up."

Mishi looked at his dad, wondering what he was trying to say.

"Father, what is the point of coming here?"

"All buildings, including this temple, are temporary. One day, that wood will rot, and these stones will crack. This floor will form holes in it, and the paint will fade. One day, all of this will fall. The man who built this temple called it 'Hevel.' It is all vapor. We reach for it when we see it, but it does not last." Mishi smiled. It seemed matter-of-factual, despite the awe that appeared as part of being this close to the Holy of Holies. It overshadowed their conversation.

"Father, I know what you said is the way of things." He wanted to say more, but he was in awe at his father's mastery of his craft as well as in reverence at where his father had worked. The two of them were within twenty paces of the Holy of Holies, a place occupied by exactly one priest for one day a year. This place was hallowed ground, stepped on by only a few people in all recorded history. Amazingly, after the tales that his father had exaggerated tales about what they had experienced on their travels to Jerusalem, he had failed to mention where he stood when he worked. Mishi looked up at his father, and his wonder shifted with a new thought.

"My father is making God's palace more beautiful than its architect, King Solomon, did." Mishi felt reverence. His father was making God's holy temple a better place, and he never thought it worthy of discussing it at dinner.

"I learned a good lesson from the architect," his father continued. It is not what I achieve, build, or earn that matters. It matters how I did it. I am proud of my work and my method, but the product belongs to someone else. And one day, when it falls to pieces, it will belong to no one."

After a deep breath, his father turned to him, put his hand on his shoulder, and said, "Go to school and learn how to use your mind, your words, and your hands so you can make a better life for yourself and your future family. I will see you tonight!"

Chapter 29: Fatherly Advice

Mishi completed his Bar Mitzvah on the day of his sixteenth birthday. The entire family from Tamar came to Jerusalem and he led the ceremony in the Temple's outer courts. As with all Bar and Bat Mitzvahs, the young man was responsible for the day's events, with the exception of the food afterward. Mishi loved the attention he received during his ceremony. He sang three songs and danced a worship dance normally performed by girls. He burned incense as he walked near the entrance to the inner sanctuary at the Temple and smiled as he passed within a stone's throw of the entrance to the Holy of Holies. If he told people he had been inside the sanctuary, everyone would call him a braggart or a liar.

His entourage of attendees extended beyond the scope of those who shared his faith. Several Lebanese tree merchants whom he had befriended also came. There were nearly 100 Roman soldiers in attendance, as well as their Centurion, as many of them were his "customers" with his letter-writing business. They also acted as his security detail, keeping out many of the pilgrims who had come to sacrifice at the Temple and were looking for entertainment. There were also many slaves from the market, as well as fellow Bar Mitzvah students from the Temple school. Moments before everything was to start, his mother approached him.

"Mishi, I am so proud of you for making so many friends. It will be very easy for your father to find a wife for you," His mother said. Her comment created a lot of anxiety and this was as good a time as any to share with her what he was thinking. She always did a better job of taking ideas to his father than he did.

"Mother, I don't want to marry into a conservative Ebreet family from our homelands. Father doesn't know anyone other than the people he works with and the people back home. They won't be a match for me, as I want to be a teacher," Mishi said. His mother looked at him.

"You want to select your wife. You want to do Erusin by yourself. Is that it?" she said. Mishi nodded yes. His mother reflected briefly before speaking to her only son.

"On the way here, the centurion politely asked to speak with me. He told me he had not met a young man with the discernment that you have. He told me to be proud of you. I always believed you needed a special sort of woman to be your wife. You need someone with your passion to be around lots of different kinds of people and learn new things all the time, and you are right. Your father and I aren't very good at finding that." Mishi kissed his mother as everything was getting ready to start.

"I would tell you good luck, but I imagine you have already memorized everything," she said. He laughed with her and began his special ceremony, happy to know that his mother understood.

After the Bar Mitzvah was complete and people were dispersing, Mishi's joy disappeared. His grandparents told him at their private meal after all the guests had been fed that they were returning to Tamar in the morning. His mother was going with them, leaving Mishi alone with his father in Jerusalem until Mishi finished school and hopefully received his calling from a senior rabbi.

His parents and grandparents knew that he could not join the Pharisees until he was aged sixteen, as he was not born to the Perishum (or the cult of the Pharisees). Starting today, he was eligible, and the whole family assumed that he would do so. He was enough of a student of people to know that he wanted no part of the world of the Pharisees. He said goodbye to his family and returned to the Temple to help the other rabbis who shared his sentiment about the segregation within their royal order.

He had seen enough of the Hillel side of the Pharisees to know that he didn't want to adopt their silly customs. He also didn't like their liberal views, including their adoption of some Roman mythology and ideology and putting it next to sacred verses from the Torah. He also didn't want any part of the Shammai side of the Pharisees, as their strict devotion to the law and obsessions with observances and food restrictions kept them from helping the average citizen. They were nearly useless to the common man and the foreigner.

The day was fast approaching when one of the current Rabbis would call the boys to follow them. With the simple phrase "follow me," a Rabbi would ask the student to abandon his current life on the Temple Mount and follow him for several years until he was ready to be a Rabbi himself. Mishi's skills as a public orator and his wonderful memory helped him find favor with the Rabbis who lived on campus next to the Temple Mount. He knew he would get selected by several Rabbis, but he also knew that he was limited to one choice. He knew that when he was asked, it would be a spontaneous decision. It would not be planned, like Erusin or marriage.

He was told that he would receive his calling in two days when the Pharisees returned from their trip to the coast. One of the administrators at the temple school told him the Temple High Priest himself would be coming and would ask him to become his disciple and follow him.

Mishi kept a straight face as the older man gave him the news, but nothing could have scared him more. Of all the Pharisees on the Temple mount who had forsaken the calling and responsibilities outlined in the law, none had strayed further from the truth than the High Priest. Phannias ben Samuel was his given name, but everyone called him Rabbi Phanni. A pleasant man, quick of wit and fast to offer blessings, he was deeply concerned with the Ebreet coffers and maintaining the peace with the Romans. He loved crowds more than he did the people in them. That was deeply troubling. Most concerning was the fact that he had refused to remove idols that the Romans had placed in the inner courts of the Temple for fear of angering the Emperor. There were rumors that there was a phallus inside the Holy of Holies that he had placed there during Rosh Hashanah two years earlier.

To his benefit, no leader was more aware of the fragile nature of the Roman occupation than Rabbi Phanni. He did what he thought necessary to maintain the peace. He greeted any Romans who approached him with a grandeur that disgusted Mishi. "Greetings! May the Living God and Emperor find great blessings from your visit to the Temple today," he would often say when Roman leadership approached him. Mishi did not want to say that or be expected to.

Mishi thought Rabbi Phanni was a blasphemous man and joked that he lived in one of those large clay pots. Phanni spoke openly and outwardly of the Emperor as a God paralleling Yahweh. This man would soon approach Mishi and publicly call him to become his disciple, perhaps to replace him. Mishi was nearly panicked at this thought.

To say no would be such an insult that no one would call him again. To say yes meant he would be groomed to become the next High Priest and a liaison between the Ebreet in Jerusalem and the Roman Empire. He knew that he didn't want to do that. The scrolls of the prophet Daniel told of the impossibility of mixing unmixable elements.

He spent the evening before his calling warming himself in front of the fire with his father. "Father, I have told you about the High Priest calling me. I have weighed this out in my mind, and I am torn."

His father looked up at his son. "What is your intention, young man?" Now that his rite of passage was complete, Mish's father no longer referred to him as "son."

"Father, I wish to honor you, our family, and God. I feel that if I do not affirm the High Priest's calling, I will be failing our family. Yet, if I choose to follow him, I will be failing my calling to Yahweh. The Emperor is not Yahweh. To treat him as such is the stuff of Golden Calf from the story of Moses. I can't say yes to Phanni and claim to love the Torah." His father laughed and let out a single deep breath before talking to his son.

"I was speaking with my co-workers today and a couple of them heard that our leaders are planning to throw out the Romans. There have been a lot of attacks on Roman troops recently."

Mishi nodded. He needed no clarification or explanation. He had seen the change in the people. He heard the same tales his father had. He knew that people from every one of the twelve tribes considered the trade of taxes for quality roads and water services to be unfair. They were planning to band together and initiate surprise attacks on Roman soldiers, most of whom had no role whatsoever in the tax collection process.

"That won't end well for us," Mishi said.

Mishi knew all about the Romans' ability to reinforce their ranks and recruit new recruits. These soldiers were better trained than any Ebreet, and they were not burdened by other jobs necessary to provide for their families. They could also organize themselves without a need for ten meetings as the Ebreet did.

"I have seen the signs of this, too." He took a bite of his food, and his father continued talking to him.

"I heard Rabbi Phanni needs someone like yourself to make his message of war palatable. You are perhaps the most influential youth in the city. That might be why he wants you." His father looked at his son with a look of anticipation as he awaited his response.

"Maybe so. I think it would be a blessing beyond words to remove the Romans from our land. There are two ways to do this. We can unite all the sects of our people and wage war, or we can wait for a Messiah to come and destroy the Romans, like what happened with Pharoah. I don't want to be a part of the first one, and I would prefer to watch from the side if Yahweh chooses the second one." Mishi's father laughed. When he finished his food, he leaned back and waited for his son to catch him.

"Son, I think it is time for us to leave this city. You have completed many years of school under many well-respected Rabbis. Leaving one day before the onset of what you believe may be a great sin does not devalue the content of your education. You are avoiding a conflict when there is no need to face it."

"So, then, what do we do?" Mishi asked.

"If you are ready to leave here and find another who may call you, then let's leave. Our promise to our village was not to see you become a High Priest but to serve those in the village who need you the most. I have no problems with your choice not to disciple under Phanni. My intention was not to stay in this city forever. We have accumulated good wealth here and we have stayed for nearly eight years. It is time for me to go home. I miss your mother and our whole family. It will be a good thing to return. You are not failing our family by following the Torah and avoiding the sins of our leadership. Yahweh repeatedly tells us to leave sinful ways and return to Him, and He will honor your repentance."

With that, the two of them began packing their belongings.

Chapter 30: Rejecting the Call

Before sunrise the next morning, Mishi's father packed everything on their camel and loaded enough provisions for the journey home. The markets were especially crowded at this time of year, as many people had been visiting the city to celebrate the upcoming Passover, which coincided with the end of the school year. Camels were cheap, but provisions were expensive.

Mishi told a dear Rabbi that he trusted him and that he intended to leave before receiving his call and returning to his village. Despite what his father said, he felt shame during his disclosure. Before the Rabbi could provide him feedback or say something hurtful, Mishi turned and began to leave. The old and venerable headmaster had watched the two of them and had heard everything. When he saw Mishi leaving, he ran after him and embraced him. Holding his face with one hand, the Rabbi looked at Mishi. "That was not an easy decision for you, was it?"

Mishi nodded his head, too shaken to speak.

"You learned that the High Priest intended to call you to follow him. Is that correct?"

Mishi again nodded.

"Mishi, I know your heart. You are of the most noble sort and our High Priest is not. Is that what you think?"

"Yes. It is." Mishi knew that sharing the truth would give him freedom, and this man could handle the truth. Talking to the headmaster helped calm his fragile nerves.

The old Rabbi pulled Mishi in closer. "If you do leave and come back, I will call you to follow me the day you return. It would be an honor to disciple you and have you replace me as the head of the school. We need educators like you." He refused to break eye contact with Mishi. This was the most powerful sort of calling, as it was done with passion and without a script.

Mishi cried out in joy and relief. All who taught him knew his story and his intention of returning to Tamar to teach. The old Rabbi knew of no better way to make that happen than to teach him everything he could about education at the Temple before he returned home to complete his family's legacy.

"I am proud of you. I will be here when you come back. I am not calling someone else as a reaction to you leaving. You can tell everyone in your family that I said, 'Follow me'. Your time here was not a waste. I know Yahweh will use you."

"Thank you, Master."

Mishi stepped away and bowed. He turned to walk and meet his father.

Mishi's father listened as his son told him all that transpired. He hugged his son and walked with him down the hill where Jerusalem sat in silence. As they traveled away from Jerusalem, Mishi wondered how he could go back to the Temple Mount without giving an account of his choice not to accept the calling of the High Priest. Mishi didn't hate the Pharisees, but he didn't like them, either. He liked the Romans more sometimes. At least the Romans were predictable. He knew there would be questions when he came home without the title of Rabbi. How could he explain to anyone that the High Priest wasn't good enough for him? At least now, he could say that one of the good guys wanted him as well. And he could see himself using the job as headmaster at the Temple School to jumpstart his career as a headmaster of a school in Tamar. He and his father continued their walk in silence as they left the hills around Jerusalem and headed back to Tamar.

Hebron was their first stop on the way south into the land of Edom. On the way, his father talked about what he looked forward to seeing and doing once he returned home. He knew that his son was upset, so he talked often to pass the time.

Mishi's father reminisced about his wife's food, the sunsets, and the quality of the water back in Tamar. He mentioned that he didn't like the water after eight years in Jerusalem. That made Mishi laugh, and he thanked his father for taking him away from the trauma of reliving his recent past.

His father poetically described the sounds of flowing water and the feeling of bathing in a river with no one watching him. He spoke of waking up to the sounds of livestock rather than those of yelling soldiers and salesmen with fresh baked goods. He missed the safety of country living and homes without iron grates over the windows. He said that he would be grateful to leave behind all the Greek and Latin words and return to Aramaic.

But Mishi could not leave his past. He continued to think about the events of the last day and his choice to leave. All his friends were at that school on the Temple Mount. He wanted to separate from the role that the High Priest proposed for him, but he didn't want to separate from everyone else. He remained quiet as he meditated on the walk on the long, dry road.

They reached the city of Hebron without any incident. Their stay in Hebron that evening was uneventful, and Mishi spoke more with the Roman soldiers at the entrance to the city than he had to anyone else that day, including his father. He soon realized that the camaraderie that he had developed with the soldiers in Jerusalem didn't help him in this new place, as the people and the leadership in Hebron were different. This exacerbated his loneliness, and he decided to tell his father about his change of heart when they sat down at the inn they had chosen for their night's lodging.

"Father, no matter where I go in the world now, the people who I will meet will be strangers. I thought that my connection with the people in Jerusalem would carry over to Hebron. It didn't. I don't know their names or anything about them. Tomorrow, when we leave, we will both be forgotten."

"Part of that is true, and no matter where you go in the world, you will be a stranger. Some will know you for skills you possessed years before. Some will recognize you by your face. You will meet a few people who get to know you on the inside. Look at that table over there."

His father pointed towards a small table where a man sat by himself, eating bread and drinking dark wine. Mishi could tell that this man was drunk and alone.

"That man has no one, and he is using that wine to substitute for what you and I have. We have a great blessing in that we have each other." He paused to take a bite. "Do you really think the High Priest will care two days from now what you have done or where you have gone? In a few short weeks, many of your schoolmates will be scattered across the twelve tribes as they finalize their studies and are chosen by Rabbis to follow in their footsteps. They would be gone from your life; your choice to stay in Jerusalem will be irrelevant."

"Yes. I know that what you are saying is true. Yet I miss Jerusalem."

"Come, let's go care for our camel and prepare for tomorrow. We will have another long day."

They left the inside of the inn and headed to the manger, where their pack animal was kept. They fed it the extra food left over from dinner and watered it. They cleaned out the rocks in its hooves and took off its traveling blanket to air out overnight. In the morning, both sides would be covered in dew. It would help to keep the animal cool in the early part of the morning when they would move the quickest.

Mishi left the stables at the inn and headed into the nearby courtyard where soldiers working the night watch were gathered, playing a shell game. He attempted to join but they would not allow him to participate. One of them mumbled obscenities in Greek under his breath, thinking Mishi couldn't understand what they had said. When all the other men began to chuckle, he stood up and left. He was tempted to address the man's racial slur, but it might result in his own death. He said nothing and walked away. He was now a stranger among strangers.

When he got back to the inn and headed up to the room, he found his father standing by a candle, counting out coins that he would need to keep on his belt for early morning purchases prior to leaving. He would need money for some dried fish and fresh bread in addition to bean paste. He had an extra amount of fodder for the camel that they would carry for the animal to eat in the middle of the day. Mishi told his father the story and how the soldiers' responses had made him feel alone. His father put his arm on his shoulder and hugged him. "You will get through this. You are called to serve in Tamar. Remember this as you sort out why you have made the decisions that you have made."

Mishi woke up early the next morning, as was his custom, and decided that he would like to meet some of his peers in Hebron, assuming they existed. "Father, I am going to the place of worship in the center of Hebron. I will be back shortly. We will be able to leave early."

And with that, he left.

Chapter 31:
Teachings from Barnabas

Mishi approached the nearest entrance to the synagogue in Hebron. The building was large, but it didn't have any of the ornaments that the Temple did or any sections for sacrificial offerings. Those were reserved for the Temple in Jerusalem.

A small group of men and women were gathered, and an old man was teaching them with authority. Mishi suspected he was from Galilee by his accent.

It was obvious that he was a practiced orator, and he spoke without anger. He was skilled at storytelling and he mesmerized Mishi, as Mishi wanted to be like this man when he was old. When Mishi paused to listen to the content of his words, Mishi froze in his tracks. This man said exactly what Mishi was feeling.

"The teachers of the law and the Pharisees sit in Moses' seat. But do not do what they do, for they do not practice what they preach. They tie up heavy, cumbersome loads and put them on other people's shoulders, but they are not willing to lift a finger to move them. Everything they do is done for people to see. They make their phylacteries wide and the tassels on their garments long. They love the place of honor at banquets and the most important seats in the synagogues. They love to be greeted with respect in the marketplaces and to be called 'Rabbi' by others."

Putting his hands on his hips, Mishi nodded in agreement as he joined in the conversation.

"That is exactly true. That is why I cannot accept the calling of the High Priest," Mishi said without enthusiasm. Everyone paused to look at Mishi and he realized that he was an intruder in their studies.

"I am sorry, but I need to tell someone this. I don't want Rabbi Phanni's traits to be my traits. I had to leave there, and now I am here. Can I sit and listen? I won't disturb you anymore," he said. Mishi looked for a seat on one of the benches and moved that way.

"Yet, you wish to be called Rabbi, do you not?" said the teacher. Mishi smiled but didn't answer him.

"But in your heart, you do not wish to be called 'Rabbi,' for you know there is only one teacher. And you do not call anyone on earth 'father,' for you have one Father, and He is in heaven. Nor are you to be called 'instructors,' for you have one Instructor, the Messiah."

"The Messiah?" Mishi blurted out.

"Yes! Yes! The greatest among you will be your servant. For those who exalt themselves will be humbled, and those who humble themselves will be exalted." Mishi was settled on the bench and felt he could now engage the old man in a debate.

"How can you say that the Messiah has come? We are as a people underneath the Romans and we have not received our King." The man smiled at Mishi and responded.

"Men sought out a King of the Ebreet. The Messiah, called Yeshua, didn't come to save us from the Romans but to save all men from sin. To save yourself from the penalty of sin, you must believe in him as the Son of Jehovah."

Mishi had heard stories of Yeshua growing up, but he knew Him as the leader of an uprising that didn't last very long. Mishi learned that Yeshua was tried and crucified and that there was a conspiracy between the High Priest and the governor of Jerusalem to have Him killed, even though He didn't do anything wrong. This story of injustice against Yeshua was another reason that Mishi did not wish to become the High Priest. Justice was not served that day. He didn't want to be a part of Ebreet culture that included injustices that he might be forced to be a part of.

"Teacher, this claim that Yeshua was the Messiah cannot be verified. You are mistaken." Mishi learned to call those who spoke in public "teacher." This show of honor early in a conversation often meant that he would get the best from the person who was speaking, not an angry rebuttal from an angry man. "You deserve to hear how we view Yeshua from the perspective of God's chosen people, sworn to protect his Temple."

Mishi's conscience reminded him that he had participated in many discussions about Yeshua and other false prophets as part of his training. He had debated this topic enough to speak with confidence. His response was rhetorical and nearly void of sincere emotion.

"We know that Yeshua entered Jerusalem on a donkey and was followed by a crowd. He performed many miracles and healed many people on His travels. He had many Ebreet men following Him, as well as women and even some Romans. They believed Him to be the Son of our Lord. I would most assuredly have appreciated His instruction, as His command of the scrolls was exemplary by all accounts. None of this is in dispute by those of us who currently serve at the Temple. That said, I can think of no fewer than three reasons why He could not have been the Messiah." Mishi took a moment to compose himself, recalling all three reasons before he started speaking.

"To begin with, Jerusalem remains under Roman occupation. Given all the events in our rich Ebreet history, the Messiah should be the one who delivers us. Yet, we remain undelivered from our foes."

Mishi looked around at the crowd, seeking eye contact, which meant they were following his argument. Once he met enough eyes, he continued.

"Second, the residents in the city that He claimed to want to help are better off since His death, not worse off. I say Ebreet peoples everywhere are in a better place without Him, not because of Him." There was less agreement on that point, but he had one more position to present.

"Third, the story of Him being resurrected has little credibility, as the claim is made that the first people to whom he spoke when He rose from the dead were women. As you know, women cannot testify in court. They are known for their propensity to gossip and provide false witness. Had this man been on a mission to convince the world that He came back from the dead, He would not have chosen women to present Himself to, but he would have selected a Roman leader like the ones who killed Him or members of the High Priest's team.

In this way, His credibility could not have been questioned. I do not believe that anyone claiming to be the Son of Jehovah would have presented Himself to humanity with a position that lacked cultural credibility."

Mishi could tell that this point had hit home with many in the crowd. He decided to keep going.

"We Ebreet have yearned for a Messiah. We have not been faithful to Yahweh's ordinances from the Torah. We chose instead to follow selfish pursuits. If Yeshua were truly our Messiah, we would be hopeless. We remain enslaved by a system that the Messiah should have freed us from. Our history records no such false deliverances if Jehovah is involved."

Several in attendance applauded, but Mishi wasn't done with his defense of his proud heritage.

"Ebreet leadership is tasked with carrying our culture from generation to generation. We do not believe in a God who does not provide hope. If our hope has come and gone, there is little reason to live. And I, for one, think that we will be saved from these seemingly unending occupations and that a Messiah that has not yet arrived on earth."

The crowd became silent as they saw the speaker walk towards Mishi. When he reached him, he embraced him like a brother. Mishi felt awkward, but he reciprocated because he was lonely.

Mishi was perplexed. This man's response to his verbal assault on his belief system was to extend affection and love to the attacker. Mishi was humbled. The Pharisees would not have done anything like this. There was no precedent for this action. He did not know how to respond other than to reciprocate.

"I would love to tell you all of Yeshua's stories, but there are so many of them that not all the pages in the books in the great library of Alexandria could hold them all. Let me tell you one of them." He told about how he watched Yeshua feed 5,000 men and their families with twelve baskets of leftovers. Mishi was mesmerized as the man's body language was convincing. This was no lie. Five loaves and two fish multiplied until it was enough for all to eat their fill with huge amounts of leftovers.

"Each basket of leftovers represented one of the twelve tribes of Judah from the desert. Yeshua had twelve disciples. These and the words that He used were signs, and all who were there said, 'Indeed, this is the prophet who was spoken of long ago.' I was there when he fed them all. I saw Yeshua hold the bread to the sky, to the Father, and ask for blessings upon the people and food. Before my eyes, he gave the bread to his young disciples. They, in turn, gave them to us. You see, each disciple sought out others in the crowd who were strong enough to carry food for 100 people. This required fifty people carrying baskets of bread and fish. My basket was light and did not grow heavy, yet as I would go into a group of people who would reach in and take food, the basket did not become lighter, even after 100 people had reached in and taken portions of fish and bread. The weight of carrying food for 100 men and their families should have fatigued me. It didn't. This remains incomprehensible to me. Had I not been there, I would not believe my own story. Now, I ask you to believe what I could not."

Before Mishi could say anything, the crowd rapidly dispersed as a group of four Roman soldiers approached. Without any hesitation, one soldier drew his sword and struck Mishi across the back with the flat side of his blade with intent. The force was so strong that it knocked him to his knees and took all the wind out of his lungs. A look of shock and pain came upon his face, and he fought to stand back up.

As soon as Mishi fell, another soldier walked over to the old man and struck him on the leg with even greater force, causing the man's leg to buckle. He yelled out in pain as he, too, slumped to his knees and finally to his back, as his leg could not hold up his weight.

The soldier spoke to the man in broken Ebreet. "Messiahs talking no more. You disturb peace. Next time, perhaps us kill you." Another soldier with a better command of Ebreet spoke to Mishi. "We told you, Palestina, no public demonstrations. Anyone who does will be struck. You are lucky that we did not use the edge of our swords. You would both be dead. Leave this place and do not behave this way again. Rome has spoken."

Mishi wanted to apologize and say that he was new to Hebron, but he had no air in his lungs. The crowd was long gone when the shock receded from both men. Once the soldiers had left, Mishi finally regained his breath. He felt rage towards the Romans who had acted first and spoken later. These soldiers didn't behave like the ones he knew in Jerusalem and he wanted, perhaps for the first time in his life, to seek retribution. He had been refuting the arguments of a man who had lost his faith and was attempting to proselytize them away from the Ebreet God of Abraham, Isaac, and Jakob.

The other man also attempted to stand up. As he tried to place weight on the leg that was hit, it collapsed. He shrieked and sat down on a stone wall meant to gather sheep for sin offerings temporarily. He found his staff, and, putting his full weight on it, he began hobbling towards Mishi. Once he had reached him, the old man extended a single hand to help him stand up while putting his weight on the staff. "It is nice to meet you, young Rabbi. My name is Barnabas. Come and sit on this wall with me. We must finish our conversation."

Mishi was speechless. This man's leg was damaged, if not broken, and he was so old that it might not heal. He had more reason to be angry at the Roman soldiers than Mishi did. Yet he desired to finish their conversation. Once the two of them were sitting on the wall and had caught their breath, the man continued his story. Mishi was even more interested in it now than he had been before.

"After we had passed out the fish and bread to the men and their families, Yeshua turned to us and spoke words that made no sense to me at the time but that are now burned into my mind and my heart: 'Blessed are the poor in Spirit, for theirs is the Kingdom of Heaven.' Today, young Rabbi, you have shown me that you are poor in spirit and have little hope. My Master always told the truth. Therefore, you must be blessed!" He reached out and put his hand on Mishi's shoulder, wincing in pain as he extended it. "Let me ask you a question, Young Rabbi. What is it that you are willing to die for?" Mishi laughed as he tried to cover up the fact that he had no answer to a very thoughtful question.

"Not the plan of the High Priest, that is certain," Mishi said, surprising himself. "But I am prepared to die for the people whom I am called to serve. Your question has caught me at a difficult time." Mishi told the man of what had happened in the Temple over the last few days and how he believed he was to be called by the High Priest either today or tomorrow.

"You are being set aside for a higher calling than to be High Priest."

"Higher than the High Priest?" Mishi asked, sounding a bit like a schoolboy.

"You haven't met the one who is calling you yet." Mishi had not considered the depth of this man's question. "Who is calling you?" seemed intuitively connected to the speaker of those words. Yet, the man's consideration of a higher thought and a higher calling engaged Mishi's mind. This was now his favorite kind of conversation, rich with safe and structured conflict.

Mishi took the time to share how the Headmaster in charge of the Temple school had said that he would call him.

"Does this man have a passion to seek the truth?"

"Absolutely. I am sure of it."

"This is wonderful news. If you study the sacred scrolls and have a passion for the truth, you will meet our Father's Son. This is inevitable." Mishi looked at him and smiled. Intellectually, he knew the man was correct. However, he was already self-aware enough to know that if the Messiah had come and gone, and he had missed it, his faith had ill-prepared him for life, let alone this moment.

"Can I pray for us?" the man asked.

Mishi looked at the man in disbelief. He knew how to pray. He had told the man how he had been trained at the Temple, yet the man was sincere in his passion to pray for them. He didn't need to ask, yet he did so. Mishi could see that he was sensitive to the possibility that his claims of a risen Messiah might have offended Mishi.

"Why not, Rabbi?" Mishi smiled. Once he used those words, he realized that he respected this man more than his questions had led him to think.

The man raised his hands in Ebreet tradition but spoke in common Greek: "Our Father, who art in Heaven, hallowed by Your name."

Mishi had not expected this. The man was calling God "father," using the same Aramaic word that Mishi used to address his earthly father. It seemed like blasphemy to use guttural language, but he let the man continue. He appeared in a close relationship with whomever he was praying to.

"May Your will be done on earth as it is in Heaven. Give us today our daily bread and forgive us our debts as we forgive our debtors. Lead us not into temptation but deliver us from evil."

"I like that," Mishi said. He gave the man a sincere and approving smile. The man said nothing at all, but he smiled back. Mishi put his hand on his shoulder and left to return to his father on earth.

When he arrived, he said, "Father, let me walk with you to complete our journey to Tamar. However, I am not staying. I have changed my mind. I am going to return to Jerusalem and accept the calling of the Headmaster. I am going to finish what I started with an honorable man, no matter what the social cost. And I need to learn more about this Messiah that an old man was talking about. He got my attention. And, the truth is always worth exploring."

Chapter 32:
The Blockade

Titus felt empowered this morning and it was obvious as he spoke to his men. They had arrived in front of the walls of Jerusalem, and it was time to begin their campaign. Out of fear, the Ebreet had closed the city gates, but they didn't know about Rome's plan to starve them into submission.

"We will need more than a slash from our swords and a stab from the tips of our javelins to take and occupy this city. Get you men to look at our plans and take wise counsel. This must be the last visit we make to this city to quell uprisings. These Ebreet resist and seldom surrender without heavy loss." Every man in leadership listened to Titus. He was their supreme leader as he inspired his troops to do their jobs with the vision of his father. Destroying the Temple was part of the command he and Rufus received. Destroying the will of the people was his priority.

With that vision now cast, Titus repeated his plan to his leadership.

"We must convey the message that Rome is in control. In order to teach them this lesson, we will not attempt to invade or attack the city for one full season. As you know, we timed our arrival to coincide with their tribal event called Passover. The city is currently overrun with pilgrims and we shall starve them into submission. The city's size doubles, if not triples, during Passover, and the entire country knows this and plans for it."

Some of the men were opposed to the idea even before leaving Rome, claiming that they could not possibly feed their armies during such an extended stay, but they got their objection answered quickly. Titus had his quartermaster's response to this fear a high priority.

"All the food and provisions that would be going into the city for the people and their sacrifices shall become our food. All the wine, spice, and cloth that normally would go through the gates into the city will be used to keep our men from getting bored. We will pay for these goods so those left behind can do commerce with Rome after this battle is complete. However, no food or supplies must be allowed to enter the city. Any Roman soldier who allows this to happen will forfeit their life."

"Are there enough prostitutes?" one of the men asked.

"I don't know. I don't care. Tell your men to do what they like," Titus said dismissively.

The men nodded and appeared to like what they heard. Titus turned to the leaders of several centuries in Legion Three. "Your orders are to keep those people behind the city walls. Those who attempt to escape must be made into examples. Take your men and cut down cedar and make crosses for crucifixions. I anticipate that many will attempt to flee. Crucify them all and hang them so their dying bodies can be seen from the tops of the city's walls. Plan for an ever-growing number of attempts to escape, for as hunger impacts the city, the number of those who discard their faith and prioritize survival will increase. They will forget their history for a loaf of bread. Of this, I promise you. Place men with the best vision on duty at night, looking for ropes coming down off of the remote sections of outer walls. This is when they will most likely attempt to escape."

The leaders of Legion 3 accepted their orders, bowed to their General, and left. When all of the men were gone, Titus did what he always did after a meeting. Titus stripped himself of all of his military garb and began to bathe at a well. Rufus joined him and they spoke as they bathed and refreshed themselves with the cool water from one of the Springs that their men had discovered.

"Rufus, I need help in Judah. I need you to be my cultural guide, as you know these people and have lived with them. Tell me when you think most of the travelers seeking entrance to the city have arrived, and we will begin." Titus thought this unique task would help his friend overcome his current emotional state, so he gave him extra power that no one else had.

"Rufus, my brother, I declare that you are the hand of the General in charge of these armies. I empower you to speak both on behalf of the Emperor. You speak the language of these people. You shall be his voice at the wall. No one in this land shall be above you, including me, as long as we serve here."

"Thank you, Brother," said Rufus, not certain what he would do with this new authority. It would not change the words the Ebreet spoke to him, nor would it change his response. His father always spoke the same way, whether he was in uniform or wearing his synagogue clothing. Rufus knew he would be like his father and treat all men equally.

And with Rufus' word that the last of the pilgrims had arrived, their siege by starvation began. All gates were barred, and no one was allowed in or out, regardless of royal decree or religious distinction. Jerusalem was now a jail cell and the jailor had deaf ears.

Several weeks into the blockade, Titus was getting the results that he had expected. The Roman hammer of economic and military strength was crushing the Judahites from the inside. The doors and walls remained void of human traffic and no one passed in either direction. He heard tales of their pleading and he knew that hopelessness was not far behind.

Rufus took ownership of communicating to the Ebreet sentries at each of the portals into the city. His skill with their language was most valuable in ensuring the Roman message was understood by leadership behind the city walls. Once a day, Rufus visited each entrance and told the guards that until the last priest and Temple worker had surrendered, the Romans would allow the residents and visitors to receive their freedom again. During the early days of his rounds, many Ebreet watchmen and Temple leaders stood on the walls and gates, trying to make deals with Rome through Rufus. Rufus remained firm and found himself combatting many of their requests using texts from his father's sacred scrolls that he remembered.

For example, more than one Ebreet Rabbi stood up and spoke, stating that what the Romans were doing wasn't fair, citing one of the Psalms of King David. Rufus would hear none of it. Yet, Rufus could see that Ebreet outside the city were being treated fairly and told to go back home to their villages, but those behind the wall were being starved because of their proximity to the Temple of Solomon. The difference created by a few layers of rock certainly seemed like injustice, but he spoke of this to no one.

Not even aware that he was doing so, Rufus spoke as his father did on days when he was sent to act as a magistrate in Ebreet affairs. He would respond to requests for judgment exactly as his father did.

"It is said in the sacred writings in the story of Jonah that salvation is of the Lord, not of man. Isn't that so?" He paused and waited for silence to do the work of forcing people to think. Once he waited long enough, he would continue.

"If this is true, I suggest that you pray to your Lord for salvation. If your God can save a man from the belly of a fish, he can save half a million starving Ebreet from four Roman Legions and their weapons of war." He would again pause and wait for the silence to become unbearable. "Unless, of course, your Lord is no match for Rome. Another day passes, and your Lord has yet to arrive. Why the delay? Aren't your people already starving or becoming sick?"

It took Rufus nearly all day to circumnavigate the outer walls and the twelve entrances into the old city, even with the help of a chariot. The walls around Jerusalem were literally a thousand years old, and they had been destroyed and rebuilt repeatedly. Rubble was everywhere. Over the following weeks, Ebreet objections became less frequent, and the time required to make his visit to each entrance took less time. His men cleared a path for him to ride, and he gave the men who did the work bonuses for their effort. Within a few weeks, he was able to start his circumnavigation of the city after the morning meal and be back in time to report to Titus and nap before the midday meal.

And the encounters with the city residents were predictable. Sometimes, Pharisees would be awaiting his arrival on the buttresses atop the walls near the gates. Some would rebuke him, cursing him in their language, but he did not respond. On occasion, he would tell them that he knew what they were saying, but that would not shut them up; when he responded to their threats of divine retribution against the children of God, he felt sadness for their state of affairs.

As the blockade wore into the second month, the speakers at the walls would plead more for mercy and spend less time rebuking him. Thankfully, the times he sat with his father proved helpful, as he knew the power of delaying the passing of judgment. Starvation would cast many votes in the days to come.

"Tell the leaders of your Temple to relinquish their control over the affairs of the city and the Temple, and those inside the city will live. Until then, you shall starve." And with that, he would move on to the next entrance to the city.

Many civilian casualties had nothing to do with the audacity of Judean leadership. As predicted, many of those on pilgrimage for Passover who were inadvertently trapped inside the city at the start of the blockade began attempting to escape at night. Some were successful. However, all who were captured met a grisly end in the most public of ways. Titus' military squeeze would start with their stomachs but would conclude in their hearts. He knew they would eventually surrender or die.

All those who were captured during nighttime escapes were tied up and held until sunrise. They would be quickly tried and crucified before the city gates. Those being crucified screamed in rage at their captors, demanding a better reason for their deaths than non-compliance with the Emperor's decrees.

Rufus trained the men on crucifixion detail so that they could speak a few phrases in Ebreet at a specific time in the process. Once the screaming began and the final nails were placed in the arms and feet, one Roman soldier would speak a single sentence in a loud voice. "By the Emperor's decree, all who attempt to escape shall pay for their disobedience with their lives." True to his word, all those crucified would be stood upright in the morning sun and left to die. None survived until sunset, and body disposal often carried into the early evening.

The crucifixion crews were not trained in any other language skills, so none of the men knew what the dying were saying. The soldiers knew that Rufus could speak Ebreet and they often asked him what the words they heard meant. He told them their responses were nonsense, nothing more than a response to their life leaving their bodies. However, sometimes, they predict the downfall of Rome and the Emperor. It would be blasphemy to repeat much of what was said, so Rufus told the men that they need not concern themselves with their final words.

As they entered the third month, the scope of starvation and sickness increased, and the scene outside of the city grew continually worse. There were a few attempted escapes during the first two weeks of the blockade, but with each additional day, literally hundreds more Ebreet tried to escape and were captured. At first, most were men and the Roman soldiers didn't struggle to carry out the Emperor's orders. However, as they ended the tenth week, many women and children began attempting to escape. Titus and Rufus privately discussed the impact it might have on the troops to kill women and children for the act of trying to save themselves. Rufus explained to the leadership that women had no role in the Temple's direction and that none of the choices made behind the walls included consultation with women or children. As such, they agreed not to kill the women and children but instead take them into captivity and use them as slaves until the city was captured.

Rufus was an empathic man. Before he spoke to them, he gave them and their children fresh water and a good meal at a special kitchen he had made for Ebreet. Once they began eating, he explained to the captured women that everyone in and around the city could escape death if they committed to two things: serving the Emperor and renouncing their faith in a false god. His delivery was dry and no one asked him to repeat himself. He knew they would do whatever was necessary to save their children and for that sacrifice, he respected most of them. Nearly all of them agreed without any thought, but some chose to die instead of worshipping another God.

For the first few days, this strategy worked well and many tasks, such as the cleaning of restrooms and the bathing of animals, were done by the newly acquired Ebreet slaves. They also made trips to the local communities to purchase supplies from the residents and bring them back with soldier escorts. The women would engage the cooking staff and find out what they needed. By the end of the first week, food quality had increased and everyone appreciated it. Some even joked about bringing home a smart Ebreet bride at the end of the siege. Rufus told no one, but he was already thinking about doing that exact thing.

One time, a group of Ebreet calling themselves members of The Way arrived, claiming to be a different Ebreet sect. They offered to buy the home of a dead widow outside the Roman encampment. When asked, they told Rufus that they wanted to use it as a gathering place each night. Rufus took a tour of the building with the purchasers. The house had a large basement and kitchen, as it was historically used as a meeting place. These people said they were from a church in Thessalonica and promised not to interfere with Roman affairs. They claimed they wanted to serve the needs of those Ebreet women and children who had escaped and had been allowed to live. Rufus heard their request and it seemed honorable and non-threatening to what he and Titus were attempting. He authorized their purchase of the structure and some of his idle men assisted them in setting up kitchens and establishing methods to bring in provisions. He gave them a month of his wages to help them purchase supplies, and some of his men agreed to contribute as well. One time, during a late evening walk, he could hear them celebrating the Ebreet tradition of Shabbat and he could not help himself. He had great childhood memories of Shabbat and he went to watch. He felt jealous that the people celebrating were speaking freely and not carrying any secrets. One of the women whom he had been kind to called for him to come and join them, offering him a cup of wine, but he politely declined and went back to his tent.

Titus especially liked the use of Ebreet women but for very different reasons. They satisfied his desire to expand his collection of foreign female experiences on the battlefield. Rufus doesn't see any value in trying to save women from Titus's attention, but it quietly upsets him with the example it sets for the men beneath him.

Bedding these foreign women became a much larger problem than anticipated. One afternoon, a woman was accused of attempting to sicken a Roman guard by offering him a mixture of human feces and rancid cooking wine. The woman who plotted this retaliation was brought before Rufus for judgment.

Even though it was unnecessary, Rufus gave her a chance to defend herself before passing judgment. It wasn't until he approached her that he realized that he was following in his father's ways as an adjudicator by listening before making a ruling. Under Roman law, anyone attempting to cause harm to Roman military personnel was guilty of treason, with no trial necessary. Yet there was something about her countenance that made him feel justified in listening before judgment.

He spoke softly, knowing her emotional defenses were working overtime. She had a child and he suspected that self-defense was part of the story. He spoke to her openly in Ebreet and Aramaic, asking her for some of the details of why she was being accused of treason.

"How is it that you know our language but do not know the one who gave it to you?" she asked him.

Her response contained equal amounts of calm and thought. Rufus was not expecting mindfulness and accommodating responses.

Rufus turned his head to the side. "What do you mean when you say 'the one who gave it to you?'"

"Our God chose us and we chose our God. He gave us our language thousands of years ago before Rome came to power. As you know, your Emperor's language comes from the Greeks and is not your own." Rufus nodded his head. His father used to say things like that. He liked her countenance in her response. She was crafty enough to debate with a senator, he thought. He smiled at her and walked until he was next to her. He took off his helmet, bracers, and armor, handing them to one of his men. He let his hair down and asked one of his men to bring two cups of water.

"My father is a Roman Centurion. He continues to serve in Caesarea. He lives in harmony with the Ebreet community and worships your God. I know the language because I grew up speaking it, as it was the primary language of our village."

None of the Roman soldiers listening to this trial understood the conversation, but they were interested in watching the faces of both speakers. They could tell that these words were unlike what they had heard when Rufus spoke to the men at the city's gates. He was smiling and had a tone with his words that he didn't use when he spoke to them.

She put her hands on her hips and spoke again. She risked a deeper resonance in her question. "How do you know the language of God yet do not know God?" She wasn't going to back away from getting him to answer her.

Rufus didn't answer her, so she changed tactics and the words she used.

"Roman, what do you remember of the God your father follows?"

"He believed that God sent his son to the earth to save us and grant us life eternal. However, his God often told him things that were not true."

She hesitated and smiled before responding. She had found hope of getting into his heart.

"What kind of things?" she asked with a sincere tone.

Rufus began telling her a story that he hadn't told anyone in many years. Perhaps he was triggered by the proximity to his native Caesarea.

"My father would often start his day by telling us what Yeshua instructed him to do. He would tell his men to go chase after a lost goat or a crippled beggar on the side of the road. He claimed he saw them in a vision that came from Yeshua. Sometimes, these visions were true, but often, they were nothing more than rolled bones."

As he continued with his stories, she sensed the shame of his youth return. He rolled his eyes as he described his father's blind allegiance to something as unpredictable as what he called "the Holy Spirit." After a moment, he moved the conversation back to the trial. "My story is not on trial here. Yours is! Give me your defense if you have one."

She spoke with advanced language and authority that came from advanced education of the sort his father said that only the men of Judah obtained. He was not expecting her to be highly educated, but it gave her credibility. He guessed that her father thought she was special and had poured into her. Looking into her added to his interest in her. He didn't realize that he had given her access to his heart until he already had. After a moment of quiet, she courageously addressed him again.

"Roman, you know our people have faced far worse than Roman blockades. As your father most certainly taught you, we lived in the desert for nearly 40 years before God saved us from the grasp of the Egyptians and Pharaoh. We have been captured and exported to Babylonia. Each time, our assailants tried to eradicate us. They failed. The Babylonians tried and failed. The Egyptians tried and failed. You try now, yet we know Yeshua has already saved us. Many will die fighting you, but we have a place in eternity because of Yeshua on the cross."

Rufus was baffled by the peace and countenance on her face. Rufus had assumed that she was a traditional Ebreet from Jerusalem. He was unprepared for what he heard next.

"Did you know that the Messiah told us of your coming? He told us that one day, Solomon's Temple would fall and no stone would be left standing. The Pharisees and Sadducees think that this is nonsense, but I think you are required to do it. You think it is from an edict of your Emperor. We know that God prophesized it as a requisite for the numbers of our faith to grow. Your act is about to open the doors of heaven for uncountable people to come to know the Messiah. It is written in Isaiah. You should read it sometime. I will wager my heart that your father has a copy of these sacred scrolls in his home unless the stories I have heard of him are lies."

Rufus was stunned. He couldn't believe she knew his father. His father had repeatedly told him that he should read the scroll and he used the same words and intonation that this woman used when he spoke to Rufus. Rufus felt alive and wanted to know more.

Yet, Rufus' breath and thoughts felt superficial. This woman knew more of the spirit world than perhaps even his father. He wanted to hear more from her, but this wasn't the forum to submit to her and let her take up her place as his teacher. But, in his heart, that was what he wanted.

"You remind me of my father," he said. He wondered if this woman might be a prophet or if she was speaking the truth that the destruction of their holy temple was recorded and on a shelf in the basement of his father's home. He had not spoken to anyone serving in the army of the Emperor's request to leave no stone standing. Her knowledge of that detail enthralled his curiosity. The other person who was present when the Emperor gave this request was Titus and the ten engineers of the 2nd Legion; none of those eleven knew her language.

"How did you know the Emperor's directive to leave no stone standing?" He found himself caught between cultures and peoples. Although the elite Roman guard standing near him couldn't understand his words, they could sense his capitulation of authority. They could sense that Rufus was not using a tone of authority but one that a peer might use, almost as if he were talking to a friend and he wanted to learn from them.

"Master, what are your orders?" one of them asked. He held up a single finger, indicating he was not yet done judging the woman. They could partially sense that this Ebreet woman had changed her trial into his trial, but none of the men could understand what was happening. All they knew was that a simple trial had become a very extended one, and no one knew what the two of them were talking about. The woman continued talking to him as if the other men weren't present.

"Your father spoke of the Messiah a lot, didn't he? He spoke in tongues and he had visions of the future," she said in the same calm voice that he used.

Rufus could not deny that her story was true. Her insight was beginning to leave a mark on his soul, and it was an uncomfortable feeling. Rufus deflected with a steady tone of the sort his father might use. Then, the spirit of humility overcame him. He took his chalice meant for wine, and he rinsed it and filled it with clean water. He walked over to her and handed her the cup. It was heavy and made of pure gold. She took and drank it all in a single gulp. She asked for more, and he gladly offered her a second cup.

"How do you know these things?" he said, humbly offering her the cup a second time.

He wanted to say more, but that didn't seem wise. He had already said too much.

"That is for another time, Roman," she said. He could tell she was done talking to him and ready to receive her punishment. She closed her eyes like he had seen his father do and she opened her palms to the sky in prayer.

Rufus remained mesmerized by her behavior. He admitted to himself that she had weakened him with ease. Now, she closed the door to sharing anything else with him and knew that her trial was all that remained. His mind returned to words his father had spoken rang out in his mind.

"Do not treat people as they treat you. You must remain fair. The history of the world is full of unfair judicial systems. Rise above that and give each person a fair trial."

He tried to rid his mind of what she was making him think about as he returned to her trial. She deserved a fair trial, even if nothing else, for this heathenistic people were fair.

"Woman, why did you attempt to harm the soldier?"

"In Yeshua, we are told that we will suffer and die for our faith and that we will not be treated fairly. Our people have always been enslaved, and He does not lie. Wouldn't your father agree with me?" He forced himself to smile. She was not done. Her question struck his heart like another gong of truth.

"Answer me. Why did you attempt to harm the soldier?" he repeated in the same tone as before. Many in his position would raise their voices or threaten her, but Rufus was bigger than that. He knew that she would eventually answer him.

"Roman, you are a successful and thoughtful man. However, I can see that nothing you have done on this earth has brought you lasting joy or true satisfaction. You have risen through the ranks and may even know the Emperor himself. That isn't helping the conviction in your heart right now, is it?"

Rufus could not answer her question. She was too far inside of him for her words to be considered meaningless. Her conclusions were correct. He had risen through the ranks. He did know the

Emperor. And, he was feeling a strong conviction. How could she have known that?

"Roman, no joy on this earth lasts. Belief in Yeshua and the salvation that He offers us is the only choice you will make that can bring joy. Cornelius the Centurion knew this from Simon Peter's visit." She smiled as she watched Rufus clench his teeth to prevent showing emotion. She knew she had shattered him, and her defense was done.

"Yes, I attempted to poison my captor. He tried to rape me while my child was watching. For my defiance, I understand that I must die. Yet none of your verdicts can take from the joy of living in Yeshua."

Rufus felt shaken and had great empathy for the woman. He immediately became mad at Titus for allowing the men to rape at will, but he knew what she had endured should not have been allowed to happen. It was legal, but it was not acceptable. He felt ashamed of his leadership and that of the men who reported to him.

He stared at the woman and was amazed by how she had humbled him. He found her to be beautiful and could not stop looking at her. Although he crucified people with nails and wooden crosses, she had crucified him with words. He was one of the most powerful men in the world, but, as the woman had said, he was not fulfilled by his accomplishments. Every goal he had sought, he had achieved, but it fell short of the mark of satisfying him. He was permanently consumed with thoughts of what was next. This woman left him perplexed. No one had blended truth and mystery together in such a way. He felt compelled to save her. She was saving him, and this was the least he could do. Privately, he desired her. She had made him recall thoughts of his father, whom he had dismissed years ago.

He turned to his men and spoke with authority, switching back to Greek.

"This woman claims that she was raped in front of her children. I believe she is telling the truth. Send the soldier who accused her of trying to poison him to me and send her back to the kitchens. Tell all men that by my decree, no Ebreet woman shall be raped during this siege." He looked back at the woman and addressed her. "Woman, what is your name?"

"My name is Gesher."

Rufus smiled. "Bridge. Your name means bridge both in Ebreet and Aramaic." She pointed at him and winked at his knowledge of her language.

"Your father taught you well," she said. He paused before continuing. He could sense that the Holy Spirit, whom his father had spoken of nearly every day of his life, was formally orbiting his soul like a summer cloud. It took everything in his being not to cry as he saw that her name and the place where he stood were the same.

"And today, He is using you to bridge between my beliefs and my fathers'." Rufus nodded at the woman as a sign of reverence, and his men took note. They had not experienced seeing him humble himself to an Ebreet before.

She retorted playfully. "Our prayers for you are already working, Roman."

Turning to his men, he said, "Lash her three times for her deed before you send her back to the kitchen. This woman did not deserve to be raped. She and her child are free to resume what she was doing." As he turned and left, he quickly changed his mind and looked back at her.

"And give her and her child double rations permanently." She bowed her head and thanked him. She had filled his soul and at least he could fill her belly.

The men obeyed, removing her shackles and striking her three times with a bamboo staff. Each strike had a loud popping sound and each time, Gesher winched under duress. When they had finished, she walked back to the kitchens.

Rufus walked away, acting as unaffected by his conversation with the woman as he could.

Not a day would pass for the rest of the blockade when he didn't find time to visit Gesher and her son, taking with him some meat and wine to share with her. Whatever she had, he wanted.

Chapter 33:
During the Siege

Mishi dropped his father at home in Tamar, greeted his family, and then began his return trip to Jerusalem. He walked alone and felt a purpose. He needed to finish what he started and not let everyone's opinion influence him. At some point, he would meet the High Priest and potentially have to explain himself. He rehearsed what he might say with different synonyms until he got a combination of words that let him feel like he was telling the truth but also being gracious with his "no, thank you."

As he entered the city, he greeted many of his old friends on the streets and walked directly to the Temple school. He saw the headmaster speaking to some of the board members, and he approached him.

"Master, I accept. I shall follow you." The headmaster kissed him and hugged him. He introduced him to all the board members, calling Mishi his "headmaster in training."

That evening at dinner, the headmaster told Mishi during his cup of wine that much had transpired in his absence. There was now an aura of violence around Jerusalem. The High Priest had mustered enough Ebreet warriors and successfully ousted the Romans from the city. Now, mercenary guards were stationed at all the city gates, denying entrance to anyone who was Roman military or a Roman citizen.

"I missed them when I entered the city. I was focused on what I had prepared to tell the High Priest."

"Mishi, Phanni has moved on and thought nothing of it. From now on, focus on what I am trying to teach you and not concern yourself with the opinions of others. The truth is more important," he said. Mishi apologized and said he had already received his first teaching from his Rabbi.

At first, the Roman battalion stationed in the province counter-attacked at the news, but the outer walls held against their siege engines. Unexpectedly, the Roman assault came to a halt after one day and the troops retreated away from the city walls and began to make fortifications and camp all around the perimeter. Many amongst them rejoiced, thinking that they had defeated the occupiers and that God had returned His blessings upon them. However, rumors circulated that Roman troops in the tens of thousands had landed by boat in Joppa and were advancing towards them. The claim was that four Legions were coming and they were led by two famous soldiers who succeeded at everything they did.

The High Priest, for his part, promised all citizens that he would take care of the Promised Land, and he used much of the Temple excesses to bring in Syrian mercenaries to protect the city. He also launched a "Come to Jerusalem" marketing campaign and pilgrims flocked to Jerusalem like no other time in history, with numbers on the register at the Temple exceeding 500,000. With no taxes leaving to go to Rome, everything was cheaper, and the city had more tourists than at any other time in recent history.

But this effort at defending the ancient city with mercenaries did not last. Without deviation, a massive Roman army arrived outside the city walls and set up a blockade while the pilgrims were inside the walls. The mercenaries all left. No food or supplies were allowed in or out, and panic overtook much of the city. Mishi was one of many who didn't know how to react, but he assumed that there would be some solution and a compromise, as that is what Rome usually did. He walked the upper walls where the Syrian mercenaries used to observe the Roman movement below the main entrance to the city. The Romans were so dense on the hillside that they reminded him of ants walking on sweet bread. Seeing no way in or out, he was one of many who struggled with depression and despair.

Mishi did what he did best: walking among the people, listening to the mood of the city. From what he heard, the Ebreet way of life was under psychological attack. The reality of hunger and thirst within the city walls permeated every part of life. No matter where he walked, he could not push the cries of starving babies and children from his mind. He had to learn to block out the cries of the people he claimed he loved and try to do his job. Soon, rationing started, and things that everyone took for granted, like clean water, clean restrooms, and a wide variety of things in the market, ceased to be common. Mishi tried to keep his routine, but it was already compromised after three weeks of the blockade.

As he finished reading a chapter of the scroll that described the creation of all things, he could hear his assistant's footsteps getting louder as he approached the Temple library. Mishi knew that Bethel did not interrupt him unless it was of utmost importance. His tone gave away that he was scared and needed Mishi to come immediately.

"Rabbi, please come! This crowd is truly crazy! The people are massing in the outer courts again, and I am concerned for our safety. Please come quickly. I fear what they might do to us in their anger and their hunger."

"Bethel, my dear, give me one more moment," said Mishi. With his back to his helper, Mishi raised a finger and held it aloft while he finished the final words of the scroll. Mishi chanted the words to himself before turning to face his long-time helper and friend. He made eye contact with Bethel, exhaled, and put on a smile.

"God has saved us from much greater things than a single army in a single place at a single time. This blockade shall pass and this conflict shall end, as it always does." He spoke the words but in his heart, he didn't believe them. He knew that someone would have to concede their pride for this to end without death, and the Pharisees in charge of the city seldom offered up their pride as a first step.

Mishi approached the exit from the library where Bethel stood and said, "Let's go see this crowd, my friend!" Mishi used his natural power with words to calm the distressed man. He held Bethel's arm like an elderly woman might hold her son as they walked toward the outer walls and the area of chaos.

As they rounded the last corner and left the guarded inner walls, Mishi could hear the cries of desperation from the crowd on the other side. They wanted food and they wanted the priests to do something to appease the Romans. This angry mob had formed every afternoon for the last two weeks. Mishi knew that he must engage the crowd as part of his role as the lead teaching Rabbi of the Temple. He knew they were starving to death and they wanted food, not words of encouragement. He was authorized to share with the crowds what could be spared. And, as of three days ago, there was none. All the remaining food stores were designated for Temple workers and their families. Mishi also knew that soon, city rations would also run out. All he had left to offer them was encouragement. He offered them the power of a loving God with a history of deliverance if the people repented of their selfish ways and turned back to Him.

"My fellow Ebreet, as I have told you every day, we serve a holy and powerful God. Otherwise, why would you have traveled to come to the Temple? Our ancestors overcame the Egyptian army, an army that pursued them into the desert. When all hope seemed lost, God parted the Red Sea, and they passed between the walls of water."

The ones most full of vigor and least impacted by starvation spoke loudly with what energy they had left.

"You go part the Red Sea. We don't care about that. We want food!" said a man in the front of the crowd.

"Yeah, give us food and not stories of the past. We know you have a store of food and we want it!" said one of the women.

Both had more fear in their voices than anger. The onset of starvation made them look weak. If these two were to lead an uprising, the well-fed guards at the entrance to the inner sanctum would not struggle to defeat them. But the day was soon coming when the guards would no longer have rations, and that protection would cease to exist.

The following morning, Mishi's Rabbi and the Headmaster suddenly died. Mishi reacted and asked the Temple School leadership to convene a meeting to select a new Headmaster for the school. No one could come to the city and participate in the meeting. Mishi was disappointed that two of the twenty members of the school management team were able to attend, and they agreed that Mishi would run all aspects of the school until the Roman blockade ended. He was given the title of temporary Headmaster and interim Rabbi, and his studies were deemed adequate to serve in the role, even though everyone knew that they were not complete. His name was recorded in the history books, making him the forty-third Headmaster in the school's long history. Bethel maintained enough strength to look and find the special robes that the headmaster was meant to wear, along with sashes. The High Priest facilitated a public gathering where he was introduced as the new Headmaster and interim Rabbi. Strangely enough, the High Priest acted as if he didn't know Mishi. Mishi withheld displaying his disgust. Instead, he forced himself to feel grateful that he avoided this man's wanton calling.

Running a school in the middle of a blockade with tens of thousands of starving people made most of Mishi's training inadequate. Mishi was not versed in crowd management during a siege. No one was. Yet he was tasked with caring for the people he served through this dark time. He felt safe when he was within the walls of the Temple and the school, but even if he was eating reduced rations, they made him feel weak. His efforts to get his people to feel the spirit of Yahweh could not help the masses overcome their plight. Atrocities were occurring all around him, and they could not be ignored. Cannibalism started being reported and some men were killing and eating the horses that carried raw sewage out of the public bathroom. Mishi tried to separate himself from these events, but his empathy for the starving made that task impossible.

Going for a walk on the city ramparts did not provide solace as it used to. Roman speakers from outside the city walls claimed that they would continue to starve the residents unless they were allowed inside and could first destroy the Temple. They claimed it was the price for defying the emperor. It was retribution. Even when looking down at the masses of men patiently waiting for food and water to run out, he would tell Bethel that the Romans were delusional. There was no way that there were enough people outside the city walls to bring down walls that had survived for the last 400 years. Yet, every day, his locus of belief would move a bit more towards empty, and he could begin to see a world when this version of Jerusalem was no more.

He watched as a few pilgrims who had traveled a longer distance than most decided to climb over the city walls at night and try to run. They left behind their possessions and attempted to circumnavigate the Roman encampments outside. Mishi speculated that some of the pilgrims probably did escape by the cover of darkness. However, most did not. The captured were brought before one of the closed gates to the city and sentenced. Each one was crucified in the morning, and they cooked in the heat of the day, with their bodies left for the crows to scavenge. After a few days, what was left was taken down from the crosses, and the crosses were recycled and used for the next escapees.

As desperation increased, so did the number of people choosing to try to escape. At one point, there were 500 active crucifixes on the hillside leading up to Jerusalem and the number of crows was uncountable. It was commonplace for crows to be seen carrying eyes from bodies while the bodies were alive, and images of these scenes even impacted the Romans who worked the crucifixes. It was rumored that every Roman soldier who worked on the crucifixions received a triple portion of wine each night to help them cope.

As food ran out, Ebreet committed sins against each other of the likes of which no one had seen. One group was cannibalistically hunting elderly men and women. These old people couldn't flee from the young men pursuing them. As soon as they were killed, they were taken to the desolate part of the city and quickly cleaned and cooked. The group would eat their fill, bring back the uneaten parts, and share them with the families as if they were offering them manna with honey. It was an abomination necessary to survive. Soon, it became routine.

The situation was dire with the city's water supply. As the blockade continued, sickness grew. The natural springs that came forth from underneath the city were inadequate to keep everyone clean and hydrated, and many suffered from loose bowels as a result of drinking unclean water. A lot of city dwellers spent much of their day in the city's public bathrooms, leaving them weak and dehydrated. The city's public bathrooms took on a new role. They became the primary food source for the dogs in the city. Dogs would gather in packs, enter the public bathrooms, and head for the trenches as groups of men would enter. The dogs would growl and bark as a man squatted above the trench, competing with one another to eat what was left once a man stood up. Often, the dogs would knock the squatter over as hunger overtook their normal domestic behavior, and people would leave the bathrooms bruised and limping.

As people died, disposal of the bodies became problematic. The Pharisees agreed that traditional burial sacraments would be bypassed to save the city. They decided on a location near the northern wall to cremate the dead. City workers were instructed to take both the city garbage and bodies to this location, and one day each week, city employees would burn everything. With the primary wind direction of travel being north, the Pharisees knew that most of the smell of burning flesh would travel up and out of the city, thereby minimizing the impact on those who were left behind the city walls. The Romans soon caught on to this plan, and on days when they were burning bodies, they would use their portable catapult to launch the heads of those crucified over the wall to invoke fear.

Throughout all the abominations, Mishi remained steadfast in his job as a teacher of the law. With most of the population now either dead or a single-digit number of days away from dying, he tried one final time to preach to them with all the strength he could develop.

"Ebreet citizens!" he would say as he addressed them. "We serve a great God and He can and will save us from this present danger. Our God has overcome the Philistines, an army that was more powerful than the Roman Legion outside our walls today. Have you forgotten our teachings?" He spoke not with anger but with authority. He reiterated the details of the story, and as he did, people stopped talking, and his storytelling skills engaged them all. "In these cases, God's people pleaded with Him for help, and He saved them from ruin. Do not think He is too weak to save you! You must have faith. You must have faith."

Most turned to walk away quietly. A few even agreed with his teachings, but they didn't know how to have faith when their stomachs were grumbling with emptiness. Women held up their children and men stood in front of their families, all indignantly claiming their share of the finite rations left in the city. On this day, the crowd that stayed behind was larger than before. Mishi could see that addressing their hunger was fast becoming more vital than their faith. He wanted them to go home and plead with their God for deliverance. Instead, they pleaded with him for food. He knew that this was not the way to God's heart. Dismay began to settle on him.

He turned to Bethel and spoke softly. "If this is the trajectory of our people, Jerusalem will fall without the Romans swinging a single sword. The burden is on me and the other Pharisees who have remained to help the Ebreet return to the heart of God."

Chapter 34: Hypocrisy

It was the 141st day of the Roman blockade. The death toll was now nearing one thousand people per day. Of the more than 500,000 visitors who had registered as they entered the city before the start of the blockade, Mishi speculated that less than a fifth remained alive. It was a nightmare that no one could awaken from. In Mishi's mind, this event had been preventable. Had the Ebreet lived by God's laws and not abandoned His commandments, they would not be in this predicament. Yet he couldn't change human nature.

He walked into the large hall and faced his remaining students. Before him sat a class of the most elite and intelligent young men in all the twelve tribes, and they were the best hope for his people. He was tasked with completing their education before they would get chosen by a Rabbi to follow. He was in their seat not many months ago, and a few of them were his friends and classmates.

"God's great test for this generation is inside our city walls, not outside the walls, as many believe."

"What do you mean, Rabbi?" asked one of the boys.

"As speakers on behalf of all Ebreet before the Holy God, we must pray for God to fulfill His promises and send us a Savior. God's chosen are designed to follow God's plan. When they do so, they prosper. You hear of these stories. King David. King Solomon. The list continues. Once our fathers began to prosper, they fell away from God's teachings. They stopped reading His sacred words in the scrolls. They built Asherah poles and evil entered their hearts. Yesterday, I spent much of the afternoon in the Temple library. You know who was in there with me?"

"Who, Rabbi?"

"No one! I am alone when I read scripture nowadays. Everyone else is doing other things. God sees this." He looked at his students ruefully. "It is not acceptable to be this way amongst us Pharisees. We are commanded to take ownership of our spiritual well-being. We are to provide you with care. We aren't usually the ones who handle it, but it is our honor to do this. How can we do it if we aren't also studying the ancient texts in the same way that we ask you to? Aren't we hypocrites for not doing what we tell you to do?"

He knew that Rabbis didn't speak negatively of any Ebreet sect while teaching. However, Mishi was in charge of their education and all events at the school, and he decided that he would expose problems that were perhaps more damaging than even the blockade.

"I tell you now, there is no place either inside or outside of this city where the leaders are not sinning against Yahweh. The Romans seek vengeance against us for defending ourselves and they do not know the history that precedes them. This short-term tactic of assaulting this city has no history of succeeding in the long term. Yet, the occupants of this city have lost their reverence for God and are committing sins against Him."

He paused. If what he was about to say reached the Roman leadership's ears, it could get him killed. The Pharisees would not protect him from their wrath. However, his students were rapt with attention.

"Our leaders have compromised our faith to comply with Roman demands. I know the Romans as no one else in this city does and they are reasonable people. They are doing as they are instructed, but not more. The Romans don't wish to be here, but they must stay here until the Temple is destroyed, as their Emperor commands it. Although many of my peers are not interested in the future of our people as they are hungry, I understand that you are a select group of boys. You are the future of our nation. You are the future of Ebreet faith. If you don't learn the words of the ancient texts, we are all doomed. Boys, remember, this city and the Temple that existed here before once collapsed. God's chosen were scattered for nearly 400 years. They were removed from the holy places and sent upon the earth like seeds in the wind. Our history was preserved by boys like you, who risked it all to learn from the Rabbis who traveled with the Ebreet to Babylon. For 400 years, Babylon was all that our people knew. Generations were born and died without leaving Babylon. Yet, have any of you seen Babylon? No. Remember, there were six generations of Hebrew people who failed to leave the confines of Babylon. Now, you tell me that none of you have seen it."

He continued walking amongst them, touching their shoulders and looking them in the eyes. He felt alive. He was doing the right thing. This moment was the reason he returned to Jerusalem from Tamar by himself.

"As we read in our scrolls, God calls out the sinful action of his people and their leaders, and He sends prophets to tell them and their leaders to repent and seek Him. If they repent and return to the sacred ways, they are saved. If they don't, they are killed. I am not a prophet, but I tell you stories that we have heard since our youth. Our leaders do not repent and do not seek Yahweh. The people in the streets aren't repenting either. If you are my students, you will learn the words of the sacred texts and we will do what is commanded of us. We shall stand in the gap, as is commanded in the writings of Ezekiel, on behalf of our people. Now, let us sharpen our minds and our tongues. Are you ready to learn?" he asked with a heightened sense of enthusiasm.

"Yes!" cheered the boys enthusiastically.

Mishi turned away from his students as they prepared to work. No matter how much impact he hoped his words might have in the lives of these boys, they could not cover his secret sins. It was when he spoke to the boys that he would forget his lack of faith.

As the day progressed and conversations delved deeper into the meaning of the writings found in the Temple library, the group began to fatigue. Mishi observed the onset of the fatigue and he asked Bethel to prepare a treat of pressed rice and corn. Each boy was also given a cupful of cold water to wash down the delicacy. When they were done eating, Mishi brought them together for a brief activity that involved mathematics before sending them back home for the day.

Once they left, Mishi turned to Bethel and said to him, "It is our turn to return to our families. Please take an ephah of grain for your family and two ephahs for mine from the Temple stores. Place each ephah in a separate bag, please."

Mishi didn't have a family in the city with him, but Bethel thought that he did. A few moments later, Bethel returned with the grain. He handed Mishi's share to him and spoke. "This is a lot of food for my family. Thank you for your kindness and generosity, Rabbi. I hope the boys know how committed you are to preserving God's word and His ways."

And with that grain, Mishi's secret festered for another day.

Chapter 35:
The Secret Room

After all the boys and staff had left, Mishi walked the halls, extinguishing the candles in the Temple and the school. The Temple Mount was not one building but a series of buildings, the second largest of which was the school. The Temple remained the tallest building in the city, and many parts of it were higher than the city walls. The school's rectangular blueprint matched the Temple's, being smaller in height and size. Inner rooms served as storage and held resources for education and instruction, and the middle courts served as classrooms.

Since the Roman occupation had begun, all of the Temple Rabbis ceased teaching classes. They told the students that it was more important to be with their families than to be in school. One Rabbi even told the youth that their lives were in jeopardy and that they should find a way out of the city. That made matters worse for everyone, especially the boys. Mishi knew the Torah instructed not to be scared. This was yet another example of Pharisees who were not doing their job, and it upset him.

Six years earlier, King Herod had begun a series of projects to expand the size of the Temple area. This "platform" project, as he called it, included a new school, an amphitheater, housing for soldiers who would protect the Temple area, and storage for the materials needed to conduct the business of the Temple. Tables, chairs, urns, candles, torches, paint, rope, wood, and tools were kept inside this area. On the outside perimeter of the new school and the foundation of the original Temple, there were many stacks of unused Lebanese cedar, as much of the supporting structure of the temple was made of the great woods from Lebanon. Stones of various sizes and types were used as part of the building's foundation. Other elements of construction, like bamboo mats and scaffolding, had piled up, and much of that which was there had started to decay. A large barrel of string made from hemp was beginning to fall apart. The carcass of the High Priest's deceased horse, buried in front of the timbers, had now begun to create a foul stench.

Despite the darkness in the space between the two structures, Mishi moved like a mountain goat on the side of Mount of Olives. He had great agility and he jumped between four years of accumulated construction trash with ease. Once he stood near the spot where the horse was buried, he lifted a large plank door lying on the ground, exposing a set of stairs leading down. He turned around cautiously, looking to see if anyone was watching him, and he entered.

With the sacks of grain in his right hand, his hand touched the left wall of the stairwell as he counted thirteen steps. He next pivoted to his left and descended another thirteen steps before reaching the bottom of the stairs. He set down the sacks of grain and felt on the left wall near his feet for a small opening. Once he found it, he reached in and pulled out a small piece of flint.

He knew there was a torch holder on the wall to his right, and he reached for it until he felt it. He struck the flint against some steel that he kept in his pocket and lit it on the first strike. As the torch glowed, he took it from its wall mount and put it in his right hand. He reached down and picked up one of the bags of grain with his left hand and pushed through a heavy burlap draper that acted as a door into a large underground chamber.

The torch illuminated the last months of his work. Mishi had been building a safe harbor for him and his best students once Jerusalem fell. This room was his secret and he could not talk to anyone about it. How could he? How much of a liar would he be if he admitted that he was as scared of Jerusalem falling as everyone else?

At first, when Mishi began furnishing this chamber with extra supplies from the Temple, he told himself that he was doing it for his students. He was creating this safe place for them. Now, his fear drove his desire to accumulate for the inevitable event to come. The supplies that he had accumulated over these last months were his refuge when the Romans finally destroyed the city walls and came inside set on vengeance. It was this room where he had put his trust.

When they reached the 100th day of the blockade, Mishi decided that he needed to have enough reserves for another 101 days. Now that 141 days had passed since the blockade had started, Mishi had counted out that he had 142 days' worth of stores in his hidden alcove. Each day, he had his servant bring him an additional day's worth of food. He had food, barrels of water, spices, pillows, night buckets, perfumes, mustard oil to last for a year, and candles beyond counting.

As the desperation of the residents increased, Mishi had to increase his efforts to protect the secrecy of this place. Unburying part of the horse next to the entrance kept away any explorers looking for food. In his heart, Mishi knew that this chamber was more than a refuge from the atrocities of the Roman occupation. It was an idol of the worst sort. It was his Asherah pole. By not talking about it, by secretly nurturing it, he allowed it to control him. Stocking this place and visiting it every day was his form of idol worship.

Holding the torch aloft, Mishi investigated the room one more time, accounting for every item and every quantity. The wall on the left side of the chamber was filled with shelves and barrels of food stores. The shelves were full of dried fruits and meats, as well as clothing that he might need in the months to come. At first, Mishi had accommodated a stay of a few weeks. Now that the blockade was into its fifth month, he decided that he needed clothing and supplies to last several seasons.

The right wall had piles of dried manure and sticks to be used as cooking fuel and a heat source as the colder months approached, and beds for six were laid out on the center wall. In the corner between the center and right wall was a pile of rubble that covered an entrance to an ancient tunnel that led into the unknown. At the top of the stairs, Mishi had dug a chimney that would direct smoke out from his secret place and over the edge of the city walls so that no one inside the city could see that someone was cooking. He examined all of the dung he brought down. It was wholly dried so as to make the least amount of smoke possible.

Mishi emptied the extra bag of grain that Bethel had given him into one of the barrels on the floor. He meticulously removed every grain from the bag before rolling it up and putting it into a pocket in his cloak. He walked the perimeter of the room. "Leather," he said to himself. "I need to bring some leather."

He reversed his steps, and when he reached the bottom of the stairs, he opened a barrel of water and prepared to extinguish the torch and go upstairs. Once the torch went out, he needed to stay down in the hidden room for fifteen minutes to allow time for his eyes to adjust. He had a small chair that he put in the room next to the water barrel.

Before he could put his torch into the water, he heard a noise from the pile of rubble on the other side of the room. His heart froze in fear, but his legs did not. He relit the torch and walked back into the room, almost too scared to breathe. He walked towards the source of the noise, holding his torch up as high as he could so as to see everything. The noise continued to get louder, and he began to see dust rise from the pile of rubble in the corner.

There was a chance that this was nothing at all. An animal in the tunnel on the other side may be digging or looking for a place to rest. But how had it gotten back there? There was also a chance that it was a person or, worse, many people. If this room were discovered, his refuge would be compromised. Involuntarily, he opened his mouth and spoke. "God, are you punishing my lack of faith?"

Without warning, a large rock from the top of the pile moved, and a small light began to shine from the other side.

This was not an animal.

It was a tiny light, and from what he could hear, it seemed likely that it was a single person. From the top of the pile, the head of a young woman emerged. Both Mishi and the girl were paralyzed as they made eye contact. The girl threw back the hood on her cloak and let her hair spin around and clear itself from where it was buried in her clothing. She was gorgeous and had deep-set eyes that mesmerized Mishi.

She looked around the room and returned her gaze to him. "Who are you?" she asked in Ebreet.

Mishi was not prepared for a conversation, and he remained silent. He was considering his options. He might have to kill her to protect his secret.

She broke the silence. "If you don't speak, I will. My name is Yael, and I am Ebreet from the village of Correae in the land of Naphtali. I have come to Jerusalem and atone for my sins. I have kept them secret for far too long, and I have risked my life to get to this damn city and find the Temple!"

Her directness demanded an equally direct response.

"It is an honor to meet you, Yael. I am Mishi, and I am the Headmaster at the Temple school. You are currently in a room under the Temple. So, you made it to Jerusalem." He climbed up the rocks and helped her clear away some rubble so she could crawl through. Once she did, she stood up and wiped all the dust and grime off of her outer cloak. Mishi gave her a cup of water and she drank it all in a single drought. She could tell by his clothing and prayer shawl that he was a Rabbi and she felt safe telling him everything.

"Rabbi, let me speak. I have kept my sin a secret. It has worn at my soul to the point that I left my village and traveled alone to get here." He gave her another cup of water and she paused long enough to drink it.

"Slow down. We aren't in a hurry," Mishi said.

"I'm sorry," said Yael. She took a deep breath and he pointed her toward one of the beds where they could sit down and talk.

"So, Colch was the nephew of one of our rabbis. His uncle was teaching in our village and Colch was staying with us for a few weeks. He and I had sex, but we were not pledged to be married. He left our village the next day. Before leaving, I told him that I thought we should marry. The jerk left anyway. I have come to Jerusalem to offer a sacrifice and pay the price for my fornication." She took a third drink of water. She spilled some of it on her dirty cloak and he wiped it off of her with part of his prayer shawl. He had seen the headmaster use his shawl to clean the little children in Bad Safir and it seemed like the right thing to do.

Yael was mesmerized at his offer to use the most sacred piece of clothing he wore to clean up her spill.

"Yael, I serve people. Cleaning up your spill is what the Pharisees are supposed to do. Continue your story. I am listening," he said. He held her hand to calm her, reminding her that she was not in a hurry.

"When I arrived, I found the city surrounded. I prayed to Yahweh and found this tunnel on the southern slopes of the walls outside of the city. I lit a candle and followed that tunnel here."

Silence again.

"Rabbi, are you listening? Can you help me, please?" she added.

"Yes and no," Mishi said.

"What do you mean?" she said. Yael was speechless as she stared at the vast array of items that had been collected in this room. It appeared as if there were food and clothing for a year and there were enough candles to burn for months at a time. Piles of blankets and huge clay containers of grains lined one wall, enough to keep half of Correae warm on the coldest of days.

"How many people live here?" she asked.

"None, yet," was all the Rabbi said.

She had no idea that shining light upon her sin meant shining light upon his.

"Rabbi, what is happening down here?" she asked.

"About the same evil as what is happening above us. I am con-victed. I have a story for you, too."

Chapter 36:
Friends

Yael exhausted all the details of her story, from her immense wealth to Colch to her journey yesterday to find a way into the city. Mishi asked questions to understand her decisions and he told her he had heard much worse. He knew that Yael wanted to atone for her sins, receive his blessing, and go home with a bead of atonement that she could use as a token from the Lord that her sins were forgiven. She still was required to make a blood sacrifice at the temple commensurate with her sin, but sleeping with one person before marriage required fractional repentance compared to many stories he had heard. Indeed, some young men in his class required this sort of blood sacrifice monthly and they were several years younger than Yael.

"Rabbi, you look anxious," Yael said. He reached out and took her hand, just as he did with everyone who came to him to repent.

"This room is my story and I cannot remain silent any longer." He took a deep breath and looked at the floor of the underground room. The torchlight was flickering, casting shadows that almost seemed to be moving. The thin yet dark black soot that came from the torch was making his eyes water and it was time to either switch to candlelight or to leave.

"I don't want to tell you my story while we are down here. It is equally shameful. Come. We are going to leave this room and return to my apartment. I will prepare food for us and we will talk some more. For now, though, please be quiet, as this is a secret place unknown to anyone in the city."

"This is a secret place? What is it used for?" Yael rhetorically asked. Based on what she knew about all the soldiers outside the wall and what she saw in this room, she finally realized she was inside some hidden bunker and was curious to know its purpose.

Instead of putting out the torch and adjusting gradually, Mishi took the torch all the way out of the tunnel before putting it out when he neared the end of the last flight of stairs. He knew the girl didn't know her way around like he did. And he wanted to be respectful and polite. There were no girls at the school and it had been a long time since he had seen a girl who was about his age and not starving to death. Yael's dark skin and voluptuous body were pleasurable to look at. Her transparency and willingness to share, though, was what he found most attractive. He led her up the stairs as respectfully as he could. He knew her soul was injured and she needed him to be meek and caring if she was to heal.

Once they left the tunnel, Yael paused to look at the enormous pillars on her left. He released his grip on her hand and let her walk into the inner courts of the temple. He pointed up to some of the work that his father had made and told her that the Holy of Holies was a mere 20 steps from where they stood. She gasped and reached out to hold one of the massive marble structures, running her hand up and down its length, amazed at how smooth it was. Then, she stared straight up in admiration of the height of God's Temple.

"So, is this King Solomon's temple?" She sounded like an eight-year-old girl when she saw her father come home from a successful hunt. Mishi looked and saw the awe in her eyes. Its splendor had no equal in the world and the marble columns that made up the outer perimeter were majestic. He smiled and told her yes. He wished he still felt the same awe that she did, but he grew up here and knew how corrupt the people who cared for the temple and its occupants had become. Yael's naivety was cute, but Mishi knew it was false. He had a lifetime of stories and experiences that would all break her heart. But that was not his job. He was a Rabbi at the Temple, and it was his job to care for and affirm God's chosen people. Yael needed him to be a nurturer and not a naysayer. She was hungry for adventure and the least he could do would be to show her God's Temple.

"God gave the requirements of this Temple to David and Solomon, and it has been destroyed and rebuilt. It is the centerpiece of our faith and you are the only one here now. It is uniquely yours to enjoy. Would you like to take a tour?"

"Oh, Rabbi! I would love that. Can we go inside and see it? I have heard about the temple since I was a little girl!" Mishi was not a tour guide, but he knew temple history.

"Of course. Follow me!" he said. He reached out and held her hand again, walking with her around the perimeter and then inside the inner courts. Yael touched everything and quickly told Mishi what she remembered from school. Everything that she had memorized was accurate, and Mishi affirmed her recanting of its dimensions and its purpose. She laughed and giggled, always returning to hold Mishi's hand. He could not tell her that there were no more animals to offer as sacrifices and, therefore, no way for her to atone appropriately, but at least she could experience the joy of the Temple and its glory.

"Yael, you are obviously a good student. Perhaps one day, you could be a good teacher. Young girls like yourself need young women to instruct them. Your enthusiasm would make you a great teacher for the next generation of women." Yael smiled. She had never thought about that before now, and the idea filled her soul. They left the temple and stepped onto the school grounds.

"This building on your right is the school where I am headmaster. There are only a few boys left whom I teach." Yael looked at him, expecting more details, but he was not about to begin breaking her heart with sadness.

"Let's go to my apartment. I am hungry," he said.

"So am I!" said Yael. Mishi was happy that Yael responded well to his efforts to care for her. He had never done it with a single woman, nor had he done it after dark, but it seemed natural and unforced. She trusted him, and he knew that there was nothing a Rabbi was more responsible for than the trust of the people whom he served. Above all things, that is what he loved the most about his oath to be Pharisee in the line of Melchizedek. He was here tonight to serve her.

The walk back to his apartment was short, but the people they passed created a grim depiction of the state of things behind the walls. A couple was leaning against the side of a building, lacking the energy to move. They were emaciated beyond recognition and they were half-naked. Mishi grumbled under his breath, "I probably knew them, but I don't know them now." He kept on walking, reminding Yael to keep up. When they reached his apartment, he looked both ways before entering. No one must be allowed to see him bring in a woman. In the not-too-distant past, it would have been a stonable offense for an unmarried Rabbi to bring a young female beyond his living threshold, regardless of intent. Now, it was nothing more than a piece of gossip. Yet, regardless of social position, Mishi knew that this girl owned his secret. He dared not risk her accidentally telling anyone about his secret place. Keeping her with him seemed like the best way to protect himself. Once they entered, he closed the door and bolted it closed for the evening. He set down his torch and both of them took off their sandals.

"I made it!" Yael said, finally taking the time to stretch. She saw the sink in his tiny kitchen and she proceeded to wash her face and hands. She dried off with an unused towel. Mishi struck up a conversation with her as he waited his turn to wash his hands and face.

"This is my apartment. This is where you will be staying for now."

Mishi started a fire and added some dung to stoke it so they could boil water for their meal. Yael didn't speak at first, but soon, she began incessantly telling him stories of her trip to Jerusalem. She had not spoken to many people and no one had heard her whole story, as she hadn't stayed anywhere long enough to tell it. She felt safe knowing she was inside the city of David. In her mind, the trip was halfway over.

Mishi was quick to discover that Yael was a fantastic storyteller, and Mishi realized that it had been a long time since he had a conversation with someone who wasn't starving. She was spirited in her delivery and quick to move on to the next event in her story's timeline. The two of them laughed and found humor in most of what they talked about.

"My instinct was correct. You are a great teacher," Mishi said, watching Yael smile. He offered her a bowl full of cooked wheat and hot lentils. Once they sat down, their conversation became more informal.

"No, it is that I haven't had anyone my age to talk to in over a week. Actually, Rabbi, I have no experience teaching. I have spent all of my time as a student," she said.

"You can call me Mishi," he said. She graciously accepted his offer and he continued.

"I was serious when I said you should consider teaching. You are better at storytelling than many of the teachers at my school," he said. Yael looked at him and smiled. She could see that he was sincere and it dawned on her that she had not had a man both cook for her and serve before.

It didn't take long before all their conversation flowed naturally. It was as if they had known each other for years. Yael offered to help him clean up and they both worked together in the kitchen, washing dishes and putting everything away. Mishi admitted that he did not use the towel and used his robe when he was in a hurry and trying to dry his hands.

"I do that, too," Yael admitted, and they both laughed. Once they finished with the dishes, Mishi poured each of them a cup of wine that he had been saving for a special moment and they sat down on the floor, leaning against the walls of the apartment.

Yael told a story of her encounter with an old man and his family by the fireside one evening. She gave few details about the man and lots of details about the riddles he spoke to her. He could tell, though, that she was perplexed by what he had shared, as it had impacted her.

"Can I ask you something? Was his name Barnabas?" Mishi asked. Yael had made a promise to protect his name and she knew that she couldn't answer him. However, Mishi was as good at reading people as a Roman soldier was with a gladius.

"I knew it!" Mishi said. Yael chuckled as she sensed his secret would be safe with Mishi.

"He made me promise not to say his name to anyone on the highway," she said.

"I met him after I had my Bar Mitzvah and was on my way to Tamar. He told some stories about a Messiah who came to save us from our sins. I sometimes think about what he said when I go to the secret room," Mishi said. Yael took a sip of wine and looked at the opposite wall, trying to formulate her words before she spoke.

"I spent one night in camp with him and he could see through me like I was an open door." She took another sip of her wine and let her words sit. She was reliving what he said to her and she was questioning why she was here. Was it to get forgiveness of sins from the temple or to meet this one man who understood her? Mishi sensed she was reliving something, so he shared his story of Barnabas.

"I didn't spend the night with him in a camp. I met him in a city a bit east of here while my father and I were walking back home. I told him everything that I learned from the Pharisees about how Yeshua could not be the Messiah, and he embraced me like a son. Even when I dismissed him and his stories, he said he was proud of me and knew that I was too smart to let the Pharisees mislead me and that I would figure the truth out on my own. He said the Messiah was already calling me," Mishi said, taking his first sip of wine. Yael was riveted to his story, and she wondered what it must have been like to hear a Temple Rabbi debate Barnabas.

"Mishi, he said that the Messiah was also calling me! This is unbelievable!" Yael said with excitement and they continued talking into the night. She told him how she found the tunnel, even after a woman tried to convince her to give up before she started. Mishi told her that there were many tunnels and there was even an ancient map of them in the Temple library. He considered burning it to leave nothing for the Romans to find, but instead hid it, knowing he and his students might need it one day. It dawned upon him that he should have known that there might be a hidden passageway behind the ruble in his secret room.

Now that she had told someone her age about Colch, Yael felt comfortable telling Mishi of the beheading and how that made her feel. She also recalled the people of her village and she admitted that she missed Despy and Nava. That made her laugh.

"I have not once in my life said one nice word about those two idiots. I am ashamed that it took traveling all the way to Jerusalem to see that they love me. I can't imagine growing up without any cousins or brothers and sisters." She looked straight ahead, and she sensed a strong connection forming with Mishi. His face showed that he wanted to understand her and wanted to listen to her. She had not seen a rabbi in such an informal light and he made her feel safe. Looking into his eyes was comforting.

"Yael, do you realize where you are at this moment? You are inside the walls of the most important city in our people's history, and it is surrounded by hostile forces intent on destroying our way of life. You are lucky to be alive, let alone found a Rabbi. You could have been killed had you been discovered by someone else. The Romans would pay a vast sum to know of the tunnel you found. You must keep it secret."

"Of course!" she said—another secret.

"I find it to be ironic that everyone wants to leave and can't while you find a way into a city. Our Lord certainly is guiding your steps," he said. He lifted his cup and toasted her.

"You think so?" she asked rhetorically. Mishi could see that his comments made her feel special. They finished their cups and leaned their backs against the apartment walls.

"When I left Correae, I took a risk. No unmarried girl has left our village on her own. As of today, I have been gone a week, and before leaving, the person I shared my plan with was my father, who was drunk when I told him."

"I, too, told my father that I was leaving by myself to return to Jerusalem to finish my training so I could start a school of my own one day," said Mishi. Yael looked at him and smiled. It was obvious that both of them were impressed with the other, but Mishi was willing to tell her first.

"I can't believe how easy it is talking to you," said Yael.

"There are other Rabbis who are real. It isn't isolated to me. The man who I replaced is my hero." Mishi told her about how the High

Priest intended to call him and train him as his replacement. He told her about how he and his father left to go home so he wouldn't shame his family by saying no to the spiritual leader of their people.

"You were going to be the next High Priest? Really?" Yael said. She was in disbelief.

"I am so glad that I didn't disciple under the High Priest. The Pharisees have been embarrassing us these last few months, and he is not following God," he said. He took a sip of wine while Yael stared at him.

"These are truly the secrets behind the walls of Jerusalem." He smiled at her. Yael had already confessed that her life was littered with secrets, and she didn't like them.

"Doesn't it feel good not to have them anymore?" Mishi asked. They both laughed.

"Mishi, something inside of me is changing. After talking to the bread lady and the old woman in the city below this one, I began to feel at peace. Certainly, I must deal with the truth that I am a sinner of the worst kind. I am here to do something about it. But, there is something bigger than my story, your story, Barnabas, and the High Priest, happening here." Yael was obviously energized by reaching her destination and the courage to finish what she started was strong. Mishi shared her insight into how quickly the world around them appeared to be changing.

"Well, you certainly are brave. However, we have no animals left inside the city for you to sacrifice so that I can give you your bead," he said. She deserved to hear the truth, and he said it as lovingly as he could. Yael smiled, but he could tell that she was hurt that all of her work appeared to be for nothing.

"Yael, perhaps it is through your arrival that God is speaking to me. I had a sin that stemmed from a lack of faith and you exposed it by arriving both when and where you did. I have been stealing and hiding away food and provisions for when the city falls. I tell everyone to be strong and trust in the Lord, but you know I am building my own Asherah pole and hiding it from everyone," he said, taking another ship.

"Except you. That is my secret as I await the fall of Jerusalem."

Now that Mishi's sin was exposed, he joined Yael in feeling relief.

"Yael, perhaps I am like you were when you could no longer live with your sin and decided to do something about it. Indeed, this very day, I am giving my confession to a stranger." Yael reached out and took Mishi's hand. She could see that he was opening up on a topic as fragile as her fornication. She smiled and lifted her cup.

"Let us make a toast appropriate for being this close to the temple. To the confession of sins!" said Yael, holding up her cup.

"To confessing sin," said Mishi, clinking his cup to hers. Mishi continued his intimate conversation.

"Each day, people come to the Temple expecting us to feed them and relieve them of the pain imposed on us by the Romans. In the months leading up to this day, I have watched men of faith become animals. Hunger does not discriminate. All men become this way as their desire for survival overtakes everything, including their faith."

Yael looked deeply at Mishi. She sensed a sincerity from him that few saw. She compared him to Rabbi Andrew but could not see Rabbi Andrew speaking to a young woman like herself so openly. She saw that he was wounded from secrets and needed healing as much as she did. And his repentance was genuine and unlike any she had seen.

"I believe God can and will save us, but I need to repent of my sins and agree to follow His ways." With that, he gave her his entire story of creating the hidden sanctuary and his intention to take his students there once the walls were breached and the temple overrun. Yael listened and could feel the pain his pain during moments when he would pause to talk about seeing a loved one starving to death.

"The truth is that I also lack faith that our Lord will intervene. As a Rabbi, I intervene on behalf of my students and fellow Pharisees. Now, who shall intervene for me?"

Yael had no response for this. She steered the conversation back to herself.

"Well, sin is the reason that I am here, too. We all know that the penalty for sin is death. Mishi, I am desperate to be cleansed. Until I do this, I can't marry. I have watched Erusin, and I want a marriage to a good man like my sister Katie has. I can't have that if I do not first atone for this sin!" Mishi broke eye contact and stared into the fire, looking for the courage of the sort Yael was showing him.

"Yael, I see your desire to heal and return to a normal life. I have given beads to men who have killed their wives and children, men who have cheated others out of money and land, and those who have deceived their parents and stolen from them. In each case, these people came with contrite hearts and full purses, hoping to rid themselves of sin. I can help you perform the ceremony of Qorbanot so you will restore yourself to God. Qorbanot is our culture, and God keeps His promises of redemption from sin by the death of a sacrificial animal. But I already told you, there are no animals available for use as sacrifices since the city is dying of starvation. There is nothing we can do tonight. Let me sleep, and perhaps I will have an idea for you in the morning."

Mishi got up and gestured for Yael to follow him. He took out blankets and laid them on the ground for her. The two of them looked each other in the eye and it was obvious that they were feeling a connection. Mishi was too shy to speak, but he was delighted to have found Yael the way that he did.

"Good night, Mishi. Thank you for being my friend." Yael took off her outer robe and slipped into the layer of blankets and the soft quilt underneath. Mishi gave her a cotton pillow and a tiny bit of Myrrh to rub on her forehead before he reached to blow out the candle. With darkness filling the room, he felt the courage to speak.

"Yael, tonight you were my first new friend in a long time. Thank you for that gift. I was fearful beyond words that someone would discover my secret place. Now that the day has come, and I have no secrets. I am at peace. Because of you, I will share the food that I have saved with everyone. There is no need to wait till the walls are breached to love my neighbors as myself."

A single tear dripped from Yael's eye and she lowered her head so that he wouldn't see it. "You are a good man, Rabbi Mishi."

Despite the near-nonexistent light, Mishi could see that Yael was crying. He reached over and wiped the tear with the clean fabric of his inner cloak. Yael looked up and he smiled.

"I don't feel like a good man," he said to her. Soon, Yael could hear him snoring.

Yael knew she could not stay. Mishi had found a feeling of peace, but she had not. She needed to leave, find a sacrificial animal, and come back. And it couldn't wait. The Romans might see her if she traveled during the day. She quietly put back on her outer robe and sandals, opened the deadbolt, and stepped into the night.

Chapter 37:
Light of the Torch

Glancing back towards the center of the Temple grounds, Yael felt almost sad that she was secretly leaving the area she had worked so diligently to reach. She connected with Mishi, but he could not free her from the bondage of her sins. He could not perform the ceremony to absolve her of her sin, as there were no animals available for sacrifice. The only possible sacrifice would have been a dying human. That would not be acceptable to Yahweh. She needed to leave, get an animal, bring it back, and give it to him as her sacrifice.

Yet, there was another choice that made her pause her steps and ponder. Wasn't a dying human the sort of sacrifice that Rabbi Barnabas had described? Was Yeshua that human sacrifice he was talking about? She found no answer and kept moving.

She needed to keep her focus. She needed to leave, find an animal to sacrifice, and bring it back. Perhaps a caged dove would be best, as the noise of a lamb or goat would increase the risk of being discovered. She would be risking her life to walk next to the Roman camps, but her internal peace was worth the risk.

The first task was to get out of the city without being detected. No one could follow her through the secret room and into the tunnel. If other Ebreet found out that there was a way to escape without being detected, the tunnel would be overrun in a matter of minutes. She needed to get out when no one was watching her.

Yale knew her way around secrets. The safety kept within secrets like this tunnel was a part of life. The gold veins on the edge of the river in Correae, her sin of fornication she committed with Colch, the hidden chamber where Mishi planned for his escape when God failed him, and the tunnel that went in and out of Jerusalem were all secrets that would cause damage if exposed. She didn't want to live a life full of secrets. The burden was something she didn't want to carry.

After talking to Mishi, she believed that all secrets held people back from their ability to connect. As Mishi had reminded her the previous evening, Adam and Eve had attempted to hide their sins from Yahweh, and the Lord saw through them. In the shame of discovery, they covered themselves, further distancing themselves from Him. She was no different. She had fled Correae and left her drunken father to explain what happened. She decided that she needed to take ownership of her decisions and speak directly to the family, specifically Katie, as soon as she got home. Her sister deserved the truth and she needed to tell her as part of her penance. Mishi already agreed with this part of her plan.

"Katie, I am so sorry that I lied to you," she said to herself as she walked towards the Temple.

She could see no other way of safely exiting the city other than the same way she had entered. She guessed that she could be outside the city walls in less than a quarter of an hour after she left Mishi's apartment. She could be back in town perhaps even before sunrise.

Her trip through town to the Temple courts went as expected. Young women walking the streets at night would typically be cause for a public trial. Still, with the town's residents and visitors literally starving to death, no one had energy for anything other than food scavenging. She made a quick detour to stand at the entrance to the Temple. There were no guards anymore and the gate appeared to be open. However, the majestic marble columns were auspicious, even with slight moonlight illuminating them.

"Jehovah, I will be back to make things right. I promise." She took a knee and bowed her head as she heard tales that her uncles would do this when they reached the Temple. She got up and made a beeline for the inner courts where she could grab a torch. Once she pulled one from the thick storage barrel that contained the burning oils, she went towards the unburied dead horse and the hidden passageway that led down to the secret room and away from Jerusalem.

She moved quickly, descending the first flight of stairs and stopping outside the entrance to the secret room. Mishi told her where he kept flint. She found it and quickly lit a torch. She looked back up and was pleased that she could hear nothing and no one had noticed her. She went through the secret room quickly, looking around at all the items Mishi had accumulated.

"Oh, we all have our secrets," she said, smiling at how much she and Mishi were alike. She climbed the rock pile and entered the first set of stairs that led down to the ancient tunnel. As she walked the length of the tunnel, she could see much more with the torch's light than she had when she had traveled by candle yesterday.

There were colored pictures on the walls, and in some places, there were iron hooks that she thought were meant to hold tapestries or war clothing. Her mind raced as she passed them, wondering what their original purpose might have been. She spoke out loud as she walked.

"Hooks on the wall! Hooks on the wall! What is your story? What purpose did you serve? Were you the hanging place of the royal robes of David and Solomon? Were you the home of scabbards and bows from the first of the tribe of Benjamin? Reveal to me your story! Otherwise, I will have to make one up like the boys do when they arrive back home!" That made her laugh. Talking to Mishi had freed her and her sense of imagination was alive again.

She liked the idea of making up stories, but at this point, her real life was interesting enough by itself. She didn't need to embellish anything. Sneaking around the armies of Rome was already a great tale. She imagined telling the boys in the village and the old men later saying, "Remember the time when Yael traveled underneath the walls of Jerusalem while it was under siege by the Romans?" She saw how the boys were continually jostling for the position of the best storyteller or the one with the most incredible adventures. If nothing else, she had finally had the adventure she had long been seeking. She returned to conversation with herself about the hooks for no reason other than to stave off fear.

"Alas, there will be no stories of ancient Ebreet hooks on the walls in the tunnel. None of you hooks are talking to me! What is your story, boys and girls?" was all she could say as she started approaching what she thought might be the end of the tunnel.

Even though she had traveled the tunnel one time, she felt like she knew her way in and out of the city well, and she soon stepped out onto the side of the mountain. Her torch was so bright that it prevented her from seeing the moon. She put it out, giving her eyes a moment to adjust, and she started moving down the mountain using the old trail. She wanted to get what she needed and return as fast as possible. Each step was a step closer to buying a dove and receiving the Temple bead that would absolve her of her sin. It reminded her of how her grandmother would tell her that a water jug is filled one drop at a time. She treated her steps to get down like drops of water filling a jug.

After a few minutes of walking, she heard something that caused her heart to stop. There were human voices above her. They were speaking in Greek, not Hebrew. She crouched down behind a large rock off the trail between herself and the direction of the sounds.

The volume increased as the speakers approached, and the light of their torches cast shadows over the rocks that she hid behind. "Keep moving, men. Rufus saw the light up here, and he wanted to know its source. If we can't find its source, he will personally kill us all. Keep looking!"

She put her hands on her face and lowered her head in disgust. Her torch! It must have been more visible than she had anticipated. Even if they didn't find her, they could find the entrance to the tunnel while they looked for her, and they would discover the secret passage into the city.

Dread came upon her. It filled her soul with darkness. She had inadvertently killed Jerusalem.

She did as she was taught and prayed. "Yahweh, you have delivered my people from great things and evil empires in the past. Please protect the people inside the city now. Do not let the Romans find the tunnel because of my foolishness and selfishness."

She prayed until the Romans could no longer be heard and the light of their torches had faded away. Once they were completely out of earshot, she stood up and ran down to the city where she hoped to buy a dove, crying the entire way.

Chapter 38:
Like Always

Yael crossed the last of the open fields between the tunnel and the lower city. She could see the city walls directly in front of her and the Roman army was beginning to stir on her left. She saw something that quickly turned her sorrow to fear, and she had to stifle a scream. Before her were two behemoths like she had not imagined. These ancient beasts were even more majestic than her Rabbis had described. The Behemoths had tails as large as Lebanese cedar trees and they were twice as tall as elephants with bodies as big around as her family's house. As they walked, each step sounded like a huge rock hitting the ground. She paused for a moment to stare, then her curiosity overtook her, and she cautiously approached the two beasts.

As she stepped closer, she could see that they had been painted. She saw patterns on their faces that she could not recognize. Were they images of war, or were those marks symbols of ownership like the tattoos that slaves got after acquisition? Each one had paintings of swords, shields, and helmets on its head. Mesmerized by the sight of the Behemoths, she overlooked a Roman soldier in full battle regalia walking directly toward her.

"Step away," was all she heard. She wrapped her scarf around her head and crouched in a submissive state, but she didn't step back as she had been ordered to do. The soldier reached for the hilt of his sword and unsheathed it as he quickened his pace towards her. Roman soldiers were taught to unsheathe their weapons if they intended to use them. She knew this, and she had seen it a week before.

"Step away," he repeated, this time in a much louder voice. Based on his horrible pronunciation, Yael surmised that this man didn't know much more of her language than that, so she did as he said. She stood up, covered her face, and backed away from the animals while maintaining partial eye contact with the young soldier. Her life was in his hands. She had heard stories of women who gave themselves to Roman soldiers to save their lives, and she thought now that she understood why they had acted as they had. "I am sorry," she said. "I have not seen one of these creatures before this moment."

She had communicated first—another mistake. Romans didn't like that.

The young man now stood next to her, his sword in his hand. She could feel his breath in her ear. Without thinking, she gave away what she had risked her life to save.

"Please do not kill me! Take my body if that will please you."

She was no longer looking at the soldier, but she heard him return his sword to its sheath. The man began speaking perfect Ebreet. "I will take your offer, village girl."

Who was this person? How did he know Ebreet?

He grabbed her wrist and pulled her up into the back of a nearby cart filled with hay. He released his grip on her arm and reached down to open his robe. "Disrobe, or my sword comes back out," he commanded.

Yael's breathing became shallow. Her arms began to tingle. He had accepted her offer. She had offered her body once before and felt the pain of that choice for seasons afterward. She had traveled across her country to atone for that act. Yet she had offered herself up again to escape death at the hands of this man. She felt like she was about to throw up. She wished she was drunk like her father so she wouldn't feel the pain.

She thought about running, reaching for the soldier's sword and striking this imposter with it, but she didn't. Her courage dissipated as it did on the sides of the Northerns too many times to count. Tears welled up again as she began to disrobe. Soon, she closed her eyes and tried to imagine being with Colch again. And again, the pain and the pleasure were blurred, and she was crying like a baby.

When they were done, the man stood up and put his clothes back on, leaving her lying in the back of the cart.

"Who are you?" Yael asked with desperation.

"I am Ebreet, like you. I am from the village of Saab near the coast," he said. "The Romans landed on our shores. They offered me the job of taking care of these beasts and trained me as a mercenary. The pay is great, but moments like what you gave me make it even better." He laughed and flashed her an evil smile. "You can go now. So that you know, I planned on letting you live even if you hadn't offered yourself to me."

Yael knew the sting of those words would wound her for the rest of her life. She hated herself now, even more than when she encouraged Colch to lay with her. The soldier jumped down off the cart and walked around the behemoths. Yael watched him as he walked away, getting smaller and smaller until, finally, he was entirely out of sight. She was isolated and alone, with her sin as her primary companion, like always.

Chapter 39:
The Old Woman's Story

Yael walked in a daze from the cart where she was raped towards the city gates. With every step, she felt dirtier and dirtier. Although she was fully dressed, she almost felt that she was walking naked. Indeed, forgiveness of her sins would now be impossible. She now needed two animals, at the very least. Perhaps she needed strong wine, like her father did.

She now knew she lacked the character to avoid sexual misconduct. She was a harlot like she read about in Sodom. Sex to anyone who wanted it was now her identity. Her body was not sacred.

Her hopes of a fruitful and joyous future were dashed. She was not to have the life of her sister or any of the other women in her village. She was going to be different. She wished Mishi was here to talk to. He would know what to say. He was a fantastic friend.

"Yael, why didn't you run, you idiot!" she said to herself. Based on his armor, she would have had a good chance of escaping him and fleeing to the edge of the city walls, where she could be lost and unlikely to be identified. His armor was heavy and he could not have run to the other side of the city walls.

Yael was face to face with her greatest shame. Why did she break her promise to Yahweh again? Yael wanted Erusin and she wanted a husband who would work night and day to build their home and provide for her. She had been on her way to find an animal to take back to the Temple to sacrifice. She knew that she needed to do this in order to give herself entirely to her future husband. But she gave away her most precious gift without a fight.

She entered the city walls and fell to her knees. Turning her hands skyward, she said, "Yahweh, why do I do these things?"

She received no answer, and asking the question gave her no solace. She hoped God had heard her plea.

People were moving all around her and she realized she was hungry. She entered the city gates and bought a loaf of hot bread and a cup of tea from a street cart, and she felt her energy returning. That feeling didn't last long for all heads turned when the Roman army camped outside the city walls sounded their battle horns. The blasts sounded as if they were right outside the walls, but she knew that they were a long distance away. However, there were so many horns that she felt that an earthquake was about to happen.

Was this now the time for the Messiah about to come, as was promised in the scrolls, or was their faith about to fail them?

And immediately after the horns ended, Yael could hear the yelling of men and their Roman battle cries. God's holy city and His Temple were under assault. Great siege engines were throwing boulders at the city walls, knocking pieces of the wall off with every strike. Pieces of the outer wall of Jerusalem tumbled to the ground. She surmised that Roman siege engineers coordinated a unified attack at sunrise, with boulders striking the wall in a concerted rhythm, each firing from a different location. The Ebreet artillery on the top of the wall could not respond with the same synchronicity, and the men on the outer walls were running for their lives.

She was startled by the touch on her left shoulder. She turned to see the older woman whose house she had stayed at, who spoke so softly that Yael could barely hear her voice. "Rabbi Mark taught us something that you need to hear. He told us that the Messiah said that not one stone in the great Temple would be left on another. All will be thrown down. I think we are seeing His prophecy being fulfilled amongst us. We must praise Yeshua for His truth." Yael was taken aback.

"Old woman, you make no sense. Solomon's Temple is about to fall and you are thanking someone for predicting it? What is wrong with you?" Yael's anger was on full display.

This woman's gibberish made Yael furious, but at least the old woman was a familiar and trustworthy face. And Yael was desperate to talk. She was desperate to rest. And with that, Yael began to cry.

The woman embraced her and held her upright, ignoring Yael's rebuke. "Come child, you are weary. I can sense that you have a story to tell."

The two of them left the crowd at the city gate and walked for several minutes until they entered the old woman's house. The old woman took Yael to a dark and cool room in the back of the house and motioned to her to lie down on a quilt on the floor.

She placed her hands on Yael and began to pray. "Loving God, You are not far from us. I pray that You comfort this young woman. Please lend me the hands of the healers who have come before me. Let her see the power of Your love, and let her find peace in You." She hummed and rocked back and forth, sitting on her knees while Yael lay on the bed of quilts.

Yael began to speak. She didn't know where to start. "You know—"

"Be still, little one. God has such a wonderful plan, and it includes you. You are redeemed by His grace, no matter what you have done. I can see now that He loves your faith. He loves your struggles. You are chosen, and he is pleased with your faith." The old woman picked up Yael's head and held it like a newborn baby.

"Yahweh knows you so well. He knows your thoughts and deeds. Yeshua came to heal you and me so we have the final word on our destiny. There is much we don't understand about life, but this I know. You need rest. We will talk when you are awake. You have my promise."

And Yael slept.

When she awoke, the sun was setting and there was no noise coming from the battlefield. She guessed the Romans must have already made their way into the city. She could hear the old woman singing a light tune. Yael got up and walked into the kitchen and saw her kneading bread and simmering a pot of beans over her small cooking fire. When she saw that Yael was awake and moving, she stopped and looked at her over her shoulder. "Come, Little One. Sit with me. God has your heart in His hand. If I remember, your name was Yael. You are from the village of Correae, and you were on your way to atone for fornication. Yes?"

Yael nodded. She hadn't actually told the old woman of her encounter with Colch, but somehow, she knew. Yael took a seat next to the old woman on the mud floor. The woman bent over and kissed her forehead like her grandmother used to. She passed a bowl of dough. She gave her no directions, but Yael knew what to do. Yael got up, washed her hands, and finished preparing the dough.

"Your choice to atone was worthy. Do not be ashamed that the evil one has distracted you from your path. But I can sense you have a huge story to tell."

"Oh, do I!"

Yael began her tale of what had happened since she had last seen the old woman. She would pause and sob, and the old woman would stir the beans and grind salt while she waited patiently for Yael to continue. She told of the discovery of the secret passage, her chance encounter with Mishi, her escape, and her shameful decision to give herself away to the Ebreet man disguised as a Roman soldier outside the city walls. Once she had blown her nose and had cried so much that she could cry no more, she stood up, handing the woman the over-kneaded dough.

"I worked so hard to reach the Temple and cleanse myself, and I risked my life to seek the atonement. Yet the harder I tried, the more unsuccessful I was. I could not keep my promise to Yahweh. I have wasted my time and some of my sister's dowry."

"Yael, daughter, there is much you need to hear, yet you must process that which has happened to you. Our Yeshua came to this earth one generation ago to atone for our sins, both the ones we have committed and the ones we will yet commit. He was crucified on a cross near here for all of our sins, as was predicted in the scrolls by our prophets nearly a thousand years ago. He is our sacrifice. You need not buy any livestock and sneak into the city to perform a ritual to be cleansed of your sins. Yeshua has done this for you and me, both now and forever. We are free of this bondage. You need only accept this gift! You don't have to work for it."

"That is what Barnabas said!" she exclaimed. Yael paused, staring into the beans for a moment, occasionally looking at the wall. This woman's idea of a free gift of salvation sounded enticing and common-sensical. No one she had known kept the Torah sacred in deed and action, even Mishi, the Rabbi at the Temple School. The woman could sense her struggle and spoke up.

"Yael, our old faith was one of rules and protocol. All of these rules define us, but they also leave us empty and feeling inadequate because we can't follow that which is taught in the Torah. We all fall short of glory. Haven't you noticed that no one, not even the Pharisees and the Rabbis, can keep the whole law?"

"I have. That was Mishi's story. I wish he were here right now. He would know what to say."

Yael continued.

"We all fall short of our expectations. Everyone knows this." She told the old woman about Mishi's secret room and how he had admitted that he lacked faith.

"Yael, that is an incredible story, and it is even more marvelous that Rabbi Mishi shared his sin with you when you were intending to share your sin with him. What a humble young man! He will make a fine husband one day." Yael looked at the woman and smiled. Her memories of Mishi were all good ones. He was humble and caring, and she felt endeared to him.

"I liked him. I liked how he treated me. He brought out the best in me," she said. The old woman smiled and even laughed.

"Yahweh is using that man, too, Little One. You might meet him again." Yael blushed as she could sense that the old woman sensed chemistry between them.

"You are missing a part of God's story. Yeshua's life and death complete what is written in the scrolls. We inherit the kingdom of Heaven from faith in Him. He doesn't replace the scrolls of the Torah; He completes them."

The old woman's breakdown of the message of the Messiah was not new. It was the same as what Barnabas had said.

"Are you sure you don't didn't learn that from Barnabas?" Yael laughed. They returned to some small talk. The old woman brought up Mishi again, wanting to know more about him. Yael's shame cut her off.

"Old woman, I am not yet of age to marry and I have already chosen to bed one man and traded my body for my life with another. Have I not broken my promises to Yahweh? I feel filthy. I can't think about a husband, let alone one as majestic as a rabbi. Mishi is above me."

"Oh, my dear, Mishi is not above you. All you need to do is confess yourself to Yeshua as your savior, and your sins are forgiven." Yael was in nearly a stupor as she listened to this woman's words and marveled at how they mirrored Barnabas's speech. Yael asked her a few questions, and each time, she gave the same answer as the old man on the side of the road.

"Both of you say that sins are forgiven through faith in Yeshua. I don't see how this is possible."

"He was the Messiah. He says to call on His name, and He will bring you peace that the world cannot understand. He is Yahweh on earth. He came to save us from our sins, not save us from the Romans." She had now finished her preparation in the kitchen and poured both of them a glass of wine. They moved to the kitchen table and sat down.

"Let me tell you a story. I was once married. I had a husband and two beautiful children. We farmed and sold livestock at the gates of Jerusalem each season. I owned gold and silver jewelry and was respected in the community. Both of my children trained with the Rabbis. However, my husband was unfaithful. He brought home a disease in his loins from one of his trips with our son to the sea. He gave it to me. It killed him and it ravaged my body for a month. Eventually, it destroyed my womb. I thought the elders in our village were a threat, as I thought they might stone me for the sins of my husband and I fled our village with the children. We reached the river Jordan after walking all night and I held my children's hands as we crossed it. I thought it would be safe."

The old woman began to shake as she entered the next part of the story. She was reliving her trauma, and it was difficult for her to share such a loss.

"The current was stronger than I thought. It carried my daughter away from me, and my son and I survived. Once we reached the other side, my son and I tried to continue, but we were weary from our loss like you are now. The next morning, all I could think about was the hope that my daughter was alive, so my son and I went back down to the river to look for any signs of her. Later that morning, a group of men from our village came looking for us. When they found us, I was petrified with fear. But when they reached us, we all embraced, and they spoke of how heartbroken they were to learn that we had thought they wished us ill. They went to the river and shaved their heads as an act of atonement, for they felt that the death of my daughter was partly their fault. They wept as much as I did and they stayed with me for days, eating when I ate and sleeping when I slept. They prayed for me and cared for my son with no regard for their own families. In their sacrifice, they continually reminded me that my husband's choices were not mine and my identity was now separate from him. Yael, girls such as yourself have given themselves up to save their lives every day since the Roman occupation started. None of today's actions are your fault. You were acting to stay alive."

Yael started feeling peace. She felt a connection with this woman like that of her grandmother. She had life stories and a heart to share them. "Thank you. That helps. I feel better."

The old woman continued her story. "I later learned that I was fearful when I didn't need to be. Those whose job it was to protect me appeared as enemies to me, and I fled them. Had I not done these things, my daughter might be alive. I must live with the results of my poor judgment all of my days. Although my son is now married and lives far to the north, I have moved to this small city outside of Jerusalem to support The Way."

Yael felt shame when she compared her problems to this old woman. Yael didn't think her problems were the most enormous hardship in all of Creation anymore. This woman had gone through a far worse tragedy. She and Yale embraced and they both cried for a moment.

"That, Little One, was twenty years ago. Not a day passes when I don't think about that decision. Perhaps I will not learn to forgive myself for that unnecessary reaction. However, God used that event, and now I see clearly how Yeshua is the father and protector whom we want our earthly father to be. He died for my sins. And He died for your sins. In our faith, when anxiety comes, we lean on rules and customs to keep us close to Yahweh. With Yeshua, we need to call on His name. Nothing else is required. He forgives all of our sins, even when we can't forgive our own. You may never come to peace about what these men did, but God can and does use all things for good. In the same way, my story impacts you, so your story may impact others one day."

"Can you teach me more about Yeshua? I have heard about him from too many people for this to be an accident."

"I can, but I would like to introduce you to our group. We are gathering at a house tonight for a time of worship and teaching. I think you will like the teacher. He is an old man and his hands are injured now, but his stories have changed us all."

Chapter 40:
Luke's Message

Yael and the old woman walked on the path from the city's outer gates toward Jerusalem's south entrance. The road leading to it was now full of activity, as the Romans had breached the city walls and were now occupying the city. Yael passed many piles of material used to construct the Roman siege engines. In the distance, she stared in wonder at the engineering required for each device to do its job. The main gates were destroyed, and she could hear the sounds of destruction going on as huge thunderous sounds rolled down the hillside as they approached the city walls.

Before they reached the entrance to the old city, they entered a large home on the road that had obviously served as a meeting place in the past. The house was two hundred steps from the entrance to the city, but it was positioned at a low point in the terrain such that none of the city sounds reached it. The Romans, for their part, did not disturb it. They allowed people to come and go, as one of the Roman commanders was himself raised in an Ebreet village and saw no harm in their gatherings, so long as they were peaceful and didn't oppose the Emperor.

The silence was eerie, considering what had happened to one of the greatest cities on earth hours before.

"We are here," she said, obviously happy to be there. Several people came out and greeted her, offering her kisses and blessings. Yael didn't understand all of what they said to each other, but she loved how the old woman introduced her to everyone, calling her a long-lost daughter.

"The synagogue in Thessalonica purchased this building a year ago when Luke heard the Lord tell him the Romans would soon be coming to destroy the Temple. It has been our safe harbor through these many months while the army was preparing. The Romans leave us alone each evening, and we often pray for our brethren who were inside the city walls." Yael was amazed at how happy everyone was, and she was amazed at the variety of people from all the tribes and even some Roman soldiers who came and left the house.

"These are the elders of The Way," she said. The old men welcomed everyone and stopped to wash everyone's feet. Women were also in their midst, singing songs and teaching the words to others as they entered so others could sing along. All in all, roughly a hundred people were present, and twenty of them were introduced to the elders as new to their gathering.

"There he is," said the old woman. An old man whose hands had been damaged was guiding two nurses as they administered aid to the injured and wounded. The old woman pulled Yael by the sleeve towards the old man, whispering into her ear. "That is our teacher. His name is Luke. He is a healer and has been here since the blockade began, healing anyone who asks him during the day and teaching us about the Messiah in the evenings."

Yael watched as the woman began talking to Luke. Luke touched him and hugged her as if she were family. The old woman pointed at Yael and Yael watched as he smiled at her.

"Yael, daughter, come here!" she said. Yael walked over to him and spoke first.

"I am sorry about your hands," she said. He casually shared that he thought that they would heal in time, but he would not be able to heal others effectively while he wore bandages on both of his hands.

"That is why I have these two young disciples helping me with the healing," he said.

The old woman introduced Yael to Luke. "Rabbi Luke, this little one has a story to share with all of us, and I can see already that she will be strong in the faith. Yahweh's hand is on her!"

Luke turned to Yael, lifted his hand, and spoke an ancient Ebreet blessing on her that she hadn't heard since her first years in Bad Safir.

"Thank you, Rabbi," was all she could say.

He laughed.

"You can call me Luke. I was raised in the ways of our people, but I share the message with both Ebreet and Roman. Indeed, there are Romans in this building right now."

Shock came over Yael. This was a Rabbi who had no interest in the privilege associated with the title. In one sense, he was like Mishi, both informal and affectionate with those who needed touch. She already liked him.

"Come by and talk to me tomorrow during the day, as I wish to hear your story. I will be praying to Yeshua tonight for you and asking the Holy Spirit to help your hesitant heart."

Yael looked at him and turned her head to the side. He could tell she was confused. She wondered how it was possible for this man to simultaneously pray to Yeshua and use ancient Ebreet prayers from the Torah. And how could he see that she had a hesitant heart? All things were new and the rules were changing in front of her.

"Thank you, Luke." She could think of nothing else to say.

Luke walked towards a group of eight who had entered ahead of them. A Roman soldier escorted them in full regalia. No one thought anything of the fact that a Roman soldier other than Yael was in the room. The soldier took off his helmet and bent forward. Luke spoke a brief prayer and sprinkled some water on the warrior before he donned his helmet and quickly left.

Yael turned and saw that a woman held a cup of water for her. Yael thanked her and drank deeply. It contained lemon and honey, and it was refreshing.

"The teacher likes you already!" the old woman said as she took the cup back and smiled.

Yael decided to share what was on her mind. "You let a Roman soldier in here?"

"Patma is from Thessalonica and he helped us purchase this building. He is one of us. He is a Centurion, with more than 100 soldiers under his command. He is dear to us all. His commander is from Caesarea and is sympathetic to our cause, as well."

Yael shook her head. "This is incredible. I have no memory of observing such a blend of people in the same room before."

"Yeshua is not only for God's chosen people. He is for all. Come, Little One, let us go to the gathering place. Tonight, you will see our numbers grow. They seem to grow every night."

The two women walked down a long flight of steps into a basement below the home. The basement had been a storage area for wine, dried meats, and cloth, and there were thin tapestries on two of the walls, obviously there to absorb moisture. There was a pair of small windows facing south, allowing sun from the end of the day to light the room, and there were candles and torch holders on each wall. Candles had already been lit, making Yael think that they were going to be there for a while.

That evening, Luke asked those present who were strong enough to tell their stories of life inside the walls for the last three months. A young man came forward and shared his perspective on the atrocities committed when the entrance to the city was closed. While others gasped in disbelief, Yael's mind wandered back to her chance meeting with Mishi. She daydreamed that she was walking the streets with Mishi, looking at how far humanity had fallen. Yael could visualize everything the storyteller said, and Luke allowed him to speak for a few minutes.

As Luke switched to allow a different person to tell a different tale, Yael's mind returned to her brief but intimate time with Mishi, when the two of them had disclosed to each other their greatest secrets and the impact of hiding those sins. It had been one of the most freeing moments of her life, even though she failed to receive the forgiveness bead that she desperately sought. Her mind stayed on the memories of Mishi. She wondered if he was safe. She pondered how he had faired during the Roman assault. She imagined him walking the destroyed Temple grounds, trying to find a way to continue his efforts to teach his boys. She visualized him bringing them into his secret room for the evening, feeding them, and reading to them from the scrolls to help them feel safe. He would probably be a great father one day if he survived this. He talked about his students a lot and she knew he loved those boys.

Her daydream ended as the storytelling ended. Luke announced to everyone that there would be food and wine upstairs as soon as they left. Before he sent them upstairs, however, he made a foreign offer to her.

"If any of you have any unconfessed sin and desire to be free of it, please speak to me as everyone goes up for food. I can provide you with solace."

Luke was missing some critical requirements to forgive her sin. There was no Temple and there were no animals to sacrifice. Yet she had heard similar statements from Barnabas and the old woman, and a pattern was starting to form. These people were Ebreet, and they quoted the sacred scrolls. But they thought differently. They all believed that the Messiah had come. They all believed that sins could be forgiven in a new way through faith in this Messiah and forgiveness of sins. Perhaps there was some credibility to this dead man and His message. Yael decided she needed to take this idea seriously. This teaching was coming to her from too many sources to dismiss.

Yael mustered her courage and walked up to Luke briskly. There was no one in front of her. She decided that she needed to call him Rabbi. That word brought her some comfort.

"Rabbi, I have sins that are weighing on me like nothing has. This old woman assured me that you would understand and have insight to share with me."

With that, she began her tale of fornication with the two different men. She described all that she had felt and all that she had done. She stopped many times to look around and saw that others were on their knees in prayer, all with their eyes closed, including the old woman. None of them were staring at her. Each time she paused in her tale, Luke repeated his message. "Continue your tale until it is done. It is by complete confession that we begin to be healed."

Revealing all things was a new concept for her. She had learned in Correae that secret-keeping was requisite to successful living and she had evidence that failure to keep secrets hurt other people. Yet this teacher was adamant that at the core of all great teachings was full disclosure of sins and faithfulness to the truth.

"Rabbi, all I want is to please Yahweh and to have a husband and children like my sister, Katie. Instead, I have had sex with two men and have no children. If I were to be with a child, it would be a bastard. How can this loving God you speak of understand me? Please tell me, how can that old woman claim that I am strong in my faith?"

Luke opened his arms and embraced her. Between him and the old woman, she felt that she had gained another set of parents. He also began to laugh. She pulled away and looked at his face, wondering how he could laugh after hearing her story.

"I am sorry, Yael. It is not funny that you speak like you do. It is evidence that God is at work. You seek to please Yahweh with the works of your hands, but you see that it shall always be an incomplete work. Fear not, as blessings shall both be poured on you that you do not yet understand. My hands are unable to write, but my intention in coming to Jerusalem was to write the story that I am about to tell you with the help of the brothers and sisters here. However, when I arrived and discovered the blockade, I decided to spend my time healing and teaching those who were in need. Now, your presence has inspired me to share with you. In fact, you are not here for your sins or your cleansing. You are here to record for all of history."

Luke stared at the ground in front of him and mumbled something under his breath. He looked back up and saw Yael and the old woman, who had come over to stand with both of them.

"I have a story for you. It is a tale of two women. One is a girl younger than you who discovers that she is pregnant. However, she has not been with any man; however, she has completed Erusin, which she has done with a man who has committed his life to her. The young man is honorable and knows that it is his right to have her stoned since she is pregnant by another. He could feel free to embark to find a new Erusin. However, he decides to keep the child as his own after choosing to believe his beautiful Erusin's story."

Yael was very surprised by this development. The story was not going as she had expected it to when Luke began.

"The other woman in this story is old. She has been barren. Her husband receives a great honor and is allowed to enter the Holy of

Holies, which is not far from where we stand right now. He experiences God like few have, but he does not respond to God's call. He discovers his wife's pregnancy by way of a messenger angel, but God makes him mute so that he cannot speak of it." Luke stopped his story and addressed Yael. "Yael, you are like the young woman in the story. Her name is Mary and she is uncertain of her role as a mother. God uses us in ways that do not always fall in line with our people's expectations."

How could Luke know how preoccupied she had been with the fear that she would be with child after her fornication? She had not told anyone of these thoughts. It was remarkable, and she was fixated on his story.

"Mary gives birth to the child in Bethlehem, not far from here, and this child is Yeshua, our Messiah. He was born of a virgin, as was foretold. The old woman gives birth to John, who is later called John the Baptist, at which time his father's speech is restored. Yeshua and John the Baptist are related. This is my story. I believe it is time to eat and drink, but in the next few days, we will begin writing this story for others to read."

"I will help you. I am very good with ink and parchment," said Yael. "I am well-schooled and have much practice. I will record your story so long as you continue to tell it."

"Indeed, you shall. Perhaps by writing down this tale for Him, you will feel His love and begin to heal. But you must stop calling me Rabbi. This story is meant for all, not separate for God's chosen. It is for the Gentile as much as it is for you.

"I will," she agreed.

"There is one thing that you must know before we start. You must record each and every word exactly as I say it. I want you to read it back to me, unaltered."

"As you wish," she replied. Yael felt like a new chapter in her life was about to begin, and she hoped it would be a little more pleasant than the previous ones.

Chapter 41:
The Fall of Jerusalem

The noise outside of Mishi's home was deafening. Mishi stepped outside into the morning sun to a unique view of Jerusalem. He had stayed up late with Yael and he must have slept through the early activity. There had been no Romans in the city since the blockade started. Yet this morning, there could be no doubt that the voices Mishi heard were those of Roman soldiers. His heart raced, and he felt adrenaline rushing through his veins.

"Yael! Wake up! Wake up!" he yelled. However, she was not there. Mishi froze, and his mind pieced together what had happened. Was the girl seeking forgiveness of sin, or was she a Roman spy trying to find a way into the city? He had connected with her so strongly. Could she be a spy? He no longer knew what was true.

Mishi panicked and ran out of his apartment and towards the school as fast as he could. There were no guards at the entrance to the Temple's outer courtyards, and he was able to enter without anyone stopping him. As he rounded the last corner before the Temple complex came into full view, he halted as if he had a chain attached to his ankle. He stared straight ahead and despaired. His selfish sense of loss was dwarfed by the greater loss that was occurring in front of him. His worst fears had come to pass.

Mishi watched as one of the pillars holding up the southeast corner of the Temple fell to the ground with a thud that sounded like thunder. In front of the Temple stood two Behemoths, each with a chain attached around their necks, with the other end wrapped around one of the supporting structures that held up the Temple.

The sound of the marble snapping like a piece of dry firewood was unlike anything Mishi had heard.

"They are really doing it. They are tearing down the Temple," he said under his breath. No one in the Ebreet leadership thought that Romans would follow through on their threat and destroy the Temple, as Rome had funded so much of its recent expansion. A mere two marble columns remained from the Temple. The surrounding buildings, including his school, remained intact.

Teams of Romans held spears and surrounded the great beasts, protecting the animals from Ebreet zealots who would not stop in their effort to deter the Romans and the animals from doing their job. Even if a wave of Ebreet marauders attacked a flank, there were three levels of trained and well-fed soldiers between them and the Behemoths. The beasts were covered in thick leather and chainmail to prevent any sword from striking the animal's hide.

Mishi did not know how long he stood there, watching the beasts tear down the Temple structures. He saw the room that held all of his father's greatest works fall to the ground in a fraction of the time it took to create. A Roman patrol squad came to him and spoke loudly enough to snap Mishi out of the trance he was experiencing.

"Do not touch any of the fallen structures. Go outside of the city and get food and water. Change your clothing and clean yourself. Once your strength is restored, come back, and your assets will be restored to you. Come back to fight us, and you and your family will die." The patrol squad repeated that message to each group of people who came to the Temple Mount to see what was happening. Mishi stared at the indifference on the faces of the men who were making the announcement. It added to his shock. He needed some moments to compose himself.

Chapter 42:
Elishar

With the sun beginning to rise, the Roman military leadership stood near the Temple Mount, relishing their success. The timeline of history shows that Titus and his Legions had traveled nearly a month to the city and waited a quarter of a year outside of its walls for this moment. This was their emotional payday.

The excitement associated with the campaign's completion was spoiled by the noise coming from the streets of Jerusalem. Whenever they could congregate, Ebreet, who had the energy to stand, was doing so, and those who could not sit, holding their heads with their hands. All were wailing. All were weak from the months of the starvation blockade, and most were sick from a lack of sanitation. Many had committed atrocities in the last ninety days that even the filthiest of Philistines would not consider. They were both dying and disgusting.

Yet many of them used the last of their strength to impede the Roman warriors from their appointed tasks. Lacking both weapons and the endurance to wield them, the amount of effort the soldiers needed to push away the starving Ebreet was humorous. They were more like mosquitoes than people protecting their heritage.

The Romans followed their plan. The walls were broken at sunrise, and before midday, leadership was standing at the top of the city. Soon, hundreds more Roman soldiers filled the Temple Mount area and one of Rufus' subcommanders called for the Behemoths and their masters to come up. Soon, these enormous creatures were brought up the windy pathway to the top of the mount. It was these animals that would make the impossible relatively simple.

Rufus loved the idea of using the largest beasts of burden in the world to finish the work Vespasian had commanded of them. These Behemoths had bodies larger than the largest elephants. Each one had chains placed around its neck, with the other end attached to the corner supports of the Temple. With a small gesture from the caretakers of these giant yet docile lizards, the animals began to pull.

No chains broke during this, as the Romans had ensured that none of their prized assets were in the vicinity where the falling Temple fragments might land. The caretakers measured sections of chains longer than the tallest trees to assist with the work. With each pull, stones as thick as tree trunks broke like small twigs and roof structures began falling to the ground with thunderous sounds that echoed throughout the city. Bit by bit, the four creatures and their masters reduced the marble that comprised the holy place of all the Ebreet pilgrimages to rubble. The Temple was coming down, and none of the Sadducees sworn to protect the Temple could stop it.

"Not one stone left standing," were Vespasian's words. And, in that regard, the soldiers and the beasts did their jobs.

With the last pull, the corner supports of what the world had called the greatest of the great temples snapped like dry firewood in a late-night campfire. The front group of four stone pillars came off the foundation and fell to the earth, shaking the ground like a small earthquake. The beautifully decorated frieze and its attached roof shattered into hundreds of pieces.

The volume of the cheers from the Roman soldiers was unmatched, for they knew what the collapse of the Temple meant: the siege was over, the Emperor would be pleased, and their return to Roman-populated lands was imminent. Additionally, the bonus promised to each man if they destroyed the Ebreet Temple now became due. That last thud meant a trip home and a big reward were not far away.

Men quickly moved to take bounties from the Temple stores and box them to send home to Vespasian. Some of Rufus' men were not interested in acting like barbarians. They sought to give their leader not merely cheers but intimate words of gratitude and praise. One young soldier who served Rufus spoke of the fight he had seen in the Ebreet. "Sir, they were quite brave despite not having much meat on their bones." Rufus smiled at the young man and gave him fatherly guidance.

"But their faith tumbled, along with their Temple. This Temple had been their most sacred place, a place Rabbis claimed that their Lord occupied. If He was there behind their sacred tapestries, He fled during the night." Rufus said.

After an hour of boxing important items from the temple and allowing his men to loot the rest, Roman engineers began the first phase of rebuilding. The post-victory procedures and protocols were as thoughtful as the pre-battle tactics. The Roman Empire did not grow by destroying the competition and leaving them in an impoverished state. Their formula for success included rebuilding the previously combative states into Roman states, which were useful to both sides, and this process began as soon as possible.

As the first wave of rebuilding engineers arrived, they discussed which parts of the Temple rubble would be removed first and what path they would take as they brought it down the mountain. Huge carts meant to be pulled by the Behemoths would require additional outer walls to be removed, and the men anticipated hauling the first rubble down the mountain no later than mid-morning the following day. Teams were sent out immediately to begin bringing in forage for the animals, and slaves who had been brought in from other campaigns started the task of hauling out dead bodies and emptying the city's sewers for the first time in three months.

Immediately adjacent to the last gateway before the inner city, there was a group of Ebreet who had recently entered the city, arriving minutes after the outer walls were breached. They stood not far away from the Roman leadership. They were behaving most unexpectedly. They were singing a song of salvation and redemption. Rufus looked at them with a curious gaze.

"Where does all this madness come from?" Rufus said aloud in Ebreet so that no one else but them would understand. He sheathed his sword, knowing that he wouldn't need it again. He took off his helmet, bracers, and gauntlets, placing them in his tent. He took a drink of water and grabbed a piece of bread. His day of combat and destruction was over.

However, he kept his focus on the Ebreet, who were singing and dancing. Their denial of the fate of their race mesmerized him. He turned to one of the men under him who was within earshot and yelled. "They are even more ridiculous than the Britons who cheered when we sank the ships that provided their only escape! Could they be so thick as not to know that their faith and their religion are dead?"

He began walking towards the Ebreet, towering over them in size and stature. At that moment, he sensed he looked like his father when he walked into the woods to speak with the Ebreet in Caesarea; he felt like him as well. As he neared the residents of Benjamin, they stopped dancing and huddled together. However, they appeared to be without fear, aware that nothing worse could happen to them. Rufus knew from his father that the onus was on him to initiate a meaningful dialogue. He went to one of the women in the group, the oldest one, and handed her the remainder of his loaf of bread and his skin of water. She bowed but said nothing. Speaking softly, in perfect Ebreet, he said, "What do you know that I do not?"

The Ebreet woman spoke up, looking directly at him as she did so.

"Did not He say, 'One of your enemies will come seeking knowledge with sincerity in his heart and sweetness on his tongue'? Is this man the one He spoke of?'

"The one who spoke of?" Rufus asked.

"Yeshua," she said.

Rufus paused. These Ebreet were of the same fabric as Gesher. He had grown fond of Gesher and her son, and he had visited her many times over the last few months. He had heard her speak of a risen Messiah repeatedly and felt he was having another conversation with her.

"There have been many who claim to be the Messiah. Which Messiah claims to know my actions?"

One Ebreet man was not intimidated by his tone or choice of words. He stood up and approached Rufus.

"Our Yeshua told of many things before He suffered, died on the cross, and rose again in fulfillment of the scriptures. I was too young to have spoken to Him or heard Him myself, so I am not an eyewitness. However, I have heard both our brothers Matthew and Luke speak of their times in His presence. Even to this day, tales of His teachings are spoken of amongst some of the Sadducees."

Another member of the group added to the conversation.

"Matthew said that when Yeshua left the Temple and was going away, He said, 'You see all these, do you not? Truly, I say to you, there shall not be left here one stone upon another that will not be thrown down.' And this has come to pass today. Your men saw Yeshua's prophecy come true this very day!" He, too, had a countenance like Gesher's, and Rufus felt paralyzed. He continued to engage them as he wanted to know more.

The woman who had taken the bread from him spoke again.

"We heard you talking to the others. We do not celebrate the fall of the Temple. Indeed, it is an awful thing for our people to lose it. But you do not understand. We are celebrating the truth that our Messiah proved that He was who He said He was."

Rufus processed what the woman said while he continued listening, as his father would. He looked at the members of this group. They all appeared to believe what they were saying.

"You say that I do not understand? Then teach me." He remained calm and resisted his desire for anger. Anger never achieved the desired result during times of judgment.

"Yeshua knew that many would hear and not believe. Even His own did not believe the story that He would die and come back to life. That is why He visited many of us in the weeks after His crucifixion, burial, and resurrection. Those visits helped our members, who had little faith, to believe in Him during the years after He ascended into heaven. With the fall of this Temple, this generation has proof that He is true and keeps His promises. They need not trust our word any longer. They can see for themselves that Yeshua is alive and His words are true."

Rufus was impressed. This logic made sense, but it was merely a story, not different from the Odyssey or the Iliad.

The eldest man continued. "You asked me early of other Messiahs who have come and gone. Yes, there have been many, but most of them did not keep the promises that they made while they were on earth. Many spoke of the immediate end of the Emperor's rule. They spoke of an escape from tyranny. Many spoke of God returning to rule and reign in this world soon. Yeshua spoke of events to come before such a Heaven appears on earth and this day, more than thirty years after his death, a promise told to many of His disciples has come true!"

Rufus wanted to hear more of this man who had prophesized what the Emperor would ask him to do. However, a younger, even more frail man in the group interrupted. He bore a look of fear on his face, but he was bold.

"Are we to be made into slaves now?

Rufus chuckled and took a moment to respond. He was a Roman leader and this one, Ebreet, was expecting judgment more than understanding.

"Fair question. The stronger among you will be taken to Rome, and the weaker will be allowed to stay and restore anything they like, so long as it does not oppose the Emperor or his rule. Based on what I see here, you all will be allowed to stay in Jerusalem and be a part of the rebuilding once your strength has returned."

None of them spoke, but all bowed their heads. Rufus had seen this before when his father passed judgment on affairs brought to him. It was a sign of respect and showed that they subordinated themselves willingly to his authority. To them, he was now their magistrate.

During this brief interchange, the bread that Rufus had given the woman had been distributed and eaten. The water was also gone. She stepped forward and returned the skin to Rufus. She was frail. As Rufus reached to take the skin from her, she spoke words that impacted him even more than the words of the Ebreet men.

"Roman, I can see that you are not our enemy. Yeshua has already captured your heart. My name is Elishar, and I think we shall meet again." Rufus' teeth clenched as emotion roared inside him. How could such a pawn of a person have such insight into his heart?

Rufus took a handful of gold and silver coins and gave them to her. "Leave the Temple courts and all this rubble. Go and replenish your supplies from the merchants outside the city walls before they run out. And, get something to eat. There is a lot of food at a house outside of the city walls occupied by people from Thessalonica. Tell them I sent you."

When they left, Rufus stood there, playing with his mustache. He turned to his men and said, "Buy a goat and give it to the cooking century. Tell them to prepare a meal for us. And send for the scribe. I need to send a message to my father, and I need it to go out tonight."

Chapter 43:
A Message Home

Dear Father,

Greetings to you and all of our family from what used to be the great city of Jerusalem. I have done our Emperor's bidding, and I shall soon inform him that I am finished with my military service. I am resigning tomorrow.

I want to let you know that I am staying and intend to settle in a valley next to Jerusalem. I have all the wealth that I need and wish no more for combat. It is now time for me to find a wife and begin a new life outside of the military. I have met a woman who lost her husband and has a small child. She can cut to my soul like you can. After speaking with an old woman, I realized that I wanted her as my wife. I look forward to introducing her. She already knows of you. I will pursue her and take her as my own.

I have met Yeshua followers here, and they are much like the ones you live near. They have said things to me that I wish to discuss with you. If possible, please travel to Jerusalem upon receipt of this letter. I have not yet told Titus of my choice to leave the military and retire. I have a heavy weight on my heart, as I think he will be hurt.

I greatly miss you and love you, mother and sister, greatly. I look forward to seeing you soon.

When you arrive outside the city walls, ask for me or a woman called Elishar. And if you happen to meet Gesher, please be as kind and gracious as you usually are. She is the one I hope will accept my marriage proposal. There is no one in the world like her, and it is because of her that I wish to quit this madness and be a father to her young boy and be her husband. I never expected to find a woman as intelligent, well-spoken, and as beautiful as she is. I don't care that she has a child. I will raise it as your grandson and my son. She humbles me and makes me into a better man. You have told me a hundred times that I can have any woman I want. I will never find a better woman than Gesher. I did not know until today that I have long since fallen in love with her, and I look forward to discarding this uniform and placing a ring on her finger in the ways of these people.

I will meet you outside the city walls.

Your son,
Rufus

Chapter 44:
Mishi meets Rufus

Mishi remained paralyzed as he stared at the temple and thought about Yael. He didn't know where she had gone or why she left in such haste. He tried to replay his conversation with her. He could not forget her desperation to be free from the consequences of her sin, and her convictions were pure and true. His heart told him that she must have left the city back through the tunnel to get an animal to sacrifice, but she never returned. He looked up at the fallen Temple. The remains of the altar that he used were already gone. Even if she came back now, he could not follow the Lord's commands and take her through the atonement ceremony. The small pedestal where he kept the heads that she wanted was also gone. Even if she did come back, he had nothing for her. And that made his heart ache.

He was interrupted by more commotion on the Temple Mount. A group of soldiers was pushing a cart of bread, giving quarter loaves to anyone who asked for them. Mishi shook his head in disbelief as he watched the Roman soldiers distribute free bread to the people they had been starving for the past 142 days.

From behind, he heard someone speaking to him in common Greek. "Are you a Rabbi?"

Mishi turned his head and saw a group of four soldiers walking towards him. Cultural awareness was his greatest strength. In his moment of grief, he instinctively did what he always did: he spoke the other party's language. "Yes, I am. I am the leader of the Temple school, responsible for education." He spoke in the most common form of Greek so the greatest number of people could understand him.

The one in charge hesitated and asked him another question.

"What languages do you speak? Can you also read and write?"

Mishi answered the questions without pride or eye contact. He knew that the wrong words could be fatal.

The men turned towards each other and spoke in a slang version of Greek that Mishi had heard many times before. Mishi understood everything that they said. "The Legate told us to take the ones who are not starving and bring them to the labor camp. This one, though, would be incorrectly used as a laborer. Let's take him directly to the Legate instead."

Mishi felt indignant and wanted to resist, but as he glanced at the building that he had dedicated his life to serving, he felt hopeless. He had nothing now to live for. He could hope that his family was safe. He went limp as two of the men grabbed his arms and began pulling him towards an area on the other side of the Temple Mount where Temple administration had previously resided, which was now being used by the heads of the four Legions present in the city. He was dropped off in front of the Roman leader. The man was large in stature, dark-skinned, and physically well-defined. The leader grabbed a chair and set it in front of him.

"Sit in this chair. I wish to talk to you, please," His Ebreet language skills were perfect and he had a northern Judah accent. He was addressing Mishi using honorable forms of the language, as well. He spoke as he took off his sword belt and sat in an adjacent chair. "Rabbi, your Temple is no more. This time, though, you will not be hauled off to Babylon. You will be going to Rome." With as much courage as Mishi had left, he closed his eyes and allowed tears to flow down his face. He took a deep breath, speaking the name "Yahweh" and allowed his breath out.

"Let every breath praise the Lord," he thought. He opened his eyes and allowed his cultural talent to take over.

"Soldier, you are well-read in the history of our people, I see," Mishi responded. He had nothing left to lose by calling them "our people." If this man knew so much of their language, perhaps a part of the heart of his people remained inside of the man.

"Can I ask who taught you our language? You have an accent that is from the North."

Rufus knew that anything he could do to help him extract information right now would be much easier than in a few days when the indignance of the Ebreet would return as their bellies filled. He took off his helmet and placed a Yamika on his head.

"Wow," Mishi said. Mishi could tell it wasn't merely the language that this man knew. But he couldn't place a thought as to why he might be doing this.

"Rabbi, my father is my teacher. He is a Roman Centurion in Caesarea, a small city near—"

"Yes, I know where it is," Mishi interrupted.

Rufus saw that this man was full of vigor. But he needed to understand his situation fully. Hopefully, Rufus wouldn't have to kill him.

"Young Rabbi, you would be wise to allow me to speak and not interrupt me. You need not fear for your life, though. I have no intention of hurting you, and I have given those instructions to my men. You need only engage me and help me understand what has happened here."

Mishi could see that this man was trained like the other ones he had known growing up near the Temple Mount. He didn't want any problems. He was doing his job. He made Mishi feel a bit safe, and he could see that this man had control of his emotions.

"I am sorry about that," Mishi said.

Mishi knew his life was already forfeit and his secrets were exposed. There was no value in withholding any information from this man.

"Start at the beginning. Tell me what you know." Rufus poured a large cup of wine for each of them and handed one to Mishi.

"I don't drink wine," Mishi said as he passed on the offer. Rufus threw it on the ground and pointed to the picture of water and a different cup.

"Suit yourself. There is water there and I haven't touched it. I am assuming you won't touch it because it says not to drink from the hands of your enemy in the scrolls of Leviticus?"

"That is correct!" said Mishi. Rufus laughed and placed his hand on Mishi's shoulder.

"Ah, a man of integrity," the large Roman said.

"Oh, not really," said Mishi, and he began to tell Rufus his story. He told of the death of his Rabbi and how he inherited the responsibilities of running the school just a few months ago. He told him of his family's return to their hometown and how he had originally planned on returning himself, but he could not abandon the calling of his Rabbi and leave the students when they needed him the most.

"Do you think your students need you now?" Rufus asked, observing how the man would respond to a challenge of his self-worth.

"Good question. No, they don't need me. They need godly leadership who will remind them of their people's great history of overcoming occupation, slavery, and adversity. Everyone else had abandoned them. I chose not to. That is what they need."

Rufus didn't know if this man was sincere or not, and he didn't know if he believed his own words. But he was smart, well-studied, and not scared to challenge him with his intellect. And he liked his courage. For that reason, Rufus liked him.

"Tell me how all Roman military was thrown out of the city," Rufus asked. Mishi told him of the Pharisee and Sadducee council that had voted to remove all Roman citizens and soldiers from the city soon after he returned from his impromptu trip to Hebron with his father.

"And how did you vote?" asked Rufus.

"I chose not to cast a vote. These were the affairs of men, not of either the schools or of God. They didn't concern me. I am the leader of a school, not of a sect of man."

Rufus paused. "I like you," he said, pointed at him, and took a deep draught of wine.

"Let me rephrase the question. How would you have voted if you had attended the council?"

"Hm.. I would not have voted to evict the Romans. You don't know this, and I don't know why you will believe me, but I had many Roman friends. Many of them attended my Bar Mitzvah, and I worked for them during my younger days as a scribe, helping them write letters home to their families. You are a soldier like them. You don't want to be a part of this, but it is your duty."

Rufus was set back. This young man had flipped the question back onto him and he was forced to look inside of himself as Keshar had done a few months earlier. That was why he told his father that he wanted to marry her.

Rufus took another drink of wine as he formulated his response.

"Yes, they were doing what people like me told them to do. Had they not complied, they would have been killed, as you can imagine." Rufus stared at the ground for a long pause before he looked up at Mishi.

"I have an offer for you that will suit you much better than sending you back to Rome."

Rufus poured another cup of wine and set it down.

"You shall call me by my given name, Rufus. I have met people and learned things over these last few months, and I need someone from around here to help me separate facts and gather information from witnesses to the events that everyone is talking about. I need someone who is trusted by people here to work with me, so I am picking you to be the Hand of the Legate."

Mishi had heard of such a title. It was usually given to a Roman soldier who had demonstrated great promise and interest in advancement. The Pharisees also had something similar. This person spoke on behalf of the person they served and could bind and commit all who served under the Legate as if he were the Legate. The title was typically temporary, but it came with great power. Rufus knew he was taking a gamble, but Gesher's words cut him like a knife each time he thought about them. He was wagering that this young Rabbi's skills with people would help him decide if Gesher's claims were true.

"Don't let this get to your head. You will not be like Joseph in Egypt."

Mishi laughed and loved that Rufus knew so much of his people's history.

"You will not be a traditional Hand. You will have no authority. You may be called Rabbi if that pleases you, but you may not tell people that you are my Hand, for that would alter people's opinion of you. For now, you must say that you are working on a special fact-finding project for me and that I am paying you a fair wage for your effort." Rufus took another sip of wine and set down the cup. That would be the last one for him today. "For now, you will restore your strength and eat and sleep in my tent. You shall be quite busy tomorrow. You are in shock, and you need food and rest."

"Legate, sir, I have a question for you on a small matter."

"Go ahead, but you only need to call me Rufus. All of my men do, and if you are going to be one of my men, you will address me in the same way."

"Did you happen to see or capture a young woman coming out of caves directly below this area?"

"We saw a brief flash of light coming from the side of the hill on which this Temple is built. We went to investigate it, but there was no young woman there. We did find an entrance to a cave that led us up to this Temple from below."

"Is that how you invaded the city?" The fear in his voice was noticeable.

"No, we began our military assault on the entrance gates and started bringing the Behemoths up the road. We decided that the starvation had done its job, and we were correct. Resistance was quite limited."

"Oh," said Mishi, with a sense of relief. The destruction of Jerusalem was neither his fault nor the girl's. He thanked Yahweh. "I will take you up on your offer of food and rest now."

Rufus got up, took off his yarmulka, and put his helmet and sword back on. He set his yamika on the table and quickly glanced at Mishi as he left. He knew that there was no reason to tell Ebreet that the discovery of the cave was what triggered Titus to initiate the final assault. He needed to keep that event secret from Mishi if he wanted to use him as a helper. Otherwise, he would live a life of shame for his past mistakes. He needed to remind Titus not to bring the discovery of the light in the tunnel up in conversation while talking to this young Rabbi. It would interfere with his intentions for him.

Perhaps one day, he would tell him. But that day was not today.

Rufus liked this Rabbi. He seemed to have a passion that didn't involve advancement or wealth, and that was novel. He wondered if some great good would come of the destruction of this Temple yet.

Chapter 45: Resignation

Rufus had not slept well the previous night. He knew that Titus would consider what he was about to do as betrayal, but he also knew that Titus was a loving and passionate man. He thought about writing his resignation letter, but that would not help him or Titus. He would do it in private with the man he loved like a brother.

He walked into the leadership meeting before sunrise that morning with Mishi directly behind him. Most of the men present were taller than Mishi, and they looked strong enough to carry a cow. They stopped speaking when one from the group stepped to the front of the table and struck it with the metal on the hilt of his sword.

Titus was the commander of the assault and he had performed his primary purpose. In the eyes of the Emperor, the hard part had passed. The Temple was destroyed, and the city of Jerusalem was again under Roman authority.

"Men, let us begin! Now comes the tedious work of rebuilding infrastructure and the restoration of the flow of Roman taxes." His authority was obvious. He hadn't needed to hit the table.

Mishi was awestruck by this man. He knew what those who served him wanted and he was ready to give it to them for being loyal to his cause. How he wished the leadership within the Pharisees had shown this instinct.

Titus was trained to apply the experience of Rome before, during, and after the battle. Roman leadership had learned that thoughtful clean-up and restoration after conquest would lead to greater compliance with Roman authority. Free handouts and promises of freedom engaged the incumbents for a limited time. New city centers, roads, clean drinking water, and employment for the masses did more to make the losers into productive parts of the empire than any other tactic.

For Titus' four legions, that meant that the fields outside Jerusalem occupied by his men these last three months would need to be scourged and cleaned before the Ebreet could plant crops or hold ceremonies on those hillsides. They would also have to remove the rubble that was now the Temple and begin reparations for what would occupy that place in the future. The act of removing dead bodies and animals of war was easy. It was the task of getting the Ebreet to use this place of great religious value to them concerned Titus. It was, in his mind, like asking a man to keep his wife after she had been raped.

The immediate need, however, was to sort out who among his leadership would volunteer to stay behind and fix that which they had broken. As was Roman policy, a small contingent of Roman troops would be left behind with the power to tax and oversee the implementation of Roman law. Fortunately for Titus, he had led meetings like this after the battles in Gaul and Britannia. Although Jerusalem was the largest city the Roman army had taken, and the Ebreet land was the most occupied land he had invaded, the protocol would not change. Titus gathered his Legions and started with an open invitation.

"Men, you have done what is asked of you and your choices now are perhaps more difficult than the ones you made these last months on the battlefield. You have earned the right to be one of those who stay here for a two-year term or return to Rome for your next assignment. Those who stay will be responsible for tax collection and local implementation of the Emperor's rule. They will have the best troops and be well-funded for their affairs. They will have all the slaves and resources that this locale can offer, and this land is agriculturally fertile. They will have no expenses while here, and all their wages will accrue in Roman awaiting their return."

He looked around the room at each man, ensuring that they understood what he said. This was a great gift for any man, let alone a soldier. He knew, though, that many men would not use this gift appropriately, as they would take whores and drink themselves to oblivion for two years. This was enjoyable, of course, but its time would be short-lived. By the end of two years, they would miss their wives and children. And many of them would be too damaged to be useful to the empire any more.

"Since this was a major victory with widespread implications for the entire Empire, the Emperor authorized me to have your family and children sent here to live with you during your governorship."

He again paused to see how the surprise of this offer would excite the men.

"He will also allow your best slaves to come to Jerusalem if you like, and he will pay for all costs associated with maintaining your estates back home while you are here."

Although he didn't say that the Emperor had authorized this, he knew that the sale of the golden cherubim they found in the temple would pay for all of that cost and more. From experience, he knew that the Emperor would hold him accountable if the men left behind were unable to tax and govern after the battle ended. These were his best, and he needed some of these men to stay.

"I ask you, who will stay in this land and take this offer? Speak!"

Without hesitation, Curtius, the Legate of the fourth Legion, spoke. "I would have stayed without these offers. The resources here are greater than the ones available in the mountains of Southern Gaul. I will stay, eat, become fat, and father many children. Why wouldn't I?"

Some men cheered, and Titus lifted his wine cup.

"To Curtius!"

As soon as the cheering stopped, two more men spoke up, and they accepted the offer as well.

"To Justus and to Dida!"

The men disbursed and Titus was grateful that he had three very good men who would be left behind to ensure that operations were successful. Rufus remained back after they left and approached his lifelong friend.

"I will stay as well," he said.

Titus was not expecting this from his best friend. He put his hand on his best friend's shoulder and closed his eyes, allowing tears to fall before speaking.

"Even the man I love the most in this entire world is staying behind! What can I say?" Titus forced himself to smile, but Rufus knew him well. Titus cried. So did Rufus. The very least he could do for his best friend was to go first. Rufus hugged his dear friend and leader and allowed himself a deep, mournful cry. Titus joined him, and the two men held each other like lovers.

Mishi stood motionless, watching the event unfold as if it were a play in an amphitheater, and he was the only person in attendance. Titus didn't know Mishi and had assumed he was a newly acquired slave.

"Let us go find a pitcher of ale in the next village and talk," Rufus said.

Titus, however, looked dismayed and was not yet done crying. He remained in a state of shock.

"My heart aches, and I must know why you are staying. My responsibilities here are great, and I can't go to the next village and drink ale with you. The armies require my presence. Yet, to me, you are more important than all of these men. Let me send for a bottle of wine and we can talk."

"Agreed. Let's eat dinner together," Rufus replied.

"And who is this?" Titus asked of Mishi.

"He is part of the reason I am staying behind, or at least he is going to help me figure something out."

Titus acknowledged Mishi and quickly left to attend to the people who were lined up outside and looking for guidance as to what to do next. Rufus and Mishi were alone in Titus' tent.

"Take a seat, Rabbi. I have some stories to tell you about, and I need a few things from you as part of our new arrangement. Let me start with the one thing and the one person that has been on my mind for a couple of months now. I met a woman named Gesher, and she told me this story."

Chapter 46:
Bellai

Mishi woke up in the morning and stared at the ceiling. When he was a boy, the sounds he heard were his father and others like his father building the Temple Mount into something grand. His father was building history. Two mornings ago, he heard the sounds of that history being torn down. He heard sounds of that history being placed on large carts and taken out of the city to be dropped off outside the city walls for some future use.

Yet, either way, history was happening. Rufus was a part of that history and he was his hand. He knew that the task he had been given carried more responsibility than any he would receive from the High Priest or any other Rabbi. He would rather be teaching young boys all about the Torah, but this task somehow seemed bigger.

"Rabbi, I need you to investigate and find evidence, if any exists, about this Messiah. Leave no stone unturned," Rufus told him.

"You mean as you did with my Temple!" was the retort Mishi wanted to use. He didn't say it in the moment, but he spoke it out loud now that Rufus wasn't here.

"I am sorry about your Temple," said Rufus. Mishi had no idea he walked in. Mishi looked at him and chuckled. He decided to let the truth lead his response.

"I was thinking about history. The Temple is a part of my people's proud past, but the building is gone. I am still hurt and a bit angry," Mishi said.

"Do you remain convinced that you don't want any wine?" Rufus asked. Mishi needed a joke to laugh and Rufus delivered.

Rufus was his master now and Mishi had no idea what expectations to have. The previous night, he watched two of the most powerful men in the world grieve together. He was told he was the hand of the Legate and could now command soldiers. As a young boy, he dreamed of doing that when he saw them striking someone. Now, that didn't seem very important.

He knew the facts of slavery within the Roman Empire. Somewhere around one-quarter of all people living in Roman-occupied lands were slaves. Sometimes, even slaves had slaves. There was no court for mistreated slaves. All Ebreet slaves were stripped of any rights they had to worship and practice their faith without permission from Roman authority.

Rufus told him that he didn't have any restrictions. Mishi knew what those restrictions were. Slaves could eat meals once all Roman citizens and non-slaves had eaten. Slaves had access to water at the start and the end of each day, and bathing was allowed with permission only. Slaves received new clothing approximately once every year, and a pair of sandals was expected to last two full years, regardless of material quality or workmanship.

"Take whatever you need from the quartermaster at any time. Here," Rufus said, placing a pin on the outer cloak of Mishi's garment.

"This lets everyone know you work directly for me. You are basically a Roman prince, and you can do whatever you want. Just get me stories from witnesses. I want information," Rufus said.

"Take today to walk around Jerusalem and listen to people. See things. Go places. Let's start with that. Let's have dinner together and you can tell me what you learned," said Rufus. The Roman put on his helmet, turned, and left the tent where Mishi had slept.

"Rufus, wait!" Mishi said. Rufus poked his head back in the tent.

"Yes, Your Grace," Rufus said in jest.

Mishi paused. He wanted to ask Rufus to tell his men to look for a beautiful Ebreet woman who might disclose that she was the one in the secret tunnel. If they found her, he wanted them to send word to him so he could find her.

"Never mind," Mishi said instead. Rufus abruptly turned and left. He feared that Yael was probably gone, if not dead.

Mishi ate a full breakfast and even had two cups of tea. He bathed and did as instructed, spending the day walking around fallen Jerusalem. At first, he watched the other slaves labor to remove the rubble and bring in supplies that would be used in the reconstruction of the city to Roman specifications. He seldom spoke and he pondered running away through the tunnel under the city that Yael had told him of. But he didn't know what he would do once he left, for once he became a slave, the act of escape and being caught meant eventual death in a most painful manner. And, he surmised that he had it better than anyone else in the city right now. He watched Roman soldiers clean out the city restrooms and make them nearly spotless, and he was fascinated by how disciplined they were. Ebreet workers would always complain about the restrooms, but the Romans didn't. They sanitized them better than any Ebreet worker had, and they smelled fresh for the first time in Mishi's memory. At dinner, Rufus listened without interruption, and Mishi told him stories of what he heard. Mishi could tell that the warrior was thinking about everything he said, and Mishi could see his mind occasionally onto something else.

On day two, Rufus gave him a new directive.

"Here is what I want you to do. Approach people and ask them to tell stories of the one they think was the Messiah and record what you hear and recount it to me. Give me what they say, word for word. Don't change it to fit some other narrative. I want real words from real people." Mishi nodded and acknowledged Rufus. In fact, he even smiled, as he liked the man's commitment to evidence. However, the request begged for an answer to a question.

"Why this man first?" he asked. Mishi stood captivated as he awaited the answer.

"You and I both know that there have been tales of many Messiahs. I think one of them was probably the real one. I want to eyewitness accounts of these stories. And everyone seems to trust you. They trust you more than they trust me." He put his hand on Mishi's shoulders and smiled. Mishi could see that he was sincere and insightful. Mishi knew this man was more than another Roman. He was different, somehow.

Mishi had never interacted with Romans at this level of authority and he asked a couple of process-related questions. He had no intentions of getting involved in skirmishes or participating in another man's death. Mishi was respectful and concerned that he didn't know if he dared to participate in atrocities that Rome was famous for. Rufus assured him that no one had any such intentions and that he would support him in walking away from anything that he hated while he walked the streets and listened to stories. Mishi left there, full of confidence in his new freedom and a desire to give Rufus what he wanted. In fact, it actually sounded like it might be fun.

Starting that first afternoon, Mishi found many groups of people, both inside and outside the city, who claimed to be part of The Way of Yeshua. As he asked them questions about what proof they had that their Messiah was the real Messiah, one answer kept emerging. Yeshua foretold of the destruction of the Temple. Mishi recorded their statements exactly as they said them, without judgment. He would sometimes make small noises to himself as he put down their exact words, and they would quote the Torah to him in their answer, sometimes getting some of the details wrong.

Above all, he was intrigued that each telling of this prediction was nearly identical. Crowds of Syrians, as well as Ebreet from as far away as Simeon to the south and Asher to the North, all said the same thing. The temple would be destroyed and not one stone would be left on top of another. Every storyteller used the same grammar and the same words. Some, however, did not reference the Torah as their source. Many groups referenced a dead disciple of Yeshua named Matthew, who spoke to many crowds on this topic long before Mishi was born. Others said that they were told this by a physician named Luke. One group said that Luke was nearby, preaching this gospel to believers right outside the city walls. Mishi circled the point that Luke was nearby each time he heard it, as he knew that Rufus would be very interested in learning it.

Still, others claimed that the Roman citizen who used to be named Saul and was now called Paul had told them. They had also heard that his body was in Rome and he had long since died. Regardless, the story was the same, even though the teller was different.

"The Messiah came to save us from our sins, not from Rome."

Mishi tried to be stoic when he heard and recorded these thoughts. However, he couldn't. Each time he heard it, his mind returned to the words of Barnabas. He couldn't deny that an old Rabbi, raised much like he was raised, also believed this story.

"So, what did you learn?" Rufus asked him at the end of the day as dinner was being served.

"Well, your future wife Gesher must have talked to some of the same people I have. I have five instances where the story she told you matched what I heard. Some were Egyptians. Two were from Asher to the North, where you are from. Here. I wrote it all down," Mishi gave him his notes and Rufus read them while he ate.

"So, they agree that Temple's purpose had been served and was no longer needed." The two of them looked at each other as Rufus handed Mishi back his notes. Mishi, though, would not agree with that conclusion.

"And, they all say that Yeshua was now the sacrifice needed to atone for sins, and your people no longer needed to kill animals to make things right with God," Rufus added.

"That is what I heard," Mishi said. Rufus took a deep breath and looked at the ceiling of their tent before responding.

"Rabbi, I have decided to compensate you at one-and-a-half times the rate that you were paid when you worked as the Headmaster."

Without thinking, Mishi blurted out, "What kind of system is this? You are paying me more than my people and the men who have worked for you for ten years!"

"You aren't a slave. I don't know how you would think that. You know how I operate. You do not have to perform manual tasks. You don't have to fill my glass, wash my clothes, or bring items to me. I need you to do my bidding and tell me what you find." Mishi nodded and thanked him. Rufus quickly had a scribe write a note authorizing Mishi's salary to the accountants and he told him he could get his first month's wages in the morning.

"Tell me stories about these Simeonites. You spoke earlier of a group who calls themselves The Way, correct?"

Mishi told the stories without any filter on his words, not hiding his disbelief at what he heard. Mishi had already had experiences with Essenes and knew to be cautious of people with religious zeal.

"I met a husband and wife from Greece, and they invited us to come and meet them. They repeated the same thing. This Messiah came to save them from their sins and the falling of this temple happened over thirty years after that prophecy was first written down. As the number of people I questioned expanded, I found that there were many people, including people new to the city, who gathered every day. This isn't a story from the past that died in the past, Rufus. This is a growing story. More people believe it every day."

Rufus took a deep breath. He had served as a magistrate many times, and he knew that the power of evidence was paramount in decision-making. There was no substitute for eyewitnesses who corroborated a story.

"You are quite good at getting people to tell you their stories. What were you going to do with your life before we arrived?" Rufus asked.

"My parents and I planned that I would train here, then go serve back in our home village when my training was complete." Rufus looked up to the sides of the tent and spoke.

"My father used to say that Yahweh can use anything for good. This is as good of a time as any to say this, but my father also talked about Yeshua being the pathway to true forgiveness of sins."

"Really?" said Mishi. He could not believe that a centurion from Caesarea could also believe in a Messiah who was not the Emperor himself. That is blasphemy, and the punishment for it is death. It was another puzzle that Mishi could not solve.

Over the next few days, latrine cleaners, leather workers, and butchers all had their words relayed to one of the most powerful men in the Roman military. And the pattern was the same. Rufus, though, would not stop. He also told Mishi to talk to women and other slaves. Rufus authorized Mishi to take a slave with him, and he carried bread, fresh hummus, and skins of water. He would offer them to anyone who would tell their stories. By the end of the fourth day, Mishi's hand was tired from all the transcription. As they gathered for dinner again, there was a silver scroll casing on the table.

"What is that?" Mishi asked.

"I cannot have you do the work that I have commanded of you under the auspices of slavery. I can't do it, even if I pay you a salary. It is neither appropriate nor moral. I know you have a perception of the morality of Roman leadership and that changing this perception will require action on my part. Since you and I are obviously changing your opinion on many things in your life, I wish to add to the list."

Rufus handed him the scroll and its case and shook Mishi's hand as if he were a Roman military leader. He looked him in the eye and said, "I hope to see you again tomorrow." Rufus turned and quickly left.

Mishi opened the scroll. It was a short decree written in Rufus' hand. In the final sentence, it declared that he was free and should be extended the rights and liberties of a Roman citizen. Mishi stopped breathing. As a Rabbi, he enjoyed great power and authority within the community of faith. However, with these words and the gift of Roman citizenship, he now had even greater power. This was a gift that he could neither earn nor repay. It reminded him of some of the stories that he was hearing from The Way, who claimed freedom by following Yeshua and His gift of forgiveness of sins. He could now travel home and to the sea, and he could find work as a teacher in any synagogue or school in the empire.

There was more. The decree stated that for some time, Mishi would work for the Roman leadership on a special mission and would have any question he asked answered immediately. He was to continue receiving his same compensation, as well as be given a camel, oxen, and a cart from the city treasury to travel and conduct his research. He was no longer part of Rufus' personal property. Before he could finish asking himself how this had happened, he recalled the last words of his conversation with Rufus the previous night.

"Rabbi, prior to our presence in this city, what was your life goal?"

Mishi had told him of his family's journey to Jerusalem, of the work his parents did, his admission into Temple school, and his rapid matriculation. He also told him of his call to disciple under the High Priest and his choice to flee the city. He ended by telling him that the hope that kept him willing to serve with an open heart was Rufus' fair treatment of him and the joy he would feel if he could return to his childhood home, marry, and build a synagogue and school. After he had finished this tale, Rufus said, "You must return to this work one day, Rabbi. For now, though, it is time to rest." Obviously, Rufus had not retired that night. Instead, he had gone to his private quarters and recorded this decree.

Once the shock had worn off and Mishi had read the decree several times, he stepped outside in the open air near the Roman military encampment and shook his head in disbelief. The moon was full and the temperature had already dropped. He felt a happiness that had not been present in his heart for a long time and, for the first time since the blockade had started, he slept through the night without interruption.

When he woke up, he lay in his warm bed, thinking. It was true that he had thought that Rufus was insincere. That was another misjudgment on his part. This Roman was different than the others. It was almost as if he wasn't a Roman. Rufus was experiencing some moral conflict that Mishi wasn't able to understand.

After getting up and putting on his rabbinical robes, Mishi took a breath and stepped outside. He began walking down the hill, where he could find members of The Way beginning their day. He passed a tailor and stopped. He was now eligible to wear the cloak and sash of a Roman citizen. He paused and contemplated what that meant.

Should he get what is now rightfully and legally his? One day that might make sense, but not today. For now, he would continue his work to find the truth. His slave approached him, already carrying a basket of bread and fish. The power of the gift he had been given overtook him. "Sit and eat," he commanded the slave, whose name he had not yet learned. The man set the basket down and began eating vigorously. The man had obviously not been stealing and eating when Mishi wasn't looking.

"Thank you, kind Rabbi," he said. His sincerity was obvious, and it moved Mishi. He wanted to get to know this man.

"What is your name?" Mishi asked.

"Bellai, from Northern Judah," he said as he finished his first piece of fish and started on his second.

Over the next five minutes, Mishi discovered that Bellai was also a follower of The Way.

"Bellai, my former master, asked me to find gatherings of the followers of The Way so that he and I could go together to investigate for ourselves the credibility of our claims."

Bellai stopped chewing and looked Mishi directly in the eyes. "We have an open gathering in the basement of a building not even five hundred paces down the hill on the Western side. It was purchased for us by the church in Thessalonica. We gather there to hear our teacher, eat a meal, and experience the power that Yeshua left for us. You are invited to join us!"

Mishi didn't know what he meant by "power Yeshua left for us," but it didn't matter. Bellai continued.

"We start before sundown and go until late in the evening. There is no city gate anymore, so we can stay as late as we would like. And we do!"

Chapter 47: Investigating The Way

While Mishi waited for Rufus to return late that afternoon for their debriefing, he stepped outside their meeting spot near the ruins of the Temple and stared at what used to be his home. "Life is new now," he said to himself, pondering what had happened to him and his faith. All the larger pieces of marble were gone, and the sandstone subflooring was being repurposed. The dead horse was gone, and seeing that the open stairs were visible, he remembered Yael.

"I wonder what she is doing now?" he wondered. Mishi had fond memories of her. He admitted that he liked her and she certainly was beautiful. He thought about how much courage it must have taken her to come to Jerusalem and leave again so quickly once she learned that there were no animals to sacrifice. And she was easy to talk to. His thoughts made him laugh out loud.

"I wonder if she found members of the Way like I have?" he said. The idea of an alternative to the sacrifice of animal life at the temple would be very attractive to a girl with her conviction, he thought.

Mishi's thoughts shifted and he formulated a new idea. In the cooler evening air, it dawned upon him that much of Ebreet history had not included a working Temple. He began listing stories of prophets who had had no experience with this Temple. He noted that nearly half of all the prophets in the Mishnah and the other books of the law had no experience of seeing the temple. He stared away from his list and wondered out loud.

"Our faith has survived moments like the destruction of the Temple or the eviction from our land. It has even survived mass enslavements and relocations. The prophets of our faith have not seen this place. Certainly, we can survive this." And, he felt peace for the first time since the fall of Jerusalem.

"Perhaps my father can help build a new temple?' he said out loud. Even though no one was listening, he told himself that his father's experience with wood and stone had equipped him for this sort of work. He had already learned that not all Roman leadership was like Caligula, looking to destroy any sense of right and wrong. Not every slave responded with resentment. He didn't. No establishments were permanent. The temple was not about to become the first exception to this rule.

Despite the loss of the Temple, the Ebreet remained Yahweh's chosen people. God had brought them through great adversity with a promise one day to deliver them with the appearance of a Messiah. And a new story was becoming clear to him. This Messiah had come, and the layman, the farmer, and the laborer had discovered Him, but the Pharisees, Sadducees, and Romans had not.

"With all my education and language skills, I missed it, too," he thought.

He left that line of thinking and returned to the present. Rufus was a good partner for him right now. Rufus was greatly interested in the affairs of those around him and what they were experiencing. But they weren't experiencing the same things. The Roman leader had willingly given up his career, whereas Mishi had had his taken from him. Rufus spent each evening with Gesher and her son, while Rufus spent his nights alone in his apartment.

Mishi looked forward to his dinners with Rufus. During those dinners, Rufus shared stories of his past life and he spoke of the trials that he had gone through on the way to becoming a Legate in the Roman military. Mishi was mesmerized as Rufus spoke of conquests in Gaul and Britannia and the methods that he and Titus had used when landing in foreign lands to interact with the locals. These methods seemed to work everywhere Rome expanded. Once they landed and conquered an area, they would find out what Roman items were of interest to the locals and offer them small amounts of them. In exchange, the natives would give them limited access to their resources. Gold for a harbor. Silver for a herd of animals.

Cinnamon for a crop of grain. Once the local leadership had become drunk on their new wealth, the Romans would offer larger sums to have unlimited access to the resource. Kings and queens would agree to the terms without contemplating what they might mean in the long term. Soon after that, thousands of Roman troops arrived and began exploiting their unlimited access to food and timber. Harbors became entire coastlines. Herds of animals became all livestock as far as the eye could see. A single crop of grain became 50% of all harvested grain. Inevitably, an uprising would start as the people sought to gain back their autonomy, and Romans like Titus and Rufus would come in and clean up the resistance. After a year or two of Roman occupation, nearly all their territories became resource delivery tools and their resources would be shipped to Romans living far away. Gaul exported food, wine, and pottery. Britannia exported wood and iron, both of which were used in construction throughout the Empire. Cotton came from Egypt. Silk and fine linens came from the Far East. Africa contributed by providing animals used in gladiator fighting. Throughout this process, Judah provided much of the gold and silver used to purchase items from these other provinces. Rome, for its part, provided safe trade pathways by providing protection on trade routes, ensuring that pirates did not interfere with their objectives.

Mishi would often wonder why Rufus was investing all of this time in educating him. Still, it quickly became apparent that Rufus needed to educate him in order to make him effective in his duties as an investigator into the credibility of The Way. Rufus fed Mishi stories in order to receive stories in return. He guided Mishi in discussing current events with merchants in the marketplace since he had no experience with this.

In exchange for these skills, Mishi was asked to memorize and record any phrases that he found people using frequently. Rufus was interested in the profanity the locals used. He needed to learn the vernacular of the people if he was going to speak with them. After all, he had recently resigned from the military and had not yet committed to a final place that he and Gesher would. He had decided that he would settle wherever was best for her and her boy; he held no strong opinion on relocating to Rome, to Manasseh, or Jusah. He had pondered Gaul and Britannia, but neither one had a climate that suited him. And he needed people who would challenge him. That is what Titus provided him, and he sensed that Gesher would do the same. The more time he spent with her and her son, the more beautiful he discovered her to be. In fact, when he closed his eyes at night, she was the lone thought he would fall asleep to.

Day after Day, Mishi reported that the number of people who had joined The Way was growing rapidly. Mishi and Rufus both thought this was related to people's desire to find something to believe in. Although there were many other choices besides The Way, The Way was the most popular.

"God uses all things to bring His glory" was one phrase that Mishi heard often. When he asked them how they came to be in Jerusalem at the time of the Temple's destruction, some told him, "God used the destruction of the Temple to spread His message and provide evidence to the next generation that Yeshua was the Messiah spoken of for a thousand years."

Yet, Roman soldiers occupied their land. That was a strong vote against the claim that Yeshua was the Messiah. What gave the followers of The Way credibility was one particular phrase that all of them used: "Not one stone would be left on top of the other." Mishi kept coming back to that. Some spoke it in Ebreet. Some spoke it in Greek. Some were Egyptian by birth and spoke in their native tongue. Others used Aramaic. However, not one story about Yeshua presented a different set of details, regardless of language. Both men found this very interesting. This was the secret behind the fall of Jerusalem. It was to make Yeshua known to those who did not know him.

As his interviews intensified, Mishi began hearing stories of miracles that this Messiah had performed. Sometimes, he would hear the same story ten times. Turning water into wine sounded like something from Exodus. Feeding the five thousand sounded like another story from Exodus. Raising the dead, though, was unique, and Mishi and Rufus had no frame of reference for this story. Throughout, no disparities were discovered.

"Rufus, I need to see the leader of these people. I am going to the gathering tonight. My slave invited me and I accepted." Mishi paused.

"You should join me," he said.

"Well, the evidence says these stories must be true. We should go. What should I wear?' Rufus asked.

"I heard that Roman soldiers attend. You can probably attend as you are now unless I have been hearing lies." Rufus laughed.

"There is no history of people lying to you. You are an approachable young man with a bright future. I shall go as I am."

Chapter 48:
The Gathering Place

It was easy for Mishi and Rufus to find the Way's gathering place. As Mishi was told, it was halfway down the western slopes of the Mount of Olives. Everyone was walking towards the building and most of them were talking and appeared happy. Rufus started laughing out loud as they got close.

"I gave permission not long ago for this building to be purchased. Now, I stand in front of it, wishing to be a student of its occupier and awaiting permission to enter. Now, that is a story for you," Rufus said to Mishi, putting his hand on the Rabbi's shoulder.

People outside were delivering the materials needed to prepare a large meal of fresh bread and hummus, as well as herbs and vegetables cooked in olive oil and spring water. As Rufus approached, the smell of the herbs reminded him of Caesarea. The smell of rosemary on cracked grains made him homesick. Never at the end of conquests in Gaul or Britannia did he wish to see his mother as much as he did right now.

After a few moments of conversation with people outside the entrance, he and Mishi were directed downstairs into the room where their services were held. Rufus felt a tug on his arm. He turned and saw Gesher, and she held Rufus' arm like a bride might hold her husband.

"We meet again, Roman soldier!" she said with a smile as she looked up into his eyes. He leaned over and embraced her, and he picked up her little boy, carrying him the rest of the way.

"Shalom," he said with a warm and friendly tone. "I wrote a letter home to my father and spoke of you," he said.

"Oh, really?" she said. She gestured to him to sit next to the other men in the dark inner chamber, and she took her place near the other women.

As Rufus sat down, he noticed that no one was looking at him. This was strange to him, as his status as a Roman leader always made him the center of attention when he entered a place in society that prioritized power and authority. This place valued both, yet it was not of the sort that he knew. Everyone seemed to be either praying with their hands held above their heads or talking with one another. Rufus turned to Mishi as he held the little boy and whispered to him.

"Just a few months ago, I let a group of Ebreet from Thessalonica purchase this building. They received my blessing. Little did I know what they would do with it!" Mishi decided to add some more information.

"I have heard that they hold their hands and speak in foreign tongues but do not know what they are saying," Rufus shook his head from side to side.

"That sounds interesting. My father spoke about that a long time ago. Maybe you and I will see it," he said.

Without any pomp or fanfare, the speaker entered. He was an elderly man who appeared to have been recently wounded, as his hands were wrapped in blood-stained cloth. Despite this, he seemed to be in good spirits as he walked down the center of the crowd. He greeted both the men and the women. He smiled often and stopped on one occasion to pray for a woman who had injured her arm.

Rufus was used to seeing men receive more attention than women, but this man appeared to regard each person as equal, regardless of gender or social status. He paused when he reached the two of them and spoke only to Mishi. "Welcome, Rabbi. Your name is Mishi, is it not?"

"It is," Mishi said enthusiastically.

Luke then spoke to Rufus. "Welcome to our gathering. I can see that you are a man in authority. The sole authority here is Yeshua and the authority that He grants to others. You are welcome here. I already know you are taking wonderful care of our widow. You are already a blessed man. I hope tonight you get to experience an even greater blessing." Rufus knew not what he meant, but it was the first time he learned that Gesher had been speaking about their developing relationship with others. He was proud that he felt no shame when she was called a widow.

Luke continued to the front of the room. He stopped walking once he reached a small pedestal at the front. After a deep breath in and out, he began to speak.

"The prophets of old spoke of the day when nations would flow into the house of Jehovah, and all flesh would be able to access the blessings of divine salvation. I tell you, those days have come. Today, it has impressed upon my heart to tell you the story of a Gentile who lives north of here and was brought into God's kingdom. He was a Roman, like some of you. Our God loves all and calls all into His kingdom. The following story comes to us from Eusebius, and he relayed it to me not long ago." The speaker looked down and whispered something no one could hear. The people who were regular listeners thought nothing of this peculiarity, but it seemed odd for Mishi and Rufus. He continued.

"The Roman man's original life path was that of a weapon in Rome's military, and he led many men. When he was young, he was zealous for blood, and the enemy used him to bring great destruction to those who are no longer in our midst." Many in the crowd murmured. "Then, God saw that good must come from this man and He sent an angel to him."

Rufus thought this story sounded much like one his father had told him when he was younger.

"The Centurion was told that the man he was to seek out was lodging in Joppa with a tanner. This was my dear friend, Simon Peter."

Rufus stopped breathing. Could this be his father's story? This could not be a coincidence. Rufus had heard this tale before, but not from a stranger. He held Gesher's hand and kissed the little boy on the forehead. He was already crying.

"The Centurion sent forth messengers to Joppa to find Simon Peter and bring him back to his house in Caesarea. These servants found Simon Peter, one of the original disciples of our Yeshua, in the home of the tanner. They were very perplexed, as they knew that Ebreet culture disdains anyone who works with dead animals, yet there was no doubt in their minds that this was the Simon Peter that they were sent to find. Simon Peter came back with the messengers. Once they arrived, they were greeted by the Centurion, some of his family, and many of his friends."

Amazed, Rufus listened to this story of the supernatural manifestation of the Spirit that fell upon his father that day. There could no longer be any doubt. This man was telling the same story Rufus' father had once told him about a man whom he had summoned. Rufus failed to comprehend his father's story because his father had always told it with great emotion and interrupted himself with prayer and song. Luke, however, was focused on details. Rufus and Mishi both needed details if they were going to believe.

"This story is evidence that our Messiah came from the Ebreet for the Ebreet. However, there is also eyewitness evidence that our Messiah came for the Romans. I laugh because I know He came for this Roman. He came to give us all unrestrained access to the blessings of His church. Yeshua makes no distinction between Ebreet and Gentile, and we must not either. It doesn't matter how you found yourself in this room today. You are all equal in the eyes of God."

Rufus stood up. Luke looked at the towering man, almost as if he had expected him to speak. Instead, Rufus appeared to freeze.

"Speak, Roman. Say what you are being called to say."

Rufus hesitated. He hadn't actually thought of what he was going to say.

Rufus handed the boy back to Gesher and stood back up. He looked straight ahead as if he were staring at the emperor, but instead, he shook like a young boy, scared for his life. He did what he always did in a large crowd, trying to introduce himself to a celebrity or a great leader. He was overwhelmed and began to weep. The room became silent as everyone stared at this giant of a man breaking down. He took a deep breath and continued.

"The man you speak about is Cornelius, the Centurion. He is my father." At once, Rufus fell to his knees and began sobbing uncontrollably. Gesher knelt with him and held him with both arms wrapped around him. He reciprocated and held her like she was his hero. He allowed his tears to continue to flow as imagery of his father's stories flooded his consciousness. His father had been telling the truth, and his heart finally admitted that he had known the stories to be true his entire life.

People began speaking in tongues, and others stood next to Rufus and Gesher, translating the messages. Luke began to shout with great enthusiasm. He raised his hands and said, "Praise Yeshua for giving us signs and miracles that He keeps his promises! Thank Him for the son of Cornelius and his future wife Gesher, who are with us today!" Mishi watched as Rufus whispered into Gesher's ear. Gesher began crying and looked Rufus in the eyes, whispering yes. Mishi was the first to see their Erusin, and he stood up and announced it to everyone.

Luke walked towards Rufus. As he reached him, he spoke loudly and embraced the towering Roman with a hug.

"Again, I say to you, 'welcome.' The Holy Spirit is working a mighty work in you, Rufus, son of Cornelius." At that moment, Rufus was grateful that he was not wearing armor or carrying a sword or javelin, for he wanted nothing to do with his past. "Everyone, let us welcome Rufus, son of Cornelius. He is one of us now and shall soon testify on our behalf."

"Gesher has just agreed to be my wife," Rufus said. The entire house erupted in laughter and song.

Chapter 49:
Yael and Mishi Reunite

Over the next two evenings, Rufus and Mishi were present every time the believers gathered. As sundown approached, Rufus gave the group enough coins that adequate food was in the kitchens. Some nights, the number of followers would grow so much that people stood at the top of the stairs on each other's shoulders so they could hear their master speak. Both Rufus and Mishi thought it was a powerful thing to watch strangers trust Luke without knowing him. For her part, Gesher served in the kitchens, but Rufus would always seek her out to kiss her when they first arrived.

Some nights, Luke would allow one of the traveling members of The Way to share their experiences. Most often, these travelers spoke of miracles. Their teachings always addressed a specific member of the crowd, as had happened with Rufus.

One night, a large contingent came from Thessalonica and the crowd more than doubled. Rufus foresaw that there would not be enough to feed everyone. During that evening's message, Luke sensed the crowd's concern, so he prayed over them and asked that the food be brought out first.

As was his custom, Luke came and ate with the crowd and mingled among them, praying for and healing the sick in their midst. This evening, he stayed at his place in front of the room while he knelt and prayed. A servant brought food for him, but he gestured to her to set it down next to him on the top stair leading to his platform. During the meal, after many had already filled their bellies and were talking amongst themselves, he gestured to his room guards to tell people to sit down and prepare to listen. "This evening, many have come to join our fellowship. It reminds me of a story that I was a part of. It is only in these last few days that it was recorded on parchment. Two among your midst have been working very diligently to record Yahweh's words, as His words are life to us. I need everyone's assistance. Would you all agree with me that you each have had a large amount of food this evening?"

People agreed that they had.

"I have heard one say, 'I am full to the top of my belly.' Give all the uneaten bread to the kitchen staff as they walk amongst you. They will take it to the poor on the other side of the fallen city." With that, the staff went among the crowd and collected the uneaten fish in one basket and the uneaten bread in another. All the while, Luke stayed in front of the room. As they gathered, he spoke to them.

"There was a time when Yeshua's apostles had retreated to Bethsaida to get away from the crowds. However, the crowds learned what they had done and where they had gone, and they followed them. Yeshua welcomed these crowds, as they needed healing, and He spoke to them about the kingdom of God." Luke looked around the room and adjusted his robe. His robe adjustment was a form of punctuation in his storytelling. However, some of the disciples objected, saying that He should send them away to the surrounding villages to find food and lodging on their own. The master replied, 'Give them something to eat.' They answered, 'We have only five loaves of bread and two fish unless we go and buy food for all this crowd.'"

A person in the room spoke up to confirm Luke's story. "I know of this crowd and have heard this tale. There were 5,000 in that crowd."

Luke looked at the man and nodded. "There were indeed. Yeshua said to the disciples, 'Have them sit down in groups of about fifty each.' The disciples did so, and everyone sat down. Taking the five loaves and the two fish and looking up to Heaven, He gave thanks and broke them. He gave them to the disciples to distribute to the people. They all ate and were satisfied, and the disciples picked up twelve basketfuls of broken pieces that were left over."

The crowd began to whisper as the story was told.

Luke asked the woman in charge of the kitchen that evening to come forward. "What did you and our Roman Rufus tell us before we began serving this meal?"

She looked up at him with fear in her face. "Master, we did not think we would be able to feed everyone."

"Tell us, how much uneaten fish and bread did you have at the end of the meal?"

She shook her head. A single tear fell from her eye. "We have five times the fish and ten times the bread we had than when we started."

After a few moments, Luke turned to the crowd and said, "Behold! The power of a risen Messiah!"

Mishi was fascinated by the old man, by his story, and by what had happened to Rufus. But he was fascinated by something else. Or, more accurately, fascinated by someone. Yael was one of the members of Luke's group tonight. She had come with an old woman and they were seated on the other aisle. Although they made eye contact frequently, something kept them from approaching each other. Was it embarrassment? Was it fear? Or was it something else, something difficult to put a name to and more difficult to confront? Neither of them knew, but somehow, they could both tell that the other person was feeling the same way, even if neither of them understood their feelings.

On the third day, after the teaching was over and as Rufus and Mishi were getting up to leave, Luke motioned to Mishi to come over to speak to him. Mishi automatically looked at Rufus. "Rabbi, you do not need my permission to speak to this man," Rufus said. "Stay as late as you want. I will meet you later."

"Tell me, what skills do you have?" said Luke to Mishi as he massaged his injured right hand.

"I was headmaster of the Temple school before it was destroyed," Mishi replied. "The headmaster before me died in the blockade, and I took over his responsibilities when no one else was available to do so."

Luke gazed deeply into his eyes. "Young Rabbi, I wish to have my stories written down so that they can be distributed and the message of Yeshua can be spread. There is no doubt in my mind that you have superior reading and writing skills. Would you be interested in doing this?"

Mishi was taken aback. He and Rufus had come to the gatherings three times, but he had not said that he actually believed anything that Luke was saying. And now the old man was asking him to be his scribe. That was very presumptive. At the same time, Mishi could not deny that Luke had seen his heart. Mishi believed in the Messiah, but he had not publicly proclaimed it. Yet, he wished to spread Luke's message. "Sure. I will help however I can."

"Interesting, you say that," Luke replied with the smile of someone who has had an epiphany. "I already have another writer, a young girl named Yael, who I believe you have eyes for. And, as the look on your face already shows, she has mentioned you to me in a most positive light." Luke motioned for Yael to come forward. Their time of avoiding each other was over. Yael was nervous and spoke first.

"Mishi, I," she started to say, but Mishi cut her off.

"Yael, let me speak first. I have thought about you every day since you left me. I have prayed for you many times each day. I didn't know what to say when I saw you. Please accept my apology for not being courageous and approaching you," Mishi said.

"Mishi so much has happened! And I have thought about you every day. I have woken up in the middle of the night thinking about you," she said. Luke watched as the two of them held eye contact. Luke put a hand on each of them and they looked up at him.

"You two shall work together and record God's words. We must make copies of His words and get them to the synagogues around the world. He will be the author and give me the words. I will give them to you, and you will be my scribes." They looked at each other, both wearing smiles as big as the walls of Jericho.

"Sure! Let's do it, Little One?" Mishi said. Mishi knew that those words were terms of endearment, and they reflected how he viewed Yael. What he didn't know was that they were also a trigger for Yael, and they immediately brought her back to her time with Colch. Mishi could see a look of panic on her face.

"What? What did I say?" Mishi asked in an equal panic.

"Mishi, one day she will tell you. For now, though, don't use those words with her, even though I can see your heart." Luke then turned and spoke exclusively to Yael. "He did not mean the same thing the last time a boy spoke them to you. Mishi is a man of God. You can trust him," Luke said. Luke didn't know that Yael had already told Mishi her deepest secret.

"Colch? Oh, Yael! I am so sorry. I am so, so sorry!" Mishi said, and he began to weep. Yael could see Mishi's heart in a new way, and she put her hand on him to comfort him. As Mishi's tears became overwhelming, she reciprocated and cried with him. She apologized in her turn, and the two of them embraced in front of Luke.

"I love you both," said Luke, allowing both of them a chance to include him in their hug.

"That was a beautiful step of healing. Tomorrow, let's get the two of you writing!" said Luke. The two of them looked at each other and smiled. They were excited to work together.

Chapter 50:
Putting It Down in Ink

The emotional intensity of last night's revelation that Rufus' father was a figure in Torah history brought the community closer. Many people hugged and cried, and everyone came to introduce themselves to Rufus. Everyone was excited to learn that Rufus had invited his father and mother to come Jerusalem to meet their future daughter-in-law. They promised to come and bless the new couple and support both of them as they entered into Erusin. Mishi stood next to Rufus all evening, and they walked back to camp together in the dark after an exhausting evening.

"Rabbi, tomorrow I want to gather all my men and tell them about what happened today," he said. Mishi loved the idea and promised to stand with him as he shared his testimony for the first time. Mishi looked up the fallen ramparts of Jerusalem's outer walls and told Rufus to stop.

"Rufus, I will share mine, too," he said. The two of them devised a plan to invite all the former students at the temple school and all the remaining military to be present. Rufus wanted to keep walking, but Mishi told him to stay.

"I think we should do it where the temple used to be," said Mishi. Mishi explained to him that he now sees that all of this had to fall for the Messiah to be ushered into the conscious world. Rufus nodded in agreement, calling Mishi wise.

"You are my new Titus," said Rufus, extending his friendship and brotherhood to the young Ebreet. They shook hands and Rufus pulled in the young Rabbi for a hug like he would give a friend he had not seen in a long time. Once Rufus let him go, Mishi wore a big smile and looked up at Rufus.

"I have never had a brother," said Mishi, and that made both of them laugh.

"Now you do!" said Rufus, and with that exchange, they entered the fallen city.

The following morning, Gesher and Yael met them for breakfast in Rufus' tent. Rufus told both women of their plan to give their testimony to the remnant left in Jerusalem. Rufus gave Gesher a bag of coins, telling her to buy food and wine for everyone and exquisite clothing for herself and Yael. Yael attempted to decline Rufus' offer, but Rufus insisted, telling her to keep her coins for a bigger and better cause.

"I will prepare the meal," said Yael. Rufus dismissed Yael's offer, telling her that his men could prepare a meal for a thousand men in their sleep. Mishi interrupted the conversation.

"Brother Yael told me stories about how she and her sister Katie prepared meals for the entire village and how much everyone enjoyed them. Let her prepare this meal, and let your tongue decide if it was the right idea to listen to me." Rufus thoughtfully looked at Mishi as he sensed his friend was defending his woman. He stood between Yael, Gesher, and himself as if he were their protector. Rufus knew the right decision was to honor his courage.

"Very well. Yael, the job is yours," he said. Gesher told Rufus that she wanted him to meet her family, and they were coming into town later today. The two of them left, leaving Mishi and Yael alone. Mishi poured each of them a cup of hot tea and they stepped outside the tent to sit at Rufus' table, which had padded chairs and a beautiful view.

"Yael, I can't explain what happened last night." He told her that Rufus and he had become brothers and that they had planned to share their faith with everyone who would listen. Yael promised that her meal would be better than the five loaves and two fishes they learned about in last night's story, and they both laughed. Mishi decided to let Yael be the first one to hear that he now believed that

Yeshua had completed the Torah, and he wished to be one of his followers.

"It was as if a picture was painted in front of the congregation, and everyone was witness to the beauty of a new sunrise. Truly, I, too, believe in this Messiah." Yael also had something to share.

"So do I. Gesher and I spoke, and I asked Yeshua to wipe me clean of my sins. I feel like a bird as it flies above the ramparts in the early morning. Mishi, I am free of the burden of my sin!" she said. Her excitement was undeniable, and she spilled her tea as she shared with abandon that her prayers had been answered. Mishi's outcome was similar but with stronger consequences.

"I am, too. I have confessed and repented my sin to the two remaining Rabbis on our school board. They took counsel and agreed that I cannot teach here any longer," said Mishi. Yael understood, and the two of them hugged.

"Let's go to work," Mishi said. They entered the basement and walked towards Luke, holding hands, and he warmly greeted them at the front of the chamber.

"Ah, you two are finally here. Please, Yael, sit down at the table and prepare yourself to be my scribe," Luke said. Mishi bristled. Certainly, Luke was not going to have Yael write first. Reading and writing were great loves of his, and he had prepared long for moments like these. How could he let someone like Yael, a girl with no experience in writing on Temple parchment, be the first one to write the story of the Messiah who completed the Torah?

"Mishi, you look upset. Are you OK?" Luke asked. Mishi felt shame that his resentment was showing in his countenance. He took a deep breath. He knew he couldn't hold it against Yael that Luke saw her in an affectionate light. He did, too, but for different reasons. He had already told everyone who had seen them spending a lot of time together that with her, he would be lost right now.

"Yael was the first one I was honest with. How can I begrudge her anything? Please accept my apology. I was jealous," he said to everyone.

Luke interrupted his reflections. "Young Rabbi, I have a job for you, as well. Find some of your former students and bring them back. Tell them whatever you feel you must and answer any questions that they may have. Just get them here."

Luke was obviously not a Pharisee. He didn't care how Mishi did things as long as they got done. The Pharisees would have focused on how to ask the students and not concerned themselves with whether or not they actually came. As he walked upstairs, the old woman Yael spent the night with when she first arrived in Jerusalem was there, and she pulled him aside.

"What are your intentions with my Yael, Rabbi?' she asked. Mishi looked at her. He had not disclosed what he was thinking, but this woman had certainly proven herself worthy of trust.

"Perhaps you can help. Here is what I am thinking," he said. With that, he told her all about the idea he had meditated on with Rufus last night when neither of them could sleep. They both had their women on their minds, and they shared many of the same thoughts.

"That is a beautiful idea. Young Rabbi, you will never regret this," she said. She turned and left. It was then he realized that he had a question for Luke, and he quickly returned to the chamber and approached Luke.

"Excuse me, but why do we need my students? You don't even need me," Mishi said. Yael looked up at him as she mixed her inks and laughed. So did Luke.

"Young Rabbi, I am compelled to tell the story of our Lord as he gives it to me, but copies must be made and sent across the kingdom for our brothers and sisters to read. We cannot make one copy and keep it for ourselves. We must share it with others in the faith, so I will also appoint you to make copies. Bring back parchment, ink, quills, and students from the Temple school that we can use in our endeavor."

That made sense. Mishi bowed his head in reverence before turning around and quickly leaving the room. He stepped outside into the morning air and smiled. "Thank you, Lord," he said in a soft but joyous voice. Luke had told him repeatedly to be joyful in all things. This was his moment to practice. He began walking towards the now-destroyed city gates to begin recruiting his former students.

With Mishi gone, Luke called for Yael to look at him. He looked at the remaining people in the room for a brief moment before dismissing them to go upstairs and begin their days.

"Young Yael, it is time to record the story given to me."

"Let us pray," Luke said. In traditional Ebreet custom, men led all prayer, but they always said "us" and not "me."

"Luke, can I lead us in prayer?" Yael asked. The importance of the task moved Luke. He took a single, deep breath. Slowly, he nodded his head in agreement before he chuckled.

"Oh, the master is again the student," he said in Aramaic, hoping she didn't understand him. He had forgotten that Yael knew many languages.

"Rabbi, you are my teacher and my master. Don't say that," she said. Luke laughed and apologized.

"I should have known that you knew Aramaic. Young Lady, I am convicted. Women can pray just like men. Lead the prayer," he said, extending his hand as a gesture of grace. He then knelt next to the chair she was sitting in.

"Yahweh, I ask you, in the name of your son, Yeshua, to please come and be with us in this room. Please heal Luke's hands and let my humble work of recording our teacher's story change our hearts and the rest of the world." Luke looked up and smiled.

"Our father loves simple prayers like yours. That was beautiful, Little One," he said, kissing her on the forehead.

Luke looked at her and smiled. He had been counseling Yael every day since they had been together, and he was proud of her progress in relationships. He also spoke to Mishi about Yael, as he knew that they both desired the other. He could sense Mishi was trying to love her the best he could, but he needed wise counsel.

After the ritual of cleansing before touching the Torah was complete, she walked towards the altar, on which were many pieces of parchment. She took one and brought it back to her small table. She put it down next to her supply of ink and feathers to record with. She was beginning to think that Luke would have a lot to say. There seemed to be enough paper to record the entire story of Exodus 100 times over. She smiled and reached for the first feather. She began sharpening the feather with a small knife. She set it down once it would serve her purpose, and she dipped in the ink.

"I am ready, Rabbi Luke," she said.

"This letter shall be addressed to my dear Brother Theophilus. I believe he is in Egypt now. He is strong in our faith, but he also needs encouragement. In some ways, his faith is stronger than my own, for he believes though his eyes did not meet Yeshua. Strong are those who have not seen yet believe."

"Wait," she said in a commanding tone. She had to mix the inks again because her first batch wouldn't stick to the quill. As she created a new potion of ink, Luke pondered a change he wanted to make to this letter.

"We shall do this in Greek. If someone else reads this message, we must maximize the chance that they will understand it. Although our Torah is in Ebreet and Aramaic, we shall deviate from that tradition. Therefore, I will also speak to you in Greek."

Yael didn't care as she was fluent in all three languages. She nodded and took a few final moments to place usable points on two feathers.

"Ready," she said in Greek as she looked up at him, awaiting his words.

"That is what you said last time," Luke said, making her laugh again.

Luke began to dictate the story of the good news of a Risen Messiah. He paused often and spoke slowly. He frequently closed his eyes and lifted his hands. He cried throughout, and when Yael asked him for the next set of words, he always provided one. He gave Yael plenty of time to record each thought before he proceeded to the next one. However, the pattern of their first chapter repeated itself with each subsequent chapter.

"Since many have undertaken to compile a narrative of the events that have been fulfilled among us, as those who were eyewitnesses from the beginning and ministers of the word have handed them down to us, I too have decided, after investigating everything accurately anew, to write it down in an orderly sequence for you, most excellent Theophilus, so that you may realize the certainty of the teachings you have received."

Yael finished and looked up at him. "Are you sure you want to say all of that? That is a long way to say, 'Greetings, dear Theo.' Can you use fewer words?"

Luke laughed so hard that he had to take a drink of water before he continued.

"Little One, you are funny. However, from now on, please write what I say. No more comments." Yael agreed and prepared to write the next thought. However, she always found herself commenting on his work, and inevitably, one of them would laugh.

"In the days of Herod, King of Judea, there was a priest named Zechariah of the priestly division of Abijah; his wife was from the daughters of Aaron, and her name was Elizabeth. Both were righteous in the eyes of God, observing all the commandments and ordinances of the Lord blamelessly. But they had no child because Elizabeth was barren and both were advanced in years. Once, when he was serving as a priest in his division's turn before God, according to the practice of the priestly service, he was chosen by lot to enter the sanctuary of the Lord to burn incense. When the whole assembly of the people was praying outside at the hour of the incense offering, the angel of the Lord appeared to him, standing at the right of the altar of incense. Zechariah was troubled by what he saw and fear came upon him. But the angel said to him, 'Do not be afraid, Zechariah, because your prayer has been heard. Your wife Elizabeth will bear you a son and you shall name him John. And you will have joy and gladness, and many will rejoice at his birth, for he will be great in the sight of the Lord. He will drink neither wine nor strong drink. He will be filled with the holy Spirit even from his mother's womb, and he will turn many of the children of Judah to the Lord their God. He will go before him in the spirit and power of Elijah to turn the hearts of fathers toward children and the disobedient to the understanding of the righteous, to prepare a people fit for the Lord.'

Zechariah said to the angel, 'How shall I know this? For I am an old man, and my wife is advanced in years.' And the angel said to him in reply, 'I am Gabriel, who stands before God. I was sent to speak to you and announce this good news to you. But now you will be speechless and unable to talk until the day these things take place because you did not believe my words, which will be fulfilled at their proper time.'"

Yael spoke without thinking as she finished the last word. She shook her hand as it was tired from such a long thought.

"Rabbi, how do you know that is what happened in the Temple?" She was sincere, and Luke saw the innocence on her face. Between her words and the look, he could not contain himself. Luke closed his eyes, trying to be reverent, but he couldn't stop laughing. Luke's laugh made Yael laugh, and she got up to pour him another cup of water. Once he stopped laughing, he shook his head and spoke to her.

"Little One, no one will know how much fun you and I are having as we write this." He was looking for the right word to describe what they were writing.

"This gospel," said Yael. Luke considered what she said and agreed.

"Why not? This Gospel. We will call it a gospel," he said.

Luke chuckled and closed his eyes.

She took up a new piece of parchment, as the first one was already full.

"Is this part of Chapter 1, or are we now on Chapter 2?" she asked. Luke laughed again.

"Little One, I have no idea. Just write." She agreed and recorded his next words.

"Meanwhile, the people were waiting for Zechariah and were amazed that he stayed so long in the sanctuary. But when he came out, he was unable to speak to them, and they realized that he had seen a vision in the sanctuary. He was gesturing to them but remained mute. When his days of ministry were completed, he went home. After this time, his wife Elizabeth conceived, and she went into seclusion for five months, saying, 'So has the Lord done for me at a time when he has seen fit to take away my disgrace before others.' In the sixth month, the angel Gabriel was sent from God to a town of Galilee called Nazareth, to a virgin betrothed to a man named Joseph of the house of David, and the virgin's name was Mary. And coming to her, he said, 'Hail, favored one! The Lord is with you.' But she was greatly troubled at what was said and pondered what sort of greeting this might be. Then the angel said to her, 'Do not be afraid, Mary, for you have found favor with God. Behold, you will conceive in your womb and bear a son, and you shall name him Jesus. He will be great and will be called Son of the Highest, and the Lord God will give him the throne of David, his father, and he will rule over the house of Jacob forever, and of his kingdom, there will be no end.' But Mary said to the angel, 'How can this be since I have no relations with a man?' And the angel said to her in reply, 'The holy Spirit will come upon you, and the power of the Most High will overshadow you. Therefore, the child to be born will be called holy, the Son of God. And behold, Elizabeth, your relative, has also conceived a son in her old age, and this is the sixth month for her who was called barren; for nothing will be impossible for God.' Mary said, Behold, I am the handmaid of the Lord. May it be done to me according to your word.' Then the angel departed from her." Again, Yael shook her hand to relax after that long passage.

"Wow, Zecariah and Mary had two very different responses to God's messengers!" Yael blurted out. Again, Luke laughed hard and asked her to keep writing as politely as he could. But first, he decided to teach her a lesson. Luke began to pace the small room.

"Young Yael, we are all like Zechariah sometimes and like Mary sometimes. We sometimes disbelieve, and we sometimes embrace God's plans with a humble heart." He stopped long enough to make eye contact with Yael before he continued pacing. "Please read your writings back to me. I have already forgotten what I said," he said. Yael laughed again. Luke was being serious and she found it amusing. As expected, that made him laugh, and they both needed more water before they could continue.

Yael focused on the pronunciation of every word as she read the story back to him.

When she was done, he stopped pacing and straightened his back, trying to crack it. "Let's go outside and walk around the city walls. We have done enough for today."

Yael looked at him, feeling a peace she had not felt in a long time. She could see at this man's feet and listen to him all day.

Chapter 51:
The Work Must Be Done

During the next two weeks, a pattern emerged in Yael, Mishi, and Luke's work to record his gospel. When Luke would finish his visitations for healing and prayer for the people, he and Yael would gather in the basement when the day was hot and continue transcribing the Word of God. Luke would share the words as God gave them to him, while Yael would write them on parchment, reading them back to him, one paragraph at a time. They often laughed deeply at how some of the words came out, and more than once, the two of them would start over as a housecat who lived down in the basement would jump on the parchment and ruin it. Yael named the cat "Steps" as she would quietly take steps on her wet parchment when no one even knew she was there.

They also cried at the meaning of what they were recording. Both of them would find themselves in awe at what God had shown Luke, and they always left feeling humbled and alive. Throughout the crying and the laughing, Luke became very fond of Yael. He loved her like a daughter, and she loved that she could speak to Luke with no filters and no concern of offending him. The interruptions by the cat always proved to be funny.

However, the story writing was long, and writing it on thick parchment was fatiguing. For his part, Mishi played an important role. Mid-afternoon, he would return with food, refreshments, and supplies from the temple school to replenish what they had depleted. Mishi made eye contact with Luke as soon as he entered, and Luke let him know that Yael was getting fatigued. Mishi would then tell a story to allow Yael's hand to recover from all the writing. On the third day, Luke could see how taxing it was on her. From that moment forward, the two of them would take turns, but Luke always allowed Yael to return to transcribing once her strength returned. Despite her unequal education and experience compared to Mishi, Yael recorded more than twice what Mishi did when the texts were completed.

But it was not a unique time of writing; it was also a time of prayer and intercession. Luke would often stand up, holding his hands high in prayer, waiting for words. Sometimes, they came quickly. Other times, Luke would appear to be suffering greatly as the Spirit would come upon him to wrestle the words from his soul. "Give me a moment alone with the Lord," he would say, and when he did, Mishi would take Yael's hand and the two of them would go outside and wait for him. They both knew they were witnessing something similar to Moses' time on the mountain when he received the Ten Commandments, and they were in awe of how hard Luke struggled to hear from God.

Mishi felt great pride holding Yael's hand and looked forward to moments when Luke would get stuck. When they walked around the gathering place, everyone who stopped to talk to them heard Mishi sing Yael's praises. He was quick to announce that Yael was beautiful, funny, courageous, and intelligent. It filled his heart when she responded with gratitude each time he did something for her. She loved how respectful Mishi was when they were both in public and alone, and it helped her push away the negative experience she had with Colch.

Yael admired Mishi's command of the languages of the twelve tribes, which was better than that of any Rabbi who had ever visited Correae. Yet Mishi was not like the other Rabbis. He treated Yael like a peer, going over her work, correcting spelling, and sometimes helping her rewrite a page when Steps left footprints in the ink.

When Luke needed time alone, they seldom strayed far from their meeting place since they didn't know when Luke would ask them to come back. They both shared anything and everything that had happened in their lives. There could be no secrets between them, and they both knew that they were destined to live their lives differently than they previously had.

Yael had time to tell Mishi many of the details that she couldn't share that night in his apartment. That time was too brief, but now they had hours per day to talk and get to know each other. She told him of her sister and cousins. She told him of her family and her village's secret and how the act of keeping that secret seemed to hurt her so. She spoke of her journey to Jerusalem and of her deepest and darkest self-demolishment of the choice she made to bed Colch.

Mishi was the first man to whom she recounted her story of offering herself to the Roman soldier in exchange for her life. Mishi mostly listened, as all good Rabbis are trained to do, and he was the first person she told that she had missed her monthly bleeding.

"Do you know what that means?" she asked. She knew Mishi had no sisters and his mother had been back in their village for many years while Mishi lived in Jerusalem with his father.

He reached out and held both of her hands. He smiled at her and wiped a tear from her eyes.

"Of course I do. It took a lot of courage for you to tell me that. You will be an outstanding mother," he said. She nodded yes, and he pulled her towards him for a real hug. The two of them cried deeply for each other until they could cry no more. Mishi looked into her eyes and poured as much into her as he could.

"Yahweh knows what he is doing. He will make good on the ill that befell you. I know it," said Mishi, unwilling to release her hand until she was ready.

Mishi told her about his family, where they lived, and his calling to return and teach at a new school that they would open, serving people from all over Judah, Benjamin, Ephraim, and Dan. He told her of his mother's closed womb and the burden he felt to honor his family as a Rabbi.

"Mishi, you are such an excellent teacher. People will travel for days in all directions to sit at your feet. Your students have told me so many times how good you are," Yael said. Her affirmation spoke into his heart, and he grew in his confidence in building a special school.

Often, their conversation focused on what they had heard Luke say. His stories about how the synagogues in remote places fascinated them. Both were in disbelief about the magnitude and number of miracles that Yeshua had performed. It was also interesting to them how many followers of Yeshua already existed around the empire and how their numbers were growing daily. They loved his stories about how the Coptic synagogues operated in Egypt and how the ministry of his friend Paul operated in the prisons underneath Rome. Yael was interested in visiting these prisons, seeing the ministry, and helping.

"We are witnessing something that is changing the world," they often remarked to each other.

On the ninth day of writing, Luke had a particularly difficult spiritual battle getting the words for them to write, and Yael and Mishi found themselves alone outside for a long time. Their affection for each other was strong, and the old woman could see that they were in love.

"Yael, we are blessed to be a part of the changing of the order of things," Mishi said. "Yet I feel more blessed to be doing this with you." Without a script or any forethought, Mishi spoke to her heart. For him, this act of courage was thoughtful and more than a reaction to their moment.

"Yael, you are dear to me, but I have a question for you. Do you continue to believe that you cannot marry and live a normal life?"

Yael didn't speak but could stare into Mishi's eyes. She could sense the courage Mishi had rallied to speak to her like that. He was not at all like Colch or the other schoolboys. He was truly invested in her. She was infatuated with the small gifts of hot tea and fresh bread he would bring her in the morning, which he thought would help her do her job. He was also open to showing her his heart. She couldn't speak, but she did reach out and interlock her fingers in his, offering him a smile. Mishi kept his heart open, choosing not to feel rejection because he did not receive the words he sought. He took her for a walk toward the destroyed city gates.

"I loved all the things that the Temple stood for, and I loved serving the people who came there. Nearly every pilgrim was sincere. However, I was unable to see how corrupt the culture that supported the Temple had become. I didn't see how corrupt the leadership in the city had become. Now that the Temple is no more, we are hearing God speak to a new generation through Rabbi Luke. Speaking and listening to you and experiencing all this change, I feel that I am see-ing God's heart in a new way." Yael nodded and added her testimony.

"If I had never sinned the way that I did, I would have never left home, traveled here, or met you. I would have missed all these stories of the Messiah and remained blind. I need this as much as you do. And Luke and I are having a lot of fun with this," she said. They reached the gates at one of the entrances to the ancient city, turning around and walking back to the house.

"I came here as what you call a pilgrim. Along the way, God tested me and showed me that I am not different than this man, Peter, whom we wrote of. I promised God that I would not fornicate again. Yet I offered my body again." As they got close, the old woman saw that the two of them were holding hands. She waved and walked towards them.

"Master Luke is ready for you again," she said. She looked at Yael and winked, making Yael blush. Yael had no words, but she could sense that the old woman was seeing her prophecy come true.

As they walked the last half stadia to the entrance, Yael held Mishi's arm as they navigated around an amphitheater that was being constructed.

Mishi spoke to her with a fondness that was now becoming more common.

"I have taught many to read and write. You have beautiful pen-manship, and you are a fast reader of both Greek and Hebrew. Luke made a good choice selecting you to write first. Yael, I know what I am going to do. Once we are done here, I am going to return to my village and build the school that I told you about. However, it will not be like the Temple school. I will teach them about what Luke has said if I can remember it all!" They both laughed. Mishi continued.

"Yeshua completes the sacred scrolls. He does not change what is written there. I can teach exactly what my forefathers have taught, but I can now finish the stories that they started to teach. The work will be great, but it must be done, and now, after working with you in recording Luke's tales, I know I can do it."

"Yes, you can do it, Mishi. I think the world needs you, too."

Chapter 52:
The Plan

Mishi's parents and grandparents immediately traveled to Jerusalem to see him once they received his letter. The events seemed too incredible to be true. Mishi enthusiastically introduced them to some of the members of The Way, Luke, Yael, Rufus, and his work staff. He had something else on his mind, and he needed them to come to Jerusalem and bring him something from the village he needed immediately. And, it was important to him that they be there in person.

Once they arrived, he outlined his plan. They all thought it was beautiful, and they approved it. His mother repeatedly embraced her son and assured him that it would be wonderful and that she couldn't wait. His father quickly sent home a letter to his uncles to come to the city.

After Mishi disclosed his plan to his parents, he looked at his father. The old craftsman took a deep breath and exhaled, pausing for a moment to look at his wife to receive some affirmation from her.

"Your mother and I both dreamed and prayed for this for you. We have what you asked for. Actually, your mother has it."

With that, Mishi's mother handed it to him. Mishi began to weep, and he bowed down in front of his mother. "I must show this to Rufus. I need his help for this plan to work." He did not walk to Rufus' tent. He ran.

Chapter 53:
The Peace the Lord Intends

The following evening, Luke and the members of The Way gathered outside their meeting place adjacent to the rapidly constructed amphitheater. The week before, Rufus asked his former soldiers who remained employed by the Roman military to bring their engineering know-how down the hill and quickly construct an amphitheater. The amphitheater was complete, and Luke himself would christen the new amphitheater. Tonight would be its first use, but not for reasons that Yael knew of.

It was semi-circular in shape and had tiered places to stand or sit. The largest pieces of broken rubble from the temple were placed on the edges of the semi-circle. Working inwardly, smaller and smaller stones were used so that everyone could see the speaker. They had dug down into ancient rubble from King Solomon's time so that the speaker would be below the audience. That way, the sound would carry further, and more people would be able to hear.

Everyone gathered before sunset, and Luke stepped into the center of the amphitheater and began to speak. This was his first experience in a Roman amphitheater and he was pleased to see how well his voice traveled. He had bathed and put on new clothing, and many people complimented him, as he normally didn't look this nice when he taught in the basement. He motioned for everyone to find a place so he could begin.

"Brothers and Sisters, please come into this new place and have a seat. Good is already becoming of the fallen Temple, as it is from its remnants that we have a new place both to share and show you how to apply God's words. Tonight, I encourage you to celebrate with us.

You will get to see the love of God with your own eyes and hear with your ears. You will see how forgiveness and love work together."

Luke had told Mishi that once he heard him say those words, it was time to get Yael and bring her to the center of the amphitheater. Mishi knew that Yael would be standing on the periphery, trying to stay out of the way so others could see and hear. Mishi knew how selfless Yael could be, and he assumed that she would be outside the main crowd, caring for others as she usually did. With the act of recording Luke's Gospel now complete, Yael would be finding something to pour herself into. Tonight was a night constructed for her alone, but she didn't know it. He grabbed her hand and told her to follow him.

"What are you doing?" she whispered, not wanting to disrupt the flow of this evening's event.

"Please follow me," he said. She set down the pitcher of water that she had been carrying and let Mishi lead her. Little did she know that she was this evening's inaugural event.

Mishi led her to the center of the amphitheater, where Luke stood waiting for them. Luke had a huge smile on his face, and he looked only at Yael. He was wearing his rabbinical robe and prayer shawl, and Yael was not used to seeing him in his formal apparel. She began to breathe quickly, looking back and forth between Mishi and Luke.

"Mishi, what is going on?" she said in disbelief. She was sensitive to the reality that everyone in attendance was looking at her, too. Nearly everyone was smiling, and a few were even crying.

Once Yael and Mishi were in the center, Luke publicly embraced both of them. Luke moved to the side, so Mishi was now the center of everyone's attention. Mishi opened his mouth and spoke loudly enough for all to hear.

"All of you have heard what is written in the law. All of you know that this law has been passed down for millennia by our fathers and their fathers before them. We are Ebreet, and our law defines us." He turned to face Yael and took both of her hands like he had been doing these last two weeks. "Yael—" he began, but his voice cracked.

He began to cry, and he repeated his best effort to speak her name without crying.

In a flash, she realized what was happening. She was not ready for it. She opened her mouth in disbelief that Mishi was about to enter into Erusin with her.

"Mishi, are you asking me?" she began to say, but Mishi raised his voice and continued courageously.

"Yael, I wish to enter into Erusin with you." He looked her in the eye, and Yael could feel the purity of his love for her. He refused to break eye contact and allowed her to see to the depth of his soul. He knew all about her, and he had fallen in love. This was his moment to proclaim publicly that he wanted her as his wife.

Before she could open her mouth, he pulled the ring his mother had given him out of his cloak and held it in the palm of his hand for her to see. She covered her face and began to cry. She was not worthy of this moment.

"Mishi, you know me. You know the real me. How could you possibly?" but he cut her off.

"Stop. The real you is who I wish to spend the rest of my life with. Yael, will you accept this ring and agree to be my wife?"

Yael's eyes froze as she looked at the ring. She wanted that ring. She always had, but ever since Colch, it had symbolized something that the law of Moses said she could never have. It was designed for people of character like her sister, who did things right. She had broken the law, kept secrets, fornicated, and cast aside God's edicts and commands. She was carrying a child who would not know his father. She was a second-rate woman.

Yet, the progression from meeting a dashing young rabbi to falling in love and now engagement was all happening too fast. Luke had told her that her sins were forgiven, but she struggled to believe. Luke told her it would be a struggle until, one magic moment, she would accept it.

Her heart was on fire with a desire to pick up the ring and allow herself to have their first kiss together. Yet, she battled the truth of her circumstances.

"Mishi! You know that I am with…" She trailed off. Her emotion was powerful. She covered her face with both hands and couldn't continue. She fought not to cry with everyone listening, and every woman in the group empathized with her pain.

Luke had counseled Mishi when he brought his intentions to the old Rabbi. Mishi learned that he should expect her resistance, and he spoke his commitment to her for all to hear. Luke told him that it was his job to be part of her healing. He was a man and it was his job to fill her with love and acceptance, regardless of what happened. He was going to marry her, for better or worse, and this was part of that commitment. And, he had a Messiah who had already provided him guidance.

"Yael, I love you just as you are. I promise to care for you and treat you as part of me for the rest of my days. I have blessings from my parents, remnants from the Temple teachers, my students, and Luke to prepare a home for us to live in. I wish to start a school, as I promised my parents, and teach children about our Lord. Let me repeat myself. I love you just as you are."

The effects of the amphitheater had made Mishi's words so loud that all could hear them. Many in the crowd, even those who did not know either Yael or her story, began to cry along with the young couple. Mishi was bold and confident as he attempted to win her heart.

"I want to spend my life with you. I am saying this in front of my family and everyone you and I know," he repeated. Yael finally smiled and began to believe him. As God's chosen people, it was required that he publicly proclaim to all who would listen to any special intent or reservation, for he could not bring it up in the future. And he saved the most powerful gift he could give her until last.

"I will raise the child you carry as my own, and my parents have agreed to raise it as their grandchild."

Yael struggled to breathe. Mishi was a rabbi and could have the baby stoned with the motion of his hand. He could reject it without any shame. Instead, he committed to pour himself into it as if it were his own. Yael now knew that he loved her.

Luke coached him on what to say next. Both of them knew that she would be paralyzed with fear and in denial of Mishi's intent.

Mishi needed to address her shame and guilt, as well. Above all, she needed to see Mishi's love for God and the example he had set.

"Little One."

His voice faltered. He knew that this phrase had been abused and caused her great harm and confusion. Despite its history, he wanted this term of endearment to be a part of their shared future. He took a deep breath and continued.

"Little one, I know who you are, and I pledge in front of all these people to be with you and only you all of my days." He wiped the tears from his eyes before he could continue.

"Please let me place this ring on your marriage finger. I am ready to take you as my wife and honor you as my father has honored his wife, and my grandfather has honored his wife before him. I care not for what you have done. I stand in this public place declaring that, as our Messiah has forgiven my sins, I forgive yours. I ask that you forgive mine." He released his hold on her hands, went down onto one knee, bowed his head so she could not see his face, and extended his palm for her to take the ring.

She looked up and saw the crowd standing motionlessly, awaiting her response. Her focus shifted, and she spoke to them without thinking.

"Is that why...how long have you people been planning this?" Her question was lost in the laughter and crying of the crowd. Her tears switched to laughter, and she reached out to take the ring. As she did, the crowd erupted. Mishi's request for her to marry him had now been accepted. Yael was now an engaged woman.

"Mishi, I accept your ring. Yes, Mishi, I shall be your wife." Mishi stood up and slipped the ring on her finger. Everyone erupted in applause. Luke began crying and laughing, telling everyone in the crowd to come forward and congratulate the new couple. Before they began to move, Yael had a few words to share, as was her responsibility at the primary subject of Erusin.

"My sister had a traditional Erusin. This most certainly is not!" said Yael, making everyone laugh again.

"This is a dream. I can't believe I am marrying a temple Rabbi!" she said, laughing herself. Mishi looked at her and lovingly corrected her.

"A former temple rabbi. But still a Rabbi!" he said, pointing at her and smiling. With the ring now on her finger, Mishi leaned in and gave Yael her first kiss, telling her that he loved her. Yael reciprocated his word and wrapped her arms around Mishi, allowing him to pick her up and spin her around, as is customary on engagement night. Luke threw a small handful of marriage dust that he had been carrying on them as they spun, thereby blessing the act of Erusin and the public commitment that each had made.

Mishi's parents, Rufus, and his family joined them at the center of the amphitheater. Luke then quieted the crowd so he could give them another blessing while everyone held hands.

"May the traditions of our great God, the blessings of His son, and the blessings of His Holy Spirit be upon you all of your days. In the name of the power of the Holy Spirit, I bind the enemy from doing damage to either you, your families, or your life's work."

Yael's future mother-in-law stepped up, put her hand around her shoulder, and whispered in Yael's ear. "Mishi's grandfather and uncles are already at work on your home. Mishi is so bad with tools that he couldn't build you a home if his life depended on it."

The lightness of her mother-in-law's comment gave Yael a moment to regain control of her feelings, and she let out a belly laugh. Soon, the crowd had finished, and they began to disperse to the basement for tonight's teaching. Once everyone was gone, Mishi spoke quietly to Yael.

"We will leave tomorrow and travel to Correae so that I can speak directly to your family. Rufus and Cornelius have agreed to travel with us and provide protection against any bandits on the road." Before she could say anything, Rufus' father and mother stepped up and hugged her. They told her that they had already heard all about her from Gesher and were pleased to know that their son had such good friends. Once Yael realized that the man in front of her was Rufus' father, she stepped away and looked at him with amazement.

"Are you Cornelius, the Centurion? I recorded your story for Luke!" she said. His story was part of the Acts of the Apostles and a large part of the second half of Luke's writing.

She remembered that Rufus told her that his father seldom withheld words when he was with strangers.

"I am. I heard that you spoke with an old friend of mine on the way here. If we catch old man Barnabas on the road, I wish to speak with him. It has been a long time since I have seen my brother! I hear that he was recently in Jerusalem, and I missed him."

Yael was puzzled and looked at everyone now in front before returning her gaze to Cornelius. "Wait. Do you know Barnabas, too?" she asked Cornelius. Luke answered the question first.

"Barnabas knows everyone alive and half of those who are dead, I think. He has come to share with our group many times. He spoke to us about meeting you on his last visit. He has been praying for you since he met you last month—all of us have. He saw you here two days ago, but you didn't see him." Yael was so embarrassed that she missed him. She needed to tell him that he was right, and she wanted him to come to their wedding.

Rufus had something of interest to add that he knew Yael would love to know. " Mishi told me of his plan several days ago. I have already traveled to Correae on horseback and spoken with your father, mother, Katie, your cousins, and the mayor. They know we are coming and they are excited to see you."

"Katie, Despy, and Nava already know that I am engaged?" Yael stepped forward, thanked him, and hugged the huge former Roman soldier. After a momentary embrace, she pushed him away.

"Wait. How did I not notice that you were gone?" she said to Rufus

"The same way you didn't notice Barnabas was here," he dryly said. Luke laughed again; she apologized for spending all of her time with Mishi. She admitted that she couldn't keep her eyes off him.

"Little One, everyone knows you fell in love with Mishi a long time ago. There is no reason to apologize. Barnabas was happy for you and loved watching the two of you together," said Luke.

The evening's message in the basement was about change. He spoke of Yeshua completing the prophecy of a Messiah coming, how the Messiah completed the stories of old, God making all things new, and God's redeeming spirit. In a moment of dramatic intent, he looked and pointed at Mishi but talked to the crowd.

"By the law, Mishi is a rabbi trained and ordained in the lines of Melchizedek. The law states he cannot marry a soiled woman unless she is his dead brother's wife. Yet Yeshua came to forgive us of our sins, both past and present. In the same way that she was forgiven and redeemed by God, Mishi extends that grace to Yael. Just as Mishi sinned by hiding his treasures from God and the people whom he served, Yeshua forgave him, and Yael extended that forgiveness to him. I tell you that before your eyes, you are seeing how God intends for us to live as husband and wife. These two are the standard that we should all live up to."

Chapter 54: Going Home

At last, it was time for everyone to leave Jerusalem and begin their new lives. They celebrated a final dinner together, and everyone celebrated the marriage commitments and the completion of the Gospel of Luke and the Acts of the Apostles. Rufus' men made toasts, all celebratory of their former leader and bestowing blessings on his new wife and son. Nearly all the followers of The Way and all of the remaining military came to wish them well, and they stayed up late, both singing and dancing.

During dinner, Gesher and Yael sat together at the head of the table. Both of their future husbands wanted to publicly display that these two women were the reason they were all together. Rufus and Mishi discussed that once they all left and began new lives, Gesher would return to her role as mother and homemaker full-time, and Rufus sought out Theophilus. Yael would begin to prepare for motherhood and move her belongings from Correae to her new home in Tamar. Their place as leaders was about to change as each would begin a new existence with the men that they loved.

The next morning, it was cold outside as winter had made its way to the hills of Jerusalem. They all met outside the city gates at sunrise after a light meal. The night before, Rufus' men prepared a cart for Mishi and Yael to use to travel to Correae and then back to Tamar. Culturally, there remained a need for a formal Erusin ceremony in the tradition of the tribe of Naphtali. Yael needed to return home to get her mother's help in sewing her veil and dress and she told Mishi that he needed to buy a nice gift for her mother and father. Without hesitating, he told her to buy whatever she wanted, as he had no idea what people from Naphtali expected, and he had to finish packing up the school supplies with his remaining students. Two of them had agreed to come to Tamar and teach at his school once construction was complete. Yael's mother-in-law pulled her aside to speak with her as everyone listened to Mishi share his plan for the future.

"Get used to shopping without him," her future mother-in-law said. Men from Dan did not enjoy shopping the way that women did.

There was a second cart filled with provisions for Rufus, Gesher, and their extended family. They also needed to travel to Correae and then to Caesarea once they were done. From Caesarea, Rufus would sail to Egypt to start his search for Theophilus. Rufus told his parents and Gesher he thought he would be gone for perhaps half a year as he sought him out and distributed copies of this gospel to the brothers and sisters in the synagogues along the way. He knew his father and mother would take care of Gesher and her son while he was gone. He gave Gesher his bonus and final year's salary to spend on anything she needed to in order to care for Nathan. Rufus had become protective of Gesher, but he was also very affectionate, the same way Cornelius was affectionate towards Valentina. Giving her his wealth was the least he could do to share his gratitude.

"You are the reason I bring home coins," he told her as she took his large pouch of coins. He kept a small portion for himself. She thanked him, and she put the bag inside of her belongings in the back of the cart. She had never experienced such a massive amount of wealth, and she was humbled. She spoke to her mother-in-law about some items she thought she might need, but her mother-in-law told her that they already had all of those things at the house.

"I will teach you what to do with extra coin, Honey. King Solomon and King David had more than a few words to say about what a woman should do with wealth. Since you can read, we will read that part of the sacred scrolls together," Valentina said, pulling the young woman next to her on the cart as if she were her daughter.

"And I will make Nathan into a centurion," said Cornelius, lifting Nathan onto the back of the cart and putting him in a makeshift seat behind his mother.

"Thank you, Centurion," Gesher said. Cornelius winked at her and kissed her on the cheek forcefully before he jumped off to help the men finish loading. His son was next to him, and he spoke to him for the first time since he arrived.

"Rufus, my boy, you are lucky to have Mishi to follow when it came to picking a woman who had children with someone else." Gesher and Yael were a bit embarrassed, but Valentina intervened to make sure the girls knew what he meant.

"Corn never seems to think before he speaks. Gesher, I promise you this old man will love your little Nathan like he was his own."

"I thought Rufus was going to kill me when we met," Gesher told Valentina.

"Kill? Oh yes, but not you. He will kill anyone who tries to harm you. You helped Rufus see what his father could not. He will give his life to defend you. Of this, I am sure," Valentina said. Gesher smiled, accepting the praise.

Finally, Luke approached the lot, as he was the last one to arrive. He awkwardly held a smaller scroll in one hand, and he approached Cornelius first.

"Cornelius, one of Mishi's school boys just recorded for you. This is your story. Keep it in that basement where you keep everything else!" said Luke, holding up a copy of the second scroll. Luke asked Yael to name it "Acts," but she suggested that it was too short. Luke prayed about it and agreed. He changed it to Acts of the Apostles. After some minor chat about the name change, Cornelius raised his voice and spoke to Luke.

"Rabbi, did you include that fact that Simon Peter did not come back to see me and answer my questions, no matter how many times I reached out to that short, little drunk?" Simon Peter's unresponsiveness hurt Cornelius and Luke only partially empathized with him.

"Cornelius! How encouraging of a story is it to tell the world that Simon Peter didn't receive or respond to your messages? I could not include that, nor did the Lord give it to me. Instead, I told them about the part that mattered.I spoke of your faithfulness, your dreams, your gift from the Holy Spirit, and the others who were saved with you." Cornelius nodded in partial agreement.

Yael was upset with Cornelius' ingratitude, and she decided to say something about it. She walked up to Cornelius and spoke to him directly, with everyone listening. She had learned that secrets require directness on occasion.

"Uncle Cornelius, don't you understand that our Lord is using your name and story to spread His message? My name is not in this scroll, even though I recorded every word. The high priest is not in it, and the emperor himself is not in this scroll. You are. You are not grateful enough." She pointed at him with one finger and put her hand on her hips with the other.

"Do you know how few names are in the Torah? Your name is spoken more than once, and your story of experiencing God is as long as the story of David and Goliath. I wrote your story down. No one knows better than I do how long your story is. Everyone in Judah knows about David and Goliath. My mother's chickens know about David and Goliath. One day, my children and their children will know the name Cornelius. They won't know Yael, the scribe. They won't know Mishi, the Rabbi. However, they will know you!" she said with passion. Cornelius looked up at Luke, looking for guidance after being reprimanded by a young woman who was half his size.

"Is the yarn as long as she says it is?" Cornelius timidly asked the old Rabbi.

"She wrote it, Old Man. She knows better than anyone else," said Luke. Cornelius was not one for accolades or attention seeking. Instead, he felt uncomfortable and wanted to leave. He turned to his wife and spoke.

"Woman, let's hurry up and go home. I don't need to hear all this. I miss my bed with you in it." Valentina rolled her eyes, and everyone laughed at her capacity to dismiss her husband yet not offend him. Yael felt a sense of power that she had not felt before as she countered a feeling that she normally would bury. She publicly reprimanded a man who was normally not reprimandable .

"Well said, Little One," Valentina whispered in her ear. Yael felt happy and complete.

Luke then turned to Rufus before he gave him the scrolls he needed to carry with him as he sought out Theophilus.

"Rufus, these two little ones are yours to protect. Keep them safe and don't let what happened to my friend Paul descend upon them. People will want to hurt them. It is your job to protect them. Can you do that?" Luke asked.

Rufus was not in the military and didn't need to salute the old rabbi. Instead, he partially unsheathed his blade and ran his finger on the edge so Luke could see that it was sharp enough to draw blood.

"Is my blade not good enough for you, Rabbi?" Luke smiled and nodded his head in approval.

"Yes, Rabbi. This is the least I can do," Rufus said, bowing and accepting Luke's charge.

Rufus' countenance had changed since he retired. He was beginning to be aware that his choices were now his own. Gesher helped him to see that long before he asked her to be his wife. This time, there would be no pay or the hope of collecting a precious relic from a foreign land. He was doing it because it was the right thing to do. He could see now that all of his experience with foreign policy was about to be used to spread the Good News and take care of his new brother and sister and their soon-to-be child. Rufus was uniquely qualified to protect his family without the backup of the Roman army. He remained a powerful warrior with an emerging faith, and he was proud to do so with a new wife and a son.

Rufus went through the contents of the carts one last time before they left the city. He wanted to confirm that there was warm clothing for Mishi's family. He knew that by the end of their journey to Correae and Caesarea, the snow might have fallen. People from Dan do not experience snow and they would be cold at the onset.

He had a larger cart for Mishi's family and Yael, as they would be carrying with them many items. It was covered since he knew that Mishi's family had limited experience in the colder airs of the northern part of the province of Naphtali. Rufus had allowed the young Rabbi to take several usable artifacts from the ruins of the Temple in addition to all the school supplies. In his cart were ancient tapestries from the inner sanctum, one of the smaller golden cherubim, one of the silver candle holders, and several bags of Roman coins that he could use to pay for all the labor and materials needed to construct the boarding school that Mishi wanted to build in Tamar. Any unused parchment, ink, and quill were also in a chest in the very center of the wagon, as those items represented the centerpiece of the new school's tools. Finally, there was a piece of woodwork that Mishi's father had worked on that he wanted to take home to give to his father. Yael had packed extra blankets and extra rations of food in their cart, including some fruits and spices. She knew that the final day into Correae would take them over the pass where she spent the night, and it would be cold and windy as they camped. Yael had also added some items to bring home to show to her family. She decided on cinnamon, coriander, and several baskets full of tangerines. She bought a large bolt of Egyptian cotton for Despy and Nava. Now, they could make their own clothes using the highest quality cotton in the region. And she admitted another secret to Mishi.

"I know I said my cousins are idiots. But they are my idiots, and I miss them," she said with a sense of shame on her face.

"Get them whatever you would like. You have hardly used the coins your father gave you. And I would be mistaken not to realize that Despy and Nava will be my idiots-in-law," said Mishi. Even Luke laughed at Mishi's joke.

Finally, Yael brought out a single silver candlestick that was retrieved from the Holy of Holies. She had kept it in the bottom of her bag. She knew its worth was immeasurable, as there were none like it.

"Rufus, I need to make one stop in the lower city. This candlestick has another purpose and is not going home with me." People wondered what she meant.

Rufus reached inside his tunic and handed Mishi an ivory scroll case.

"I want you and Yael to have this artifact. I took it as my share of the pillage on one of my missions to the coast a few years ago. It contains the writings of Yeshua's half-brother, James. Apparently, he was here in Jerusalem and was an early member of The Way. I don't know why I brought it to Judah, but I did. Take it and make good use of it."

Mishi opened the scroll. "Rufus!" he exclaimed, disbelieving that he had been hiding this from him the whole time. Rufus spoke to the crowd as Mishi read the scroll.

"When I acquired this scroll after our battle, I was told that the author was stoned to death in Jerusalem. I find it ironic and painful to consider his fate. Jerusalem is destroyed and no stone has been left on top of any other stone, all because of my effort. Perhaps there is something in this writing that you can use at your new school to help others avoid falling into sin." Mishi listened to what Rufus said, finished reading it, and handed it to Yael. She read it quickly and spoke to Rufus with enthusiasm even before she finished.

"I like that these are fewer words here than in Luke's gospel. It will be easy to make copies of this. Perhaps you can take one or two of them with you when you go meet with Theophilus? I will start making a copy when we stop for the night," she said, not waiting for his answer. She took the scroll from Mishi and put it in her bag, then she took out a few pieces of parchment and a bottle of ink, placing all the items in the same place. Everyone watched her as if she were performing magic.

"If I organize everything here, it will take less time to find everything tonight and get started," Yael said in justification of her breaking of all the structure that Rufus had imposed on their packing.

Rufus smiled at Yael and spoke to Mishi. "I like your woman," Yael looked up at him and stuck her tongue out at him for using the derogatory word for woman, but she knew his heart.

"I love you, too, Rufus," she said as Rufus walked to his horse by his family's cart.

Finally, it was Luke's turn to say goodbye. It was an emotional moment for him, and two of Mishi's former students walked with him, carrying a large tray with eight ornate scrolls. Luke's hands were still in bandages and he needed their help to distribute the scrolls. Luke waited for everyone to be quiet.

"Brothers and Sisters, it is time for me to leave this place and visit the other synagogues and encourage them, as I have done with you. The task of recording the story of Yeshua and the early congregation of believers is complete, and now it is time for me to deliver this story to the rest of the world." He looked at Mishi and Yael, closing his eyes and bowing. He was crying and could not express his gratitude for all the help they had given him in any other way than tears. He and Yael had cried and laughed together too many times to count, and Yael leaned in and hugged the old Rabbi, telling him out loud that she loved him. When she stepped back, both Cornelius and Rufus put their hands on Yael's and Mishi's shoulders. Everyone was aware that Luke's work would not have been complete without these two young seekers who gave him their best effort.

"The Lord gave these words to an old doctor who could not write, with two young Ebreet hiding great sins as his scribes and a Roman warrior who helped destroy the Temple in logistics and transportation. That is also a story for the ages!" He shook his head, laughing and in disbelief at what his life had become these last weeks.

Luke motioned to the two students carrying the scrolls to begin distributing them. Luke told the boy to give three of the eight copies to Rufus. As Rufus took them, Luke provided guidance.

"Rufus, take three copies to Egypt. Cornelius here is one for you and the people of Caesarea. Mishi and Yael, there is one for each of you."

"Why each of us?" said Yael. Luke then looked at Rufus and Mishi, nodding at them to help Yael get off the cart. She stood in front of him, knowing she was being set up again.

"Yael, I can't tell you how proud I am of you. I give you two copies of this teaching. One is meant for Mishi to use to instruct the boys at your new school and one is meant for you, Yael, to instruct the girls. Perhaps you will have a niece you can pour your heart into." He smiled at her and kissed her on the cheek, whispering into her ear.

"I love you," he said, wiping a tear from Yael's eye.

"I have something else for you. This one you earned," he said. He then motioned for one of the boys to reach into his robe and pull out Luke's original prayer shawl, a garment worn only by those in the sacred line of priests.

"And since all things are new in Yeshua, so is the line of Melchizedek made new and those who follow it. I name you the first woman Rabbi in the faith. You shall teach the next generation alongside your husband, and the sacred writings are for you to share as much as him. I know these are very old, but these are the ones given to me a long time ago." Luke's hands remained wounded; instead, Mishi put it on her, aligning both sides so they extended the same length. Yael pulled her hair out so all of it was on top of the sacred material and she stood up straight. Everyone began to clap as Yael proudly accepted the most sacred title that could be bestowed in any of the twelve tribes. She was a Rabbi and priest in the Levites.

"That is my only one, so take good care of it. I am an old man and don't need it anymore. You are a young woman, and it will help the older people accept you as being as capable as your husband," Luke said. Yael looked at him, completely speechless.

"Yael, I said you earned it. You know the words on these two scrolls better than anyone, and you will be a great teacher to the younger girls." Luke had asked Mishi's permission to extend the power and responsibility of becoming a rabbi to his fiancé, and Mishi proudly approved. It was his turn to pour into his woman.

"No woman has taught at an Ebreet school. You will be the first one," Mishi said. They each took their scrolls and bowed in reverence to Luke. Yael then climbed into the wagon, and her mother-in-law whispered to her that she was proud of her. Yael's heart was full, but she was also a bit scared of what this title would mean to her future life as a wife and mother.

Rufus' sister could see that Yael was thriving on all the accolades, and she wanted to add one of her own. She spoke to Yael loudly enough for all to hear.

"My husband and I shall send our two daughters to study with you, Rabbi Yael."

Yael beamed. It was not her husband who believed she was good enough; Rufus' sister did, too. She had never heard the words " Rabbi

Yael" before now, and she loved how they sounded. Yael's heart was overflowing, and she accepted the challenge.

"I will teach your girls the Torah and everything I learned from Luke. I will also teach them what is on this new scroll from James. It reads much like the Torah, but the laws seem to be focused on the teachings of the Messiah," Yael said.

With that, the two carts departed, traveling down the hill away from Jerusalem. They reached the outpost city and entered through the city gates. The city was busy rebuilding, and there were vendors and suppliers all over the main city square. Yael saw the old woman who had first loved her like a daughter. She was there working her cart and looking the same as she always had.

"Stop the cart. I owe this woman something," she yelled at Rufus, and she jumped off and ran towards her. The old woman opened her arms and they embraced.

The old woman spoke first. "My dear, the Roman who travels with you already told me about your Erusin. I am happy for you."

Yael was ready to tell the woman her stories and invite her to their wedding, but Yael didn't know that Rufus had followed her. The old woman released her hold on Yael and embraced Rufus, kissing him on the forehead as he bent over. Yael could see that Rufus was as much of a son to her as she was a daughter. Yael stared at them and their embrace, not knowing what to say. Rufus placed her arm over her shoulder like a son might do to his mother and the two of them looked at Yael.

"Without this wonderful person," Rufus said to Yael, "I would still be looking for your family to tell them that you were coming home. She told me where you were from, what your family's names were, and even about your idiot cousins. I felt that I had already met Despy and Nava because of her stories!" Yael laughed at the simple explanation. Yael walked to the old woman and embraced her, just as Rufus embraced her.

"I have a gift for you," Yael said. She reached under her cloak and handed the old woman the silver candlestick that she had taken from the Holy of Holies.

"Keep it in your kitchen where I told you my darkest secrets. When I was at my lowest point in my life, you ministered to me and gave me light. Without you, none of this would have happened." She gestured to the two carts full of her family members, and she pointed at her Erusin ring.

"This candlestick came from the Holy of Holies and was meant to shed light on the greatest creation on earth. And that is who you are to me." The woman graciously accepted it and put one of her hands on Yael's cheek, speaking to her.

"Did I not tell you that you had great faith?"

Yael looked down in reverence. "Yes, Mother, you did. I'm sorry I didn't believe you."

The old woman took her hand, stepped closer to her, and whispered into her ear. "That ring looks beautiful on you. I always knew that you would wear one."

Yael chuckled. "I didn't think I would ever wear one." Now that everyone was listening, the laughter was as loud as last night. Once it stopped, Gesher approached the old woman and gave her half of all of Rufus' coins. Rufus stared at her with his mouth wide open. He gave those to her to care for her and her child while he was away. Instead, she decided to tithe half of it to this woman. Before anyone could speak, Gesher turned to Rufus and spoke.

"Your mother told me to do it." Everyone laughed.

"You have already learned how to avoid my wrath!" Rufus said. He leaned over and kissed Gesher, publicly declaring that he loved her.

"Come, let me serve everyone a cup of tea," she said. They all sat on the wall around the city manager, laughed, and told stories. After some more hugs, Rufus stood up and walked to Yael and Mishi.

"Come, you two, we must leave. I will come to get her when your wedding day approaches and personally take her to Correae and Tamar," Rufus told the couple. "As you asked, she shall stand beside you under the canopy as an honored guest."

"I could not think of a better person to be a part of my wedding party as I marry. Thank you," Yael said.

Yael savored the moment as their group left Jerusalem and the land of Benjamin. Before this moment, she would have thought that the fall of the Temple was the worst thing that could happen to her and her people. Now, she knew that Yahweh was going to use it to save people from their sins in a new way. And, more incredibly, despite her sins, she was going to be the wife of an incredibly talented Rabbi and the mother of a child who would be deeply loved.

Yael's mind returned to thoughts of the girl she had been in Correae before any of this had happened. Before Colch, before her trip to Jerusalem, before the fall of the Temple, before Mishi, that girl had longed for adventure. She had certainly gotten what she wanted.

"Take me home, General," she said to Rufus. He bowed his head in reverence. His life's job was to protect them and do their bidding, and today was his first day on the job.

"Of course," he said. He turned his horse to lead them back to where this journey had started.

Epilogue

The morning air of Correae was cold and crisp. As anticipated, Mishi's family was freezing, but Mishi was there with a purpose and didn't care about the cold. Everyone knew that Mishi needed to speak to Yael's family before their Erusin could be accepted, and they started traveling early in the morning to reach Yael's childhood home before their father went to work.

When he reached the outskirts of Correae and entered the home with Yael and his parents, he wasted no time. Yael led them to the kitchen. Katie now lived next door, but when she saw her sister walking in with someone she thought was her sister's fiancé, she ran over and hugged Yael, congratulating her and introducing herself to Mishi before her father made it to the kitchen.

"Father gave me your dowry before he left. Here," Yael extended the purse that held over a hundred gold coins that she never used.

"Keep it for your school. Consider it mine and Matthew's first tithe," Katie said. Yael thanked Katie and handed the purse to Mishi.

Jakob then entered and listened as Mishi recited his desire to marry Yael. Yakob was happy to give his daughter in marriage to Mishi, and Yael's mother ran into the village square screaming just as she did when Katie became engaged. Soon, half of the village was outside of Yael's home, all waiting to congratulate the young couple. Word had spread since Rufus' visit and no one had any resentments about Yael leaving the wedding to save her soul.

After receiving Yakob's blessings and exchanging gifts, Mishi and Yael stepped outside and Yael introduced Mishi and his family to everyone in Correae. Mishi introduced the village to Cornelius, Rufus, and their families. Gesher and Nathan went into the kitchen with Katie to prepare tea for everyone while everyone else got their first iteration of Yael's story. Her skills at telling her tale were refined by all the time she spent recording Luke's message, and her skills as an orator were impressive. She had great stories about her time on the Jerusalem highway and she shared a song about the nail hooks she found in the tunnel leading out of David's secret tunnel. Her father was impressed and he proudly told everyone that he could not believe that his daughter had become an adventurer.

"She speaks like one," said the village mayor.

As Katie and Gesher gave everyone a cup of tea, Mishi spoke again.

"I have a story to tell you before you leave to go to the mines," he said. They agreed, and everyone walked to the town center. Mishi stood on the top of the wagon and addressed the crowd.

"Many, if not all of you, have read the Torah and know what is said there. We have been promised a Messiah. All of us, myself included, believed that this Messiah would be the one to deliver us from the oppression that our people have experienced for thousands of years. Most recently, we thought that our Messiah would save us from the Romans." He motioned to Rufus and Cornelius to stand and join him atop the wagon. They dwarfed him like he was a child.

"It is not the Roman warriors such as these two whom we should seek to be saved from. These men are leaders of the highest level. They stood with me these last weeks and encouraged me. They protected us on our travels, and one of them came in advance to speak to my Erusin's father and mother." Mishi paused, knowing that what he was about to say would have a powerful impact on his listeners.

"He was also the Roman Legate in charge of the destruction of the Temple."

The crowd gasped. Mishi knew this was coming, and he had prayed for guidance.

"Do not judge. Both of these men are my brothers. What all of us have in common is that we have each had a powerful encounter with a living God and the Messiah he promised. Our individual stories are anecdotal. What I want to tell you is the story of the Messiah that all of us missed. It is the story of a humble man, born in a manger." He reached for the parchment given to him by Luke and held it up. "This story was given to us by our Brother Luke. It was written on these scrolls by this village's daughter, Yael."

More gasps. Before this moment, no one had ever heard of a woman recording words in the Torah. Mishi waited for them to stop before continuing.

"This is a letter from Luke to his dear friend, Theophilus. It tells the story of the origin, birth, ministry, death, and resurrection of our Messiah. I believe this is the first time this scroll has been read out loud. May the Lord bless all those who hear!"

He opened the scroll and read. Cornelius and Rufus sat side by side. Yael was holding Katie and Gesher's hands.

"Is this the truth, Yael? Did you write this?" Katie asked.

"I did."

"Are you wearing a Rabbinical prayer shawl, too?" Katie rhetorically asked.

"I am," Yael said with happiness on her face.

"Yael, are you a Rabbi? How is this possible?" Katie asked, no longer whispering.

"I will tell you all about it later," Yael said quietly. She hoped Katie would be excited for her. Mishi began to read out loud the words the Lord had given to Luke, who had dictated them to Yael.

"Many have undertaken to draw up an account of the things that have been fulfilled among us, as they were handed down to us by those who from the first were eyewitnesses and servants of the Word..."

He continued until he was finished, frequently looking up at his wife when he knew there was a small story that only the two of them shared. Soon, Yael stood up and walked towards her future husband, standing next to him and not behind. Mishi nodded at her, accepting her as his equal and proud to call her soon his wife.

Once done, he called everyone to pick up everything and follow the Messiah. Nearly everyone in the hamlet of Correae followed Mishi and Yael to the Jabbok River. Yael baptized the women, and Mishi baptized the men into the Kingdom of God. Once done, Mishi and Yael went to her sister's house to relax and tell her sister and brother-in-law everything that happened. The burden of secrecy was too much, and Yael was convicted not to sleep until her sister knew everything. Luke told her everything. Mishi told her everything. Kayta deserved an honest sister. And she told her everything.

"My sister is not only marrying a temple Rabbi. She, too, is a Rabbi!" said Katie. Yael smiled, and she could feel how proud Katie was of her.

Little did Yael know that her sister had the same idea. She, too, had a secret that she was protecting, awaiting the right moment to share with the ones she thought would be impacted the most. The days of secrets were over for both women.

Katie looked at Yael.

"I also have a story. I am with child!"

Yael smiled and took her sister's hand. She let fly a few tears of sheer joy. She had been set up to succeed as her veil of secrets finally came tumbling down. Jerusalem was not the home of her people. It was the place where secrets came tumbling down.

"Katie, so am I!"

The story continues in book 2, The Emperor and the Ring.

About the Author

Jeff Gaura is a retired IT executive who has always gravitated to storytelling and imagery as he built and eventually sold his company. He grew up in the great outdoors, first as a boy scout and later as a Peace Corps volunteer in the Himalaya of Nepal. He competes in endurance racing events like marathons, ultra-marathons, and duathlons. He has participated as a member of TeamUSA no less than eight times.

Jeff operates Threshold Academy, Inc., to promote the endurance sports lifestyle and to lead adventure travel, both cycling and hiking, worldwide. His epic tour offerings can be found at https://thresholdacademy.com.

https://jeffgaura.com

www.ingramcontent.com/pod-product-compliance
Lightning Source LLC
Chambersburg PA
CBHW060429310726
48977CB00001B/111